THE SUSPECT LIST

I exit Alvetta's office with my mind aflutter. She has given me so much to think about. Despite her apparent grief, I still wonder if she knows about Raynell's affair with Michael. Your supposed best friend sleeping with your husband is certainly motive for murder.

I also wonder if Terrence knew about Raynell's affairs with Michael . . . and/or Gregory. (Sister *got around*. That's for sure). Another motive for murder.

Then I consider whether or not an old high school wound is enough motive for Gregory . . . or Kimberly to kill Raynell. And, as I make my way to my van, I can't help but think about what Alvetta said . . . how, with Raynell out of the picture, whoever helps Gregory close some real estate deals stands to make out like a bandit. If Christy has been Gregory's go-to girl all along, wouldn't she be his logical choice to assist him now that Raynell is dead? Is being positioned as the next in line to a hefty real estate commission enough reason for Christy to kill Raynell?

Alvetta, Terrence, Gregory, Kimberly, Christy— they all had reasons to do away with Raynell.

I guess it's now up to me to figure out if any of them actually acted upon those reasons . . .

Books by A.L. Herbert

MURDER WITH FRIED CHICKEN AND
WAFFLES

MURDER WITH MACARONI AND CHEESE

MURDER WITH COLLARD GREENS
AND HOT SAUCE

Published by Kensington Publishing Corporation

Murder with Macaroni and Cheese

A.L. HERBERT

KENSINGTON BOOKS
www.kensingtonbooks.com

KENSINGTON BOOKS are published by

Kensington Publishing Corp.
119 West 40th Street
New York, NY 10018

All Kensington titles, imprints and distributed lines are available at special quantity discounts for bulk purchases for sales promotion, premiums, fund-raising, educational or institutional use. Special book excerpts or customized printings can also be created to fit specific needs. For details, write or phone the office of the Kensington Special Sales Manager: Kensington Publishing Corp., 119 West 40th Street, New York, NY 10018. Attn. Special Sales Department. Phone: 1-800-221-2647.

Kensington and the K logo Reg. U.S. Pat. & TM Off.

ISBN-13: 978-1-4967-1127-4
ISBN-10: 1-4967-1127-0
First Kensington Trade Edition: September 2016
First Kensington Mass Market Edition: January 2019

eISBN-13: 978-1-61773-177-8
eISBN-10: 1-61773-177-3
Kensington Electronic Edition: September 2016

10 9 8 7 6 5 4 3 2 1

Printed in the United States of America

CHAPTER 1

"Someone needs to turn the heat down out there. I'm about to sweat my wig off," Wavonne says as she comes through the front door of Mahalia's Sweet Tea. "But it sure feels good in here." She leans her head and shoulders back, rolls her neck from side to side, and takes in the cool air pumping through the vents from three air conditioners toiling at maximum capacity on the roof above my restaurant.

"It is a scorcher." I look at my watch. "You were supposed to be here an hour ago and help us set up for lunch. We'll be busy today. People will want to get out of the heat and into the air conditioning. We'll go through iced tea like crazy."

"Speakin' of iced tea. What kind we got on special today? I need to get me a glass."

"It's strawberry. Laura brewed the syrup early this morning."

Laura is my assistant manager and, thankfully,

a morning person. She usually gets in around eight a.m. and starts working with my kitchen prep staff to have us ready for our lunch opening at eleven. I generally come in after ten and stay until after we close. On weeknights it's often past eleven p.m. when I leave and usually later than that on Friday and Saturday nights.

"Strawberry! That's my fave!" Wavonne hurries toward the back of the restaurant where we keep the tea dispensers.

I stand by the bar as I watch Wavonne scoop some ice, drop it into a tall glass, add a big serving of homemade strawberry syrup, and fill the whole thing with sweet tea. For customers, we add the syrup to unsweetened tea—the strawberry flavoring is made from berries and plenty of sugar, so it adds a nice touch of sweetness to regular tea. But Wavonne likes her tea so sweet the straw practically stands up on its own.

"You *do* realize you are here to work, Wavonne, no?" I watch her linger by the drink station, alternating between sipping and stirring her tea with a straw as if she's a customer on a leisurely lunch break rather than a paid employee.

Wavonne is my significantly younger cousin and, after a troubled youth that involved only sporadic amounts of supervision from my alcoholic aunt, came to live with Momma and me when she was thirteen and has been a handful ever since. She's in her twenties now, but I still find myself reprimanding her as often as I did when she was a teenager.

"All right, all right. Slow your roll, boss lady." She pulls a lavender tie from her pocket and starts tying it around her neck. All my servers wear black pants, long-sleeve white shirts, and pastel ties. But all my servers certainly do not tell me to "slow my roll" or call me "boss lady." As a member of the family I allow Wavonne a certain amount of slack, and, knowing that I'll never fire her, she takes every bit of it. But, honestly, given her history, most days I'm happy that she manages to show up for work at all.

I'm about to ask Wavonne to make sure we have enough rolled silverware on hand for the lunch crowd when I see Saundra, my afternoon hostess, with the phone in her hand, motioning for me to come to the hostess stand.

"There's a call for you. I said I'd take a message, but she insisted on speaking with you now. She said she's Raynell Rollins's assistant."

"Raynell Rollins?" It takes a moment for the name to register. It's not a name I've *heard* in quite some time—I have, however, *seen* it all over town. I haven't been in touch with her since high school, but Raynell Rollins is a local real estate agent—you can hardly visit any of the better neighborhoods here in Prince George's County, Maryland, without running into one of her "For Sale" signs with her photo plastered on it. "Wonder what she wants," I say more to myself than Saundra, remembering how my friend Nicole, the only person from high school with whom I've kept in regular contact, gave me an update on Raynell a while back. She told me that Raynell married Terrence Rollins shortly after college when he was starting for the Washington Redskins. Nicole, who loves to gossip and has way more time to surf Facebook than I do, also recently informed me that Terrence, who has since retired from playing football, is now a sports anchor on a local station. I don't really follow sports, but I've seen him on the news a few times. Per Nicole, thanks to Terrence's past as a star football player and his current presence as an on-air personality, Raynell has managed to build quite the little real estate sales empire—mostly by tapping Terrence's network of broadcasting and professional-sport-player friends as clients.

I take the phone from Saundra and lift it to my ear. "This is Halia."

"Ms. Watkins?"

"Yes."

"My name is Christy Garner. I'm Raynell Rollins's assistant. She asked me to set up a lunch date with you."

"Really? Any particular reason? I haven't seen Raynell since high school." I'm considering adding that you can count on one hand the number of times Raynell and I spoke to each other while we actually were in high school, but I decide not to go there. Although I don't recall Raynell being a particularly nice person, it's not like there was any animosity between the two of us or anything like that—we just didn't run in the same circles.

"Ms. Rollins is scouting venues for her . . . and I guess *your* high school reunion. She would like to discuss possibly holding the event in your restaurant."

"I thought the reunion was going to be at Colony South Hotel. It's in less than two weeks, isn't it?"

I got an invite to the event months ago and sent my regrets. I rarely take off Saturday nights, and, aside from Nicole, who I already see all the time, there isn't really anyone who I'm terribly eager to reconnect with, so I decided not to bother attending.

"There was a water main break at the hotel. They won't have the event space repaired in time."

"Really? That's a shame."

"Raynell heard that you owned a local restaurant and thought you might be able to host the affair."

"I'd be happy to discuss it with Raynell."

I wonder why Raynell didn't just call me herself, but if memory serves me correct, Raynell was one for putting on airs—using an assistant as an intermediary is probably just one of those wealth and status things I don't understand.

"Why don't you ask her to come by for lunch tomorrow, and we'll talk about it?" I offer even though it's highly unlikely that I'll agree to host the event at Sweet Tea. Depending on how many members of our graduating class are attending, hosting the reunion might mean closing the whole restaurant for an entire evening to accommodate the crowd. I doubt the reunion committee has the kind of money I would have to charge to make up for a Saturday night's worth of lost receipts. Besides, I learned the hard way that closing Sweet Tea for a private event is not a great idea. A few years ago, for a hefty sum, I agreed to close the place to host a wedding reception for the daughter of the owner of King Town Center, which houses Sweet Tea. He agreed to more than cover any lost revenue and, when the man who can raise your rent come lease-renewal time makes a request, you think long and hard before saying no. I tried to get the word out to my clientele about the closure that particular night a few weeks prior to the reception. Among other things, I displayed a poster at the hostess stand and put a notice on our Web site. I even sent e-mails to patrons on our contact list, but my efforts proved to be of no avail. Customer after customer came through the front door wanting a table the night of the reception. Believe me, you have not seen *angry* until you've had to turn away mouths that were all set to bite into crispy fried chicken and fluffy waffles. And some of the customers I had to deny entry to seemed to take it as a personal offense and posted some rather unpleasant commentary on Yelp. I just don't feel like going through all that commotion again.

"Raynell is available at twelve thirty tomorrow afternoon."

"That would be fine. Please tell her to come by Sweet Tea then."

"Sure. I will likely accompany her, and she may invite Alvetta Marshall, who has also been involved in the reunion planning. If that's okay?"

"Of course."

Alvetta registers in my head—another one I haven't seen since high school. I'm sure she's referring to the girl I knew as Alvetta Jordan. I remember Alvetta being nicer than Raynell, and, although she was prettier than Raynell, she was definitely the "number two" girl at my high school. Raynell was the clear leader of the gang of "it" girls, and Alvetta was her primary minion. I think there were six or seven girls in Raynell's little squadron. They all followed Raynell around like newborn ducklings waddling behind their mother. Raynell said "jump," and Alvetta and the others said "How high . . . and in what kind of shoes?" I remember when Raynell got that horrible asymmetrical 'shroom haircut that was big in the eighties—next thing you knew, Alvetta and the other underlings were chopping one side of their hair and leaving the other side long to match their queen. Raynell bought an acid-wash denim jacket and, within days, it became like a new uniform for her girls. When neon was popular the whole lot of them wandered the halls like a walking advertisement for Day-Glo highlighters. I remember them going through a phase when each of them constantly sported a neon beaded necklace. They each had a different color—Raynell probably assigned them. I can't recall the colors the other girls wore, but I do remember that Raynell's necklace was bright green—only because the intense color reminded me of a St. Patrick's Day leprechaun. Raynell isn't much taller than a leprechaun, and seeing her roam the school halls in her colored necklace always made me picture her with a green top hat and pointy-toe green shoes with gold buckles on them. The image was always good for a laugh.

"Okay. I will confirm with Raynell, and we'll plan to see you tomorrow."

"Sounds good."

"Who was that?" Wavonne asks after I hang up the phone.

"The assistant to one Raynell Rollins. I went to

high school with her—Raynell—not the assistant. Apparently, Raynell is on the reunion committee. Remember? I told you about the invite I got for it?"

"Yep. And I still don't get why you ain't goin'—all those former classmates who are likely eligible brothas. By the time people get to your age, Halia . . . you know . . . all old and creaky . . . half of them have been divorced and are on the prowl again."

I laugh. "You'll be in your forties one day, too, Wavonne. I hope to be there the first time some-one calls you 'old and creaky.' "

She rolls her eyes at me. "You know some of those brothas have been beaten down by naggin' wives for years. They probably all damaged . . . ripe for the pickin'. If nothin' else, you could at least get a weekend fling out of it."

"Just what I need—a weekend fling with some man weighed down with more baggage than a bell-man. Thanks, but no thanks!"

"Well then, don't you want to go just to show off? You own one of the most successful restau-rants in town. If it were me, I'd go just to rub it in the faces of any nasty heifers who thought they were better than me in high school."

"What are you talking about?" I hear Momma say as she comes out of the kitchen into the main dining room. At seventy-four, she doesn't move as fast as she used to, but she still bakes up some mean desserts. She gets in early and whips up the cakes and pies for Sweet Tea. She's probably fin-ished with her baking for the day and is about to head home.

"I can honestly say I have no idea, Momma."

"Halia was just remindin' me that she's skippin' her high school reunion."

"Why would you do that, Halia? Go. Mingle." Then she adds under her breath, "Find a husband . . ."

"What did you say?" I ask even though I heard her. Momma is forever trying to find me a love life.

"I said for you to go and mingle . . . and if you happen to find a potential romantic interest, so be it."

"You don't ever give up, do you, Momma?"

She ignores my questions. "Just go for Pete's sake . . . and think like a lion while you're there—wait until an eligible man is separated from the herd and then move in for the kill. Stick with the divorced ones. Anyone who's never been married by the time they reach your age must have something wrong with them." She notices the look on my face. "Except for you, dear. You've just been . . . well . . . busy."

"Not that it has anything to do with your badgering, Momma, but I may be going to the event after all. Apparently, there was a water main break at the hotel where they planned to have the reunion, and they need a new venue. I just got a phone call about it. One of my old classmates who is on the reunion committee wants to host the event here at Sweet Tea. She's coming by tomorrow to discuss it."

"Do you think that's a good idea, Halia?" Momma asks. "You don't need perspective suitors knowing you own a restaurant right off the bat. Men can be funny about dating women who are successful in business. Let them get to know you first," she adds as if my status as a restaurant owner is akin to a case of herpes or a prison record . . . or whatever else you wouldn't mention on a first date.

"I just agreed to meet with her. I didn't say I was definitely going to host it here. I'm not keen on shutting this place down for an evening . . . especially on a Saturday night. I think I'll make a few phone calls instead, and see if I might be able to secure another location. Then I can just cater the reunion. That way I can help out without having to close Sweet Tea for an evening."

"That sounds like a good idea," Momma says. "You can have staff supervise the catering, and then you can go as a guest. We'll get you a new dress—"

Wavonne cuts her off. "And maybe we can do somethin' with that hair of hers," she says to Momma, and then turns to me. "Let me give you a full makeover, Halia. I'll do your makeup and loan you a wig . . . one of the good ones with the European hair. I'll have you lookin' straight-up pimp in no time."

"I don't think 'straight-up pimp,' whatever that means, is exactly my style. But thanks all the same, Wavonne."

"Suit yourself, but that Eddie Bauer/L.L. Bean getup you got goin' on is not goin' to get you noticed."

"I'm on my feet and moving around this restaurant all day. I like to be comfortable, Wavonne."

"Fine. Be comfortable. But you ain't gonna land no man at your reunion lookin' all frumpadump."

"Whatever, Wavonne. My 'frumpadump' self

has work to do, and so do you." I turn to Momma. "And isn't it time for you to get on out of here?"

Momma looks at her watch. "Why, yes. It really is. I've got to run, girls," she says to Wavonne and me before focusing her eyes on just me. "I do hope you attend the reunion, Halia. And remember what I said: you're the lion, and the single men are the gazelles. As soon as one lags behind—"

My back is already turned to her as I cut her off on my way to my office to make some calls and see about finding a venue for the reunion. "I know, Momma: 'Move in for the kill.' "

CHAPTER 2

"Wavonne! If I catch you doing that one more time ..." I let my voice trail off as we both know whatever I say is no more than an empty threat. She just used a glass to scoop herself a cup of ice out of the well instead of the metal scooper. She does this all the time, and last year, in the middle of the dinner rush, she broke a glass in the process—we had to pour hot water in the well to melt all the ice and make sure we didn't miss any shards. Then restock the whole thing.

"My bad, my bad." Wavonne dumps the ice back into the cooler and uses the scooper to fill her glass before placing it under the sweet tea dispenser. "What time your high school friends comin' over?"

"They should be here soon. And I wouldn't call them 'friends.' They are just former class-mates. We barely interacted in high school at all."

"Oh ... so they were the *popular* girls?"

"What makes you think I didn't hang out with the popular girls?"

"'Cause you were probably always cookin' with Grandmommy or had your nose buried in some book."

"So what if I spent time in the kitchen as a teenager and liked to read? I turned out okay."

"How about the chicks you have comin' in here? How'd they turn out?"

"I don't really know. I haven't seen them in over twenty years."

"What are their names again?" Wavonne pulls out her phone.

"Raynell Rollins and Alvetta Marshall. Why?"

Wavonne starts typing on her phone. "Here's Alvetta." She places her phone under my nose.

"Ah . . . the magic of Facebook." I take the phone, click on Alvetta's main photo, and watch it enlarge on the screen. "She looks good . . . *really* good."

Wavonne grabs the phone back from me and looks herself. "She's all right . . . considerin' she's like forty-somethin'." She clicks on her phone again. "Says here she's First Lady of Rebirth Christian Church."

"Is that so?" I ask. "I guess that mean's she's married to the pastor. Rebirth is one of those mega churches, isn't it? With a few *thousand* members?"

"Yeah. It's not too far from here . . . over in Fort Washington."

"Didn't we just have a bunch of Rebirth members in here last Sunday?"

"Yep. The ones who hoarded three tables for over two hours."

"They do tend to be some of our lesser-behaved after-churchers." I don't know exactly when we started simply referring to them as "after-churchers," but the folks who come in here after services for Sunday brunch are one of the prime reasons I have the rare thought of getting out of the restaurant business. Diana Ross herself could walk into Sweet Tea wearing a diamond tiara, and I bet she'd be less demanding than some of the after-churchers. The ones who come from the gigantic mega churches like Rebirth are typically the worst.

Now don't get me wrong—I'm a Christian, and I'm all for giving God his due on the infrequent Sunday that I can get away from Sweet Tea to attend service—but some of these mega churches just leave a bad taste in my mouth. Momma attends one in Camp Springs. The few times I've gone with her, the collection basket went around more times than a tip jar at a strip club, which wouldn't be so bad if I didn't suspect that half the money deposited in the basket was going toward the pastor's Mercedes G-Class or to keep his wife, who, like Alvetta, refers to herself as the "First Lady," in all the latest fashions from Saks and Neiman Marcus.

"Those Rebirthers were here forever last Sunday. They about ran Darius and me ragged with special requests. Thank God you implemented that tip policy, or we'd have been left with their usual five percent tip."

Wavonne is not one for math, but it wasn't long after she started working at Sweet Tea that she learned how to calculate percentages—working for tips will do that for a person. People really should leave at least twenty percent of the total bill for good service, and no server likes to get less than fifteen percent. But if Wavonne is on the other side of a five or ten percent tip, we all know to batten down the hatches. Even with her poor impulse control she knows better than to chase after a customer who's stiffed her. So instead, she complains to no end to whichever staff member is within earshot. Usually words like "project ho" or "thot" are involved.

"I hated to do it, but I had to do *something.*" I'm referring to the Sunday brunch tipping policy I implemented last year that automatically adds an eighteen percent gratuity to all parties. We've always added gratuity to parties of six or more, but some of our less refined customers started breaking up into smaller parties to avoid the charge, and it was becoming a particular problem on Sundays. Most of my customers are decent tippers, but certain after-churchers see it fit to leave well below the industry standard tip amounts. And I'm all for spreading God's word or what have you, but I'm sorry, religious literature left on the table after a customer departs does *not* constitute a tip and is certainly not going to pay my servers' rent or their car payments.

"Let's see what else we can find out about her." Wavonne starts tapping on her phone again.

I'm about to lean my head over and see if she's found a profile for Raynell when I spot a slick black Hyundai Equus glide into a parking space in front of the restaurant. I move closer to the door, and, as the car comes to a stop, I see one of those clear stickers on the back window with a drawing of a church outlined in white. I lean toward the glass to make out the writing underneath the sketch—it says *Rebirth Christian Church.*

"I guess the *First Lady* has arrived."

"Think she's upset that we ain't got a red carpet?" Wavonne asks, walking toward me.

I chuckle. "Maybe so. I guess a tall glass of iced tea will have to do."

CHAPTER 3

Wavonne stands next to me as we watch the door to Alvetta's luxury sedan open. My eyes are initially drawn to her towering pink heels as they make contact with the pavement. I follow them up to a lovely floral dress paired with a short light blue jacket—a bolero jacket, I think it's called.

"Oh *hail* no!" Wavonne says. "I just saw that outfit online."

"The dress?"

"It's not just a *dress*, Halia. That is some *Oscar de la Renta*. Costs like two thousand dollars. I bet those Blahniks on her feet were another thousand, easy."

One of Wavonne's favorite things to do, often when she should be waiting on customers, is to look at high fashion online, snap screen shots of what she likes, and then try to find lookalikes at T.J. Maxx or Ross.

"I guess I'm in the wrong business. Clearly religion is much more lucrative than owning a restaurant."

"You ain't kiddin'. If I'd known landin' a minister would get me all up in some de la Renta, I'd go to church with Aunt Celia more often."

"Oh you would, would you?" I ask as I open the door to greet Alvetta.

"Halia Watkins!" Alvetta calls to me as she carefully navigates her heels on to the raised sidewalk in front of Sweet Tea.

"Alvetta!" I smile. "You look amazing. The picture of summer," I add, eyeing her dress of pastel flowers. And, considering it's nearly ninety degrees today, being dressed for sunshine is certainly appropriate.

As she makes her final approach toward the door, I'm reminded of how beautiful she was in high school . . . and still is. She has the same long legs and hourglass figure . . . the same dewy brown skin, high cheekbones, and full eyelashes framing her hazel eyes. Clicking her heels along the sidewalk with her long black hair pushed back with a pair of oversized white sunglasses, she looks like she's about to board a private jet bound for some exotic location.

"Thank you." She leans in, grabs both my hands, and gives me a kiss on each cheek.

"It's so nice to see you. Please. Come in."

"It's great to see you as well." She steps inside Sweet Tea and begins to look around. "What a lovely place. I'd heard you'd become a successful restaurateur. I can't believe I've never been here . . . especially considering I only live a few miles away."

"That is a shame, but we'll make up for it today. We'll indulge you with the finest soul food in town." I notice Wavonne hovering next to me. "This is my cousin, Wavonne. She works as a server here."

"Nice to meet you."

"Please. Let's have a seat." I gesture for Alvetta to follow me as I walk toward a four top by one of the front windows.

"What would you like to drink? A cocktail or a glass of wine? Or we have a watermelon mint iced tea on special—it's perfect on a hot day like this."

"That sounds delightful."

"Wavonne, could you get us a couple of glasses of the watermelon mint tea?"

Wavonne, who followed us to the table, finally diverts her envious eyes from Alvetta's attire, nods, and heads toward the drink station.

"So, how are you? What have you been up to?" Alvetta asks.

"This." I look around me. "Keeping this place running leaves little time for much else. How about you? I heard you married a church pastor." I figure that sounded better than telling her Wavonne and I were just snooping around on Facebook for details about her.

"Yes. My husband, Michael, is the pastor of Rebirth Christian Church in Fort Washington. We have a congregation of more than ten thousand. It keeps both of us very busy."

"I'm sure it does."

"You should come to service sometime. I'll reserve you a seat in the Pastor's Circle."

"The Pastor's Circle?"

"It's the seating area closest to the stage. The seats are reserved for special guests and VIPs."

"How nice," I reply, even though the idea of a VIP section seems more appropriate for a nightclub rather than a church. "I'd love to, but it's hard to get away on Sunday mornings. Preparing to feed church attendees after the service doesn't give us much time to actually attend ourselves."

"Well . . . when you can get away, I hope you'll come."

"Of course," I respond before switching gears. "So. The reunion?"

"Yes. I'm so excited. It will be a real treat to get the old gang back together again." She seems to be saying this as if I were part of the "old gang." By no means was I part of the "Whitleys," a name bestowed upon Raynell and Alvetta's gaggle of snooty girls in honor of Whitley Gilbert, the spoiled elitist character played by Jasmine Guy on *A Different World,* the spinoff of *The Cosby Show* that was popular back in my high school days. I'm not sure Raynell and Alvetta ever knew that the Whitleys is what they were called by most of the school. It wasn't a name *necessarily* used in a derogatory fashion, but it was always said with a hint of distaste by those of us who were not part of the exclusive clique. I was reasonably popular in high school, but more in a studious "class president" sort of way rather than the fast-partying, latest-fashion-wearing way of the Whitleys.

"I'm sure it will be a fun night. I've lost touch with most of our classmates. Occasionally, some alumni I recognize will come in here for lunch or dinner, but Nicole is the only former classmate I'm still in regular contact with."

"Nicole Baxter? How is she?"

"She's good. She's planning on attending. She lives in Bowie now. She—"

Wavonne interrupts me. "Here we go." She set three glasses of tea down on the table. I'm curious who the third glass of tea is for until I see her grab a chair from a neighboring table, slide it over, and plop herself down on it. "Your other friend who's comin' over . . . you said her name was Raynell Rollins?"

"Yes."

"I thought that name sounded familiar. Then I was pourin' the tea, and it came to me—*Raynell Rollins*. She wouldn't happen to be the wife of Terrence Rollins?"

"Yes," Alvetta responds. "That's her."

"Get out?! She's the wife of *Terrence Rollins*? Former wide receiver of the Washington Redskins?"

Alvetta smiles. "Yes indeed. He retired from the Redskins years ago. He's a sports anchor on the local news now. I'm sure you've seen him. He's on every night at six and eleven."

"I've seen him," I say. "He certainly is a nice-looking man."

"Do you really think Raynell would have it any other way?"

I laugh. "No, I guess not."

"I think that's Raynell now." Alvetta directs her eyes over my shoulder.

I turn around and look out the window at a

white Cadillac Escalade easing into the parking space next to Alvetta's car.

"Great. We can start figuring out a plan for the event." I turn to Wavonne. "Is there something I can help you with?" I'm wondering why she is still sitting with us when we had arranged for her to be the server for this table, not to mention the two or three other tables she should be waiting on at this very moment.

"Nope. I'm good."

"Wavonne, you are supposed to be serving this table—not sitting at it. And you have other tables that need tending."

"I got it covered. Darius said he'd look after my tables for a few mins." She leans in and whispers to me. "You need to hook me up with this Raynell sista. She and her husband may be my ticket to finding a professional sports playa boyfriend."

I don't want to have an argument with Wavonne in front of Alvetta, so I just nod at Wavonne and get up to greet Raynell. As I watch her step out of the SUV I'm reminded of how short she is, even in the high heels she's sporting. I often remember women like Raynell—woman with big personalities and bigger egos—taller than they actually are. Absent her stilettos she barely clears five feet.

Unlike Alvetta, Raynell, with her wide nose and square jaw, is not a natural beauty. You wouldn't call her obese, but words like "stout" or "solid" come to mind when you look at her. She doesn't have much of a waistline. Somehow she manages to be plump without having curves—her figure is more in line with . . . say a tree trunk rather than an hourglass. But you have to give the girl credit for doing the best she can with what God gave her. As she gets closer to the door, I can see that her hair and makeup are meticulous, and her lavender pantsuit flatters her less than curvaceous figure as best it can.

Raynell's power never did stem from her looks. It was always her confidence and authoritarian manner that made her the empress of my high school. And I'm guessing it's those same traits that landed her a handsome rich husband.

Raynell's boxy stature is made even more apparent when a petite, much younger woman rounds the corner from the passenger side of Raynell's SUV, carrying what appears to be a very heavy bag in one hand and an iPad in the other.

The pair reaches the door, which I open for them, and, as Raynell's eyes meet mine, I suddenly remember how she was sort of a bitch in high school. I wonder if she still is.

I welcome her, and she extends her hand in a fashion that makes it seem as though I'm supposed to kiss it rather than shake it. Confused, I decide not to do either and just say, "Hello, Raynell. It's good to see you again."

"You too, Halia." She turns her head from left to right, looking around Sweet Tea. "Such a cozy little . . . little lunch counter you run here," she says of my restaurant, which seats nearly two hundred customers and regularly makes local top restaurant lists. She then looks me up and down. "And who can blame you for putting on a few pounds . . . who wouldn't, working in a restaurant."

Yep, still sort of a bitch.

CHAPTER 4

"Alvetta," Raynell says as we approach the table. "How are you?"

"I'm just fine. You?"

"Trying to survive this heat. You know how I *hate* summer." Raynell reaches into her designer bag, pulls out a handkerchief, and dabs at her forehead. The brief walk from her car to the restaurant was enough to make her faintly perspire in the August warmth.

"Please have a seat," I say to Raynell and her companion. "Raynell, this is my cousin, Wavonne, one of the servers here at Sweet Tea."

Wavonne stands to greet her. "I'll be helping with the reunion planning."

"You will?" I ask. This is news to me.

"Of course. You know how I like to help out as much as I can around here."

I let out a quick laugh before I can stop myself.

"Of course." I figure this is a better response than "Since when?"

Raynell gives Wavonne (and her poufy wig, heavy makeup, and tight clothing) a once-over and apparently decides she is not worth a handshake or a hello. She just offers Wavonne a quick smile as she sets her purse down, slides into a chair next to Alvetta, and plops a gaudy gold and sparkly-stone Michael Kors keychain on the table. "You sit over there," she says to the young lady with her, who I assume is the assistant who called me to set up the lunch date, but I can't be sure as Raynell hasn't introduced her to any of us.

"Halia Watkins." I extend my hand toward the young lady. "And this is Wavonne."

She gives my hand a shake and nods politely in Wavonne's direction. "Hi. I'm Christy. Raynell's assistant." She's a pretty girl with a tiny frame, light brown skin, and short black hair. I'd be surprised if she were over twenty-five.

"She can take notes or make calls . . . or whatever needs to be done while we talk," Raynell says.

"Great. That will be a big help."

"Alvetta, sweetie. Are you using that eye cream I gave you? The bags under your eyes don't look much better than the last time I saw you," Raynell says as I sit down next to Christy. I guess I shouldn't be surprised. I didn't spend much time with them, but I observed the girls enough to recall that Raynell worked overtime at destroying Alvetta's self esteem in high school. Why should things be any different now? Alvetta doesn't have so much as a hint of any bags under her eyes, but the ends of her hair were not split or frayed either back in high school when Raynell convinced her she needed to cut her hair.

It was always clear that Raynell was jealous of Alvetta's good looks and seemed to go to great lengths to convince Alvetta she was an ugly duckling when the exact opposite was true. I can't be sure of her motives, but Raynell was queen bee of the Whitleys, and my guess is she wanted the status of having the prettiest girl in school as her best friend, but, at the same time, was afraid Alvetta would challenge her authority if she was actually aware of what a knockout she was.

I don't recall the complete details, but from what I remember, Alvetta came from *very* modest roots. She was the daughter of a single mother who served as a live-in housekeeper for a more fortunate family. The rumor around school was that Alvetta actually shared a room with her mother in the employer's home.

My high school was largely made up of students from working-class and middle-class families. There were certainly poor kids at my school, but many parts of Prince George's County were more affluent in the eighties than they are now. Being so close to D.C., many of us, including Raynell, had parents who made healthy incomes as government employees or by working for government contractors. Andrews Air Force Base (now Joint Base Andrews) in Camp Springs, not far up the road from my school, was also a big employer.

It had to be hard for Alvetta to be the daughter of a maid who didn't even have her own home.

But two things kept Alvetta from being derided—her good looks and her friendship with Raynell. At some point, while Raynell was assembling her little empire of fashion conscious she-devils during the early part of our freshman year, the two of them became inseparable. Raynell's cronies consisted of a whole gaggle of girls, but Alvetta was her closest friend—Raynell's most loyal and trusted subject. Raynell protected Alvetta from jeering based on her upbringing (no one dared cross Raynell Spector—she was known by her maiden name in high school), but, at the same time, she made a hobby out of criticizing Alvetta herself in a constant effort to remind Alvetta who was in charge.

"You look lovely, Alvetta," I say before she has a chance to respond to Raynell's rude question. "You haven't aged a day." Raynell looks momentarily annoyed with me for complimenting Alvetta. "I can say the same about you, Raynell," I offer, trying to make a quick save. And Raynell really hasn't changed that much, either, but, in her case, that's not necessarily a good thing—in high school her features, and really her whole demeanor, reminded me of a bulldog, and they still do.

"This menu is killer," Alvetta says. "I want to try everything."

"It's nice," Raynell chimes in. "You know, for a *casual* dining establishment. I had so wanted to hold the event at a different . . . a different *type* of restaurant . . . some place high-end with white tablecloths and palette-cleansing sorbet between courses. But, considering many of our classmates may be . . . how shall I put it . . . 'financially challenged,' we booked the Cotillion Ballroom at that raggedy little motel in Clinton. And then they go and let a pipe burst, leaving us in quite a lurch."

I'm familiar with the venue she's referring to, and, while Colony South may not be the Four Seasons, it is a quaint little hotel (not motel) with a small conference center and nice amenities. To hear Raynell talk, you'd think it was Red Roof Inn with bedbugs.

"Do you think you can accommodate us here, Halia?" Alvetta asks.

"I did give it some thought, but I don't think I can shut down Sweet Tea for the evening; however, I spoke with a friend of mine who books the ballrooms at that Marriott in Greenbelt. They have availability and can accommodate up to two hundred guests . . . and I'd be happy to give the reunion committee a deal on catering."

"That sounds like a viable plan," Alvetta says.

"I don't know," Raynell groans. "Marriotts are so . . . so *ordinary*."

"The space may be ordinary, but I can assure you the food will not be. I can put together a stellar menu for the event and work with your budget."

"And I'll help with all the arrangements. I can keep an eye on the buffet while Halia's busy minglin' with all her old classmates," says Wavonne.

Raynell just glares at Wavonne as if she is not keen on her involvement. "I suppose we don't have much choice at this point," she says. "Christy, make a note to call the Marriott and make the arrangements."

"I can call my contact there if you'd like. They

don't usually allow outside caterers, but she owes me a favor and—" I'm about to continue with my offer to make the arrangements myself when Raynell interrupts me.

"Christy can do it," she says as Christy types a note on her iPad.

I'm about to talk menu options when Darius shows up at the table looking hurried.

"Hello, everyone." He starts refilling the three glasses on the table with more iced tea. "What may I get you two ladies to drink?" he asks Raynell and Christy.

"What's that?" Raynell points to Alvetta's glass.

"That's our watermelon mint iced tea."

"I'll have one of those, but, given it's past noon, slip a shot of vodka in it for me," Raynell says. Christy requests the same minus the octane.

"Sure, but before I get those drinks, let me tell you about our specials today. We have soft-shell crabs dusted with a Cajun cornmeal batter and lightly fried. They're served with twice-fried French fries and coleslaw. We also have butter-baked chicken. There's barely a need for a knife and fork—the meat practically falls off the bone for you. We serve that with macaroni and cheese and collard greens."

"Thanks, Darius," I say. "We'll let the ladies look at the menu a bit more thoroughly, and then I'll ask Wavonne to take their orders and serve the table." I turn to Wavonne. "And the two other tables you've punted off on Darius."

"How am I supposed to help you with the re-union if I'm not at the table to hear the deets?"

"I'll give you a complete rundown on everything we discuss. Now *get*."

Wavonne moans before slurping down the rest of her iced tea and getting up from the table.

"She's quite the character," Raynell says. And, while this is true, there is a condescending tone in Raynell's voice when she says this that I don't appreciate.

"She's a good kid, but she tests me sometimes," I say with a laugh. "She's lived with my momma and me since she was thirteen. My aunt, her mother . . ." I'm about to give them Wavonne's backstory, but then I decide it's none of their business. "Let's just say she had a complicated family situation before that."

"How sweet," Raynell says. "You still live with your mother."

"I guess we do still share a house. Momma needed my help when she became Wavonne's guardian, so I moved back in. These days I'm rarely home at all. This place keeps me very busy." I'm finding myself on the defense. Maybe I'm reading too much into it, but Raynell seems to be saying, "Oh so you're a spinster with no man and live with your mother . . . how pathetic." Rather than continue to justify my living situation, I decide to move on. "So, the reunion. Sounds like we have the place nailed down. Why don't we talk menu?"

"Fried chicken and waffles, catfish, spare ribs, pot roast," Alvetta says, running her finger down one side of my menu as she reads out loud. "It all sounds so good. I don't know where to begin."

"There are a lot of choices." Raynell looks casually disinterested. "But everything is laden with calories. We'll need some options for those us who haven't let our bodies go completely to hell since high school and—" Her cell phone ring interrupts. As it continues to chime, she looks at the screen and hands the phone to Christy. "It's Gregory. Handle it."

"Of course." Christy takes the phone from Raynell, gets up from the table, and bypasses Wavonne as she heads toward the hostess station to take the call.

I watch Christy walk away and then return my attention to Raynell, who's chattering on about the fat content of some of the selections on my menu. I try not to laugh as her stout self blabs to Alvetta and me about how she'd have to double her treadmill time if she were to eat most of the items we serve. But from the looks of Raynell's thick middle, I suspect doubling her treadmill time wouldn't require that much exertion—after all, doubling zero minutes still nets you zero minutes.

I find myself barely paying attention as she blathers on. I think more about how some things never change—Raynell is just as bossy, unpleasant, and condescending as she was in high school. And then, as if she can read my mind and wants to confirm my thoughts, she takes a quick breather from relentlessly critiquing my menu before she shoots her mouth off again.

"So, Halia," she says. "Your hair's almost the same as it was in high school. All this time and you never thought about updating it or switching to a more stylish cut?"

CHAPTER 5

"One watermelon mint tea with a kick," Wavonne says as she sets a glass in front of Raynell. After she places a second glass in front of Christy, who has returned to the table after "handling" one of Raynell's phone calls, she lifts a black cast-iron pan from the tray it shared with the drinks and places it in the center of the table.

"What's this?" There's a touch of excitement in Alvetta's voice.

"It's *just* cornbread," is Raynell's response.

"It smells heavenly."

"And that's coming from the wife of a minister." I smile at Alvetta. "It's my grandmommy's sour cream cornbread." I cut into the pan of golden goodness and place a slice on everyone's plate.

Alvetta takes a bite. "Oh my. That is some *good* stuff."

"It's not bad," Raynell says before taking a second bite, and a third, and then polishing off the whole slice with one last chomp.

"Are you ready to order?" Wavonne asks.

"I'll have the chicken," Raynell barks.

"The butter-baked chicken on special?"

"No. The roasted chicken. With green beans . . . no oil, and a baked potato . . . no butter or sour cream. I'm watching my figure."

"Got it."

"I'll have the pot roast with mashed potatoes and gravy," Alvetta says.

"Oh . . . get the butter-baked chicken, Alvetta," Raynell says. I bet you'll like that better."

"Um . . . okay."

Some things never change, I think to myself yet again. *Once a loyal subject—always a loyal subject.*

"And for you?" Wavonne asks Christy. Before she can answer Raynell pipes up. "Bring her the soft-shell crab special. That sounds good, Christy, right?"

"Sure . . . of course."

I pause for a moment before giving Wavonne my order, wondering if Raynell is going to tell me what to have as well. "Bring me the butter-baked chicken too, please."

Wavonne nods and turns from the table.

"So back to the menu for the reunion," Raynell says, cutting off a second large slice of the cornbread and bringing it to her lips. For something she called "not bad" a few moments ago, she sure seems to be scarfing it down.

"What if we went with some eighties-themed foods?" Alvetta asks.

"That's silly." Raynell offers her standard look

of disapproval. "What are we going to serve? Capri Sun and Fruit Roll-Ups?"

"Actually, that doesn't sound half bad," I joke.

"Back then, lunch sometimes consisted of an order of fries and a Diet Coke . . . and maybe some Ho Hos for dessert. I'd slice a finger off to have that metabolism back again," Alvetta says.

"You and me both," Raynell agrees. "It sounds so cliché, but those really were the days."

"You know it. The clothes . . . and the hair."

"The acid-wash jeans, the big earrings, over-sized sweaters . . . and those stupid Dwayne Wayne flip-top sunglasses the brothers wore . . . thought they were fly as hell in those things," Raynell says.

"I remember when Lee Trainer walked into school wearing that suit with the stripes and a pink tie like he was Rico Tubbs," Alvetta says

"Please. You thought . . . *we all* thought he was *all that*," Raynell says.

"Remember the rolled-up jeans?" I ask.

"Not just rolled up," Raynell corrects. "They had to be folded over at the bottom before you rolled them up. That way they set nicely on your high-top Air Jordans."

I chuckle. "I didn't have Air Jordans. I had the Converse Weapon. Boy, did I think I was some-thing else in those things. I remember getting those shoes for Christmas along with a new Walk-man." I turn to Christy, who has been quiet up to this point. "Do you even know what a Walkman is?"

Christy smiles. "Yes. Those portable cassette players."

"We're probably boring you to tears. I'm sure the eighties are long before your time."

"She's fine," Raynell says before Christy can respond. Even by Raynell standards she seems to treat this Christy girl pretty bad.

"I am. Really. It's fun to watch you guys reminisce."

I doubt she meant it, but if Christy was telling the truth, we decide to give her a rocking good time and launch into a series of chats about everything from Lisa Lisa and Cult Jam to Salt-N-Pepa to the hair bands the white kids listened to. We are deep into a discussion about Brenda K. Starr and "I Still Believe," which Christy admits to knowing only as a Mariah Carey song from her teen years, when Wavonne and Darius show up with our entrées.

I see eyes go wide as Wavonne sets the butter-baked chicken down in front of Alvetta and me. Raynell appears unimpressed when Darius serves her the roasted chicken, but I can't say I blame her. It's a nice dish, and the chicken is tender, but it's really just one of a few items I added to the menu with little enthusiasm to meet the occasional requests we get for lighter fare. I'll be the first to admit that much of the food we serve at Sweet Tea is not for calorie watchers or people monitoring their cholesterol, but we do offer a few dishes for the more health-conscious. In addition to Raynell's roasted chicken, we have several salads, a low-calorie but flavorful steamed shrimp dish, a grilled fresh fish that changes daily, and we'll (albeit grudgingly) broil our crab cakes rather than fry them upon request.

I turn to Christy and see her eyeing her soft-shell crabs curiously and recall how Raynell essentially forced her to order them.

"Where are you from originally, Christy?" I ask as if I'm just trying to get the conversation rolling again.

"I grew up outside of Hartford."

"Connecticut? So that explains why you're looking at those soft shells so apprehensively. Soft-shell crabs are definitely a Maryland thing. I don't imagine they were terribly common in New England."

"No. I've never had them before."

"You'll like them." Raynell reaches over and breaks off a crispy batter-coated claw from one of the crabs on Christy's plate.

"Do you want to switch?" I ask her. "How about you take my chicken? I'd love to have the crabs." Soft-shell crabs are one of those "love 'em or hate 'em" foods. If you were brought up on them, there are few things better than a Maryland blue crab freshly caught just after shedding its hard shell, seasoned, battered, and fried-up golden brown. And if you really want to eat it like a local, you'd slip it between two pieces of soft white bread. But if they are unfamiliar to you, the idea of biting into what looks like a giant deep-fried spider can be less than appetizing.

"Are you sure?" She seems to look at Raynell for her approval.

"Of course." I go ahead and switch the plates before Raynell has a chance to offer or decline to give her blessing.

"That's very nice of you," Christy says.

I sense Raynell is about to reprimand Christy

for not eating what she ordered when her phone rings for the second time since she arrived.

"It's Gregory again." She hands the phone to Christy. "Tell him I'll meet him after lunch in about an hour and a half."

"Mr. Simms. Hello," I hear Christy say as she steps away from the table with Raynell's phone.

"Clients. They expect you to be available twenty-four seven."

"That's the price of being one of the top real estate agents in all of Prince George's County," Alvetta coos.

"Not *all* of Prince George's County, Alvetta," Raynell says, and then looks at me. "I only work Mitchellville, Fort Washington, and Upper Marlboro . . . sometimes Brandywine," Raynell says, spouting off the names of Prince George's County's nicer neighborhoods. "Occasionally, I'll accept some clients in Accokeek or University Park. And, of course, I take listings at National Harbor," she adds, referring to the luxurious waterfront community in Oxon Hill.

"Yeah . . . she don't work in none of the Heights," Alvetta says with a laugh.

"You ain't kiddin'," Raynell replies as she pokes her fork onto Alvetta's plate and scoops up some macaroni and cheese.

Jokes about the "The Heights" are commonplace inside and outside of Prince George's County— made mostly by people who don't live in them. The Heights refer to various communities in Prince George's County with "Heights" in the name: Marlow Heights, Capitol Heights, Hillcrest Heights, District Heights . . . People like Raynell and Alvetta, who, like me, grew up just south of most of the Heights themselves, stick their noses up at these areas, which tend to be poorer and have higher crime rates than the more uppity "outside the Beltway" locales in the county. The Heights are generally the areas of Prince George's County that are being referred to when you hear lame jokes about PG County standing for "Pistol Grip County" or "Poor Ghetto County."

"Mmm-mmm!" Raynell crows before she has a chance to stop herself . . . and before her fork, once again, finds it way over to Alvetta's macaroni and cheese. "Girl, this is *good!*"

The compliment surprises me, and I think it surprises Raynell as well.

"It's my grandmother's recipe. Cheddar cheese, heavy cream, and butter. How can you go wrong? And adding cream cheese makes it extra smooth."

"What's this crispy stuff on top?"

"Bacon and panko bread crumbs. Grandmommy used cracker crumbs, but I think the panko crumbs give it more of a crunch. That's the only change I've made to the recipe. Back in the day, I helped my grandmother make it every weekend for Sunday dinner."

"Are you going to leave some for me?" Alvetta teases as Raynell pilfers more mac and cheese. I look on as Raynell starts helping herself to Alvetta's chicken as well, and without thinking, I find myself pushing my own plate closer to me before Raynell starts pilfering my lunch too.

CHAPTER 6

"**W**here is that waitress? Wavy? Wolfie?"

"Wavonne," I correct her, before signaling for Wavonne.

"We're going to need another order of this," Raynell says after Wavonne approaches the table.

"Another order of what?" Wavonne asks as Raynell points to an empty spot on Alvetta's plate.

"Bring Raynell a side of mac and cheese, Wavonne, would you, please?" I ask.

"Mac and cheese?" Wavonne asks, eyeing Raynell. "I thought Sasha Fierce here was watchin' her figure."

"Wavonne!" I reprimand as Alvetta lets out a quick laugh—a laugh she immediately halts when Raynell's disapproving eyes dart toward her.

"Not for me," Raynell says. "For the table to share."

"One mac and cheese comin' up."

As Wavonne heads to one of the terminals to

put in the order, our conversation returns to high school memories—football games, dances, the McDonald's on Stuart Lane where so many students hung out after school and loitered in the parking lot on Friday and Saturday nights to watch the occasional brawl or find out who had parents out of town and a keg tapped in the backyard.

Long after the à la carte order of mac and cheese arrived, and we've finished our meals . . . and Raynell has helped herself to half the food on everyone else's plate, Wavonne returns to the table. "How about dessert? My aunt Celia has made a mean coconut custard pie. We also have her famous chocolate marshmallow cake and banana pudding."

"I couldn't possibly eat another bite," Alvetta says.

"Me either," I hear Christy say next to me.

"I don't really have much of a sweet tooth," Raynell says as she grabs a spoon and scraps the last bits of macaroni and cheese from the metal casserole dish. "And I've got to run for a meeting."

"Just the check then?" Wavonnne asks.

"No check, Wavonne," I say. "The ladies were my guests today."

"Thank you, Halia. That's very nice," Alvetta says

Wavonne is about to walk away when Raynell stops her. "What was it you said about a chocolate marshmallow cake?"

"It really is a lovely dessert," I say, before Wavonne has a chance to describe it as "dope" or "straight-up pimp." "Momma makes all the desserts here. Her marshmallow cake is one of my favorites—it's a very rich chocolate cake topped with a fluffy marshmallow frosting."

I see Raynell's lips involuntarily part as I describe the cake.

"Not for me, but I'd love a slice to take to my husband."

"Of course." I turn to Wavonnne. "Wavonne, honey, why don't you box some desserts for each of the ladies to take home."

"Oh, that's not necessary," Christy says.

"I'm happy to do it. Take it home. Enjoy it with a nice cup of coffee," I insist.

"Thank you."

"Yes, thank you, Halia," Alvetta says. "For everything."

So many thank-yous today, but not a single one from Raynell, I think to myself as I catch her looking at her watch, which I noticed earlier had the word "Rolex" on it.

"I really do have to get moving," Raynell says. "It doesn't look like we got that much planning done for the reunion—too much talk of Jody Watley's big hoop earrings, and Jane Child's nose ring/chain thing . . . and Kid's hi-top fade. We still need to discuss the menu for the evening." She turns to Christy. "Christy, set up another meeting for us."

"Why don't I put a menu together with some prices? I can e-mail it to you."

"I'd really like to discuss it a bit more," Raynell says as Christy scrolls through Raynell's calendar on her iPad. "Christy, what have I got open tomorrow or early next week?"

"You're pretty booked. You're showing properties to Gregory all day tomorrow and—"

"I have an idea," Alvetta interjects, and seems to look to Raynell for permission to share it. Raynell nods at her, and she continues. "Why don't you come to service on Sunday, and then we can meet in the café afterward and discuss the final details."

"That would work for me," Raynell agrees.

I hesitate for a moment. "It's hard for me to get away from here on Sunday mornings, but let me check with my assistant manager. I may be able to sneak off for a little while."

"Great, I'll reserve you a seat in the Pastor's Circle."

"Two seats," I hear from behind me as Wavonne returns to the table with three brown bags with the Sweet Tea logo on them. "If I'm going to help Halia with the event, I should be there, too."

"Two seats it is," Alvetta says.

"Let me call you later today to confirm," I say to Alvetta.

Wavonne hands a bag to Alvetta and one to Raynell, who also snatches the bag meant for Christy out of Wavonne's hand.

"Get the car and cool it down, would you?" Raynell hands her keys to Christy. It seems odd to me that Raynell would ask Christy to retrieve her car like she's a valet given that Raynell parked in the front of the lot, but then I remember how Raynell was perspiring just from the short walk into the restaurant. If she stepped into her Escalade after it's been sitting in the August afternoon sun, she might just melt altogether.

We get up from the table, say our good-byes, and my guests head toward the exit with Christy scurrying ahead of Raynell and Alvetta. Wavonne and I linger behind and watch Raynell and Alvetta hover next to the door, waiting for Christy to cool down Raynell's car.

"For her *husband*," Wavonne says, eyeing the bags Raynell has in her hand with Momma's cake packed in them. "You know her husband's gonna come home to nothin' but a crumpled bag, an empty Styrofoam container, and a chunky wife with marshmallow breath."

RECIPE FROM HALIA'S KITCHEN

Halia's Macaroni and Cheese

Ingredients

1 pound large elbow macaroni
8 slices of bacon
1 garlic clove, minced
3 tablespoons all-purpose flour
3 cups whole milk
1 cup half-and-half
1 teaspoon hot pepper sauce
½ teaspoon salt
½ teaspoon black pepper
4 cups sharp cheddar cheese (grated)
1 pound softened cream cheese
1 cup panko (Japanese) bread crumbs
3 tablespoons melted butter

- Preheat oven to 375 degrees Fahrenheit.

- Boil pasta with a pinch of salt for 7 minutes, or according to package directions. Drain. Set aside.

- Fry bacon in a large frying pan until crispy. Remove bacon from pan, blot with paper towels, and chop into thin strips. Set aside.

- Add three tablespoons bacon grease to large saucepan. Add minced garlic and sauté over medium heat for 1 minute. Slowly add flour while constantly stirring mixture until a roux or paste forms.

- Add milk, half-and-half, hot sauce, salt, and pepper. Continue stirring until sauce thickens (8–10 minutes).

- Remove pan from heat and drain sauce through sieve (to remove any lumps) into large glass or metal bowl. Add cheddar and cream cheese. Stir until sauce is smooth.

- Add cooked pasta and blend. Transfer to well-greased 13-by-9-inch baking dish.

- Mix bread crumbs with butter and chopped bacon and sprinkle over macaroni and cheese.

- Bake until bread crumbs are crispy, about 30 minutes.

Eight Servings

CHAPTER 7

"Oh my," I say as traffic stalls and I realize we are likely not headed toward a typical church service—cars don't come to a near standstill before the building is even in view at a typical church service.

"Ain't he fine," Wavonne says from the passenger seat next to me about one of the police officers directing traffic. "We should have brought some of your honey butter, Halia . . . put a little on him and eat him right up!"

"Wavonne!" Momma calls from the backseat. "We're heading to *church,* for goodness sake."

"Sorry, Aunt Celia," Wavonne says. "I'll ask the minister to bless the butter first."

I chuckle as we're guided through a maze of orange cones. As the van creeps forward, we eventually round a corner, and Rebirth Christian Church comes into view. The land in the general area is flat, which makes the enormous circular-shaped church resemble Ayers rock rising from the Australian outback.

"It looks like the Verizon Center with a steeple on it," Momma says.

"That is one big place. I bet they could host the BET awards in there."

"The parking lot . . . or should I say *lots* . . . look completely full," I say as our forward motion comes to yet another halt.

Momma lowers her window. "Excuse me," she says to one of the men directing cars. "What's causing the delay?"

"It's like this every Sunday, ma'am. You need to wait for the current service to wrap. The parking spaces will open up when the nine a.m. worshippers start to leave. Then we'll get you moving."

Momma thanks the man and puts the window back up.

"All that parking." I'm eyeing the vast lots surrounding the church. "And there still isn't enough to ease this backup."

"Says here more than ten thousand people attend services here every Sunday," Wavonne says, staring down at her phone. "Ooh, let's check out the pastor." She taps on her phone. "Mmmm . . . not bad for an older guy." She turns her phone toward me.

"He's a good-looking man."

"Let's see what they say about Ms. Thang." Wavonne taps a few more times. "Well, la-te-da." She turns the phone toward me again.

I view the photo of Alvetta in a conservative navy blue suit and white blouse. She's accented the outfit with a simple strand of pearls. "She looks nice, and I have to hand it to her, if she was going for a 'minister's wife' look, she nailed it."

"Says here she's a graduate of Howard University, where she received a bachelor's degree in psychology, which she's found to be an asset when called upon to counsel church members," Wavonne reads aloud from Alvetta's bio. "Oh lawd—girlfriend's a headshrinker."

"Since when did an undergraduate degree in psychology qualify you to counsel people?" Momma asks. "Don't you need at least a master's degree or a PhD?"

"I suspect just being the wife of the pastor qualifies you for all sorts of things."

We wait a few minutes longer, and departing church attendees finally start to make their way out of the lots and traffic begins to move. When we eventually secure a spot in Lot D to the left of the church I text Alvetta to let her know we are here.

Momma and I walk toward the building, moving slowly in an effort to let Wavonne keep up as she tries not to tumble over in the ridiculously high heels she's wearing.

I examine the crowd as we approach the entrance. I was expecting to see worshippers dressed to the nines—especially the women. I was anticipating regal suits and big showy church hats. But, while most of the people walking toward the church are smartly dressed, women in full suits are in the minority. I don't see a single hat, and some people are dressed rather casually in slacks or even jeans.

We step through the main entrance and see

nothing even reminiscent of the churches I'm used to attending. While Momma now attends another mega church across town, she came from a Methodist background, and Daddy was Catholic, so we dabbled between the two religions when I was growing up. I'm used to dimly lit, almost somber interiors . . . stained glass windows, organ music, uncomfortable pews, and people talking in a whisper if they are talking at all.

Rebirth is designed like a sports arena with a brightly lit wide corridor that appears to circle the perimeter of the building. To the left of the vast hallway, which is lined, trade-fair style, with various booths and tables promoting church activities, I get a peek through some double doors into the . . . I'm not sure what to call the area where the service is actually held—the terms "theater" or "stadium" come to mind, though. We're about to start perusing the various promotional stalls when I see Alvetta walking toward us.

"Halia!" She strides forward on a pair of exquisite pointed-toe pumps. "So glad you could make it." As usual, she looks flawless in a close-fitting skirt somewhere between pink and peach and a white silk blouse.

"Me too. You remember Wavonne, and this is my mother, Celia Watkins."

"Yes. Of course. Hello, Wavonne." She turns to Momma. "Alvetta Marshall." Alvetta extends her hand to Momma. "Welcome to Rebirth Christian Church."

"Thank you. I'm looking forward to the service. I'm the only regular churchgoer in this bunch." Momma casts disapproving eyes on me

and Wavonne. "Good luck with these two hea-
thens."

Alvetta laughs. "How about I show you around?"

We follow Alvetta down the main walkway.

"This is the Grand Hall. It loops around the
worship center. As you can see, our ministries set
up tables to recruit new members before and after
the services. We have over a hundred different ministries." Alvetta starts pointing to various tables.
"That's the artist ministry, the fitness ministry, the
photography ministry . . . over there is the magazine ministry—"

"Magazine ministry? Can I get me a free copy
of *Us Weekly*?" Wavonne asks.

"Afraid not. The magazine ministry produces
the church's monthly magazine. It's full color and
has a readership of over twenty thousand people."

"Full color? That sounds expensive," I say,
thinking of how much money I've spent on color
printing for the restaurant.

"Not at all. We sell advertising that more than
covers the costs of production and distribution."

As we continue to walk through the Grand
Hall Alvetta smiles and waves at the other church-
goers. She even stops to hug or offer a quick kiss
on the cheek to some of them. She has a confidence about her as her heels click along the pris-
tine hardwood floors that was absent when she was
at the restaurant with Raynell a few days ago.

"Let me show you the kids' area."

We follow Alvetta a few more steps down the
hall, make a right through some doors, and I swear
we've fallen through a hole into Wonderland or a
Smurf village.

"Damn." Wavonne looks around and catches sight of the cartoonish-looking artificial tree in the center of the room. Its painted leaves go up to the high ceiling and continue outward, creating a canopy over the room that is dotted with oversized multicolored mushrooms, rabbits, deer, and other woodland creatures. The forest theme is continued on the walls in the form of a vibrant mural. There is a reception area on the far side of the room where parents are checking in their children.

Wavonne leans in and, oddly, exercises some discretion by lowering her voice. "Forget the service. I bet some of them be droppin' the little rugrats off here for some free babysittin' and headin' to the mall."

"This is quite something," I say to Alvetta, hoping she didn't hear Wavonne's comment.

"This is just the play area. We have six classrooms behind the reception desk. Volunteers teach bible class to the older kids, and we offer supervised play for toddlers and babysitting for infants."

"I've never seen anything like it. I mostly went to a Catholic church growing up. Our plan for children involved parents hurriedly taking them to the back of the church if they starting misbehaving during the Mass," I say.

"Our children's program lets parents focus on their worship. It's very popular." Alvetta signals for us to follow her yet again. We step back in to the main hallway, and Alvetta continues the tour. She whizzes us past a fully equipped gymnasium, several coffee kiosks that seem to be as well outfitted as any Starbucks I've been in, a spacious book and media retail store with long lines at the registers, and a surplus of multipurpose meeting rooms before guiding us up two flights of steps that lead into what she calls "the control room." From the view through the floor-to-ceiling glass in front of us I can see we are behind the back wall of the worship center just above the balcony seating area.

"I bet the control room at CNN doesn't look much different than this," Momma says, watching the multitude of video monitors, microphones, and switch panels operated by five people wearing headsets at their respective stations.

"We control all the special effects from up here," Alvetta says. "The lighting, sound, fog, the curtains . . . there's a button for everything."

"Well, I'll be . . ." is all I can muster. I look through the panes of glass and feel like I'm backstage at a Bruno Mars concert. Church attendees are starting to file into their seats on both the main level and the balcony. A few minutes later, men and women in weighty burgundy robes begin their procession into the seats behind the main stage. I do some quick calculating and determine that the choir loft alone seats more than two hundred people.

"We should head back downstairs. The service will be starting shortly."

"Sure," I say, surprised to find myself excited for the service. After getting a tour of the building and an insider's look at the control room I'm eager to see how everything comes together for the main event. Something tells me we are not in store for the kind of sleepy church service I grew up attending. Other than it likely being grand and maybe theatrical, I'm not really sure what to expect or how the whole thing will unfold, but given the over-the-top nature of everything else I've seen this morning, I can't wait to find out.

CHAPTER 8

Wavonne, Momma, and I briskly follow Alvetta
down the stairs and eventually enter the worship
center. Alvetta continues to offer quick waves and
hellos to the people she passes as she leads us to a
small seating area directly in front of the stage.

"This is the Pastor's Circle. We reserve it for
special guests."

Unlike the rest of the seating in the worship
center, the chairs in the Pastor's Circle have a sig-
nificant amount of leg room and side tables next
to them—each one equipped with a bottle of
water, a crystal glass, a small bible, a church bulletin, and some mints.

"Girl, we flyin' first class," Wavonne says as we
all take our seats, and I must admit it is fun, for the
first time in my life, to be in the VIP section of
something. "Look at all those jealous heifers givin'
us the eye. That's right, hookers, we in the Pastor's
Circle! How you like that?"

"My God! We can't take you anywhere," Momma whispers to Wavonne.

"Isn't that the truth," I agree. "Now settle down and behave yourself, Wavonne."

Wavonne raises her eyebrows at me before looking toward Alvetta. "Where's Omarosa Manigault-Stallworth? Won't she be joining us?" Wavonne says this in a hoity-toity voice, as if she's Tina Turner on one of her British accent kicks. I wonder who she's talking about, but Alvetta doesn't seem to have the same trouble.

"Raynell will join us after service. She doesn't really *do* mornings," Alvetta responds.

Thinking about how there are probably all sorts of things Raynell doesn't do, I grab the church bulletin on the table next to me and start skimming it. There are notices about group meetings, church finances, and community events. There's also a column called "The Word" by Pastor Michael Marshall. It strikes me as clever that he writes it in longhand, and the church publishes it "as is" rather than typing it up. The cursive writing sets it apart from the rest of the word-processed text and gives his message a very personal tone. I'm about to give "The Word" a read when there's a dinging noise over the speaker that apparently is a signal for everyone to stand. As Momma, Wavonne, and I follow along with the crowd and rise from our chairs, we see no fewer than ten people take their seats on the left side of the stage and pick up their instruments . . . guitars, horns, saxophones . . . you name it. Growing up, my church had Mrs. Tebbler . . . and *only* Mrs. Tebbler, who played the organ at the nine- and eleven-o'clock services. Rebirth appears to have a full orchestra. We continue to look on as six people, two men and four women, all dressed in black, take their places behind as many microphones in front of the choir loft.

The orchestra begins to play an up-tempo melody, and the singers in black with *their own* microphones (I can only imagine what kind of church politics are involved in getting one of those coveted spots) begin to sing. It's not long before the entire choir, more than two hundred members strong, joins in, and the worship center fills with music emitting from a state-of-the-art sound system.

I'm not sure this type of over-the-top service is for me, but I can't help but feel . . . feel *something* with the sound of a few hundred stellar voices, accompanied by a talented orchestra, going at full volume.

"Sing it, girl!" Wavonne calls out as one of the vocalists dives into a solo.

I look around and see people swaying to the music—some with their arms raised like Eva Peron on the balcony of Casa Rosada. And, just when I think my senses of sound and sight have received their delights for the day, a team of women march in from all sides with glittery flags. They take positions at various spots around the main level and begin twirling the flags every which way to the beat of the music. I must say, the effect is striking. Alvetta catches me marveling over the whole grand display and beams with pride as if to say, "I may be the illegitimate daughter of a maid, but look at me now, presiding over one of the biggest congregations in the state of Maryland."

When the music quiets we take our seats, and Michael steps forward from the back of the stage. He's more handsome than his photo online led us to believe, and he's only a few words into his address, when I realize why he packs them in by the thousands every Sunday. He's a gifted speaker with a deep baritone voice and immediately sets the crowd at ease with some self-deprecating humor. He moves about the stage with a headset microphone rather than speaking from behind a podium. Calls of "Preach, Preacher, preach!" and "Amen!" boom from behind us when he makes key points during his sermon. He talks about the heat of the summer and how everyone sweats . . . and then makes a joke about how he misspoke, and everyone but his lovely wife, Alvetta, sweats—"Alvetta's skin," he says, "just gets more dewy and lustrous." A silly joke, but it works because of his good looks, charisma, and command of the stage. He goes on to speak about how we really sweat when faced with temptations from the devil, and I'm not quite sure how he did it, but he uses this segue to seamlessly request that attendees give generously today to keep the air conditioning flowing in the building.

When the collection basket comes around Momma drops in ten dollars, Wavonne passes it to me without making a donation, and I, mindful of Alvetta's eyes right next to me, drop in forty dollars, and wonder if it's enough. *Should I have done fifty? A hundred?*

After some additional singing from the choir and some general announcements about the church's ministries and classes, the service wraps with a final hymn. As I listen to the choir, I make a mental note to try and come back to Rebirth over the holidays. I don't think I'll be joining as a tithing member any time soon, but I'd definitely be up for a return visit in December—I bet this choir puts on a Christmas concert the likes of which I've never heard before.

At the close of the service, Michael descends the stage, walks toward us, and takes Alvetta's hand.

"We'll just be a few minutes," Alvetta says as she steps away from her seat and joins Michael at the foot of the stage where they stand in a makeshift receiving line. Most of the church attendees are exiting the worship center from a number of doors on all sides, but a handful come down the walkways toward Michael and Alvetta, who graciously greet them with hugs and handshakes. Wavonne and I watch for a few moments as the two of them interact with church patrons like a well-oiled machine—an extremely good-looking well-oiled machine.

"If you two want to walk around for a few minutes while Michael and I finish up here, feel free," Alvetta says after excusing herself from her adoring fans. "I'll meet you in the café in about twenty minutes."

"Sure," I reply, and, just before our little trio starts to make our way out to the main hall, we catch a glimpse of Alvetta returning to Michael's side. He's talking to two young ladies, both wearing short skirts and heels that might be even higher than Wavonne's. But, even in the towering pumps, the girls still look up at Michael, who stands at about six foot four. You can see the infatuation in their eyes as they listen to whatever words of wisdom he's sharing with them.

As we turn to leave, Wavonne leans in. "So which one of those thirsty hos you think he's cheatin' on Alvetta with?"

unten in their ease as they hang over having
works of redemptive destiny still them
As we draw nearer, however, I get the
which one of these tables display thank to
chosen salvation with

CHAPTER 9

Once we're out in the Grand Hall we meander around, scan the various booths, and eventually stumble upon a large table promoting a retreat. The banner hanging along the front of the display says: POINT AND CLICK YOUR WAY TO THE LORD: USING TECHNOLOGY TO BRING US CLOSER TO GOD. We're about to continue walking right on past the "point-and-click" table when Wavonne gets a look at the man behind all the promotional materials—a nicely built thirtysomething brother with an angled razor part on one side of his neatly cropped Afro.

"Hold up." Wavonne stops in front of the table. "I need to check me out this retreat." She looks the young man up and down. "What was it Salt-N-Pepa said about bein' *stacked and packed*?" she mutters to me.

"Shoop!" I say with a laugh. The upcoming reunion sparked me to pull out an old Salt-N-Pepa CD. I've had it going in the van lately as Wavonne and I drive to the restaurant.

"Hello, ladies," the young man says to us.

"Hello yourself," Wavonne replies as Momma and I stand behind her.

"I'm Rick Stevens. I'm part of the church's Retreat Ministry. We still have a few openings for next weekend's session if you're interested."

Wavonne shamelessly looks him up and down a second time. "Oh, I'm *interested*," she coos. "Tell me more."

"We'll be spending the weekend at The Williamsburg Inn. It's really an impressive hotel." He hands Wavonne a hotel brochure, and she begins to look through it. "There's a welcome reception on Friday evening, seminars throughout the day on Saturday, and an early breakfast on Sunday. We'll be discussing, among other things, the church's strategy to expand our outreach via social media. We'll be holding classes for members about how to effectively use Facebook, Twitter, Instagram, and such to promote God's word and attract new members to the church."

"Mmmm . . . fancy," Wavonne says as she continues to thumb through the brochure. I look over her shoulder and see photos of the hotel—lots of wainscoting, colonial furniture, and heavy drapes. "Will you be attendin', Rick?"

"I will. I'm leading a focus group about the church's Web site. We'll be reviewing the site in detail . . . determining what works well, and what can be improved."

"I know all about Web sites," Wavonne brags. "I help my girl Jereme with her blog. It's called 'Real, Wig, or Weave?' We put up photos of celebrities, and viewers post commentaries about whether Beyoncé or Viola or Mary J . . . or whoever are sportin' their own hair, a weave, or a wig. We've got hair-care tips and let readers know about specials on products. You should check it out."

"Sure."

"I think I'd like to attend this retreat. How much does it cost?"

"The church subsidizes some of the expenses, so it's only five hundred dollars for the weekend, which includes your hotel room, a complimentary breakfast on Saturday and Sunday morning, and access to all the classes, seminars, and discussion groups. And it's a great way to meet other church members."

"Halia." Wavonne turns to me. "Loan me five hundred dollars, would ya? So I can go on this retreat with Rick and help him with the church's Web site . . . and *anything else* he may need some help with."

Knowing that one, Wavonne has no interest in the helping with the church's outreach via technology and just wants to go to Williamsburg to get all up in Rick's business, and two, that "loan" and "give" mean the same thing to Wavonne, I respond, "Umm . . . no."

"Come on, Halia. Tell her, Aunt Celia, I'll be doin' the Lord's work."

"Not getting involved," Momma says.

"We have the reunion next weekend anyway, Wavonne. You promised to help me with that."

I watch as Wavonne tries to determine if her time will be better spent chasing Rick around at a retreat in which she has no interest or tagging along with me to my reunion where she can spend some time with a retired professional football player who may be able to introduce her to some real live Redskins.

"That's right." She puts the brochure back down on the table. "I need Raynell's husband to set me up with some football. . . ." She lets her voice trail off as she notices Rick looking at her. "With some *footballs* . . . yeah, some footballs . . . to give to needy kids."

"Yes, we all know you are all about helping needy kids." I try not to roll my eyes as I say this.

Wavonne glares at me before turning back to Rick. "How about I leave you my phone number, and you can call me if you ever want to talk Web sites . . . or whateveh."

"Sure. Of course." Rick taps a few times on his phone and hands it to Wavonne. She grabs it from him, enters her contact information, and gives it back to him.

"Whatever happened to a pen and paper?" Momma asks, looking on.

Rick extends his hand to Wavonne. She shakes it and then holds it a tad longer than is really appropriate before I remind her it's time for us to meet Alvetta in the café.

"There's a bible-study group meeting now," Momma says, looking down at the bulletin as we walk through the hall. "I'll check that out while you two discuss reunion plans with your friends."

"Okay. Why don't we plan to meet in front of the bookstore in an hour?"

Momma nods and goes looking for the bible-study group while Wavonne and I continue to walk the lengthy perimeter of the church in search of the café.

CHAPTER 10

Wavonne and I reach the café, and as we step inside, we realize the *café* is really more of a full *cafeteria* with a long line of people making their way through the serving area.

"Over here," Alvetta calls to us from a table along the wall. Raynell is seated with her. Michael and another man who I recognize from TV as Terrence are standing next to the table.

"Hello again," I say to Alvetta as we reach the table and turn and smile at Raynell. "Hey there," Alvetta says. "This is my husband, Michael, and Raynell's husband, Terrence."

"Halia Watkins." I shake their hands. "And this is my cousin, Wavonne Hix."

The gentlemen smile, and we exchange a few words. I tell Michael how much I enjoyed his sermon, and how beautifully I thought the choir sang. Then I chat a bit more with Michael about how impressive the church is while Wavonne cozies up to Terrence.

"So, you're a former Redskins wide receiver?" Wavonne asks him.

Terrence is slighter than I imagined. By no means is he a little guy, but when I think "football players" I think of big burly men—Terrence is built more like a baseball or soccer player. I'm guessing he stands at around six feet tall, and I wouldn't put him at any more than one hundred and eighty pounds or so.

"Yes," Terrence says. "Guilty."

"What a career. Three hundred and one catches for 5,220 yards and forty-one touchdowns."

Wavonne knows less about football than I do, which is almost nothing. Clearly, she's been studying up on Terrence.

Terrence laughs. "Very impressive."

"I've followed your career since you started with the Skins in ninety-five," Wavonne lies. She was probably scanning his Wikipedia page when I saw her sneaking looks at her phone during the service.

"Ninety-five? You had to have still been a child."

While Wavonne laughs and curls a strand of synthetic hair, Raynell, who has barely acknowledged us thus far, decides it's time to put the kibosh on Wavonne's flirting. "I hate to break up Wendy's little rehash of my husband's career, but—"

"My *name* is *Wavonne.*"

"Yes. *Wavonne,*" Raynell says, then looks at her husband. "Aren't you and Michael due in the theater for the big football game?"

"It's just a preseason game, but I guess we are," Terrence says.

"Theater?" I ask

"It's more of a large media room," Alvetta clarifies. "It has a big projection screen . . . seats forty people . . . leather recliners . . . it's quite nice."

"It was good to meet you." Terrence shakes my hand again and then Wavonne's.

"You too," Wavonne says. "Before you jet, let me axe you somethin'. Do many Redskins players attend church here? Ever have any . . . any meet and greets?"

"We actually do have quite a few players on the rolls here. Meet and greets? Hmm . . . we don't have anything specific planned with the players at the moment, but if you join some of the church's ministries and come to service regularly, you're bound to run into some of them."

Raynell rolls her eyes at Wavonne's obvious attempt to gain some introductions to professional sports players. "Terrence. Get!" she says. "We have reunion plans to discuss."

Terrence smiles and looks at Michael. "Guess we better do as the boss tells us."

"Pleasure meeting you," Michael says before he and Terrence make their exit.

"Please have a seat," Alvetta says, and Wavonne and I slide into the booth across from her and Raynell. We've barely gotten settled when a lanky young man wearing an apron appears at the table.

"Good morning, Mrs. Marshall," he says to Alvetta while setting down a coffeepot, a bowl of creamers, various sweeteners, and a carafe of orange juice. "What may I get for you and your guests?" He fills each of our mugs with steaming coffee and pours orange juice into four crystal glasses.

"Why don't you just fix us a few plates with the works?"

"Of course, Mrs. Marshall."

As the young man steps away I see Raynell discreetly elbow Alvetta.

"Kenny," Alvetta calls. "Extra bacon please for Mrs. Rollins."

"For the *table*. Not just for me," Raynell says. "So, let's talk reunion plans. Is everything all set at the Marriott?"

"Yes. My connection there gave the committee a very nice rate, but that's about all I know. Christy was managing the details."

"Where is Christy?" Raynell asks no one in particular, irritation in her voice. "She was supposed to be here by now."

"There she is," Alvetta says as Christy hurriedly makes her way to the table.

"Sorry, Raynell. Traffic getting into the parking lot was crazy."

"What's the latest on the venue for the reunion on Saturday?" Raynell says, not bothering to greet Christy properly or even reprimand her for being late.

Christy grabs a chair from a neighboring table, sits down at the end of the booth, and pulls a manila folder from her bag. "It's all set. We have the Grand Ballroom reserved. Twenty-five round tables. Each table seats eight people. Standard centerpieces and candles. The buffet tables—"

"Fine, fine." Raynell cuts Christy off. "Sounds

like it's under control. You've confirmed the dee-jay?"

"Yes."

"The staging area for the silent auction?"

"Yes. There's a small conference room next to the ballroom. We'll display the items there."

"Silent auction?" I ask.

"Yes. I thought it would be a good idea for classmates and some local businesses to donate items. All the proceeds will go to the Raynell Rollins Foundation for Children in Need."

"It's a great charity. Raynell raised sixty thousand dollars last year." Alvetta beams.

"Well, you know, I'm a giver."

"You are, Raynell. You do so many good things."

I stifle a laugh while Wavonne leans in and whispers in my ear. "Was Alvetta this far up Raynell's ass in high school?"

I ignore her question. "So, Raynell. Tell us more about the charity."

"We focus outreach on children in the D.C. metro area, but it's open to everyone. We identify children of unfortunate means and provide funds for virtually anything that might improve their situation: food, clothing, school supplies, scholarships, summer camps, you name it."

"Sounds like a great resource." I can't help but notice the way she looked directly at Alvetta when she spoke of "children of unfortunate means."

"It is. The silent auction at the reunion will be the perfect way for us to raise funds," Raynell says. "You'll have to donate an evening at your restaurant. What's it called again? Salty Tea?"

"Sweet Tea," I correct. "Of course, I'd be happy to donate a gift card."

"Great. We've collected several donations so far." Raynell looks to Christy. "Remind me of some of the items."

"Everything from free dry cleaning to a complimentary oil change at Middleton's Garage . . . to a dozen roses from Sienna's Floral Arrangements in Oxon Hill. One of your classmates donated a sculpture, and John Thomson, who owns a photography studio, donated a free portrait setting. Another classmate—"

"Meh," Raynell groans. "Such paltry items. Meanwhile I'm donating an antique desk worth a couple thousand dollars."

"Not everyone is as successful as you," Alvetta says. "And the reunion is still a week away. I'm sure more donations will come in."

Alvetta is about to continue reassuring Raynell when Christy's phone rings.

"Raynell Rollins Real Estate. This is Christy. How may I help you?" Christy is silent for a moment before she nicely asks the caller to hold. "Raynell, it's Gregory. Confirming you are meeting him to show properties at two."

"Yes. Tell him I'll meet him at the Brandywine location."

As Christy passes on Raynell's words to the gentleman on the phone, I realize I haven't once heard her use the word "please" or phrase anything as a question when she speaks to Christy. Everything she says to the poor girl is simply a command.

"Like I was saying," Alvetta interjects when Christy wraps up the call. "Michael and I will make some donations, and while I doubt we'll get anything as valuable as the desk you contributed, as some of our former classmates who live outside the area arrive for the event, I'm sure they'll check in and make some donations."

"I hope so. I'll have Christy make some more calls this week . . . shake a few trees," Raynell says, her eyes suddenly pointed in my direction. "Speaking of the desk. I was going to hire someone to take it to the hotel to display at the reunion, but it's not that large and, surely, you must have a van or a truck or something for that little lunch counter of yours . . . no? Would you mind picking it up on Saturday and taking it over to the hotel?"

"Um . . ." I'm not sure what to say. She already has Christy and Alvetta acting as her lackeys. I'm really not eager to add my name to the list, but it is for charity and, honestly, I'm a little curious to see Raynell's house. "I guess so. I'm sure we'll be running back and forth to the hotel a few times on Saturday anyway to get the catering set up."

"Great. Christy, write the address down for Halia."

As Christy writes Raynell's address down on a piece of paper, the young man who approached the table earlier returns with two others, and the three of them, all holding trays, begin laying down plates. While I watch people who were in line at the counter when we first stepped inside the cafeteria continue to wait for their turn at the serving station we enjoy table service—the perks of being guests of the First Lady I suppose. Dishes loaded with eggs, bacon (pork *and* turkey), sausage, English muffins, pancakes, and oatmeal land in front of us. They're accompanied by containers of whipped butter, syrup, and a selection of jellies.

We enjoy our breakfast and begin discussing the menu for the reunion. I present Raynell and Alvetta with a list of options for appetizers to be passed around during the cocktail hour, main and side dishes for the buffet, and desserts. I also suggest that I whip up a few pitchers of our house cocktail to be served at the cash bars.

Generally this approach works well when planning a menu for catered events—customers review the options, make a few selections, and we wrap things up. Such is not the case with Raynell Rollins, though. Alvetta is mostly agreeable to my suggestions, but Raynell doesn't like any of the appetizer recommendations. She wants to know if I can arrange for chilled shrimp cocktails, but when I inform her of the cost of quality fresh shrimp and the effect it will have on my catering price, she lets it go. She's decided she doesn't want fried chicken on the buffet as "fried chicken has no business at a formal event." But apparently macaroni and cheese does have every business at a formal event because she insists that it be part of the menu. She goes on like this for about an hour, and I politely explain why most of her requests (e.g., a staffed raw oyster bar, chocolate soufflés, Kobe beef sliders) are not feasible within the available budget.

I think she believed she was going to be able to bully me into taking a loss on the event and preparing dishes way beyond what my fee would cover. I might have been a little timid around Raynell in high school, but I'm certainly not afraid of her now. I'm not looking to make money on this catering job, but I'm not going to lose money, either. So, after a lot of hemming and hawing, we eventually finalize the menu and come to an agreement over a nice selection of appetizers, entrées, and desserts. And, if I do say so myself, come Saturday night, my old high school classmates are in for a real treat when they get a sampling of some of my tastiest recipes.

CHAPTER 11

"Those look divine," I say to Momma as she starts popping chocolate cakes out of their pans. She's been at Sweet Tea since five this morning. It's eight now, which is actually early for me to be at the restaurant. I'm generally here until well after we close, so I try not to start my workday too early. Coming in during the late morning also allows very little overlap between Momma's time in the Sweet Tea kitchen baking all of her delicious goodies and my time in the Sweet Tea kitchen supervising the rest of our creations, which, believe me, helps keep the peace around here. Momma usually starts her baking at six a.m. and wraps about four hours later, but like me, she came in early today to get a jump on the catering order for the reunion.

Raynell's husband (at least Raynell said it was her husband) loved Momma's chocolate marshmallow cake so much that Raynell asked . . . well, more like insisted, that we serve it as the featured dessert for the reunion.

Momma has twelve layers of chocolate cake cooling on the counter—enough for four cakes. As the smell of rich cocoa reaches my nose, I have to fight the urge to press my hands on them just to feel their warm velvety texture.

As there's always an occasional freak . . . yeah, I said it . . . an occasional "freak" who doesn't like chocolate, to supplement the chocolate marsh-mallow cakes, we'll also be serving sour cream co-conut cakes. And that's just the desserts. We'll be starting the affair with mini corn muffins and fried chicken salad tartlets during the cocktail hour. These will be followed by a full dinner buffet of herb baked chicken, salmon cakes, and host of yummy sides. Of course, this spread is way beyond the budget of the reunion committee, but I agreed to offer a substantial discount. I'll barely break even with this job, but I guess it's okay considering it's for my alma mater.

"Let me get started on the frosting while they cool. Wavonne, start opening those jars of marsh-mallow cream, would you?" Momma calls over to Wavonne, who couldn't have been any less helpful since she arrived with me a few hours ago. She's currently sitting on a stool with her head against the wall and her eyes shut.

"Wavonne!" I call to wake her up.

"Huh?" She slowly opens her eyes.

"Help Momma with the frosting, please."

"I'm so tired." She sluggishly lifts herself from the stool. "Why'd we have to come in so early? I was up late watchin' a *Basketball Wives* marathon.

Those sistas live the life, Halia. They got it all—money, big houses, cars, clothes, jew-reys . . . everything. That's the life I was meant to have . . . not being up at no damn six a.m. to make cakes. Now I just need Raynell's husband to hook me up with a football player, and it will be me on TV covered in bling when they launch a show about football wives."

"You know, Wavonne. Has it ever occurred to you that maybe you could earn your *own* money and have your *own* career to pay for all those big houses and big cars . . . and all that other stuff?"

Wavonne looks at me like I have horns. "What kind of fool would work when she can land a man to pay her bills?"

"The kind that knows she might not ever find that rich brother."

"Oh, I'll find me a rich brotha all right."

"Well, until such time, you need to earn your keep around here." I nod toward the jars Momma asked her to open.

"She doesn't have it *all* wrong, Halia," Momma chimes in, and I'm reminded of why I prefer not to share the kitchen with her. "A little less career and a little more husband hunting isn't the worst idea in the world."

I sigh. "Yes, Momma."

"Don't moan at me. This reunion is a perfect opportunity for you to get out there. There must be an old high school flame . . . or someone who's recently divorced . . . or someone . . . *anyone* for you to connect with."

"Halia had a flame in high school?" Wavonne

looks up from the jars toward me. "Ooh girl, gimme the deets."

"There are no old flames, Wavonne. Other than the occasional homecoming or prom date with guys who were usually more friends than boyfriends, my high school years were pretty devoid of romance."

"So, in other words, your love life was as borin' then as it is now."

"My love life is not that bad," I protest. "I date."

Momma lets out a loud dramatic laugh. "Since when?"

"I went out with Jeremy Hughes just . . . well, okay . . . it was like a year ago. And there was Timothy Jenkins."

"That was even before Jeremy, and we all know that was more a bidness meetin' than a date. You just wanted to get a discount on some kitchen equipment," Wavonne says. "And as for Jeremy . . . any man who wears more foundation and concealer than I do . . . and who takes you to a freakin' *Sound of Music* sing-along at Wolf Trap is hardly husband material."

"I tried to set her up with Stan, the UPS driver," Momma says to Wavonne as if I'm not in the room. "But she didn't move fast enough, and now he's dating that mousey little thing who manages the Walgreens."

"Martha Brennen? That tiny lil' rodent?" Wavonne, who is always combing the aisles of the Walgreens next door for cheap makeup or accessories, asks. "That ho-bag follows me around whenever I go in there like I'm gonna steal somethin'. I don't know what that little Polly Pocket thinks she would do if I did take anything—she barely comes up to my rack. Even Halia could take her in a fight," she adds, turning to me. "Run down there and fight for your man, Halia. Go on."

"Stan is hardly my man." I laugh. "Why don't you both focus on your own love lives, which, if I recall correctly, are no more existent than mine."

"That may be, but I'm gonna get that Raynell to set me up with a Redskin. Then I won't have to be all up in here at the butt crack of dawn makin' cakes."

Momma takes the jars from Wavonne and scoops their contents in a large metal bowl she's already filled with softened butter, secures the bowl into one of my favorite kitchen gadgets, my five-quart stainless steel Hobart N50 mixer. I just upgraded to it a few months ago. It cost a mint, but it works beautifully. Some people get excited over the Audi A6 and the BMW 500 . . . or Versace and Ferragamo. But if you want to see me light up, let's talk about the Hobart N50 mixer or the Kolpak P7-068-CT Walk-In Cooler . . . or the Duke E102-G Double Full Size Gas Convection Oven. Some girls dream of fancy cars and jewelry—for me, a freshly sharpened Misono 440 Molybdenum Santoku knife makes me positively giddy. I'm a sucker for a freshly seasoned Tomlinson cast-iron skillet . . . and don't get me started on the Manitowoc QM-30 Series Self-Contained Cube Ice Machine that's been on my wish list for a couple of years now.

Momma starts the mixer and begins to whip the frosting. As the butter and marshmallow cream blend together she slowly adds powdered sugar to the whirling bowl. When the icing has creamed together nicely, she adds a touch of vanilla, gives it a final mix, and *voilà*, we have Momma's famous marshmallow frosting.

"Yeah . . . good luck with that, Wavonne. From what I know about Raynell, she isn't keen on helping anyone but Raynell. Not to mention she doesn't seem to be terribly fond of you in particular."

I grab two serrated knifes from the knife block, hand one to Wavonne, and we both help Momma slice the small domes off of the tops of the cake layers, so they will lay smoothly on top of each other.

"My knees are not what they used to be. Give them an eye-level look and make sure they are even," Momma asks me.

"Let me do that for you two old hens," Wavonne offers. "Drop it like it's hot," she says as she squats down to get her face level with the cakes. "Perfect."

We've helped Momma enough with her baking to know the drill from here. We take four circular pieces of plywood that I've already covered with decorative purple foil and lay them on the counter. These will function as the serving platters. We place four strips of parchment paper on each platter, so they lie just underneath the edges of the cakes to keep icing off the foil while we work. We then place a dollop of frosting on the center of the boards to anchor the cakes before we flip a moist chocolate layer onto it.

"Now, you girls be careful," Momma says as she goes down the line with a pastry brush and sweeps away any loose crumbs so they don't get in the frosting.

"That's too much, Wavonne!" Momma calls as she watches Wavonne haphazardly plop a glob of frosting onto one of the layers. "These are for Halia's former classmates. We want them to be perfect."

Wavonne removes some of the icing with her spatula and starts to spread it around. "I wanna slice up one of these for breakfast, Aunt Celia," she says as we begin on the second layer. "Girl, hook me up with a slice of this cake and maybe a caramel flan latte, and I'd be like a pig in—"

"Don't even think about it, Wavonne. We need four for the reunion, and that's all Momma's made."

"'Bring me those jars.' 'Too much icing.' 'No cake for you,'" Wavonne mutters under her breath, mimicking Momma and me. "That Russian woman who runs the prison kitchen on TV barks fewer orders."

Momma and I ignore her as we continue to pull the cakes together. When we finally get all three layers assembled and frosted, Momma, ever the perfectionist, slips a thin spatula in hot water, quickly dries it, and uses the heated tool to carefully smooth out the cakes.

"You can tell people you made them, Halia," Momma says as we stand back and admire our finished work. "If these cakes can't land you a man, nothing can."

CHAPTER 12

I can't believe I'm pulling up in front of Raynell's house to pick up the desk she's donated to the silent auction like I'm some sort of moving service. I'm already catering the reunion at zero profit. You'd think that would be enough. I guess I could have just said no and told Raynell to make other arrangements, but she's a hard person to say no to. Besides, I did want to see her house, which I now see I correctly assumed would be quite impressive. And yes, I thought of asking Wavonne to make this run, but my understanding is that this desk is an antique and might be fragile. Wavonne can be careless, and I'm sure I'd never hear the end of it from Raynell if the desk ended up being scratched or otherwise damaged in transit.

Oh well . . . I guess it's for a good cause—at least I hope the Raynell Rollins Foundation is a good cause and not one of those charities with operating expenses sucking up all the donations before they get to the people they are actually supposed to help. For all I know, the donations go to subsidize Raynell's salon appointments and first-class vacations.

I step out of my van and take in the sheer size of Raynell's home. My first thought is *damn, that's a lot of windows.* I start counting them—fifteen windows along just the front of the house and three more in the rooftop dormers overlooking the expertly landscaped yard. Most of houses in newer suburban neighborhoods have brick facades in the front, but the sides and rear are generally covered in siding to save on cost. But this is not the case for the residence of Mr. and Mrs. Terrence Rollins. I can't see the back, but both sides are brick from the roof to the ground.

I walk toward the double front doors, and, based on my experience shopping for wooden tables and chairs for the restaurant, I suspect they are mahogany.

I press the doorbell and hear it chime inside the house. A moment later I'm surprised to see Raynell open the door. I was sure it would be a housekeeper.

"Halia. Hello." Her eyes veer past me toward the driveway. "Gosh. The neighbors are going to wonder who's here in that ramshackle thing," she says of my van, which I'll admit is no Mercedes, but it's only five years old with a few minor nicks on it. "Come in."

I step inside onto gleaming hardwood floors and look up at the foyer ceiling that goes clear to the top of the house. A large window above the front doors carries beams of light onto a mammoth contemporary chandelier dripping with a few hundred thin rectangular crystals. To the left I see a formal dining room with yet another smaller, but no less exquisite, chandelier hanging over a shiny dark wood table (also mahogany I believe) that seats ten people. To the right is a formal sitting room with lush carpet and contemporary furniture.

"The desk is in the family room."

I follow Raynell as we walk alongside the staircase to the kitchen, which opens into a two-story family room with exposed beams and a stone fireplace. The entire wall along the back of the kitchen and the family room consists of floor-to-ceiling windows. I remind myself to lift my jaw back up as I examine the kitchen. It's better equipped than some of the commercial kitchens I worked in earlier in my career. It's a regular utopia of rich wooden cabinets offset with metal hardware, stainless-steel appliances, and glossy granite countertops. There's a large island in the middle and a long glass-top table in the dining area in front of the windows. I guess you might call the area with the table "the breakfast nook," but that term doesn't seem to do it justice.

"I love your kitchen."

"We never use it," Raynell says with zero enthusiasm, and continues walking toward the adjoining family room.

I want to shout what a crime that is—to let such a lovely well-appointed kitchen go to waste— but I keep my mouth shut and follow Raynell.

"Here it is."

I look down and see an ornate piece of furniture . . . what you might call a "period piece."

While quite handsome, it is decidedly out of place among all the modern furnishings in Raynell's home. It hosts a bunch of cubbies and drawers and stands on thin legs that descend into claws—I think they are called ball-and-claw Chippendale legs. It's adorned with metal pulls and outlined with a trim that looks like a detailed wooden rope.

"It's lovely," I say. "How old is it?"

"I had it appraised a few weeks ago. The appraiser thought it was at least two hundred years old. I gave Christy the paperwork with the details. She put together a description that we can display with the desk at the auction. It's valued at more than a thousand dollars, so I've suggested twelve hundred as the minimum bid. We'll see who of the trifling fools we went to high school with has that kind of money."

"That's nice of you to donate it," I say, wondering what her angle is. Raynell is not the kind of person who does things out of the goodness of her heart. Maybe she's tried to sell it and can't, or maybe she's lying about its worth . . . who knows.

"It's nothing. And honestly I'll be glad to have it out of my house. I'm all about clean lines and modern furniture. This thing just clashes with my whole decorating theme."

"What made you buy it if it's so dissimilar to the rest of your décor?"

"Oh, I'm always picking up things that I think might have value—not necessarily to keep. One of the perks of being a real estate agent is I often get first dibs on the possessions divorcing couples are trying to get rid of. They put their house on the market after the divorce papers are filed. Often one of the spouses will sell me things below market value just to be spiteful—the stories I could tell. There's less drama on an episode of *Scandal* than in some of my business dealings with couples who've decided to separate." She looks to the right of the desk. "I bought that painting from the same client who sold me the desk." Raynell points to what can only be described as a stunning portrait of a young black woman in a lovely one-shoulder evening gown. She's poised in front of an old-fashioned microphone. The painting manages to capture her both singing and smiling at the same time. It immediately makes me think of the 1940s . . . or maybe the early fifties.

"Wow," I say. "What a beautiful painting . . ." My voice trails off as I realize that beautiful doesn't really do it justice. "Exquisite . . . it's truly exquisite," I add as I think about what a shame it is to see it just sitting on the floor leaning against a bookcase rather than being displayed on the wall.

"Meh," Raynell says, unimpressed. "It's worthless, and I overpaid for it. I'm not sure if I'll keep it."

"Who is the painting of? She looks familiar."

"Sarah Vaughan. Apparently, she was a jazz singer or something back in the day."

"Sarah Vaughan!" I exclaim. "My mother played her version of 'Send in the Clowns' when I was a kid. She had an amazing voice. I remember Momma referring to her as 'The Divine One.' "

"I thought her heyday was more in the forties and fifties."

"Her career spanned decades. I only know because Momma is a big fan. 'If You Could See Me Now' was another big song of hers—that's a really old one I think . . . from the forties, maybe."

"Well, apparently she's dead."

"She must be dead for more than twenty years now."

"You'd think that would make the painting worth something—even if it isn't a Keckley."

"Keckley?"

"I thought the painting might be an original Keckley. Arthur Keckley was a well-known black artist who painted portraits of performers at the Lincoln Theatre on U Street in D.C. during its prime. He painted all the greats: Duke Ellington, Pearl Bailey, Ella Fitzgerald, Cab Calloway, Billie Holiday . . . and I was hoping that this one was the rendition he did of Sarah Vaughan."

"It's not, I take it?"

"No. I had Christy find me an appraiser. He evaluated the desk as well. I was actually more excited about the painting, but it turns out only the desk has any real value. And even that is only worth a couple of thousand dollars. The painting is just one of many copies of the Lincoln Theater portraits that were done by unknowns. I could probably sell the painting for a few hundred bucks. But, really, I guess it's not half bad. I'm thinking of switching it out of the antique-looking gold frame into something more modern. Maybe then I'll hang it and see if I want to keep it.

"You should keep it. It's rich with history even if it's not an original."

"History shmistory. Show me the money."

I'm about to offer to buy it from her, thinking that Momma would love it, or that it might be a nice addition to the artwork at Sweet Tea, when there's a faint knock on the front door.

"Hello?" we hear Christy call out.

"In here," Raynell responds.

Christy walks into the family room. "Hi," she says to me.

I'm about to say hi back, but Raynell starts running her mouth before I have a chance. "Christy's here to help you move the desk. I would lend a hand, but I just had my manicure done. Doesn't it look nice? OPI's Vampsterdam." Raynell holds up one hand with nails done in a deep reddish brown polish.

"Yes." Somehow the color fits her—much like Raynell, it's sort of dark and witchy.

"Christy will also help you transport it and unload it at the hotel. I need to stay back and get ready."

I guess she assumes I don't need any time to get ready, or that I'm planning on showing up to the reunion in a garbage bag and a pair of Birkenstocks.

Christy looks at me, nods, and we both grab a side of the desk from underneath the top. Raynell watches as we lift it out of the room and past the staircase toward the front door.

"Careful," Raynell says as she opens the front door for us.

Christy and I carefully descend the front steps

with the desk, maneuver it out to the van, and set it down for a moment while I open the hatch. We take a breath, manage to raise it level with the floor of the vehicle, and slide it inside. As I close the hatch I see Raynell disappear back into the house, and think it's rude of her to not even say good-bye or thank you, but then again, it's Raynell.

Christy and I walk around to the front of the van, get inside, and buckle up.

"I hate to ask, but since you have the van, Raynell wanted me to see if we could swing by my place and pick up a few more items your class-mates have donated."

"Why is the stuff at your place?"

"Raynell didn't want people bringing things here. I believe her words were something to the effect of, 'I don't want those trifling fools I went to school with coming here. They're liable to case the place and rob me blind when I'm not at home.' "

"Sure. No problem."

I'm about to drive off, when, once again, it dawns on me how out of character it is for Raynell to be donating a desk worth more than a thousand dollars to charity. I'm still wondering what's in it for her when I see her scampering out of the house holding a glossy poster the size of a large pizza box.

"Be sure to display this on the desk," she says as Christy opens the door and accepts the sign. It has an inappropriately large (and heavily Photo-shopped) photo of Raynell and her contact infor-mation, and reads "Donated by Raynell Rollins, Realtor. Please contact Raynell for all your real estate needs in the finer neighborhoods of Prince George's County."

Raynell heads back into the house, and after reading the sign I look at Christy. "Well, I guess it's better than saying, 'Donated by Raynell Rollins. I don't work in none of the Heights.' "

RECIPE FROM HALIA'S KITCHEN

Celia's Chocolate Marshmallow Cake

Chocolate Cake Ingredients

2 cups all-purpose flour
1 teaspoon salt
1 teaspoon baking powder
1½ teaspoons baking soda
1¾ cups sugar
¾ cup unsweetened cocoa powder
½ cup whole milk
½ cup sour cream
1 stick of butter (½ cup)
3 eggs
1 teaspoon pure vanilla extract
1 cup strong hot coffee

- Preheat the oven to 350 degrees Fahrenheit.

- Generously grease and lightly flour two 9-inch round cake pans.

- Sift flour, salt, baking powder, baking soda, sugar, and cocoa into bowl. Mix on low speed until combined.

- In another bowl, combine milk, sour cream, butter, eggs, and vanilla. With the mixer on low speed, slowly add the dry ingredients to the wet until well combined.

- With mixer still on low speed, add coffee and mix until well combined.

- Pour batter into the prepared pans and bake for 25–35 minutes, until a toothpick comes out clean.

- Cool in the pans for 30 minutes, then turn out onto rack and cool completely.

Marshmallow Icing Ingredients

4 sticks of butter, softened (2 cups)
2 cups powdered/confectioners' sugar
1 teaspoon vanilla
2 jars marshmallow creme (14 ounces total)

- Cream butter in a mixing bowl with an electric mixer on medium speed until soft and fluffy.

- Gradually beat in powdered sugar.

- Beat in vanilla extract.

- Add marshmallow creme until thoroughly incorporated.

Eight Servings

CHAPTER 13

"Would you come on," I say to Wavonne as we approach the hotel from the parking lot. As usual, she's moving at a snail's pace as she tries to balance her Rubenesque frame on a pair of heels that clearly value form over function.

We've just stepped out of Momma's Toyota Avalon—it's not exactly a Mercedes, but it's better than showing up to the reunion in my aging utilitarian minivan. I had some things to take care of at the restaurant and was then running behind getting ready for the event, so we are later than I had wanted us to be. My catering team has been onsite for more than three hours setting everything in motion, but I had hoped to be here at least an hour ago to supervise the final food and serving preparations. I'm technically a guest at this event, but I'm sure I won't be able to help myself from checking in on the food here and there.

I don't like to think of myself as one of those women who cares what former classmates she hasn't seen in more than twenty years think of her, but I have to admit I made way more of a fuss over my appearance tonight than I have in a long time. Wavonne and I went for hair and makeup at my friend Latasha's salon this afternoon, and I bought a new outfit from Nordstrom last week—an Adrianna Papell purple lace overlay dress. It's lovely and a bargain at less than two hundred dollars. The sales lady in the Encore section even talked me into a Spanx waist and thigh shaper. It was quite the devil to get on, and it's not the most comfortable thing in the world, but it does help smooth out my curves. I think it even gives my caboose a lift. I thought it might help me squeeze my size fourteen frame into a size twelve dress, but I guess even Spanx has its limits. I've paired the dress with some low-key gold hoop earrings and simple black pumps. Tomorrow I'll be back in my khakis and no-slip unisex kitchen shoes, but, I must say, it does feel nice to be gussied-up like a real woman for the first time in a long while.

"These shoes are made for posin', Halia. Not walkin'. When Terrence tells all his football player friends about me the description needs to be off the chain."

I guess my pumps would be considered high heels, but I'm managing a more hurried pace as mine are maybe two inches or so compared to the five- or six-inch beasts Wavonne has shoved those canoes of hers into. I don't even know how to describe them. I think Wavonne called them "platform booties." They are bright yellow and, with no fewer than six straps, one wouldn't think they'd need a zipper in the back, but apparently they do. The outlandish shoes are an appropriate match for her dress—an ankle-length fitted sheath of a thing with a multicolored zigzagging pattern and a wide scoop neck that shows off Wavonne's ample cleavage.

"How do I look?" I ask Wavonne when we reach the door to the hotel lobby.

"Dope as hell. You might just get lucky tonight, Halia."

I laugh. "Okay. Let's do this."

We walk through the main entrance and down the hall, and I immediately recognize my friend Nicole Baxter sitting behind a welcome table in front of the main reception room.

"Halia!" She hops out of her chair, shimmies her full-figured self around the table toward me, and wraps me in her arms. "You look gorgeous!"

"Thanks. So do you."

Nicole, who's white, was one of a handful of students, like myself, who crossed the racial divide at my high school. While the student body there is now almost exclusively African American, back in the late eighties there were still a fair number of white kids on the rolls. And, by and large, the black kids socialized with the black kids and the white kids socialized with the white kids. The few Asian and Hispanic students were generally lumped in with the white students. Outside of class, we mostly only crossed paths through student activities and sports. Off-campus outings and parties were not known for their racial diversity. But Nicole and I

were both joiners with no athletic ability, so we
served together on the debate team and the poster
club and the drama club . . . and the student coun-
cil . . . and who can remember what else. Nicole is
naturally very social and, while I'm not exactly shy,
her gift of gab was a good match for my somewhat
reserved personality. We both share a sharp (some
may say "caustic") sense of humor. We became fast
friends, and she's actually the only person from
my senior class that I'm still in regular touch with.
And, if there's one person to still be in touch with,
it's Nicole.

Nicole married well, doesn't work, and has no
kids—all of which leaves lots of time for collecting
gossip. She knows the skinny on all our former
schoolmates. A few days ago she and her husband
came to Sweet Tea for dinner, and I got an earful
about how Candy Bennett and John Moore are
now engaged, but only after a torrid affair in which
they were sleeping together while still married to
other people. I learned that Tim Bell, who is not
expected at the reunion, is now Tina Bell, an advo-
cate for transgender rights. Nicole also told me
that Sasha Montgomery probably won't make it to
the reunion, either, as this soon after her surgery
even the best concealer won't cover the scars
along her hairline.

"You look lovely as well, Wavonne." Nicole hugs
Wavonne and starts shuffling through the name
tags on the table before handing one to each of us.
Mine has my senior photo on it, while Wavonne's
simply has the word "Guest" under her name.

"Go on in. I'm going to staff the table just a bit
longer. I'll find you."

"Okay."

As I pin on my name tag, I see Wavonne shove hers in her purse. "I'm not pinnin' nothin' on this dress. I'm takin' it back to Gussini tomorrow and gettin' my nineteen dollars back."

I take a second look at the dress and, even at nineteen dollars, I suppress the urge to tell Wavonne that she overpaid. One look, and you can see how poorly the stitching has been done around the neckline, and the fabric is so sheer that . . . well, let's just say I'm glad Wavonne has Spanx on as well. The shapewear is performing double duty tonight—not only is it smoothing out all of Wavonne's lumps and bumps, but it's also keeping certain anatomical parts from being visible through the thin material.

We walk through a set of double doors into the ballroom and see that the party is already in full swing. We stop by the bar and order two servings of Sweet Tea's signature drink, Mahalia's House Cocktail, a refreshing blend of my homemade berry syrup, Sprite, grapefruit vodka, and lemon juice (Check out *Murder with Fried Chicken and Waffles* for the recipe. ☺). As I take a sip of my drink, I'm pleased to see my servers, dressed in black pants, crisp white shirts, and pink ties, making the rounds with the hors d'oeuvre trays.

"Hi, Joslyn," I say to one of the servers who approaches as soon as she recognizes us. "How's it going?"

"Good. We're passing out the appetizers now and dinner preparations are in progress."

I take a moment to examine the selections on her tray and admire my handiwork. My team and I were up late last night preparing the finger food. While I do love the peapods' stuffed cheese filling and the smoked salmon deviled eggs, I decide to taste test one of the fried chicken salad tartlets while we are still on the sidelines of the room. I take a bite and am reminded why they are such a favorite of mine—shredded fried chicken (seasonings, breading, and all), a bit of mayonnaise, sour cream, some sliced seedless red grapes, and a touch of salt and sugar—all mixed together, delicately placed into crispy mini-tart shells made from Grandmommy's pie crust recipe, and topped with a sprinkle of chopped candied pecans.

"That is *good!*" I say as Wavonne takes a napkin from Joslyn and begins to pile it with a hefty sampling of items from the tray.

"All the starters seem to be going over very well with everyone."

"Great. I'll check in with the kitchen in a little bit."

Joslyn steps away, and I take a moment to give the ballroom a once over. I know it's more than two decades since graduation, but you'd think I'd recognize more than just a handful of faces. I see Beverly Wolfe, who was on the debate team with me, and Matthew Dyer, who I remember routinely getting shoved into his locker by some of the school bullies . . . and Tisha Hammond, who sat next to me in home economics and was completely worthless when it came to cooking. I'm still scanning the crowd when Alvetta, who is standing with Raynell and two other women, catches sight of us and waves us over.

I approach Alvetta and Wavonne toddles behind me as best she can given her snug dress, steep shoes, beverage glass, and napkin full of food.

"Hello, ladies," Alvetta says when we reach her little gaggle. "Halia, the appetizers are exquisite."

"Yes," Raynell chimes in, and almost spills her cranberry-colored cocktail on me when she leans in and gives me a quick air kiss. "This bunch does seem to be enjoying them. Perhaps the more sophisticated cuisine I suggested on Sunday would have been wasted on this crowd after all. Your . . . how do I put it . . . 'down home' vittles seem to be more their speed."

"*Down home vittles?!*" Wavonne questions. "You gonna let her talk about your food like that?" Alvetta and the other girls suddenly look uncomfortable. I vaguely recognize them as former Whitleys, and, no doubt, they are not used to people who don't shamelessly cater to Raynell.

I laugh. "Oh, Wavonne. Raynell is only . . . well . . . being Raynell." I give Raynell a little wink. "I'm glad everyone is enjoying the food."

"Halia," Alvetta says. "You remember Tamika and Nesha." She nods toward the two ladies standing next to her.

"Of course." I extend my hand to each of them, and we exchange greetings. "This is my cousin, Wavonne. She's my date for the evening."

Raynell looks at Wavonne and then me. "Your date? I guess the man shortage is affecting so many these days."

"Speakin' of men," Wavonne says to Raynell. "Where's yours?" Wavonne looks around the room.

"Terrence couldn't make it tonight."

"He and Michael are at the church retreat this weekend," Alvetta says. "They are both leading some discussion groups, and Michael is giving the keynote address at the main reception tonight. They wouldn't have known too many people here anyway. They would have been bored."

"What do you mean Terrence ain't here?" The disappointment shows in Wavonne's voice.

"He's away for the whole weekend," Raynell says. "Sorry, no football player introductions tonight. Walter, over there," she adds, pointing toward an overweight bald man popping a deviled egg in his mouth, "is an appliance salesman. You'd probably stand a better chance with him anyway."

I can sense Wavonne about to counter Raynell's catty comment, so I pull her aside, excuse us, and take her for a little walk to the other side of the ballroom before she has a chance to really start something with Raynell.

"That stubby little oompa loompa be trippin', Halia. I got a mind—"

"Let it go, Wavonne. She's not worth it," I advise. "Why don't we go check out the auction room?"

Wavonne lets out a long groan before responding. "Fine . . . as long as it's a ho-bag-free zone."

I begin to lead the way out of the ballroom with Wavonne following. "I can't make any promises with regard to ho-bags, Wavonne, but let's hope for the best."

CHAPTER 14

"I see Raynell snagged the best spot to display her desk and all her real estate promotional crap," Wavonne says as we step into a room about a quarter of the size of the one we just left.

"Wow. She really is shameless." I eye the desk, which, of course, is exhibited closer to the ballroom entrance than any other item. Christy and I displayed the poster that Raynell gave us when we were leaving her house earlier today on one side of the desk, but, since then, it has been joined by a multitude of business cards, brochures of homes Raynell is listing, and promotional magnets, calendars, and notepads.

"Some retoucher worked overtime on that." Wavonne takes note of Raynell's oversized photo on the poster. "Who ever did it should get an award. She almost doesn't look like a Rottweiler."

"Almost," I agree. "Let's see if this desk has gotten any bids." I find the sheet of paper where people write down their bids among all of Raynell's marketing paraphernalia and review the numbers. "So far, the desk has only fetched two bids: one for five hundred dollars and one for five hundred fifty dollars."

"That's not even the minimum bid. Sista girl is not gonna be happy about that."

"I'm not sure she cares what the desk fetches. Clearly her donation was just a vehicle for marketing her business."

We step away from the desk and begin perusing the other items on display and find there is quite a variety. Leonard Durey donated a certificate for complete auto detailing at his car wash in Marlow Heights. Jamie Stacks (who is apparently a massage therapist these days) is giving away a sixty-minute massage. Karla Sable is offering a dozen cupcakes from her bakery to the highest bidder, the list goes on and on. . . .

"Here's yours," Wavonne says when she comes across the display for the one-hundred-dollar Sweet Tea gift card I donated. It includes the gift card (unactivated in case some fool tries to steal it) and a Sweet Tea menu. "Look, it's already reached ninety dollars."

"Really?" I walk over and take a look. I'm pleased to find that seven people have bid on it already.

"Who are the dummies who've bid a bunch of money on this tacky-assed T-shirt?" I hear Wavonne say a few steps ahead of me. I look up and see her bent over to take a better look at the shirt. "The bidding is up seventy dollars."

I join her in front of the table and smile. "Oh

my God! I have not seen one of those in forever." I take in the white T-shirt featuring a black Mickey and Minnie Mouse decked out in FILA sportswear with the words "Yo Baby, Yo Baby Yo" across the top and "Mickey & Minnie, Good to Go" across the bottom. "These shirts were all the rage back in the day." I laugh thinking about it. "Everyone had one. I think Disney ended up suing whoever made them." I lift the shirt from the table. "This looks brand new . . . like it's never been worn."

"Probably cause it's butt ugly."

"We didn't think it was ugly in the eighties."

"No, we sure didn't," I hear a voice behind me say.

I turn around. "Robin Fillmore."

I wouldn't have called Robin and I great friends. She was more of a partier than I was, but she also had a studious side and served in the student government with me, so we were sort of casual friends.

"Hi, Halia. So good to see you again."

"You too."

"I was just telling my cousin Wavonne here about how popular these shirts were when we were in high school."

Robin smiles at Wavonne. "Believe it or not, she's telling the truth. They were just one of many stupid things we took a liking to in the eighties." She looks back at me. "Remember those horrible jelly shoes . . . and stirrup pants . . . sneaking out to an M.C. Hammer concert . . . driving down to freakin Waldorf to cruise the parking lot at Waldorf Shoppers World?"

"I had forgotten all about that." It wasn't something I did often as I really was pretty straightlaced in high school, and cruising Waldorf Shoppers World was mostly a white-people thing, but I did partake a time or two.

"Cruise Waldorf Shoppers World?" Wavonne asks.

"We'd just circle . . . and circle . . . and circle the parking lot of a strip mall down in Charles County. On the first loop you might notice a guy you like the looks of in another car, make eye contact with him on the second loop, maybe exchange a few words with him on the third loop. People did it for hours . . . often until the police came and cleared us all out."

Wavonne looks at us, decidedly unimpressed. "You circled a parking lot to get dates?"

"I guess we did," I confirm. "We didn't have iPhones back then, Wavonne. We couldn't just fire up Tinder and start swiping through photos."

Wavonne rolls her eyes. "Life in the olden days."

"If we weren't cruising and no one had a party we were usually at The Oak Tree drinking and smoking . . . and doing God knows what else."

"I don't think I ever went," I say to Robin, but I do remember hearing about the infamous tree. It was a big tree in a field that everyone just called The Oak Tree . . . over in Cheltenham I think . . . where a lot of the area high school kids would converge to blare boomboxes and party. The field was down a hill, so drivers couldn't see it from the road.

"Really? Why?" Robin asks.

"Because, just like now, she's a stick in the mud," Wavonne says.

"I wasn't . . . *am* not a stick in the mud, Wavonne." I turn back to Robin. "But I didn't really run with the kind of crowd that hung out at The Oak Tree."

"I wonder if that tree is still there."

"I doubt it. That field is probably a tract housing development by now," I say, and Robin and I continue to chat as we move along to the next display table with Wavonne.

"This is nice," Robin says when we come upon a small painting of a farm scene. It's an oil painting of a pasture with a big red barn in the distance. There are some animals grazing in the field—a horse, two cows, some chickens, and a pig. "It's quite well done. The artist perfectly captured the feeling of early evening with the sun setting behind the barn."

I took an art class in high school, and I remember being taught how to capture light using yellow and orange paints. I was never good at it, but I do recall sitting next to a girl who was good at it—*very* good, actually.

I leaned over to read the place card describing the donated painting, and, as I suspected, it was painted by my former painting classmate. "Well, look here." I say. "Kimberly Butler painted it."

"Really?" Robin asks as the three of us take a closer look at the canvas.

"Yes. She was in painting class with me. She definitely had an artistic talent back then. It looks like she's really continued to develop it. The painting really is lovely," I say, but as I continue to look at Kimberly's work something about it is bothering me—I can't put my finger on what it is, but there is just something odd about the painting.

We give the painting a last look before continuing to peruse the rest of the auction items. Before too long we reach the end of the rows of display tables, and Wavonne and I decide to make our way back to the main ballroom while Robin stays behind to place a few bids.

"You ain't goin' to bid on anything?" Wavonne asks me.

"No. Nothing really interested me," I say as we rejoin the party. "Now just try to have a good time and stay away from Raynell. You two seem to bring out the worst in each other. There are plenty of other people to talk to." And no sooner have the words left my lips when a striking woman with flawless medium-brown skin moves toward us. She's wearing a "barely there" red strappy slip dress that shows off a near perfect figure.

"Halia? Halia Watkins, right?" the woman says to me.

"Yes." My eyes linger on her face. I look for a name tag, but she's not wearing one. "I'm sorry. Offhand I don't recognize you."

"Kimberly. Kimberly Butler."

"Oh my gosh! We were just talking about you. We saw your painting in the auction room. It looks lovely . . . and so do you, I might add. Really, you look amazing," I say, and actually mean it. "What a difference from when we were . . . I mean you looked nice back then, but *now* . . ."

Kimberly smiles. "Thank you. I guess it just sort of happens . . . one eventually fills out."

And "happen" it did indeed. In high school Kimberly was shapeless and dowdy. I remember her hiding her flat chest and nonexistent behind under heavy sweaters and baggy corduroys. The white girls could get away with boyish bodies, and some of them actually dieted themselves down to boney petite frames, but a black girl without curves—that had to be a tough pill to swallow.

"You look great as well, Halia."

"That's sweet of you," I say. "Kimberly, this is my cousin Wavonne. I'm actually catering the event tonight, and Wavonne works at my restaurant with me. She came to help me keep an eye on things, so I could enjoy being a guest."

Kimberly greets Wavonne, shakes her hand, and then turns back to me. She looks at me awkwardly for a moment before speaking. "While I have a chance, Halia, I just want to say thanks."

"For?"

"I don't know . . . for being one of the nice ones. I know we weren't exactly friends, but at least you were never mean to me. Let's face it—I wasn't the most popular girl in school to say the least. Hell, I hate half the people here . . . especially the women. The only reason I came is to show these bitches that I turned out pretty well in spite of them and their nastiness."

I'm about to agree that she did turn out pretty well and maybe compliment her on her dress when a male classmate on his way to the bar, unlike me at first, actually does seem to recognize her. He taps her on the arm and begins to engage her in conversation. He ignores Wavonne and me.

"*Rude*," Wavonne says as the man continues to pay us zero attention and keep his focus on Kimberly and her voluptuous figure. She really seems to shine these days, and it appears Wavonne and me are getting lost in her light.

"Come on, Halia. We ain't gonna stand here bein' treated like no Kelly and Michelle." Wavonne grabs my arm and pulls me a few steps back.

It actually works out well that we've put a little distance between us and Kimberly, so I can give Wavonne a little backstory on Ms. Skimpy Red Dress. I'm about to tell her how homely Kimberly looked in high school and what a dramatic transformation she's made, but before I do, I catch Kimberly's eyes scanning the room as her companion speaks to her. As he's going on and on about God knows what, I see Kimberly's pleasant expression suddenly evaporate. I wonder what the gentleman she's speaking to said to make her look so abruptly agitated, but then I realize that it wasn't something she *heard* that distressed her. I can tell from her eyes that it's something she *saw* . . . something she's *seeing* at this moment. I turn around to find exactly who or what her line of vision is fixed on, and, let me tell you, if I could draw a line from Kimberly's eyes to the focus of her hostile attention, it would run straight as an arrow to one Raynell Rollins.

CHAPTER 15

Wavonne also notices the unsettled look on Kimberly's face. "What's wrong with her? Why's her face all gnarled up all the sudden?"

"Her demeanor went sour when she spotted Raynell."

"Well, that would make anyone's demeanor go sour."

"Yeah . . . well, she and Raynell have a *history*."

"Ooh, girl, I smell me some gossip. Lay it on me."

"Hmm . . . where to begin?" I pause for a moment. "Like I said, Kimberly wasn't much to look at in high school. She was sort of gawky, and boy, was she shy."

"So, the type of girl Raynell ate for lunch?"

"You've got that right. People like Raynell have a homing device on girls like Kimberly. They seek them out to use and abuse—that whole search-and-destroy dynamic. Actually, I don't remember Raynell paying much attention to Kimberly during the first couple of years of high school. It wasn't until later when Kimberly made the mistake of developing a crush on whatever buffoon Raynell was dating at the time—I think it was Eddie Wicks . . . yeah, it was Eddie . . . he was on the football team and played whatever position requires the big hulky brothers. He was built like a refrigerator and, if I recall correctly, about as dumb as one. It's all coming back to me now—he and Kimberly were thrown together as chemistry lab partners. He needed a lot of help from Kimberly, and she took a liking to him. Poor girl made the foolish error of telling someone—I can't remember who—about her feelings for him. Well, whoever she told was a blabbermouth, and you know how quickly word gets around a high school cafeteria."

"You ain't lyin'. A girl borrows one pair of Chanel sunglasses from someone's locker without axin', and, next thing you know, the whole school be callin' her a thief."

I give Wavonne a look.

"Don't be judgin' me, Halia. Turns out they weren't even real Chanel . . . and I was gonna give them back . . . I *was* . . . especially after I found out they were bobos."

"*Anyway*. Word quickly got around that Kimberly had a thing for Raynell's boyfriend. Everyone, including Raynell, knew that Kimberly never stood a chance of snagging Eddie, but bullying was a hobby for Raynell, so it didn't take much for her to go on the attack.

"She took Kimberly's crush as a license to kill. She would bark like a dog at Kimberly in the hallway, get others to hold their noses when she walked by, and even spread rumors about Kimberly having a tail. Everyone was afraid to cross Raynell, so no one stood up to her or told her to knock it off. As if the harassment wasn't enough, Kimberly became an 'untouchable' on top of it—other students kept their distance from her for fear of becoming a Raynell-target themselves. And while I never participated in any of the bullying, I'm sorry to say I never made an effort to stop it, either. I guess I was as afraid of Raynell as everyone else.

"The worst was when Raynell switched Kimberly's shampoo after gym class with Nair hair removal cream. I wasn't in the locker room when it happened, but I heard the story—the whole school heard the story of how Raynell stood laughing as Kimberly emerged from the showers in tears with patches of hair missing. Kimberly wore a head scarf to school for the rest of the year."

"Her hair looks pretty good now," Wavonne says as we watch Kimberly's new admirer give her a kiss on the cheek before continuing on to the bar.

"That was Brian Clarke," she says, re-approaching us. "He sat behind me in homeroom two years in a row and never said so much as hello to me. Now he's asking for my number and wants to have dinner while I'm in town."

"What did you say?" I ask.

"I gave him *a* number . . . not mine, but if he needs a pizza delivered it will come in handy."

"Ooh, I *like* you," Wavonne says.

Kimberly laughs. "That guy was a tool in high school, and he's still one now. We only talked for a few minutes, and he managed to slip in something

about his BMW and how he only wears Hugo Boss
suits. If only having money could make up for
being a jackass."

"He has money?" Wavonne shifts her eyes toward Brian, who is in line at the bar. "Excuse me,
ladies. I think I needs me a cocktail."

As Wavonne saunters toward the bar I continue to engage Kimberly in conversation. I tell
her all about Sweet Tea and my years in the restaurant business, and she gives me the scoop on what
she's been up to since graduation. She tells me
that after high school, she attended the Pratt Insti-
tute in Brooklyn and stayed in New York after college. While working a series of odd jobs she slowly
made a name for herself as an artist. She beams
with pride when she tells me about the early years
after college that she spent banging on doors trying to get galleries to show her paintings. And
how, now, after much persistence and hard work,
New York's finest galleries approach her and out-
bid each other by reducing their commissions for
a chance to show her work.

"Congratulations," I say. "That's really impressive. Maybe I can see more of your work sometime.
Your paintings are probably out of my price range,
but I occasionally switch out the artwork in Sweet
Tea to keep things fresh. Who knows—I might buy
something to hang in the restaurant."

"Sure," Kimberly says. "Let me give you my
card." She retrieves a glossy full-color business
card from her purse and hands it to me.

I give it a quick look. "That's a lovely photo of
you."

"Thanks. It has my contact information and a

link to my Web site. I'll be in town for a couple more weeks if you'd like to talk about some of the pieces I have available . . . or even commission an original."

"An original? Wouldn't that be fun." As I drop the card in my purse I see Raynell hurriedly making her way toward us—her cranberry cocktail replaced with what appears to be a sour apple martini. I notice Kimberly stiffen when she catches sight of her.

"Halia, I think it's about time we open the buffet. Hopefully the main course will go over as well as the appetizers. Clearly, these people have no experience with fine dining, so it should be okay."

"Sure. Let me check in with my team," I say, before I bring up the uncomfortable topic of money. I usually require at least half my catering fee up front with the outstanding balance due the day of the event, but given that this job was for my own reunion I agreed to forgo the deposit and collect my full fee today. "Do you have the check for the catering?"

"I was in such a rush today I forgot all about it. Christy's my chauffeur for the evening. I'll write a check when we get back to my house tonight, and give it to her. She can drop it at the restaurant for you tomorrow."

"Why don't I just swing by your house in the morning and get it?"

"Oh God, no. Get it from Christy. Let her get up early."

While I grudgingly agree I notice Kimberly still standing next to me, glaring at Raynell. "Um, Raynell

. . . this is Kimberly. You remember her? Kimberly Butler?"

Kimberly and I wait for a flood of recognition and maybe an outpouring of apology—we get neither.

"Yes, yes, of course," Raynell says, but you can tell from the look on her face that she doesn't remember her. She extends her hand while giving Kimberly a good once-over. "You were on the cheer squad, right?"

"Yes," Kimberly lies. "Go Hornets!"

I laugh quietly, knowing full well that Kimberly was never a cheerleader, and she's just screwing with Raynell.

"I wonder why we didn't hang out more?" Raynell says, clearly confused as to why someone as attractive as Kimberly was not part of the Whitleys.

"Oh . . . I wasn't really into the whole skanky slut thing," Kimberly says with a laugh and just the right amount of inflection, so you can't quite tell if she's serious or joking.

Bewildered, Raynell decides to laugh it off. "So what are you up to these days, Kimberly?"

"I live in New York. I'm an artist . . . oil paintings mostly, but I also work with watercolors, and I've been experimenting with an airbrush lately just for fun."

"How nice," Raynell says with a condescending tone. "Sounds like a fun hobby."

"I thinks it much more than a hobby," I say. "Kimberly's art has been shown in galleries all over New York City."

"Really?" There's a change in Raynell's demeanor—the sort of change that happens to Raynell-types when they realize the person they've been talking to might be of use to them. "So you're really a pro?"

"I would like to think so. My last painting sold for more than twenty thousand dollars at the Leslie Miller Gallery in Chelsea."

"Hmm." Raynell puts her finger to her chin. "Do you know much about appraising art? I have this painting of Sarah Vaughan . . . you know, the famous jazz singer. I recently purchased it. I thought it might be a Keckley. Arthur Keckley was—"

"The famous painter who did renditions of singers who played the Lincoln Theater back in the day. Yes, I know who he is. His originals are worth a hefty sum."

Not one who's used to being interrupted, Raynell stammers for a moment. "Um . . . yes. That's him. Unfortunately, I was told by one appraiser that it's not an original, but I'd love to get a second opinion just to make sure."

"I'm not an art appraiser by any means, but I may know enough to be able to tell you if it's real. Maybe we can set something up while I'm in town."

As I watch Kimberly hand Raynell a business card, I wonder what she's up to. I can't imagine she has any real interest in helping out her high school tormenter.

"Thanks." Raynell turns her head and yells to Christy, who's a few feet away chatting with Alvetta. "Christy. Give Kimberly here my contact information. She's going to come by and give me a second appraisal on the Sarah Vaughan painting," she says, takes a last sip of her martini, and departs for the bar to get a refill.

Christy rushes over looking exhausted, which isn't surprising. She's been here all day getting the silent auction set up and helping out with other details.

As Christy digs for a card in her purse, I take a moment to excuse myself to make sure the buffet is ready to make its debut. I start to walk away when I notice a hush come over the ladies I'm leaving behind—all their gazes fixed in the same location over my shoulder. I look behind me to see what all the fuss is about, and there *he* is—a brother so fine, it's no wonder conversations have stopped and all eyes are on him.

CHAPTER 16

"Gregory Simms," I hear coming from behind me. I flip around and see Nicole. "The man you and the rest of this room are staring at—it's Gregory Simms."

"Really?" My eyes are still fixed on his handsome face. He's wearing a snug pair of dress pants that outline a behind you could set your drink on. I suspect he decided to forgo the suit and tie that most of our former gentlemen classmates are wearing as the tight polo shirt he's sporting shows off an impressive chest. "The Gregory Simms that always had his nose in the book? The one all the jocks made fun of because he couldn't even do one pull-up in gym class?"

"From the looks of those biceps now, I bet he can do a hell of a lot more than one pull-up these days."

"Who's that?" Wavonne has returned from the

bar with a fresh drink. She must have decided to ditch Brian to head back over here and get some details on Gregory.

"The man who looks like he just stepped out of a cover of *GQ*?"

"Uh-huh."

"That's Gregory Simms," Nicole answers. "He was in our class—a quiet academic type back then. I doubt he weighed more than a buck thirty in high school."

"Now that is a *man*," Wavonne says.

"He lives in Miami now," Nicole extols. "I got the skinny when he checked in at the welcome table. He owns a chain of gourmet burger restaurants called South Beach Burgers—handmade burgers, fresh cut fries, shakes . . . all that stuff."

"Really? A fellow restaurant owner."

"And a successful one, too." Wavonne's already tapped on her phone a few times and must have found her way to the South Beach Burger Web site. "Twelve locations from Florida stretching up to North Carolina."

"Well, good for him," I say. "He was always a nice guy. I'm glad he's doing well."

"Doing well is right. That's a Burberry polo he's got on, and those pants are Moschino. That's more than a thousand bucks in clothes right there. Factor in those Ferragamo loafers, and you're looking at another five or six hundred bucks."

"How does she know the designers of everything he's wearing?" Nicole asks me.

"Hell if I know. She can't remember that table three wants another iced tea, but ask her to name the designer of a blouse some random woman across the street has on, and she'll get it right every time."

"Don't worry," Wavonne says, looking at Nicole's dress. "I don't do Kohl's designers."

"Really?" I say. "This from someone who bought her dress at Gu—"

"Guess," Wavonne lies, glaring at me before I can finish the word "Gussini." "I bought this at the Guess store . . . the one in Montgomery Mall."

"No one cares where you bought your dress, Wavonne," I say. "Certainly not me or Nicole anyway."

"Why are we wastin' time talking about clothes anyway? Take me over there and introduce me," Wavonne says to Nicole.

"Me? If anyone should do the introducing, it should be Halia. She's the one who went to prom with him."

"What you mean, she went to prom with him?!" Wavonne turns to me. "You mean to tell me you got all up in *that*?"

"All that was not . . . well, *all that*, in high school. We were in honors English together. He needed a date. I needed a date. We were just friends. I don't even think there was a good-night kiss."

"Wait . . . wait. He's the guy who looked like Urkel with you in that photo Aunt Celia has on the bookcase . . . where you're wearin' that poufy pink Puerto Rican bridesmaid's dress?"

"That was the style back then, Wavonne. All the prom dresses were poufy in the eighties."

"You looked like a big pink balloon. I'm surprised nobody tried to pop you."

"Don't worry, from what she's said about her and Gregory that night, nobody did," Nicole says with a laugh.

"Very funny, Nicole," I say. "Come on, let's go say hello."

Kimberly lingers behind and as Nicole, Wavonne, and I begin to make our move, or as Momma said a few days ago, "move in for the kill," I notice that Gregory has caught Raynell's attention as well. I see her also making a beeline toward him. We speed up our gait accordingly to beat her to the target, but Raynell takes notice of our ascent toward Gregory, and picks up her pace, too. For a stout sister, the girl can move when she wants to.

"That thirsty heifer's tryin' to move in on my man," Wavonne says.

We speed up some more. Raynell speeds up some more. You can almost hear the movie chase scene music playing in the background. Me, Wavonne, Nicole, Raynell—anyone watching all these thick ladies moving at top speed probably thinks the buffet just opened.

I continue to scurry as I look back and see Wavonne struggling in her heels.

"Leave her," Nicole says. "She's dead weight."

I laugh but fail to heed her words. I give Wavonne a chance to catch up, which, unfortunately, causes us to lose the de facto race. By the time we reach Gregory, Raynell is already giving him a hug.

"Did you ladies just get out of prison?" Raynell asks once she's released Gregory from her embrace. I detect a slight slur in her words. Her affinity for colored cocktails seems to be catching up

with her. "It's like you've never seen a man before."

"Look who's talkin'. You're the one who beat
us over here," Wavonne says. "And ain't you got a
husband?"

I ignore both Wavonne and Raynell. "Hello,
Gregory."

"Halia Watkins!" Much to Raynell's dismay he
leans in and gives me a long hug. "It is *good* to see
you."

"You too." I have to admit I'm smiling from ear
to ear. It *is* good to see him. "This is my cousin,
Wavonne, and you know Nicole."

"Yes, yes," Gregory says, and shakes Wavonne's
hand. "Pleasure to meet you."

"Let go of his hand, Wavonne," I say as she
continues to clasp Gregory's palm with seemingly
no intention of releasing it.

"Wavonne and Halia are our caterers for the
night," Raynell says as if we're the hired help. She
catches Gregory taking a quick peek at Wavonne's
cleavage and adds, "Wavonne's a *waitress* at this little hole-in-the-wall Halia runs." She says waitress
with the tone someone might use when saying the
word "prostitute" or "drug dealer."

"Oh, I know of Mahalia's Sweet Tea. It's hardly
a hole-in-the-wall. I hear it has the best fried
chicken and waffles south of Sylvia's in Harlem."

"I'm flattered you've heard of it."

"Of course I've heard of it. I'm in the business
as well. Correct me if I'm wrong, but I believe I've
seen Sweet Tea on some of the local top restaurant
lists."

"We've made the *Washington Post* and *Washing-*

tonian Magazine lists since we opened," Wavonne brags.

"That's all very nice, but I have a little business I'd liked to discuss with Gregory if you'd excuse us," Raynell interrupts.

When she says this it dawns on me that Gregory Simms must be the Gregory she was getting some calls from when she was at Sweet Tea, and, then again, when we met her at church on Sunday.

"It can wait, Raynell," Gregory says.

"I'm helping Gregory find some retail space." Raynell interlocks her arm with his in a way that seems a tad inappropriate for a married woman to be doing. "He's looking to expand his restaurant and add locations in Maryland. His restaurant is a *chain,* Halia, with multiple locations . . . not just one."

"Why would you want to discuss business tonight with a *real estate agent.*" Wavonne mimics Raynell's earlier tone when she condescendingly referred to Wavonne as a waitress. "Tonight should be about having fun. Let's get you a drink? I bet you're a Cîroc man."

"I'm good right now," Gregory says politely. "I really don't need a drink, and I guess if I'm going to talk business with anyone, it should be with Halia, a fellow restaurateur."

Gregory's comment makes me smile. It's funny to see Raynell hanging off Gregory on one side, and Wavonne trying to put the moves on him on the other. They are both working him hard, but, if I didn't know better, I'd swear the one he has eyes for is me.

CHAPTER 17

"I'd be happy to talk shop with you anytime," I say to Gregory.

"Gregory, are you sure you don't want to hear about some of the new locations I've found for you?" Raynell asks. "And *Halia,* aren't you supposed to be opening the buffet?"

"She's got staff here to do that," Wavonne says.

"Aren't *you* part of that staff? Isn't there some macaroni and cheese or *something* that requires your attention?"

"Come on, Wavonne," I say, trying to diffuse yet another war of words that's about to erupt between her and Raynell. "We really should check on the food."

"I'd love to come along and see what you've prepared," Gregory says.

"What about the potential restaurant sites?" Raynell continues to play tug-of-war with us.

"He can go over those with you later," Wavonne says. "Right now, he's comin' with us . . . and, besides, I think you need to visit the little ho's room and fix your weave . . . some tracks are showin'."

"Wavonne!" I shriek.

"I'll have you know there are no tracks on this head." Raynell starts running her fingers through her hair, lifting sections up to reveal nothing but scalp. "This is all *mine*. I doubt you can say the same."

"Well smack my ass and call me Janeka," Wavonne says, her disdain for Raynell abruptly transforming into genuine curiosity. She sidles closer to Raynell and leans in to inspect her head. "That is some *good* hair. What's your secret?"

"Girl, you have to condition, condition, condition." Raynell's own dislike for Wavonne seems to be temporarily sidelined as well. I guess a compliment about one's hair can soften even the most ferocious of women.

As the ladies continue to suspend their mutual distaste for one another over a discussion of holding sprays and pomades, I notice Kimberly. She's lingering by the bar, eyeing the two of them. She watches as Raynell tosses her hair to show Wavonne its volume. I can only imagine what Kimberly is thinking while Raynell, the woman who so cruelly robbed her of her hair in high school, stands showing off her flowing mane to Wavonne.

"Shall we check out the food?" Gregory says to me while Raynell and Wavonne are still distracted with hair talk.

"Sure."

"I had some of the appetizers. Were those your doing as well?" Gregory asks as we walk toward the serving tables.

"Yes."

"Those deviled eggs were killer. I wouldn't have thought to pair smoked salmon with deviled eggs, but it definitely works."

"Thanks! That's one of the things I like about catering gigs—they give me a chance to try out some new recipes."

When we reach the buffet I see my team putting out the last of the chafing dishes.

"So we've got the salad station over there." I point to the far end of the line. "Then my famous sour cream cornbread and some dinner rolls."

"Nice."

I lift the lid off the serving tray closest to me. "My herb-baked chicken. I wanted to go with fried, but Raynell insisted on baked."

"It smells really good."

"Then we have my salmon cakes, mashed potatoes and gravy, macaroni and cheese, and green beans with ham hock."

"I'm glad I came hungry."

"Wait until you see the dessert spread—chocolate marshmallow cake and sour cream coconut cake."

"I guess I should have worn pants with an elastic waist," Gregory jokes.

"Please. You look like you can more than afford an indulgence or two." I try not to let my eyes linger on his body as I say this.

"It's a balance," he says. "Some indulgences amass calories." His eyes give me a quick once over. "And I guess certain other indulgences burn them."

I let out a quick laugh and feel my face get hot. I'm not used to flirting, and I'm certainly not good at it. I'm at a loss for anything to say in response to his suggestive comment when Raynell intrudes on our banter.

"Everything ready to go?"

"Yep."

Raynell gives a signal to the deejay, and he announces that the buffet is open.

As Gregory, Raynell, and I watch people line up and start moving through the serving stations, Wavonne appears with a fresh cocktail in her hand. "I told you to tell me before you opened the buffet to everyone, so I could get a good place in line."

"Sorry, I forgot."

"You know I can't move fast in these heels. Now I'm gonna be stuck behind this herd of cows . . . there'll probably only be scraps left by the time I get up there."

"There's plenty of food, Wavonne. Let's all go get in line."

As we move to take our place behind my old classmates, I notice Raynell's a little unsteady on her feet. She stumbles on her heels and, at one point, grabs hold of me to keep from falling over.

"Girl's drunk as a skunk," Wavonne says.

"I am not. I'm just a little dizzy. I need to eat something."

"I think that's a good idea," I say. "Wavonne, why don't you help Raynell to a table, and Gregory and I will fix plates for all of us?"

"Why I gotta take that mess to a table?"

"Because I asked you to."

Wavonne is about to protest further, but then she shifts her eyes from me to Gregory and then back to me again. "Oh. Okay. I got you, Halia." She leans in and whispers, "I'll let you have this one. You go on . . . get you some."

She grabs Raynell by the elbow. "Come on. Let's sit your drunk ass down."

I vaguely hear Raynell insist, once again, that's she's not intoxicated as Wavonne leads her to a table.

While we wait for our turn at the buffet, Gregory and I get a chance to catch up. I tell him about Sweet Tea, and how it sucks up most of my time. He gives me the lowdown on how he started South Beach Burgers and leveraged it into a regional chain. Conversation between us flows naturally, and I find myself glad we are at the end of the line—it gives us more time to talk.

We eventually make it to the table with four loaded plates and sit down with Wavonne and Raynell. Alvetta is seated at the table as well with a few of Raynell's other former high school minions. As I unwrap my silverware I notice that Raynell and her comrades have on colored neon necklaces. Alvetta's is pink and Raynell's, just like in high school, is green.

"You didn't have those on earlier, did you? Where did you get them?" I ask Alvetta, pointing to her necklace.

"I brought them," Janelle Sanders says before Alvetta can respond. "I got them online. A little nostalgia for the evening."

"How fun," I say before I catch sight of yet another cocktail in Raynell's hand. "How'd she get that?" I ask Wavonne.

"She said she pay for my drink if I got one for her, too."

I groan. "The last thing Raynell needed was another drink, and it wouldn't be the worst idea in the world for you to slow down with the booze, either," I suggest. But despite my displeasure with Wavonne contributing to Raynell's further intoxication, I must say, drunk Raynell is way more pleasant than sober Raynell. The booze seems to have mellowed her out—she even compliments my food. "Halia, this macaroni and cheese is *so* good!" She takes another bite. "You were right." The slight slur in her speech that I detected earlier in the evening has progressed, and her words are starting to become garbled. "This baked chicken . . . chicken . . . it's nice chicken . . . but, like you said, we should have gone with the fried . . . yeah . . . the fried."

"You can come by Sweet Tea for fried chicken anytime."

"I can?" she asks. "Thank you, Halia. You're so nice." *Boy, is she drunk.*

Raynell spends the remainder of the meal saying things that only half make sense while the rest of us at the table chat about high school and flashback to the eighties. As we begin to finish up dinner, the deejay cranks up the volume on the music, and the lights above the dance floor come alive.

"That's my jam!" Raynell yells when Pebbles's "Mercedes Boy" starts blaring from the speakers. She hops up from her seat and hurriedly staggers to the dance floor. She's the only one out there, but that doesn't stop her from busting a move . . . or, quite frankly, stop her from making a fool of herself. She more fumbles than dances as everyone looks on. She twirls around and lifts her hands over her head, swinging them from left to right. Then she starts doing a clumsy move that resembles the funky chicken. Finally, when she starts lifting her dress and swinging it back and forth like a cancan girl, I see Christy and Alvetta get up from the table and approach her. Raynell is not ready to call it quits and protests their attempts to remove her from the dance floor, but she eventually concedes and lets the two of them help her across the room.

When they come back to the table to get Raynell's things, Alvetta suggests that Christy retrieve Raynell's car and bring it around.

"I'm not ready to go home. I'm having fun. I haven't even danced with Gregory yet," Raynell slurs while putting her hands on Gregory's shoulders.

"No more dancing, Raynell," Alvetta says. "We need to get you home. Come with me."

Gregory and I stand up to say our good-byes and offer any help that might be necessary to safely get Raynell to her car.

"At least let me say good night," Raynell insists, and gives Gregory a hug—a hug that's tighter and lasts longer than it should considering it's between a married woman and a man who is not her husband. She even takes a moment to move her arms up and down his sides, feeling his back muscles. "I'll see *you* later," she says. "Good night, ladies . . . and

Wavonne." She starts laughing hysterically. "Did you hear that? Ladies . . . *and Wavonne.*"

"Yes, I heard it," Alvetta replies disinterestedly. As she starts to lead Raynell out of the ballroom I catch sight of Raynell's neon green necklace, which, thanks to her antics on the dance floor, is hanging down her back rather than her chest. Raynell and Alvetta are about to clear the exit when it suddenly occurs to me what was amiss about Kimberly's painting.

"Excuse me," I say, and get up from the table. I quickly bypass Raynell and Alvetta and stride toward the auction room.

"Kimberly, you little devil, you," I say under my breath once I'm in the room standing in front of her canvass. I can't help but laugh as I take in the painting a second time. I get a good look at the green pasture, the barn, the horse, the chickens . . . but it's when my eyes zero in on the pig that my hunch about what was odd about the painting is confirmed—the pig is wearing a collar. That's what must have struck me as unusual earlier. I'm no country girl, but I don't think farm pigs generally wear collars. Oh, and did I mention the collar is neon green?

I'm still laughing as I pick up a pen and place a bid on the painting.

CHAPTER 18

After placing my bid on Kimberly's painting I return to the main ballroom. By this time, without Raynell scaring everyone off by gyrating like a crazy woman, the dance floor has started to fill.

"Shall we?" Gregory asks when I reach the table and Billy Ocean's "Get Outta My Dreams, Get Into My Car" begins to play.

"Sure."

"I'm comin', too," Wavonne says, and the three of us hit the dance floor. I haven't been dancing in years, but boy, is it fun. When you own a restaurant your nights out are few and far between, so an evening of cocktails and dancing is a real treat. The deejay plays a mix of Top 40 and R & B hits from the late eighties. We get down to Janet Jackson, and Bobby Brown, and Madonna, and Morris Day, and Whitney Houston . . . and, yes, even Tony! Toni! Toné! and J. J. Fad. We're all having a good time until Roxette's "She's Got the Look" hits the speakers. While not quite as intoxicated as Raynell, Wavonne, too, has been a frequent visitor to the bar and, let's be honest, she's not exactly the most inhibited person sober. The longer we stay on the dance floor the more, shall we say "ill-mannered," her moves become—she jiggles her breasts back and forth, waves her hands in the air, and shakes her booty like a go-go dancer in a rap video.

"Look at me doin' the Stanky Leg to white people music," Wavonne says as she brings her knee in and pushes it out to the music of a white Swedish rock band. I definitely know it's time to go home when I hear her call to Gregory, "Come on, let's do the ghetto booty freak." Wavonne maneuvers herself in front of him, and, I swear it couldn't have been timed any better in a *Saturday Night Live* sketch—right when "She's Got the Look" hits its pause . . . you know, when the music completely cuts out between "And I go la la la la la" and picks up again with "Na na na na na," Wavonne bends over in front of Gregory—she bends over in front of Gregory, and all of us within earshot are treated to the tearing sound of nineteen dollars worth of multicolored zigzagging fabric.

My mouth drops as I see her dress literally split right along the middle of her behind. Gregory looks on, bemused, as Wavonne straightens herself up.

"Oh, Halia, please tell me what I think just happened didn't just happen."

I don't answer. I just wince in response to her question.

"Those bitches at Gussini are gonna get a piece of my mind tomorrow," she says before directing her attention to the people next to us on the dance floor. "What are you look-in' at?!"

I refrain from saying, "It's not Gussini's fault you were trying to shove a size-sixteen woman into a size-fourteen dress." Instead, I turn to Gregory. "I think it's time to take Wavonné home," I say to him as I watch Wavonne reach behind and try to pull the fabric back together, but the dress is too tight for her efforts to be productive. "Come on," I say to her. "I'll walk behind you."

"Can I reach you at Sweet Tea? I would love to connect again before I go back to Miami."

"Sure. Of course."

Right then, for the first time all night, the dee-jay plays a ballad—Exposé's "Seasons Change." I hate to admit it, but I'm silently cursing Wavonne. It's bad enough that she imposed herself on us for the upbeat songs, but now she's wrecked my chance to get a slow dance in with Gregory.

"I'll call you."

"Great." I lean in, give him a quick hug, and begin to try to discreetly remove Wavonne and her torn dress from the premises.

"All those times . . . those *many, many* times I've told you to stop 'showin' your ass' . . . ." I say to her as we approach the exit. "And this time I get to really mean it."

CHAPTER 19

"Well, look what the cat dragged in," I say to Wavonne. We're at home the morning after the reunion, and I'm sitting at the kitchen table.

"Shhh," she says, rubbing her temples. She's still in the oversized T-shirt she slept in.

"I told you to slow down with the liquor last night."

She directs a hungover stare at me before making her way to the coffee pot.

I'm not sure most people who know her would recognize Wavonne when she first gets up—before she paints on the heavy makeup, plunks a wig on her head, and accessorizes herself to high heaven with flashy costume jewelry. She's getting close to thirty, but, at the moment, without all of her trademark razzle-dazzle, she still looks like a teenager.

"Why'd you get me up so early?" She sits down across from me with a cup of coffee.

"It's seven thirty, Wavonne. Not five a.m. I want

to go by Christy's this morning and pick up the check for the reunion catering before we head to Sweet Tea. It's out of the way, and I'd like to be at the restaurant by nine thirty to help set up for brunch. We need to get moving shortly. Laura covered for us last night, so she's taking the morning off today."

I get up from the table and set my mug in the sink. "You better get in the shower. I want to be on the road by eight thirty."

Wavonne yawns, slowly gets up from her chair, tops off her coffee, and heads out of the kitchen with her cup.

While she's getting showered I get up to reach for my phone, lean against the counter, and start swiping through last night's photos. Looking at the images, I recall that I had originally planned not to go to the reunion, but now I'm certainly glad I did. It turned out to be a fun evening. I liked having a night off from the restaurant, catching up with some old friends, and especially enjoyed reconnecting with Gregory. I feel like he was flirting with me, but I'm so out of practice in that arena I may be completely off base. I'm also not sure if he has something going with Raynell. I know she's married, but married women cheat all the time. And I don't think she would get as territorial about Gregory as she seemed to last night if he were just a casual friend or real estate client— and the way she hugged him before she left was pretty intense for platonic friends. But, who knows— Raynell was highly intoxicated, so her behavior may have been a result of the alcohol.

I'm about to brush off the whole evening and

let go of any expectations where Gregory is concerned when my phone buzzes with a text from him.

gregory here . . . got your cell number from christy . . . good to see you last night . . .
still up for getting together to trade restaurant stories?

I have to say I can feel my pulse quicken when I read his words. As Wavonne and Momma love to point out, I don't date much, and once you've crossed the line over to the less desirable side of forty without landing a man, your hopes for a relationship aren't exactly lofty. In my twenties I was optimistic about getting married and very picky about who I dated. During my thirties the pessimism started to set in, and I began giving guys who weren't "attractive enough" or "smart enough" . . . or "ambitious enough" a few years earlier a second look, but nothing ever panned out. By the time I hit forty, and after one too many dates with men who still lived with their mommas or thought I was supposed to be their nursemaid, I pretty much gave up on romance and decided a single life focused on family, friends, and a thriving restaurant career wasn't so bad.

I text back.

Sure

The moment I hit send, I wonder if I responded too soon. *Do I seem too eager? Maybe I should have let some time pass before I replied.* Like I said, I'm not good at this.

I wait for him to text me back, but when I don't get a response after a few seconds, I drop my phone on the table and walk down the hall to hurry up Wavonne. With a little cajoling from me, I manage to get her ready to roll just shy of eight thirty.

"So, are you going to see him while he's still in town?" Wavonne asks as I throw a few things in my purse.

"Who?"

"What you mean, *who*? Gregory."

I refrain from telling her about his text. "I don't know, Wavonne. I think he's only here for a few days, and I've already taken one night off from the restaurant."

We're about to head out the door when I hear some quick scurrying coming from the hallway.

"Gregory? Who's Gregory?" Momma asks, hurriedly turning the corner. We had a dachshund growing up who I swear could hear you unwrap a piece of cheese from the other side of the house and show up at your feet in a nanosecond wanting his share. Momma's ears have a similar talent when any mention of a possible man in my life materializes.

"Nobody," I say. "We're late, Momma. We have to run."

Momma maneuvers herself between me and the front door. "*Who* is Gregory?"

"He's one of Halia's old classmates who was puttin' the moves on her last night."

"Really? What's he look like? Employed? Father material? Is he a Christian?"

"We were just friends in high school, Momma."

"She went to prom with him."

"That lanky fellow with the big ears?"

"He's not so lanky anymore," Wavonne says. "Brotha is fine these days."

"And he's interested in *Halia?*"

I glare at Momma. "Don't act so surprised!"

"Single? Divorced? Never married?"

"We didn't talk about that, Momma, but he was not wearing a wedding band, and I'm sure Nicole would have told me if he were married."

"Are you going to see him again? What's he do?"

"I don't know. And he owns a chain of restaurants."

"He's in the restaurant business as well. He sounds perfect for you."

"He lives in Florida, Momma. He's only in town for a few days."

"Well, you better jump on board that train before it leaves the station then. This is no time to dawdle." She says this as if Gregory is the last helicopter out of Saigon.

"I agree with Aunt Celia. He was into you, Halia. I could tell. Some brothas dig the full-figured matronly types . . . go figure," Wavonne says with an evil grin.

As I scowl back at her, my phone buzzes again. I grab it from my purse, take a look at the screen, and see another text from Gregory suggesting a date tomorrow evening.

"If you must know, he just asked me out, so I guess we are getting together after all."

I see the excitement in Momma's face. "Fantastic! You'll need to get your hair done, and Wavonne and I will help you with your makeup."

"Whatever, Momma. We're late."

Hopeful that her only daughter may not be an old maid after all, Momma steps out of our way and let's Wavonne and me pass. We walk out to the van and finally hit the road. Sunday traffic is light, so it doesn't take us too long to get to Christy's building.

Her apartment is in an older garden community of three-story buildings in Temple Hills. There are no elevators, so Wavonne and I walk up three flights of stairs to her unit on the top floor. When I knock on the door, there's no response, so Wavonne knocks a second time. A few moments later we hear some stumbling on the other side of the door and see the knob turn.

"Halia," Christy says after opening the door. She appears groggy, like she's just gotten out of bed. There are even sleep lines from her pillow on her face. She clearly was not expecting us.

"I'm sorry. Did we wake you? Raynell said to come by this morning to get a check for the catering."

She narrows her brow. "No. Raynell didn't say anything to me about it."

"So you don't have our money?" Wavonne asks.

I turn to Wavonne. "*Our* money?"

"No, I'm afraid I don't. I'll see Raynell on Monday. I can get a check from her then and drop it by the restaurant."

"Raynell's house isn't too far from here. Why don't Wavonne and I just drop by on our way to the restaurant?"

"Okay. I'll call her and let her know you're on

your way. But I must warn you, she's not really a morning person, and I'm sure she's hurting from last night."

"Thanks. I'm sorry we woke you."

"It's okay. I have a lot to do today, and it's time to get moving."

"Why don't you just let Christy bring you the check on Monday?" Wavonne asks after Christy closes her door. "You really wanna wake up the dragon lady so early on a Sunday? She might breathe fire at us."

"I've been in this business for a long time, Wavonne. And if I've learned nothing else, it's that people have a short memory where owed-money is concerned. First it's 'I'll pay you on Monday.' Then it's 'I have appointments all week. Can I pay you on Friday?' Then they stop answering the phone when you call altogether. For all we know, Raynell has dipped into the reunion fund to cover a new pair of shoes or one of her fancy designer outfits you're so infatuated with."

"Fine, but you know Medusa's gonna be in a mood."

We get in the van and buckle up. Before I start the ignition and back out of the parking space, I say to Wavonne, "She can be mad as a wet hen for all I care as long as she can sign her name on a check made out to Mahalia's Sweet Tea."

CHAPTER 20

"This is where Raynell lives?" Wavonne asks as we pull up in front of her house, and I park on the street. "Fancy!"

"It is quite nice, isn't it?"

We step out of the van and walk up the driveway.

"How much you think this house is worth? A million bucks?"

"I have no idea, Wavonne."

When we reach the front door, I press the bell and hear it chime on the other side. We wait a few moments. When there is no response, we press the button again. We linger a tad longer, and when there is still no answer, I start to get a little suspicious. First Raynell tells me to pick up a nonexistent check from Christy, and then she conveniently doesn't answer the door when I come by to get it from her directly.

While we stand outside waiting for someone to

answer the door, I notice that the window next to the door is open . . . actually all the windows along the front of the house are open.

"Raynell?" I call through the open window closest to us. "It's Halia. I'm here to settle the bill for the catering."

"Want me to pull up Rihanna's 'Bitch Better Have My Money' on my phone and blast it at full volume? That should get her moving."

"I don't think we're quite to that point yet, Wavonne, but I'll let you know."

"Have it your way." Wavonne steps away and peeks into the garage. "Her Escalade's in there."

I look through the window next to the door and see Raynell's gold Michael Kors keychain on a console in the foyer. "I see her keys on the table. Her car's here . . . and she wouldn't leave the house without her keys. I think she's just ignoring us."

"Maybe she really did dip her greedy hooves into the reunion fund. I bet that's why she ain't answerin' the door. She don't have your money."

I knock forcefully on the door rather than hitting the bell for a third time. "Raynell!" I yell through the window again. When my voice is, once again, met with silence, I instinctively try the doorknob and find it unlocked. I give it a full turn and open the door just enough to poke my head in.

"Raynell, it's Halia and Wavonne. Christy said she'd call you to let you know to expect us." I open the door wider. "I see your keys on the table. You must be here."

I hate to think the worst about people, but I'm now convinced that Raynell is indeed trying to put one over on me, and get out of paying the bill for my catering services. She was a conniving little monster in high school, and clearly she's no different today.

"All right . . . enough." I throw the door open and step inside. "Raynell!" I call up the steps. "We know you're here. I need to collect payment for services rendered."

"Yeah! Fool!" Wavonne says.

"Shut up, Wavonne," I say as we stand in the foyer waiting for Raynell to show herself.

"If she's not comin' down, then we're goin' up," Wavonne says. "If we happen upon her closet and stop to check out some of her clothes, then so be it."

"You stay out of her closet," I command, and follow Wavonne up the steps. "Raynell!" I call again, and begin to wonder if maybe she isn't hiding from us . . . maybe she isn't well from all her drinking last night and is still passed out.

"Yo! Raynell! Show your tired ass."

"Wavonne!"

"What?"

"Take it down a notch. You're not helping," I scold. "Let's look down there."

We walk down a long hall past a large bathroom and what appear to be a few guest rooms. When we reach the doorway at the end of the hall, we see what is obviously the master bedroom. It's a cavernous space with a long row of picture windows that frame a seating area in front of a fire place. A large flat-screen TV hangs on the wall across from a king-size canopy bed.

I look at the disheveled linens on the bed. "Where is she?"

Chapter Twenty-three

Saturday morning dawned sunny, and Susan put on her sunglasses as she drove Raz to baseball practice. He kept his head turned to the window, cell phone in hand and listening to music through his earbuds. She'd hardly slept a wink, her thoughts on Raz and Ryan, torn between the two of them like when they were young and fought over the same toy. They'd tantrum, and she'd tended to get down in the weeds with them, but Neil would tell her:

Honey, when they fight, they spiral down. Don't go into the spiral. You're the parent, remember? If you go down the spiral, you'll all end up in the toilet.

Susan remembered his words as clearly as if it were yesterday, which was the problem. She remembered everything about Neil, how he had acted, what he had said, the jokes he'd made, the way they'd made love. She wished she remembered less. She wished he wasn't so present all the time, in her head and her heart.

Susan drove ahead, her thoughts churning. It had been almost a year since Neil died, and a year was the grief cutoff. He died in August and it was already April, so she had only four months left. Nobody said so explicitly, but she got the message. She saw an article in the paper that said most widows return to their "pre-loss level of life satisfaction" after a year. So she knew she had four months to become a normal person. Still she didn't believe there could be a deadline to mourning the dead.

Susan stopped at a light. She knew what they were saying at work, behind her back. She was *milking it. She just wanted the sympathy.* She was *wallowing in grief* and not *moving on.* She was *dragging down* her sons, too. They're spiraling down to get *swallowed up* by the grief toilet.

The light turned green, and Susan glanced over at Raz. They were only a few blocks from school, and she wanted to make sure they understood each other.

You're the parent, remember?

"Raz?" Susan said, but there was no reply. "Raz."

"What?" Raz turned to her, his expression slack and his skin pale. His eyes looked bloodshot and puffy. His hair was wet from the shower, dripping onto his blue Musketeers T-shirt, darkening it around the neckline. He had on his gym shorts and sneakers, his feet resting on his backpack in the well of the passenger seat.

"I want to talk to you."

"So, talk." Raz blinked.

"Please take out your earphones."

"I can hear you."

"I'm not going to talk to you with your ears plugged up. This is important."

"Fine," Raz said tonelessly. He pulled out one of his earphones.

"Both, please."

Raz pulled out the other one.

Susan reminded herself to be patient. Neil had been, above all things, unbelievably patient. "Okay, so first thing this morning, what are you supposed to do?"

"Mom, I know."

"Yes, but tell me. I want to hear what you'll say."

"You mean like a rehearsal?" Raz's weary eyes flared in disbelief.

"Yes, exactly." Susan returned her attention to the road because his expression only made her angry. She drove ahead, passing the tall oaks, the clipped hedges, and the clapboard colonials with their shiny PVC fences.

"Okay, well, whatever, first I'm going to Coach Hardwick. I'm going to tell him I'm sorry I threw the bat."

"Right." Susan kept her eyes on the road. "Remember, the first words out of your mouth are 'I'm sorry.' Lead with 'I'm sorry.'"

"I know that. I *said that*."

"I want you to go to him before practice even starts."

Raz sighed heavily. "That's not going to be that easy, Mom. He's busy."

"Just go up to him and say 'excuse me.'"

"He doesn't like to be interrupted."

"He won't mind after he hears you say 'I'm sorry.'"

"Should I say I'm sorry for interrupting, too? How many things am I sorry for, Mom? Am I sorry for *breathing*?"

"Don't be fresh," Susan said, then an awful thought struck her.

I'm sorry for breathing.

It was true. She was sorry that she was breathing, when Neil was not. She wished she were dead, and her husband was the one dealing with these angry, thankless children, who acted like they were the only ones who lost him, when exactly the opposite was true. Neil might have been their father, but he was her husband. She'd been there first. She'd loved him longer. He was more hers than theirs. She was his lover, his *wife*.

Susan's fingers tightened on the steering wheel, and she gritted her teeth not to turn around to Raz and *smack him in the face.* That's what she actually thought, a vicious notion that came out of nowhere, shocking her. *My son is driving me so crazy that I want to smack him.*

"Then I have to go to Coach Brennan and tell him I'm sorry that I ruined his party, even though I didn't ruin his party. They stayed after. They had a good time. It didn't end or anything. Jordan was fine, he didn't have to get stitches."

Susan roiled inside, enraged at his freshness, at his attitude, at his *selfishness.* He used to be a fun little boy, but he had turned into a total brat.

"Then I go to Jordan and tell him I'm sorry that I hit him. I'm not allowed to say that I didn't mean to hit him, because like you always say, 'When you do the act, the consequences always go with it.'"

Susan tried to press away her horrible thoughts. The high school was in sight. She breathed in and out, trying to calm down.

"Then, after I apologize to everybody at practice, I have to call Mrs. Larkin and apologize. I have to tell her I'm happy for Jordan if he's the starting pitcher because 'that's what friends are for.'" Raz made air quotes, and Susan turned left into the school grounds.

The road ran uphill, and she passed the student parking lot on her left. She glanced over at the entrance, where several Central Valley police cruisers sat in front of the school. She looked away, having seen quite enough police cars recently.

"Cops?" Raz frowned at the cruisers. "Wonder what's up."

Susan drove forward, having a schedule to keep. She had to drop Raz off, go home, and pull Ryan out of bed because she was taking him to a therapist at eleven o'clock. Susan would be meeting with her own therapist at the very same time, so two-thirds of the Sematovs' Shit Show would be on expensive couches.

"Mom, look, something's the matter," Raz said, alarmed, and Susan stopped the car. A group of uniformed police, teachers, and staff were leaving the school building, and some of the teachers were crying.

"Oh, my." Susan took one look and knew that someone had died. She had *lived* that scene. She *still* lived it, in her mind.

"That's Dr. McElroy, and Mr. Pannerman. And Madame Wheeler's freaking out."

"Who's Madame Wheeler?" Susan didn't know who Raz meant for a minute. Neil was the one who went to Parents' Night.

"The French teacher. Ryan had her, remember? She's the one in the front."

"Poor woman," Susan said, touched at the sight of the stricken teacher, holding a Kleenex to her nose. She left the building next to Dr. McElroy, whom Susan did recognize, with a bearded male teacher, also weepy. Three female students held each other as they cried, and a baseball player in a Musketeers T-shirt and gym shorts hurried from the entrance and started jogging toward the field.

"Hey, that's Dylan. Maybe he knows what's going on." Raz slid down the window, waving to get the attention of the tall, wiry kid. "Dylan!"

"Raz!" Dylan hustled toward the car, his backpack bouncing. "Hi, Raz, hi, Mrs. Sematov."

"Dude, what's up with Madame Wheeler? Why are the cops here?"

"Oh man, it's bad." Dylan bent over to peer inside the car, pushing up his glasses. Wrinkles creased his forehead. "Mr. Y died last night. Dr. McElroy's crying. They're all crying."

"What?" Raz gasped, shocked. "That can't be! I just saw him! How did he die?"

"Mr. Y is dead?" Susan recoiled. It was horrible news. Mr. Y was Raz's Language Arts teacher, and Ryan had him, too. They both loved him. That's how she knew the name, they talked about him so much.

"He committed *suicide*," Dylan answered, blinking behind his glasses.

Step Two

Chapter Twenty-four

Chris hurried up the sidewalk, his head down. The last thing he needed was another meet with Alek, especially one he had to drive to Philly for. Alek had set it for two o'clock, and Chris had barely had time to change after practice. It had been an awful morning, with the team distraught over Abe's death.

Chris hustled toward the massive sandstone-and-brick tower, rising seventeen stories and occupying the entire block of Second and Chestnut Streets, in the colonial section of the city. The building was on the National Register of Historic Places, though its history was undoubtedly irrelevant to the people outside, enjoying the last few puffs of their cigarettes.

He reached the building and hustled up the steps, through the stainless-steel doors, and inside to the metal detector, while his eyes adjusted to the darkness. There were no windows in the entrance area, and the brass fixtures were vintage, shedding little light. He slid his wallet from his back pocket—not his Chris Brennan wallet with his fake driver's license, but his real wallet with his true

Curt Abbott ID, his true address in South Philly, and his heavy chrome badge, with a laminated card identifying him as a Special Agent in the Philadelphia Field Division of the Bureau of Alcohol, Tobacco, Firearms, & Explosives, or ATF.

Chris handed his open wallet to the guard, who scrutinized his ID and handed it back. He worked undercover, and he had to show his ID because he wasn't at the office enough to be recognized by the security guards, especially on the weekends. He put his ID on the conveyor belt with his keys, walked through the metal detector, and collected his belongings; then entered the lobby. He experienced a sense of awe every time he crossed the dark marble floor, starting from twelve years ago, when he was first hired by ATF.

The massive space was flanked by two carved staircases and topped by an ornate plasterwork rotunda that soared three stories high. At its apex shone a circle of daylight rimmed by an upper deck with a stainless-steel railing. To Chris, the history of the building mirrored the history of ATF, and he was proud to be an ATF agent, even though he had to report to Alek Ivanov, who acted like a gangster even though he was a Washington bureaucrat transferred to the Philadelphia office.

Chris pressed the elevator button, uncomfortable to be in public as himself, as if he were wearing the wrong skin. He hated coming in while he was undercover. It wasn't procedure, and he knew it wouldn't have happened during any other operation, further evidence of the lack of support he was getting from Alek.

The elevator arrived, and he stepped inside and pressed the button, his thoughts churning. As a child, he hadn't known what he wanted to be when he grew up, but he wanted to help the underdog—maybe because he *was* the underdog, raised in so many different foster homes. He'd been drawn to law enforcement and after college, had chosen ATF, an underdog of an agency that lived in the shadow of the FBI. Chris's favorite movie was *The Untouchables* about the legendary ATF agent Eliot Ness, and after a string of successful operations, he'd felt honored when everyone started calling him The Untouchable. But lately, the nickname bothered him, reminding him that he was literally untouchable, disconnected from people.

He got off the elevator, took a right, and walked down a hallway that ended in a locked door, intentionally unmarked so that no member of the public would know it was ATF. For the same reason, ATF wasn't listed on the directory downstairs and none of the security guards would confirm that ATF was even in this building, having been instructed not to do so. ATF's Philadelphia Field Division employed two hundred people—Supervisors, Special Agents, Task Force Officers, Detectives, Certified Explosives Specialists, Fire Marshals, Intelligence Research Analysts, and many others, but none of their names was on the directory, either. Unsung didn't begin to describe their status. Unknown was closer to the truth.

Chris unlocked the door and let himself into the office, which was as quiet as expected on a Saturday afternoon. He went down a gray-carpeted hallway past walls of institutional yellow, unadorned with any artwork. The hallway led to a large room of gray cubicles that looked like an insurance office except for the Glock G22 or subcompact Glock G27, agency-issued weapons, hanging in a shoulder holster on the cubicle's corner, evidence that an agent was in.

Chris reached the conference room and opened the door to see Alek sitting at the head of the round table. The Rabbi was nowhere in evidence, though he was supposed to be here, too. "Hey, Alek."

"Curt, thanks for coming in." Alek half-rose and extended a hand, which Chris shook, though he could barely bring himself to meet Alek's small, dark eyes, set deep in a long face. His dark hair thinned in front, and a thin scar on his cheek looked like it was from a knife fight, but it was from a car accident at the mall.

"Where's the Rabbi?"

"He'll be right back." Alek sat down. "You know, that's all you ever ask me. 'Where's the Rabbi?' 'Where's the Rabbi?'"

Suddenly the door opened and the Rabbi came in, holding his laptop. "Curt, so good to see you!" he said with a broad grin, showing teeth stained from excessive coffee. His real name was David Levitz, but everyone called him the Rabbi because he was the smartest agent in the Division.

"Hey!" Chris gave the Rabbi a bear hug, almost lifting him off his feet, since the Rabbi was only five-foot-five and maybe 160 pounds. He was fiftysomething with frizzy gray hair, sharp, dark brown eyes behind thick, wire-rimmed bifocals, and his thin lips were bracketed by deep laugh lines, earned over the years.

"Sorry I missed you last night," the Rabbi said, which was code for *Sorry I didn't rescue you from Alek*.

"No worries," Chris said, which meant, *Can we shoot our boss and get away with it?*

"Let's get started, lovebirds." Alek gestured Chris into the seat opposite the Rabbi, rather than next to him, and it struck Chris that Alek was the Coach Hardwick of ATF. Technically, Aleksandr Ivanov was the Group Supervisor, or GS, of the Violent Crimes Task Force, and the Rabbi was Chris's contact agent, to whom he reported when he worked undercover.

"Okay, so Alek, why did you call me in?"

"I'm pulling the plug."

"On my operation?" Chris wasn't completely surprised. "There's no reason to do that, Alek. I disagree—"

"I went out there to meet you. Sleepy little town in the middle of nowhere. It's nothing but a total waste of time, and now that some teacher offed himself last night, there's a possibility of you being blown."

"I won't be, and anyway, I'm not so sure it's a suicide. The jury's out for me, and it could be connected to the case." Chris still couldn't believe that Abe Yomes was really gone. He had liked Abe, and it had shocked him to the marrow to hear that he was dead, much less by his own hand. It was awful, and it sent up red flags in terms of the operation, which had been dubbed Operation Varsity Letter.

"What facts do you base that on?"

"His personality. It doesn't make sense that he would commit suicide."

"You didn't know him that well. You've been there two days."

"I get the guy. He's a fun, upbeat guy. Connected to friends and students. They all loved him, they called him Mr. Y." Chris flashed on the scene at practice this morning. The players had been so distraught when they heard the news. Raz had been dropped off by his mother, after he had obviously been crying. Coach Hardwick had made them practice anyway, but they played horribly and left crestfallen.

"I don't see the point."

"That's because you never heard the justification for the operation. You were in D.C. when I got the authorization—"

"I read the file. I'm completely up-to-date on your reports."

"It's not the same thing, and besides, there's no downside. It costs nothing. My rent is $450, and I buy my own clothes."

"Don't forget we had to pay to place you in the school. The superintendent wanted four grand to send the teacher and her old man on a vacation." Alek rolled his eyes. "Your tax dollars at work."

"But still, it's cheaper than a house or a boat, and the upside is great."

"You know what your problem is, Curt? Your premise is wrong."

"How? It's cost–benefit. The typical budgetary analysis—"

"No, your premise is that you're the one who makes that analysis. But you're not. I am. I'm shutting you down."

"You haven't given it a chance. Let me break it down." Chris commandeered the Rabbi's laptop, logged into the network using his password to get beyond the ATF firewall, then found his private files. "Did you see the video? Did you even look at it?"

"I read—"

"It'll take fifteen seconds. Watch." Chris hit PLAY, and the video showed a shadowy image of a tall figure forcing open a door in a dark shed, then hurrying toward bags of ammonium nitrate fertilizer. The figure reached for one of the bags, and as he did so, he came closer to the camera. The man's features were obscured by a ball cap, but it captured the lettering of his blue T-shirt, which read Musketeers Baseball.

"So?" Alek sighed theatrically.

Chris hit STOP. "We know that ammonium nitrate fertilizer is the go-to ingredient for IEDs made by domestic terrorists and that its purchase, transport, and storage is strictly monitored by Homeland Security and it's restricted to those with a permit, mostly farmers. The only other way to get it is theft." Chris pointed to the screen. "This video was taken by Herb Vrasaya, one of the farmers in Central Valley, whose farm is located five miles from the high school. Mr. Vrasaya grows corn and he has a permit to buy and store the fertilizer. He installed the camera two weeks ago, because he thought rats were getting into the shed and he wanted to see how."

"I read that part."

"Mr. Vrasaya sent the video to our office, like a good citizen. 'If you see something, say something,' and he didn't want his permit jeopardized. I think this video is evidence of a bomb plot that has a connection to the baseball team at CVHS. The blue Musketeers T-shirt is only issued to the varsity players, the boys I coach. It's a badge of honor. I'm infiltrating the team to identify this kid and learn why he's stealing fertilizer. And it would be no problem at all for an underage kid to rent a box truck in Central Valley. All the locals know where to go, to a guy named Zeke. I went there myself to see how hard it would be to rent a truck and what the pitfalls would be. I met the guy. He always has them available, and there's no paperwork."

The Rabbi interjected, "Remember that it's April, Alek. April 19 is the anniversary of the Oklahoma City bombing. Anybody trying to blow something up would be stockpiling fertilizer now. It takes a ton of fertilizer for a major explosion. That's fifty bags. Bottom line, I agree with Curt. I'm backing him."

Alek threw up his hands. "Why? Because some kid has a T-shirt? He could've gotten it at Target. Curt, you said so in your own report, didn't you?"

"What I wrote in my report was that I talked to the manager at Target, and he told me that only the Booster moms buy T-shirts at Target. The store never sells any large or the extra large, only the extra small and small." Chris thought ahead to preempt Alek's next objection. "And don't think that the kid in the video wore the T-shirt to frame a member of the baseball team, because there's no way they could've known about the security camera."

Alek scoffed. "But what kind of an idiot would wear a team uniform to steal something?"

"Not an idiot, a kid. I've been a teacher for two days and I can tell you they do dumb stuff. Especially the boys. They don't think anything through."

"Not that dumb. All it takes is one kid to buy the T-shirt or one mom to buy a larger size."

"Then assign another agent to follow up with Target. I can't do it myself with my cover, and the video alone isn't enough for probable cause. We can get the name, address, and credit card of everybody who bought a Musketeers T-shirt in the past five years. I think it was a newish one because the color stayed true." Chris had washed four T-shirts thirty times to see when the color faded. The answer was, the twenty-third time.

"We don't have the agent to spare."

"I'm making progress. Like I told you, I'm in: I picked my guy, Jordan Larkin."

"Is that the name of your unwitting?" the Rabbi asked. An unwitting was the ATF term for an informant who was being pumped for information without knowing that he was part of an undercover operation.

"Yes, and he's perfect. It took me only two days to befriend him, that's step one, and step two, I'll cast my net wider to find who stole the fertilizer." Chris hit REWIND, stopping the video when the shadowy image first entered the room. "The height of the doorway in the shed is eighty inches, and this figure is over six feet tall, between six-one and six-five. There are five boys on my varsity team who are over six feet tall. Three of them are the ones in my AP Government class, including my unwitting—Jordan Larkin, Raz Sematov, and Evan Kostis." Chris kept talking, though Alek glanced at his watch. "Step two is to get to know the other two players who are over six feet tall, Trevor Kiefermann and Dylan McPhee. I'm investigating them and I know I'm going to get a break."

"When?" Alek snapped.

"I have three days left until the nineteenth, if what they're planning is an anniversary bombing. Give me three days." Chris pointed again at the video. "In addition to which, the timing makes absolute sense for it to be a baseball player. A player leaving practice when it was over would arrive at Mr. Vrasaya's farm, park his car, and run to the shed exactly when this happens, which is 6:20. I drove the distance myself. Then he still gets home in time, and nobody is the wiser, except for the fact that his trunk is filled with ammonium nitrate."

"What does he do with it then? Does he hand it off? Does he store it at his house?"

"I don't know but I'm gonna find out."

"One question, Curt," the Rabbi interjected. "What about your unwitting, Larkin? Do you suspect him?"

"No," Chris answered. "Again, I'm going with my gut. Jordan Larkin doesn't fit the profile for a domestic terrorist. He's quiet, a rules follower, and a good kid."

Alek ignored them both. "I still don't understand what the teacher had to do with it. Yomes, the one who committed suicide."

"Maybe Abe knew something. Maybe he saw something. Maybe he overheard something. He was a connected, inquisitive guy. It's too coincidental otherwise." Chris hadn't yet found the connection, but he'd asked around at practice and determined that all five boys had Abe Yomes for Language Arts. "He was the one who asked me about Wyoming."

"So it was a lucky break he died."

"No, it wasn't," Chris shot back, cringing inwardly. He couldn't think of Abe's death that way, and before Abe had died, Chris had decided to immerse himself in Wyoming trivia, in order to answer Abe's many questions.

"It's a suicide, no question, according to the locals. Yomes hung himself. His boyfriend told them he had a history of depression."

The Rabbi interjected, "Curt, I understand that Yomes was African-American and gay. Did you see any facts that would suggest the possibily of a hate crime? Any evidence of a neo-Nazi group? Are you seeing anything like that at the high school, or on the team?"

"Not yet," Chris answered, then turned back to Alek. "Let the locals think whatever they think. Yomes told me about his depression himself, but it sounded like it was in the past. I'm going to follow up."

"But Yomes has no connection to the baseball team, does he?"

"Other than he taught my five guys? No, not that I know of, yet." Chris had been wondering if there was some secret connection there, maybe one of the players was in the closet, but he didn't have enough information on which to float a theory.

"Curt, I'm unconvinced." Alek shook his head. "We have bigger cases."

"The Oklahoma City bombing was the most deadly act of domestic terrorism in the country. It doesn't get much bigger than that. In this political climate, with feelings against the government, it's only a matter of time until it happens again."

"We're not hearing anything. Nothing unusual, no chatter, no leads."

"That could mean they're good at it. Or a small group. Or a loner. I've got my eye on a few kids on the team who spoke against the government in one of my classes. I did an exercise to see who felt that way. I'm asking for three

lays. Three more days, until the anniversary on the nine-
eenth."

Alek frowned. "Curt, you're killing me. You've made
a name for yourself in the most dangerous operations. I
can't believe you want this one, with a bunch of high-
school kids. It's like Jump Street, for God's sake!"

"The hell it is," Chris said, simmering.

The Rabbi turned to Alek. "Let him see it through. We
owe him that, don't we? After Eleventh Street?"

Alek kept frowning, but said nothing.

Chris thought back to the Eleventh Street Operation,
in which he'd gone undercover as a Kyle Rogan, a low-
level cocaine dealer, infiltrating a gang of violent dealers
near Wilmington, Delaware, believed to have connec-
tions to the Sinaloa cartel. Chris had been about to make
a "buy-bust" in a run-down house on Eleventh Street, but
the moment of truth had come when the drug dealers had
insisted that Chris sample the product, which was one of
the few things that the movies actually got correct—
undercover ATF and FBI agents were typically asked to
sample the product to prove they weren't cops. In theory,
it was otherwise illegal activity, or OIA, since the government had an acronym for everything. But refusing could
endanger their lives. Chris had thought of another way
out.

No can do, Chris/Kyle had said to the three thugs sitting opposite him, behind the black duffel bag of bricks
wrapped in plastic, which the bearded drug dealer had
split open with a key.

You won't try some? Why?

I can't. No liquor, no drugs. I'm a Muslim.

*Who are you kidding? You're white as a sheet. A Ku
Klux Klan sheet.* The bearded dude had burst into coarse
laughter, and so had his cohorts.

So? Chris/Kyle had-shrugged. *I'm a Muslim. Muslim can be white.*

I don't believe for one minute you're a Muslim, said skinny black man on the end, the only African-America in the room.

So Chris/Kyle had launched into a recital of the mos important passages of the Koran, which he had memo rized in anticipation of being quizzed. It had convince the thugs of his bona fides, and they made the buy. After wards, they'd left the house, where ATF agents had a rested them all, including Chris, to preserve his cover.

The Rabbi was saying, "Alek, look at it this way. I Curt is right, you come out looking like a rose becaus you gave him the approval. If he's wrong, everybody wil understand why you gave him a freebie. It's win-win, fo you."

Alek sighed heavily, then turned to Chris. "Thre days. That's it."

Chapter Twenty-five

Chris walked next to the Rabbi past the well-maintained stone row houses, reflexively keeping his head down through Fairmount, an artsy city neighborhood with indie coffeehouses, historic pubs, and used bookstores, as well as the Philadelphia Museum of Art, Barnes Foundation, and Free Library. The Rabbi and his Portuguese wife, Flavia, were always nagging him to go to author lectures at the Free Library or folk dancing at the Art Museum, which would never, ever happen.

Chris was going to the Rabbi's for dinner only because he wouldn't take no for an answer, but Chris felt out of sorts. He was angry at Alek's attempt to shut down the operation, and Abe's death was beginning to haunt him. Heather was at the back of his mind, too, but he pressed her away as they reached the Rabbi's house, which was different from the others, since Flavia was an artist and had wanted their window trim to be purple, pink, and green.

"Flavia is so excited you're here," the Rabbi said, unlocking the front door.

"Me, too." They went inside, and Chris found himself surrounded by chatter, music, and delicious aromas of broiled fish. Soft bossa nova music played on an old-fashioned stereo system, and the sound of laughter and women talking floated from the kitchen.

"And the girls are home," the Rabbi said, meaning his twin daughters, Leah and Lina, who shared an apartment in Center City.

"Terrific." Chris looked up as their chubby brown mutt, Fred, ran barking toward them, his long ears and pink tongue flying.

"We're home, honey!" the Rabbi called, bending down as the dog jumped up on his shins and got a scratch behind the ear.

"In the kitchen!" Flavia called back, and the Rabbi headed toward the back of the house with Chris and Fred on his heels. They walked through the large, funky living room, with its green tufted couch and hot pink chairs grouped around a glass coffee table covered with books, drawing pads, and colored pencils. The walls were a soft turquoise, and vivid oil paintings covered every square inch with abstract scenes of flowers, fruits, and pottery.

"Curt!" Flavia appeared at the threshold of her aromatic kitchen, threw open her arms, and hugged Chris, barely coming up to his chest because she was as short as the Rabbi.

"Hello, Flavia," Chris said, hugging her back. She felt warm and soft, and he breathed her spicy perfume and garlic smells from cooking. Inwardly, he struggled to cross the Chris/Curt divide to her, the family, and the house. It was an occupational hazard of an undercover cop to always be inside himself, but Flavia and the Rabbi reached into his heart and yanked until he gave it to them, so Chris surrendered as best as he could. At least he knew he wanted to, even though he was The Untouchable.

"How have you been, Curt? Long time, no see!"

"Wonderful, you?"

"Terrific. I'm so glad you could come. You know we love when you hang with us."

"I love to hang with you."

"Yet you won't come dancing with us? David told me he asks you."

"I can't right now—"

"You always say that!" Flavia pouted, pretending to be offended, her dark eyes flashing. Her features were beautiful in an exotic way, with a large curved nose, full lips, and striking cheekbones. Her figure was part of the same package, voluptuous in a flowing peasant dress. Black curls trailed freely to her shoulders, framing her lovely face.

"Curt!" the twins said in unison, looking up as they set the table. They were a matching mixture of Flavia and the Rabbi, with their mother's round brown eyes, the same dark curls, and a ready smile from their dad.

"Ladies!" Chris couldn't tell them apart for a minute, though he had known them a long time. He felt a pride in them as if they were his own daughters, which he knew was a ridiculous thought, even as he had it.

They laughed, coming over and giving him a quick hug. "I'm Leah, she's Lina," Leah said, smiling up at him.

"Wow! When did you two grow up?"

"When you got old!" Leah shot back, laughing.

"Curt, meet our friend Melissa Babcek." Lina gestured behind her, and a slim blonde came out of the pantry with some cans.

"Hi, I've heard a lot about you," Melissa said, and Chris realized that Flavia and the Rabbi were trying to set him up, yet again.

"Nice to meet you too. I'm—" Chris was about to say Chris Brennan, but he stopped himself. "Curt Abbott."

"I hear you're, like, the best ATF agent ever."

"Not exactly," Chris said, eyeing the Rabbi. "So much for confidentiality."

The Rabbi waved him off. "Don't give me that, Curt. She doesn't need clearance to know you're a star."

Chris laughed it off, and they all sat down to a delicious dinner of vegetarian risotto and roasted branzino, covered with tomatoes, onions, and red peppers. He wolfed down a second helping as the conversation circulated easily, lubricated by chilled Sancerre. Melissa was a nice woman, telling funny stories about her life as an associate at a big law firm, and although Chris gave the right responses and said the right words, he felt apart from everyone. It was as if he could go only so far but no further, and by the end of dinner, Chris could feel the Rabbi's eyes on him.

"Curt, let's go outside. I need a cigar."

"Sure, okay." Chris followed him from the kitchen, through a set of French doors, and out to their back patio, a flagstone rectangle framed by a privacy fence covered by ivy and climbing rosebushes. At the center of the patio was a table and wire chairs painted red, and on the table sat a blown-glass ashtray with a half-smoked cigar and a Bic lighter.

"Sit down, please." The Rabbi sat down, picked up his cigar, lit it, and took a long drag to bring it back to life. "So what did you think of Melissa?"

"I think she's a lovely young woman who will make some guy a great wife." Chris sat down.

"But not you?" The Rabbi's cigar flared orange-red, and he leaned back in his chair.

"Not me." Chris could see inside the kitchen through

the glass doors, and Flavia and the three girls were talking, laughing, and feeding Fred bits of fish, which he kept dropping on the tile floor. A warm golden glow emanated from the kitchen, and soft jazzy music floated through the screen door.

"What's going on, Curt?"

Curt. Chris. He tried to reposition himself in space and time. "Nothing."

"I'm not buying that." The Rabbi tilted his head back and exhaled a wispy funnel of cigar smoke, which was swept away by the city air.

"Alek ticks me off. I appreciate your going to bat for me."

"Happy to do it, you know that. I think you're right."

"Thank you." Chris glanced inside the kitchen, through the window, and he could see Fred walking on his hind legs for more fish. The women burst into laughter.

"Why do you want to stay with the operation so much?"

"Like I said. Something's not right, and we've gotten away with too many peaceful Oklahoma anniversaries. We're pressing our luck and—"

"And that would be the party line."

"What do you mean?" Chris looked over, surprised at a new skepticism in the Rabbi's tone.

"Don't get me wrong, I believe you. But you've been undercover for years. There's no operation you turn down, no matter how big or how small. And this one, you reached for, as soon as that video came in. You wouldn't be denied."

"Is something the matter with that?" Chris felt stung. "I'm doing my job."

"Curt." The Rabbi took another drag on his cigar, and

its thick ash flared at the fat tip. "As your boss, I appreciate your dedication and your commitment. But as your friend, I don't like it."

"Why?" Chris scoffed. "Don't treat me like I'm some cliché, the undercover burnout. I'm not that at all. I'm fine. I'm stable. I'm not showing any signs of PTSD."

"That's *exactly* what bothers me." The Rabbi's dark gaze narrowed behind his glasses. "You like undercover work too much. You don't want to leave it."

"Because I like what I do. I'm a workaholic, like you."

"No, wrong, I hated undercover work. You know why? I like who I am and I love my life. I love Flavia and the girls, and I even love that fat dog." The Rabbi gestured to the kitchen, but his gaze remained on Chris. "You like being under too much because it gives you an identity. Someone to be. A role to play."

Chris's mouth went dry, and the Rabbi's words resonated in his chest. But he didn't know if he could admit it, not even to himself, much less to the Rabbi.

"I think that's why you want to continue this operation, and why you leapt on the opportunity. The operation was your idea, and you rammed the authorization down Alek's throat. That's why he's coughing it back up. You want to be under forever, that's what I worry about."

Chris didn't know what to say, so he didn't say anything. He wished he had a cigar so he had something to do with his hands, something that would distract him from the sweetly domestic scene on the other side of the window. It struck him that he'd lived his entire life on the wrong side of the window, with everyone else on the other side, the normal side, easy to see and within reach, but only through glass, separated from him. The Rabbi was right. Still Chris couldn't say anything.

"And the question is, if that's true, what do you do

about it? The answer is simple—come in, for good. You can't start figuring out who you are until you get rid of Chris Brennan, Kyle Rogan, Calvin Avery, and the other aliases. They're not you. They're just roles you played. I want you to stop before you lose yourself."

Chris swallowed hard. "I'm not sure if that's possible," he said, quietly.

"Stopping or losing yourself?"

"Stopping." Chris knew the other one was possible. That, he knew.

"Of course it is." The Rabbi gestured at the kitchen window again. "You can have everything that I have. A wonderful wife, two great kids to drive you crazy, a dog on a diet—"

"What if I need to play a role to be the best agent possible?" Chris heard himself say. It must've been the wine, loosening him up.

"You don't. You're already the best agent possible. The rest is just dressing. Like clothes or a scarf. Overlay. The distinction is form over substance." The Rabbi eyed him. "And Curt, you're all substance. Always have been."

Chris warmed inside, almost believing him. "So I won't lose my superpowers?"

"No." The Rabbi chuckled.

"I met someone," Chris said, after a moment

"Really?" the Rabbi asked, intrigued. "Who?"

"One of the moms. Larkin's mother. Heather." Chris liked her name. It was so feminine. He hadn't said it aloud until this very minute.

"You like her?"

"Yes." Chris had to admit it. He liked Heather. He flushed. It felt like high school, which, in a way, it was.

"You're sure the son's not a suspect?"

"Pretty sure."

"You're not letting your feelings for the mom cloud your judgment about the kid, are you? I'd hate to see you get hurt."

"I'm sure."

"So then. You know the rules." The Rabbi emitted a puff of cigar smoke. "A man's got to do what a man's got to do."

Chris burst into laughter, like a relief of a pressure valve. He'd never gotten involved with any woman on an operation before, but he knew it happened. "I wouldn't do anything, and it's not going anywhere. Nothing can jeopardize this operation now that Alek's on my ass."

"But even wanting it, that's a step in the right direction." The Rabbi's expression softened. "It's good to want a relationship. You're getting older. You're entitled to a family."

Chris didn't know if he was entitled to a family. He had gotten this far without one.

"I want you to think about what I'm saying. Curt Abbott is one helluva guy, and I really like him. So does Flavia, and she's smarter than I am, and the girls, and Fred. Don't stay out because you're afraid to come in."

"I'm not," Chris shot back, but he wasn't sure which was in and which was out. To him, he was in, and they were out.

"Then why? Why this operation, really? This is just us, now. You're going toe-to-toe with Alek, for what?"

"I know why," Chris said, thinking aloud. "I want to protect my kids. These kids. One of them is mixed up in something, maybe more than one of them. But they're good kids and they can't know what they're getting into."

"You don't know that."

"True, but it's a hunch. They're young. Naïve. They're *all* unwitting." Chris felt a new conviction and heard the truth in his own words. Maybe the kids were standing in for him, for all of his boyhood. No one had protected him, and he knew how that had felt. Now he could protect them. He hadn't realized it until this minute, clarifying his mission anew.

"Then stay. And however it ends, I hope that woman is still there for you."

"We'll see." Chris checked his watch. "Gotta go."

Chapter Twenty-six

The neon sign glowed **REGAL CINEMA MULTIPLEX CENTRAL VALLEY**, and Chris joined the back of the crowd swelling into the theater, mostly teenage boys. He had learned from his audiotapes that Evan and Jordan were going to the movies tonight, and after he'd left the Rabbi's house, he'd had just enough time to wire himself. He'd taped the microphone to his chest under his polo shirt, and the controller was in his pocket so he could turn it off and on remotely, saving him hours of listening to irrelevant details of a target's everyday conversation.

Jordan and Evan shuffled ahead in the middle of the throng, visible because they were so tall, and Jordan had on his Musketeers baseball cap, worn twisted backwards. The crowd shifted forward, and Chris kept his eye on them as they went through the door. He watched them join the line at the concession stand, where every teenage boy was buying oversized tubs of popcorn and sodas.

Chris lingered at the back of the lobby, pretending he was reading the menu, which was endless, including nachos, hummus, and pizza. He couldn't remember what they sold in the movies when he was little; he'd been to the movies only once, as a child. He didn't even remember which movie he'd seen. All he remembered was that when he'd looked over, his foster mother's eyes had been teary. He hadn't had to ask why.

Evan and Jordan got their popcorn and sodas, headed to the ticket taker, and had their phones scanned, and Chris followed. Jordan and Evan went down the hall to the theater and went inside, and Chris let a few people pass before he entered and took the first seat on the left. He passed the next few hours watching the movie, a decibel-blasting superhero sequel, but in the back of his mind was his conversation with the Rabbi.

It's okay to want a relationship. You're getting older. You're entitled to a family.

After the movie was over, Chris got a bead on Jordan and Evan, heading toward the side exit. It was time to make his move, and he left his seat just as they were reaching the line. "Jordan, Evan!" Chris called to them, managing a look of surprise.

"Hi, Coach!" Jordan smiled, but he looked unusually drawn, and Chris flashed on the scene at practice this morning, remembering how upset they'd been over Abe's death.

"Yo, Coach," Evan said, already looking down at his phone, and the three of them left the theater together, squeezing into the hallway.

"How's your face feel, Jordan?" Chris gestured to the injury on his cheek, which had scabbed over.

"A lot better."

"Good. What did you think of the movie?"

"Awesome," Jordan answered.

"Totally," Evan answered, still looking at his phone. They trundled out to the main lobby, to the exit doors, and out of the building. People passed them, lighting cigarettes, checking phones, and pulling out car keys as they left for the parking lot.

Chris stayed close to Jordan. "Hey guys, you want to go out and grab a coffee or something? It's not that late, and I know you've had a tough day, after what happened to Mr. Y. We could go next door. We don't have to move the cars."

"Okay." Jordan smiled with a shrug.

"Why not?" Evan said, texting.

The night was dark and cool, and they walked the length of the multiplex with Evan texting on his phone. Jordan fell into step with Chris, who put his hand in his pocket, found the remote control for the wire, and pressed ON. "It's so sad about Mr. Y," Chris said after a moment.

"Yeah." Jordan walked with his head down, the flat lid of his backwards-baseball cap pointing up at a moonlit sky.

"How are you feeling about it?"

"It's sad, like you say."

"Obviously I didn't know him that well, but he took the time to welcome me. Suicide is a terrible thing, an awful thing."

"I know. How can you *hang* yourself? That's, like, hard to do."

"It must be." Chris didn't explain that, in fact, the opposite was true. It wasn't that difficult to hang yourself, and if the ligature were positioned correctly, it wouldn't be suffocation that would be fatal, but the breaking of the hyoid bone at the base of the throat, crushing the windpipe.

"God, it sucks," Jordan said, as they approached the restaurant. "It's so hard to believe that Mr. Y is dead. It's, like, final. You can't change it or take it back."

"Right, I know." Chris had actually had the same

thought about death. That it was final, and forever. "It's difficult to wrap your mind around."

"Is this place any good?" Evan asked, still texting as Chris opened the door to the restaurant, which was packed.

"My mom likes it," Jordan said, and Chris felt a twinge at the mention of Heather. He pointed at an empty table, and a harried waitress gave him a nod. They went over and sat down at a tiled circle, fitting with the island scheme of the restaurant.

Chris eyed both boys, but only Jordan was paying attention. "Sorry you had to practice this morning, guys. I was surprised that Coach Hardwick held it after the news about Mr. Y."

Jordan nodded sadly, but didn't reply. Chris could see Heather's features in her son's face, the warmth of her eyes and the shyness of her smile. He wondered what it would be like to have Jordan as a son. Or to have a son at all.

Evan glanced up. "Coach Hardwick holds practice, no matter what. I think his wife could die and we'd still have practice."

"Jordan, Evan, you know, the school's worried that any time you have a suicide, you guys are going to start getting strange ideas. They're going to have grief counselors there on Monday." Chris wasn't lying. He'd already gotten a flurry of emails from Dr. McElroy informing the CVHS community of Abe's death and setting up preventative counseling for CVHS students. "Do I have to worry about you guys? You wanna talk about it?"

"You don't have to worry about me, Coach." Jordan managed a smile.

"Me, either," Evan said, still texting away, his thumbs flying.

"I'm glad to hear that. But just let me know, don't be

ashamed. Everybody gets down sometimes, when you just don't feel like yourself." Chris sensed he was talking about himself, but stayed on track. He needed information about his four suspects—Evan, Raz, Trevor, and Dylan. "You know, being new, I don't know the team very well, but what about some of the other guys? Raz, for example. And Trevor and Dylan?"

Jordan sighed. "Raz was upset, but I don't think he would ever do anything like that. I hope not, but since his dad died, you know, he's been down."

"No way, he wouldn't." Evan shook his head as he texted.

"I'll keep an eye on Raz. I know he's got some trouble at home he's dealing with, so this is a hard time. But I've got his back."

"Good, Coach." Jordan smiled, and Chris wanted him reassured so that the two boys didn't become close again. Raz was on Chris's list of suspects and had chosen the Bill-of-Rights side in Chris's classroom exercise. The profile of his suspect would be a kid with a grudge against the government, which had been Timothy McVeigh's motivation in blowing up the Alfred P. Murrah Federal Building in Oklahoma City.

"Jordan, tell me about Trevor. He's a helluva third baseman, and I got to talk to him a little at the game. What's he like?"

"Beef, he's a nice guy," Jordan answered, as the waitress came over with a tray of water glasses, setting them in front of them with a hurried "be right back," which made Chris think about Heather.

I quit my job!

Suddenly Evan looked up from his phone with an excited grin. "Dude! Looks like Brittany freed up. She wants me to come over."

Jordan's gaze shifted sideways. "You mean Miss Booty Call?"

"Ha! Coach, you mind if I bounce? She goes to a different school, and I never get to see her. Check her out." Evan scrolled through his phone, swiping through photos, then held one up of a pretty blonde making a duckface kiss. "I mean, you feel me? This girl is haaawwwt!"

"Go ahead, Evan. As between me or her, I'd choose her too." Chris turned to Jordan. "I'm assuming you guys took Evan's new car. If you did, I can take you home, so Evan can go."

"Uh, okay." Jordan smiled. "We did take his car. He loves that car. He'd sleep in it if he could."

"Dude, you love my ride, too." Evan jumped up. "Coach, sorry. Later, Jordan." Evan took off, leaving Jordan alone with Chris, who paused before he resumed the conversation.

"How about Evan? You ever worry about him becoming depressed?"

"No, are you kidding?" Jordan looked at Chris like he was crazy. "He has too much to live for. He's dating, like, four girls in rotation."

"He's got a varsity and a JV?"

"Hell, he's got a farm team."

"Ha!" Chris wanted to know more about Evan, who was on his suspect list. "He seems like a pretty happy guy to me. Is he?"

"Yes, totally. He's, like, so popular."

"But Mr. Y was popular, so that doesn't tell you anything."

"Right." Jordan's face fell.

"What's Evan like?"

"Like what you see. Easy, cool. I'm not that friendly with him, but he's got nothing to be bummed about. His family is rich, and his dad is a big deal. They belong to the country club my mom works at, er, quit from."

"She told me. Good for her."

"Right." Jordan brightened. "She hated that job."

Chris felt fleetingly the warmth of the bond he shared with Jordan, especially in Heather, but he put her out of his mind. "So does Evan have a lot of friends outside of school?"

"Not friends, just girls. If it's a girl, he's there. They come to him."

Chris moved on, so it wouldn't seem like an interrogation. "Tell me about Trevor. What's he like? He seems so outgoing."

"He is. He gets along with everybody. He's a farm boy."

"You mean he lives on a farm?" Chris didn't understand. He had researched Trevor online and learned that the boy lived with his family in a development in Central Valley. Trevor's social media was sparse except for the weight lifting videos.

"Oh, whoops, I guess I shouldn't have said anything." Jordan grimaced. "It's, like, secret."

"What's secret about it? I won't tell anybody."

"Trevor doesn't live at the address they have for him at school." Jordan leaned over. "Like, it's the wrong address in the Booster directory. His family has a farm but it's outside the school district, near Rocky Springs. They told the school he lives at his uncle's address in town so he could go to CVHS."

"Is it a dairy farm or what?" Chris's ears pricked up. If Trevor lived on a farm, he could have access to fertilizer and a place to store it. But he'd need fifty bags or so to make an IED powerful enough to blow up a building, which would explain why he'd be stealing more from Herb Vrasaya's farm.

"I don't know, I've never been to the farm. But that's

how he got so big. He can bench press, like, 250. He's a monster."

"What's his personality like? You don't think he would be the kind of guy to get depressed, do you know?"

"Nah. The only thing is he's got a temper."

"I saw, at the party. How about Dylan?" Chris was ticking off the names on his suspect list. He'd pump Jordan until he struck oil.

"Dylan's a nice guy."

"He seems it." Chris was starting to see the shortcomings of his unwitting. Jordan liked everything and everybody, and Chris would have to pull teeth to get better information. "But he's the quiet type, isn't he?"

"Totally. He works so hard. He gets really good grades. Evan thinks he's a total geek."

"Do you know Dylan?"

"Yes, him, I know. He played JV with me, too. He's not superhard-core into baseball. Don't get me wrong, he's a great player and I don't want to dis him to you—"

"No, I get that."

"He plays because his parents make him, and he's so tall, like the tallest on the team, and it helps him in the outfield. And he can hit. His mechanics are good."

"Right. Where are they tonight, Dylan and Trevor? Do you know?"

"I don't know."

"Who do they hang with?"

Jordan shook his head. "Nobody I know. They're both, like, loners. Trevor especially. He never goes anywhere because he has so many farm chores."

"Where's the farm?"

"On Skinny Lane Road. It's called Skinny Lane Farm. I remember the name because Raz said it should be called Meathead Lane Farm, for him." Jordan sipped his water, chuckling.

"How about Dylan? Who's he friendly with?" Chris's research on Dylan's social media had shown that the boy had only six friends who were people and the other fifteen were scientific organizations like CERN, NASA's Hubble Space Telescope, and Curiosity Rover. Chris thought it didn't get lonelier than having an inanimate object for a friend.

"Nobody, he studies all the time. Like on the bus to away games, he puts his headphones on and keeps studying. Once I asked him what he was listening to, and he said 'nothing, I just want to block you guys out.'"

Chris had another thought. "I wonder why he's not in our AP Government class. He must be on the AP track, right?"

"Yes, but he took Government last year. He takes everything ahead of everybody else. He's on an independent study now. He took Physics last year, too."

"How about Chemistry?" Chris asked, since Dylan's interest in the sciences was a red flag.

"I don't know." Jordan shrugged. "Come to think of it, Dylan is kind of weird. Maybe you should be worried about him, with depression and all. He seemed weird this morning when we heard about Mr. Y. Everybody was upset, but he wasn't. He told all of us about it like it was a news story."

"Yeah, I noticed that," Chris said, meaning it. Dylan showed a marked lack of empathy when he told everyone about the scene at the high school, with the crying teachers. In contrast, Raz had been holding back tears, his face mottled with emotion, not to cry in front of the team.

Jordan wheeled his head around. "Wonder what happened to the waitress? Maybe we should just go?"

"Okay, it's getting late. Your mom's probably wondering where you are." Chris didn't want to arouse Jordan's suspicions and he was looking forward to seeing Heather again. Maybe they'd have another talk over water and cookies.

"No, not tonight." Jordan stood up. "She's out on a date."

"Oh, good," Chris forced himself to say, rising.

Chapter Twenty-seven

For Heather, the check couldn't come fast enough. She hadn't ordered dessert, but her date had, oblivious to the fact that she was having a horrible time. She sat across from him, muting him in her mind, like a commercial she couldn't fast-forward. He was decent-looking and had a great job, but she didn't want looks or even money. What she wanted was a man who was interested in *her,* and she knew that her date wasn't interested in her by the appetizer, a mixed green salad.

It only went downhill from there, when, in response to her *so what do you do for a living,* he started mansplaining title insurance. They'd ordered entrees, and she'd listened to him drone on through her poached salmon with yogurt dill dressing. She could've put up with it if he had just asked one question about her. That was her test for first dates—whether he learned as much about her as she did about him.

But by the time the check came, he still had no idea whether she had children, a job, a dog, or preexisting illness. That didn't stop him from pawing her in the parking lot on the way to her car and forcing his tongue into her mouth. She pushed him away, got in the car, and drove home, looking forward to taking off her bra, getting into her pajamas, and watching her DVRed shows, which were backing up like a Things To Do List for the unemployed.

Suddenly her cell phone rang, and she glanced at the screen, surprised to see it was Raz, so she answered. "Raz? How are you?"

"Sorry to call you so late, Ms. Larkin."

"That's okay." Heather didn't know what was going on, but Raz sounded upset, his voice shaky.

"I've been calling Jordan. Do you know where he is?"

Heather hesitated. She didn't relish being the one to tell Raz that Jordan was with Evan. She wondered if he and Jordan had talked since practice. Jordan had been upset about Mr. Y's suicide and had spent the day in his room, on his computer and doing homework. She told Raz, "I think he's at the movies. Maybe he has his phone on silent."

"Who did he go with?"

"Evan, I think," Heather answered, because it couldn't be avoided. She didn't know what Raz could have expected after he'd punched Jordan. She heard a woman's voice in the background, probably Susan, but the words were indistinct, like it said on closed captioning. WORDS INDISTINCT.

Raz cleared his throat. "See, uh, I wanted to say I'm sorry to you, too. I lost my temper and I didn't mean to hit Jordan, I'm sorry about that."

"Well, that's nice of you to say. But I think Jordan is the one you owe the apology to."

"That's why I'm trying to reach him."

"Well, good. It's between the two of you. You have to make it right."

"I know, I went too far."

"Yes, you did." Heather felt a pang of sympathy for him, he sounded so upset. But still, she'd been happier knowing that Jordan was out with Evan and she sensed Jordan had been looking forward to it, too. Not that he'd told her as much, but he'd put on a clean T-shirt and jeans. And Heather couldn't believe it when she saw Jordan and Evan driving off in a BMW that cost more than she made all last year.

"Mrs. Larkin, my mother wants to talk to you."

"Okay, no problem, good night."

"Good night," Raz said miserably, then Susan came on. "Heather? I'm so sorry about what Raz did. I hope you accept his apology."

"Of course I do," Heather said, softening up. She felt guilty that she hadn't gone up to Susan at the game. "I'm so sorry about Neil, and you have my sympathies. I know that couldn't have been easy for you yesterday."

"Right, thanks." Susan sounded shaky, too. "It's been so hard, and I'm not saying this is an excuse, but Raz has been very upset about losing his father."

"I can't imagine," Heather said, though she could. Jordan never knew his father, but he still never punched his friend in the face.

"He's been so angry lately and withdrawn, and he spends a lot of time in his room on the laptop. I'm beginning to worry what he's up to." Susan's tone turned vulnerable, which surprised Heather. They didn't know each other at all.

"Jordan spends a lot of time in his room too. They all do. They're growing up."

"I know, but this is different. I think he's withdrawing and I don't know who he's online with, all the time."

"Tell me about it." Heather steered onto Central Valley Road, almost home.

"I hope that what happened won't affect his friendship to Jordan. I always liked that they were friends. Jordan is such a good influence on Raz."

"Thank you." Heather didn't think Jordan should have to raise Raz, but whatever. The traffic on Central Valley was light since most of the businesses were closed, the storefronts darkened and their signs turned off. Only the Friendly's sign was still on, blasting into her apartment. She always thought, *Not so Friendly, are you?*

"Heather, I need to ask you a favor. I'm hoping there's something you could do to facilitate things between the boys. You could broker a peace."

"How?" Heather asked, unprepared for the request. Susan had a big job at ValleyCo, so maybe she was used to asking for things. Heather had always wished she could be more like that. She never asked anybody for anything. She relied on herself. She *waited*. As Dr. Phil would say, *How's that working for you?*

"Please talk to Jordan and tell him that Raz is having a hard time. I don't know if you heard, but his brother Ryan was arrested last night for vandalism, and that's upsetting everybody."

"Oh, my," Heather said, as if she hadn't heard, though she had.

"I hope you'll try to just get us through this time. It's a rough patch and I think Jordan would really be key to helping Raz. Jordan hasn't answered his calls."

"He was at the movie, so maybe he didn't get it."

"Raz has been calling him all afternoon, too. And texting. Jordan's not responding. He would've apologized to him at practice but for the news about Mr. Y. It's so terrible. I feel like we're all in a bad patch lately, don't you?"

"In a way, yes. I just left my job." Heather reached her apartment building and turned left into the driveway, then had a thought. "Susan, you work for ValleyCo, don't you?"

"Yes, I'm Marketing Manager."

Heather hesitated, then thought of Dr. Phil. "Do you know of any openings, for me?"

Chapter Twenty-eight

Mindy scrolled through Facebook on her phone in bed, not bothering to comment on the funny animal videos, baby pictures, or inspirational sayings. Usually she was a Facebook slut, liking all her friends' posts and counting the likes on her posts. But not tonight. She was completely preoccupied, waiting for Paul to come home. He was late, the second night in a row. And again, he'd only texted, **got held up at the hosp, sry.**

She kept scrolling, watching the posts flip by like a slot machine. She remembered when she used to read in bed, but Facebook had replaced books. She'd been happier back then, but that could have been a coincidence. Finally she heard Paul's car pull into the driveway and glanced at the bedside clock: 12:15.

The house was quiet, and Mindy waited for him to get inside, so that when he finally did, she could almost hear the mechanical *ca-chunk* of his key turning in the lock downstairs, then the slight squeak of the front door opening, and the comforting sealing sound as it was shut and the deadbolt thrown. She knew Paul's routines so well, the way a wife does a husband's, so that she knew he would drop his keys jingling on the console table, which he did, then his messenger bag on the chair beside the console table, *thud,* then he'd turn off the light she'd left on for him, and last would come a sigh, which she used to think of as a sigh of contentment. But after he'd had his affair, she wondered if his sigh was one of resignation, like, *I'm home, having no other choice.*

Mindy focused her attention on Paul's heavy tread on the steps. One footfall then the other, each beat like the tick of a clock, signaling that she was running out of time on a decision. She hadn't decided what to do about the mysterious jewelry charge. She could let it go or she could confront him—but she couldn't be accusatory, she had to use I-words, and not point her finger, literally. Their ground rules had been laid down by their marriage counselor, though Mindy couldn't believe that her husband was threatened by her manicured fingernail.

Mindy knew that when she forgave Paul, she was letting him off the hook, but she didn't want him thinking that he was off the hook forever. She had consulted a divorce lawyer, unbeknownst to him even to this day, and the lawyer had told her about the "one free bite" rule, which was the law in Pennsylvania with respect to dog bites—every dog gets one free bite before the owner is liable. Well, her dog had had his free bite, and after the next one, he was getting neutered.

Mindy tried to make a decision. To confront or not to confront? The footfalls disappeared, which meant that Paul was crossing the carpeted hallway, then he materialized in the doorway, looking tired, though she didn't know if that was an act.

"Hey honey, sorry I'm late," Paul said, flashing her a tired smile, though he barely met her eye.

"It's okay." Mindy's instant impression was *he's hiding*

something. He was tall, a trim six-footer with dark hair going prematurely gray, and it looked slightly greasy, since he had a nervous habit of raking his hair. His dark brown eyes were small, set far apart, and slightly hooded for a forty-five-year-old, with deep crow's-feet. Mindy always thought he had the weight of the world on his shoulders, being an oncology surgeon, but now she was wondering where he had been. She asked him, lightly, "What kept you?"

"The last case took forever. My feet are killing me."

"You poor thing. What was it?"

"The case?" Paul slid out of his suit jacket, which he tossed on the cushioned bench at the foot of the bed. "Lawson. I think I told you about him. He'll make it, Thank God."

"Great. I don't remember you mentioning a Lawson. What was the problem?"

"Honey, you know I don't like to talk about my cases. Let me leave it at the hospital, please." Paul came around the bed and gave her a quick peck on the cheek.

"Mm, okay." Mindy received his kiss like a happy wife, though she sniffed him like a hound dog. Or maybe a cadaver dog. Was their marriage dead or alive? Was it buried under some rocks, waiting to be rescued?

"How was your day?" Paul kicked off his shoes.

"We had some bad news."

"What?" Paul slid out of his tie and threw it on top of his suit, then began to unbutton his shirt around his growing paunch, which pleased Mindy more than it should have. She hated that Paul did nothing to stay thin, which was metabolically unfair. Plus he would've been dieting if he were having another affair. Last time, he'd started going to a gym and dyeing his hair, a Hubby Renaissance that would've tipped off any wife but her.

"You know Mr. Y, Evan's Language Arts teacher? He committed suicide."

"Whoa." Paul frowned. "That's terrible. How?"

"I know, isn't it? He hung himself." Mindy felt terrible about Mr. Y's death, but she was happy to have some actual news to tell Paul. Ever since the affair, she'd worried that she was boring. She tried to think of stories that happened to her during the day, just to have something to tell him. Sometimes she even made them up. *See, I'm not just a housewife. I'm fascinating!*

"Wait. Language Arts is English, right?"

"Right."

"Why don't they call it that?"

"Progress?" Mindy answered, as Paul slid out of his pants, hopping around in his socks to stay on balance. She bit her tongue not to tell him to sit down when he took his pants off, because he always said she sounded like his mother. She wondered if every man married his mother, then hated his wife for being his mother, or if he didn't marry his mother, then he would eventually act like such a child that he would turn his wife into his mother.

"Be right back." Paul stripped to his undershirt and boxers, then went into the bathroom and closed the door behind him, which he never did. Hmmm.

Mindy eyed her phone without seeing a word. She realized she was tallying the clues about whether Paul was having another affair, like an Infidelity Ledger. In the No Affair column he was *gaining weight,* and in the Divorce column was *home late, lame explanation, oddly tired, shut the bathroom door,* and *mysterious jewelry charge.* Mindy heard him washing his face, buzzing his teeth clean, flushing the toilet, then he left the bathroom and was back in the bedroom.

"God, I'm beat," Paul said, which Mindy knew was

marital code for *I don't want to have sex*. He walked around the bed, climbed in, and pulled up the covers with a grunt. Of satisfaction? Of pain? Why hadn't she noticed before that he made so many noises?

"Me, too," Mindy said, which communicated, *I don't want to have sex either, so don't sweat it, I won't hold this one against you—unless you don't want to have sex because you just had sex with someone else. In which case, I've got a divorce lawyer who's dying to take half of your money, and I'm keeping Evan and the house. And I'm melting your Porsche for scrap metal.*

"How was your day?"

"Fine, but it's so sad about Mr. Y. The school is having grief counselors on Monday, and Evan was upset about it, too. He really liked Mr. Y. He spent most of the day in his room."

"Bastard!"

"Who? Evan?"

"No, the teacher." Paul inched down in bed. "What kind of teacher does that? He's not thinking about the kids."

"Well, I think people who commit suicide are in despair. They don't see a way out."

"Yes, there is one. Work through your problems like an adult."

"It's not that easy—"

"Of course it is. Mindy, you're too soft."

Mindy cringed. She heard everything he said as a criticism of her weight, ever since he told the therapist he wanted her to lose thirty pounds. She had to stop the drinking, that's what did it, the sugar. Then the thought struck her. She was too soft, and Paul was too hard.

"I see my cases, like Lawson tonight, fighting for his life. If these people spent one day in my OR, they'd see what life is worth. Everything."

Mindy didn't reply, because he didn't need any encouragement to talk anyway. She *was* too soft. Her hand went to her tummy, and she squeezed the roll under her T-shirt. She held it like a security blanket, trying to decide whether to confront him. He seemed irritable tonight. Maybe he really had been at the hospital.

"People don't have a governor anymore. They do whatever they please. They don't control themselves. They don't think of the consequences. They lack discipline. Willpower."

Mindy cringed again. Once Paul had told her that she was fat because she didn't have willpower.

"So what's the school going to do for a *Language Arts* teacher now? What about the class? These are high-school juniors. Can't screw with their grades right now." Paul turned over, his back to her.

"I suppose they'll figure out something." Mindy switched off the bedside lamp, plunging the bedroom into darkness, the way Paul liked it. He would've been perfectly content to sleep in a cave, and she used to call him Batman. The consolation prize was that she had custom curtains made with a lovely Schumacher fabric that she'd used for the headboard, bench, and two side chairs.

"Good night, honey."

"Paul, there's something I wanted to mention," Mindy said, making her decision to confront him.

"I know, I forgot to bring up the recycling bin when I came in. Does it really matter?"

"No, it's not that." Mindy lightened her tone, as if she were a violinist playing a Stradivarius instead of a wife asking her husband a legitimate question.

"What is it?" Paul said, staccato, and Mindy wished she could see his face, but she couldn't. He was turned away, and it was dark, the only bright spot in the room was his undershirt.

"I was going through the Visa bill and I noticed a charge I didn't understand."

"Like what?"

"A three-hundred-twenty-seven-dollar charge at the jewelers, you know, the one in that strip mall? Do you know if that was Evan or you? Because if it was Evan, I told him to ask me before he bought any more jewelry."

Paul fell silent a beat. "That was my charge."

"For what?" Mindy felt relieved and nervous, both at once, and it was a struggle to maintain her falsely light tone. He wasn't denying it, which was a good sign. It went into the No Affair column on the Infidelity Ledger.

"Carole's birthday, remember? The new secretary? I got her a fancy picture frame. I picked it up on the way to the hospital. I thought I paid cash for that, but I was short that day. I charged it."

"Oh, well, thanks." Mindy's chest eased. That was a reasonable explanation, and more important, a verifiable one. She could double-check Carole's birthday. She used to note all of the staff's birthdays to buy them their gifts, but after therapy, they decided that Paul should buy his own gifts, since he never liked what she picked out anyway.

"It really bothers me that you do that," Paul said coldly, after a minute.

"Do what?" Mindy said, but she knew. *Here it comes.*

"You question me."

"I wasn't questioning you." Mindy hated Paul's habit of construing every question as an accusation. Except this time it was.

"You *were* questioning me. You're questioning me all the time. I mean, I do a nice thing, handle my own people myself, even though I have *no time.* I got the present myself, and here you are, fly-specking the credit cards."

"I'm entitled to that—"

"No, you're not, you're not at all." Paul huffed. "What the hell, Min? I'm walking on eggshells around here!"

"*I'm* the one walking on eggshells, not you." Mindy would never understand how he always accused her of things he did, but he got it out first, so he won.

"I don't deserve this, not in the least. I get called in on a Saturday, no less, and I work my ass off. I'm in the OR all day, then this pain-in-the-ass daughter of one of my cases is asking me four hundred questions. I barely get dinner and when I finally get to bed, you question my integrity."

Mindy rolled her eyes, since he was turned away. Sometimes she gave him the finger behind his back or when they were on the phone. "Look, I'm sorry, but you can understand it—"

"No, I can't."

"A jewelry store charge? From the *same store*?"

"Okay, listen, Min." Paul flopped over in the darkness, facing her. "You have to let it go. We've been through the mill. We've worked through it and we did everything we're supposed to do. We're past it now."

"Are we?" Mindy heard herself say, her genuine voice poking through her self-editing, like a blade of grass peeking through a crack in a pavement.

"Yes, we absolutely are. I love you." Paul's tone softened, and Mindy felt her heart ease.

"I love you, too. I really do."

"Okay, so remember that, Min. You love me, I love you."

"But I worry—"

"So, don't. Don't worry so much. You have absolutely nothing to worry about." Paul reached out, pulling her to him for a hug.

"Well, good." Mindy hugged him back, burying her face in his undershirt, which was when she realized something. He didn't smell like he'd been in the OR. Those odors always clung to his undershirt, an acrid anti-bacterial tang and even the metallic scent of blood. And he always took his undershirt off when he'd been in the OR, a habit he probably didn't even know he had. Then she thought back to when he'd first come in the bedroom. His hair had been greasy, but he hadn't had helmet head from his surgical cap, like he always did. She would've bet money that he hadn't been in any OR tonight.

"Good night, honey." Paul kissed her again on the cheek, then flopped back over.

"Good night." Mindy lay in the darkness, looking up at the ceiling, her heart sinking as she added another two items to the Divorce side of the Infidelity Ledger.

Which only made her think about what she would do next.

Chapter Twenty-nine

Chris hunched over his computer and watched the videotape of Trevor Kiefermann at the team party, his suspicions beginning to focus on the boy because of what Jordan had told him. Chris had called the office to see if the Kiefermanns or Skinny Lane Farm was registered with Homeland Security to purchase and store ammonium nitrate fertilizer, but he hadn't gotten a call back yet. It always frustrated him that it took so long to get answers, not like in the movies with split-second replies, magical indexes, and seamlessly shared intel. In truth, federal law enforcement too often functioned like any other government bureaucracy. Except that lives were at stake.

Chris watched the video, and the scene changed to Trevor standing in front of the gun case, telling his teammates about the weapons. The boy seemed to have a working knowledge of firearms, which was consistent with the profile of a domestic terrorist, though not dispositive. And Trevor and his family had lied to school authorities about his true address. That wasn't proof either, but it sent up red flags. It was likely that any bomber would be part of a conspiracy, even a family conspiracy like the Tsarnaevs in Boston and Bundys in Montana.

Chris eyed the screen, concerned. He didn't know Trevor's political leanings because the boy wasn't in his Government class, but there was an array of antigovernment groups on ATF's radar: neo-Nazis, Ku Klux Klan, skinheads, Nationalists, Christian Identity, Originalists, Constitutionalists, and militia groups. Plenty of them were in rural Pennsylvania, and Trevor and his family could belong to any one of them. Or be lone wolves.

Chris checked the clock, which read 2:03 A.M. He wasn't tired, but jazzed. He closed out the computer file and grabbed his phones, keys, and windbreaker on the way out. He hurried from the apartment, left the town house, and hustled to the Jeep as he thumbed his phone to Google maps and plugged in Skinny Lane Farm Rocky Springs PA.

Fifteen minutes later, he was driving the deserted streets of Central Valley, then leaving town behind as he headed north. The outlet malls and chain restaurants gradually gave way to open farmland, and he rolled down the car window. He passed barns and farmhouses set far from the road, their windows black. There was no traffic and no ambient light. The moon hid behind a dense cloud cover, and only Chris's high beams illuminated the road. Bugs dive-bombed in the jittery cones of light, and dark fields of new corn rustled in the chilly breeze.

He drove on and on, following the twists and turns, and the only sound was the coarse thrum of the Jeep's engine, the mechanical voice of the GPS app, and outside the window, the constant chorus of crickets. Chris's nostrils filled with the earthy scent of cow manure and the medicinal odor of chemical fertilizer, and he breathed deeply, letting his thoughts run free.

Scraps of memories floated into his consciousness, and

they were times he didn't want to remember, especially not on the job. He wasn't a little boy anymore, a ten-year-old on a ramshackle farm in the middle of nowhere, the only foster son of the Walshes, chosen by the local DHS for their allegedly wholesome life.

You don't listen, boy.

Chris kept going as he approached the sign, SKINNY LANE FARM, HORSES BOARDED, SELF-CARE, at the end of a dirt road. Up ahead, the road bottomed in a compound that included a small gray farmhouse, nestled among two white outbuildings, a chicken coop, and a large red barn. He turned off his headlights and steered onto a narrow dirt road between vast cornfields. Corn was the primary crop fertilized with ammonium nitrate, but ammonium nitrate wasn't generally used by farmers on the East Coast, where humidity turned it to rock quickly, rendering it less spreadable. It wasn't impossible that Trevor's family could legitimately have ammonium nitrate fertilizer, and there was only one way to find out.

Chris traveled up the dirt road slowly, and when he was about a quarter of the way toward the house, he cut the engine. He got out of the car, closed the door, and stayed still for a moment, waiting for the bark of a dog. There was no sound. He ran down the road toward the house, turned into the cornfield so he wouldn't be seen, and kept going. It was pitch-black, and he ran with his hands in front of him, got the pattern of the rows, then angled to the right toward the main house. Bugs flew into his face, and dust filled his nostrils. He reached the end of the corn rows and peeked out. The farmhouse was to the right, and the barn and the outbuildings were to the left. There was still no barking dog, so he hurried from the cornfield, and ran to the barn, where the smell was unmistakable. Horses.

You don't listen, boy.

Chris used to love horses, one horse in particular, an old mare. The Walshes had been horse brokers, of the worst sort, and the mare didn't even have a name. She was a brown quarterhorse from some third-rate racetrack, on her way to a kill pen, for horsemeat to Canada or other countries. He had named her Mary, for which the Walshes had teased him.

Chris put the thoughts out of his mind as he walked down the center aisle of the barn, four stalls on each side, and he could see the shadows of the horses, the graceful curve of their necks and their peaked ears wheeling in his direction. He hustled to the end of the barn, knowing that there would be a feed room and hayloft. He opened the door, slid out his phone, scrolled to the flashlight function, and cast it around. There was nothing untoward, only galvanized cans of feed, labeled with duct tape, Purina Senior, Flax Seed, Alfalfa Cubes.

The Walshes never had treats like alfalfa cubes, but he used to pull grass to feed to Mary, and she had loved it, following him everywhere. He would find excuses to stop his chores and groom her, pick her feet, or pull her mane, imagining she enjoyed the attention. It was when she developed a cut that started to fester that was the beginning of the end. But Chris refused to think about that now.

His flashlight found a stairwell in the corner, and he hurried up the stairs. He shined the flashlight around the neatly stacked bales of hay on both sides of the loft, next to a pile of extra feed. He went over to make sure nothing was hidden behind them, then hurried back downstairs and out the feed-room door. He glanced around, but there was no sound, except for the horses' occasional shuffling in their stalls. There was another door across the way, presumably the tack room. He opened the door, closed it behind him, and shined his flashlight on saddles, grooming boxes, and blankets, then shelves of the typical supplies—Ventrolin, Corona hoof dressing, and a white jar of Swat, a salve for wounds.

On impulse, Chris walked over, picked up the Swat, and unscrewed the lid, releasing the pungent smell, and for a second felt lost in a reverie of emotion. It all came rushing back to him then, and he couldn't stop it if he tried. His mare had cut herself on a nail on the fence, a cut that would've healed if he'd been able to treat her. It had been the height of summer, hot as hell, and the horseflies were biting the mare alive, laying eggs in the wound. All it would've taken to heal her was Swat, which he'd seen an ad for in one of the farm newspapers. The salve only cost nine dollars then, and it would've fixed everything.

Walsh wouldn't spend the money, and so one day, Chris had bought Swat himself with money he'd saved and covered Mary's wound, before he turned her out at night. But the telltale pink stain on her neck showed Walsh that Chris had been treating the wound, and Walsh had smacked him so hard that he went flying down the aisle of the barn. Then Walsh found the Swat, dug his dirty fingers inside, and smeared two pink globs on Chris's cheeks, like rouge.

You don't listen, boy.

Chris hustled out of the barn and went past the chicken coop, also well maintained. Ahead lay the two outbuildings, the first a white woodshed with a peaked roof. He went to the door, which had a galvanized turn handle, but stopped before he opened it. Going inside the shed was an unlawful search, and he never would have been able to get a subpoena. The fact that Trevor was on the baseball team, lived on a farm, and was the requisite height wasn't sufficient for probable cause.

Chris couldn't break and enter, under the law. Undercover ATF agents weren't allowed to engage in otherwise illegal activity, OIA. If they needed to engage in OIA, they were supposed to get prior approval, which was laughably impractical. Chris remembered the time he'd infiltrated a human-trafficking ring smuggling young women from the Philippines, and he'd been offered one of the girls. It not only revolted him, but it would've constituted OIA. He'd declined, coming up with what became a classic line around the office—*I never paid for it in my life.* He took a special pride when those traffickers were convicted and sent to jail for twenty years.

But with the outbuilding, Chris was willing to bend the rules. It wasn't locked, so he wasn't breaking in, and it could prevent an impending bombing. He opened the door, stepped inside, and flicked on his flashlight. He looked around for fertilizer or anything suspicious, but it looked normal, even first-rate. Just an old tractor and a Kubota front-end loader with keys in the ignition. Hanging neatly were pitchforks, brooms, shovels, a hedge clipper, blowers, and the like.

He left the shed and hustled ahead to the other outbuilding, with a similar type of door, but it was padlocked. The shed could be used to store fertilizer, it was a cool location and it would be prudent to be kept under lock and key. He didn't smell anything but ammonium nitrate fertilizer was odorless. Chris thought about breaking the padlock, but didn't. It would be discovered, and even so, he made a distinction between going through an open door and breaking into a locked one. It drove him crazy that law didn't always lead to justice, and often thwarted justice, like now.

Chris needed a work-around. The situation came up on undercover operations, and the way that ATF dealt with it was through a "walled-off" operation. Most common was when he knew there were suspects driving around with contraband or explosives, but they couldn't be stopped without blowing an agent's cover, so the higher-ups at ATF would call the local constabulary. The locals would then make a traffic stop on the vehicle, finding a broken taillight, cracked windshield, or expired inspection sticker. It happened every day, but Chris couldn't do it without a call to the Rabbi, and he couldn't get it done tonight. He turned from the door, which would stay locked another day.

And he ran back toward the Jeep.

Chapter Thirty

Mindy reached for her phone and touched the screen, which came to life—3:23 A.M. She had been awake since Paul had told her that the mysterious charge at the jewelry store was for Carole's birthday. Mindy hadn't been sure whether she wanted to know the truth, but she had reached a decision.

She thumbed to the calendar function, scrolled to March, and scanned the entries on her calendar, color-coded: red for family, blue for Boosters, pink for Hospital Auxiliary, and green for Miscellaneous. An entry for Carole's birthday would have been Miscellaneous, but she scanned the entries with a sinking heart. There was no entry for Carole's birthday.

She scrolled to April, and there was no entry for Carole's birthday there either. She searched the calendar under "Carole," because she remembered entering the secretary's birthday, and the entry came up, October 23. Mindy got a sick feeling in the pit of her stomach. Carole's birthday wasn't last month. It hadn't even come yet. No amount of staring at the phone would change that fact. Paul had lied to her.

Tears came to her eyes, but she was more angry than sad. What did Paul think, that she wouldn't check the bill? How stupid did he think she was? Even brain-dead housewives can read Visa bills. Why did she let him handle all the money in the first place? In fact, she had offered to handle their household finances more than once, but Paul felt strongly that it was *his money*.

Mindy wondered how many other charges had gone unnoticed. Questions flooded her brain, and she had the sickening realization that it was happening all over again. Did he take her out to eat? Who was she? Was she married? The reason he'd gotten caught last time was that the nurse had started calling him. Maybe this time he'd wised up. Practice made perfect.

Mindy's phone blinked into darkness, and she glanced over at Paul, snoring soundly away. Then she remembered something he had said.

I thought I paid cash for that, but now I remember. I was short that day. I guess I charged it.

Mindy thought it was an odd thing to say. It got her thinking. Maybe *that* was his improvement, that he started paying cash. Maybe *that* was why she hadn't seen any other charges. He wasn't charging anymore. Her heartbeat quickened. It made perfect sense. If he was paying cash, he would have been using his ATM card to withdraw cash. She never checked those before because she'd been so focused on the charges.

Mindy got out of bed, padded out of the bedroom, and went back downstairs to the kitchen. She flipped on the light and went directly to the drawers in a pocket office off the kitchen, where they kept bank statements, which she had rifled through only this afternoon. She'd been looking for the wrong thing, for canceled checks and charges. She should have been looking at cash.

She went to the first stack of envelopes, which she kept in chronological order with the most recent on top. March was the first statement, and she grabbed the thick envelope, slid out the three pages, and scanned for cash withdrawals that looked unusual. Paul generally withdrew cash in two-hundred-dollar amounts, and she saw one on March 7, March 14, then March 21, and then another on March 28, also two hundred dollars. In other words, nothing unusual or suspicious.

She felt stumped. She replaced the March statements, refilled the envelope, and reached back for February. She withdrew the February statements, another three pages, and scanned them as well. There was a two-hundred-dollar cash withdrawal on February 1, 8, 15, 22, and 28. She noticed they were all around lunchtime at the same ATM, Blakemore Plaza, at the hospital. Again, not suspicious.

Mindy put the February statement back and reached into the drawer for the January statement. But when she pulled it out, she noticed that it wasn't from their joint account—it was a February statement from Evan's account. They had opened the account for him, and the balance was about $32,000. Evan deposited money he got from them and from Paul's wealthy parents, who had been generous with gifts for their only grandson. The statement was still sealed, since she never bothered to open them when they came in. Evan didn't bother either, evidently taking it for granted, defeating her purpose in opening the account in the first place. She could almost hear her father's voice, saying, *you have to teach him the value of money,* and that had been her intent, but somehow she ended up with a son who had affluenza.

Mindy tore open the envelope, which read at the top, **Dr. Paul & Mrs. Mindy Kostis in custodianship for Evan R. Kostis,** and she scanned down to the bottom for the balance, which was $22,918. That was a lower balance than she remembered, but she could have been mistaken. There had been no deposits that month, but oddly, there had been a withdrawal, in the amount of $5,000.

Mindy gasped. Why had there been such a large withdrawal, or any withdrawal at all? Who had withdrawn it? She, Paul, and Evan were all authorized to make withdrawals, and no permissions were required. Mindy hadn't withdrawn the money, so that left Paul or Evan. She didn't know if Paul had withdrawn the money to buy his new girlfriend a present, or if Evan had withdrawn the money to buy whatever girlfriend he had a present.

Mindy felt flabbergasted. In the past, Evan had bought presents for his girlfriends at Central Valley and other high schools, probably five gifts in total, but he had never used his money to do it and the most he'd ever charged was three hundred dollars, which was when she'd laid down the law that he had to ask first. So what could Evan have possibly done with $5,000? Or Paul, for that matter?

She set the statement aside, went back in the drawer, and started looking for the previous statement, which she found, also unopened. She was kicking herself now. She'd simply assumed Evan's account was dormant.

She examined the envelope, postmarked February 12, then extracted the statement, scanning it. She spotted a withdrawal of $3,000 on January 16. She couldn't believe what she was seeing. Why would Evan take so much money out of his account? Why would Paul? How many gifts where they buying? What was going on? Where was all of Evan's money going?

Mindy's heart began to hammer. What was going on in her own house? Her own family? She set the statement aside, went back in the drawer, and rummaged until she found the December statement for Evan's account. She tore it open, pulling out the single-page statement with hands that had begun to shake. Again, on December 13, about a month previous, there was another withdrawal, for $2,000.

Mindy's mind raced with possibilities. Drugs? Gambling? She went back to the drawer, collected all of the statements from Evan's account, and opened every envelope, checking to see if there were any cash withdrawals. Half an hour later, she'd found none earlier than December.

Mindy sat cross-legged on the floor, the statements around her in a circle. So there had been three withdrawals, totaling $10,000 in cash, but she didn't know if they were by Evan or Paul. Her heart told her that they had to have been made by Paul, but she knew a way to answer her own question.

She returned the statements to their envelopes, put them back in the kitchen drawer, then hurried from the kitchen and headed for Evan's room.

She was going to get to the bottom of this, right now.

Chapter Thirty-one

Chris sped toward town, his head pounding. It drove him crazy that there could be ammonium nitrate fertilizer in the Kiefermanns' shed and he was leaving it behind. He'd already called and texted the Rabbi to set up a work-around, but the Rabbi hadn't called or texted back yet, and Chris suspected it couldn't happen until tomorrow or the next day. Which could be too late.

Chris accelerated down the country road, racing past dark farms and fields. He gripped the wheel tight, grinding his teeth and clenching his jaw. He *knew* he was right about a bomb plot at CVHS and he wasn't going to stop digging until he stopped *them*. He felt a rush of adrenaline that focused his thoughts and clarified his mission, a drive that dedicated him to a higher purpose—protecting people, saving lives, serving *justice*.

He glanced at the speedometer and saw he was nearing a hundred miles an hour. He let off the gas. Central Valley lay ahead, and he followed the route to Dylan McPhee's house. Chris had been making nocturnal rounds of the four suspects since he moved to town, regularly cruising their homes. Now he knew that with Trevor, he'd been staking out the wrong house, a split-level in Central Valley proper. No wonder he hadn't seen Trevor there. Trevor didn't live there. Chris was kicking himself, but it showed why an undercover needed an unwitting.

He took a right turn off the main road, then wended his way through the upscale Golfing Park neighborhood, where the homes were large, with a stone or brick façade. Most were built fifteen years ago, when the developers came in to support the outlet boom. He turned onto Dylan's street, Markham Road, and parked at the corner, giving him a diagonal view of the house, number 283, three doors down.

He cut the engine, not wanting to wake anyone up. The street was quiet and still. Houses lined up behind the hedges, and perennials sprouted through fresh mulch. Newer cars sat in the driveways, though some houses had garages. Several of the garage doors were left open, indicating that the residents felt safe and secure, but Chris knew otherwise. People thought no harm could ever come to them, but the harm was already here.

He sat eyeing Dylan's house, a standard four-bedroom on two acres, bordered by a high stone wall that enclosed a kidney-shaped pool and a small putting green—Chris knew from Google Earth, which had given him every detail of the homes he staked out. Dylan's bedroom was around the back, and the boy's was the only window that stayed lighted after the family had gone to bed. Chris had binoculars and he used them to see Dylan through the open curtains, the boy's head bent over the lighted screen of his laptop, sitting at his desk until almost one in the morning, every night.

Chris glanced at Dylan's window, but it was dark, which made sense since it was 4:15 A.M. The kid had to sleep sometime. Chris picked up his phone, thumbed to the camera function, enlarged the view, and took a picture, reviewing what he knew about Dylan's family. The father, David McPhee, was a workmen's comp lawyer in town who had no website and little social media. His mother was a dental hygienist, also in town, but she had no activity on social media, and the other kids were younger, Michael, age ten, Allison, age nine, who had been in the local newspaper for winning a spelling bee. There were two cars in the driveway; a green Subaru Outback and a new Honda Fit, a shiny eggplant color.

Chris had a bad feeling about the McPhee family, not because of anything he saw, but because of what he didn't. It was strange that even the mother wasn't on social media, especially with kids who had academic and sports success. It struck him as secretive, and he'd also noticed that the family only rarely went out, except to church on Sundays, attending United Methodist in Central Valley. Chris had been making the rounds to different churches, temporarily becoming the religion his suspects were, but so far, it had been impossible to keep track of everybody on Sunday morning, which was why he needed more manpower.

Suddenly, he spotted something in motion behind the hedges at the house next to the McPhees'. It was moving fast, maybe a deer. He reached inside the glove box, retrieved his binoculars, and aimed where the shadow had been. It took him only a second to focus the lens, and he saw something race across the McPhees' driveway behind the cars.

Chris watched through the binoculars, astonished. It was a person, and in the next minute, a figure climbed on top of the stucco wall and walked along the edge to the house, climbed a trellis affixed to the wall, and used it like a ladder toward the window. It had to be Dylan, because in the next minute, the boy reached his window and scrambled inside.

"Holy shit," Chris said under his breath. He kept his binoculars trained on the window as Dylan closed the sash. A moment later, the bluish light of the laptop screen went on, and the boy appeared in view, his profile silhouetted as he sat down at his desk.

Chris tried to make sense of what he had seen. He'd been here many nights and seen Dylan at the computer, but there had never been any suspicious activity. Dylan had obviously sneaked out somewhere, which didn't fit his nerdy profile. It wasn't inherently suspicious that Dylan was sneaking out, but the questions were obvious.

Chris kept an eye on the window, and Dylan stayed on his laptop. Chris wished that he could legally get inside the kids' computers, but again, the law thwarted him. He didn't have probable cause for a subpoena and even the Rabbi wouldn't let him go phishing, that is, sending the boys a false link to hack into their computers. Again Chris understood the reason for the law, but it kept thwarting him when he was trying to save lives. He would just have to keep investigating the old-fashioned way, around the clock.

Chris waited, watching, and in the next few minutes, Dylan got up from his desk and disappeared from view. The laptop screen blinked to darkness, and the window went black. Chris stayed waiting and watching, just in case anything else happened. After twenty minutes, he turned on the ignition, pulled out of the space, and left the street, heading home with another set of questions to answer.

The anniversary of the Oklahoma bombing was less than three days away.

Chapter Thirty-two

Mindy reached the door to Evan's room, listening. No sound came from inside, so she twisted the knob as quietly as she could and entered. Moonlight shone through the open window, and she could see the familiar form of her son, his breathing soft and regular. Evan's iPhone was recharging on his night table, and she tiptoed over, unplugged it, then backed toward the door, and slipped outside, closing it again.

She hurried across the hall into Paul's home office, then ducked into its bathroom, and closed the door behind her. She didn't know Paul's phone password, but she knew Evan's—and Evan didn't even know she knew. She had been curious who he was texting all the time, so one day, when he didn't realize she was looking, she'd watched him plug his password into his phone. A not-so-dumb housewife, after all.

She sat on the toilet lid and touched the phone screen, then plugged in the passcode 0701, the birthday of their old Lab, Sam. The passcode worked, revealing the home screen, a photo of Miley Cyrus in a wacky outfit, with her tongue out and showing a dream-catcher tattoo on her side. Mindy thumbed to the text function and scanned the list. The boys' names jumped out at her because there were so few of them and they were his teammates—Jordan, Trevor, Raz. Mindy didn't bother to look at those texts because Evan wasn't buying presents for his teammates. Then she had a second, scary thought. What if Evan was doing drugs and buying them from one of the boys? She didn't know Jordan or Trevor very well, but Raz was a wacko and his brother had just been arrested.

Mindy was just about to take a screenshot of the people Evan texted with, but she realized that if she did that and sent it to herself, Evan could tell from his Sent email box, so she got her phone and took a picture of the screen, then scrolled down and took another picture, then another, and finally a fourth, until the names finally started to repeat. She couldn't believe how many people Evan texted with. It was a miracle that he got anything else done.

Mindy started with the girls, opening the text from the first girl, Brittany, and reading the text bubbles:

Brittany: where r u? i thot u were coming over
Evan: cant
Brittany: why not? what r u doing?
Evan: movies
Brittany: w who? r u w maddie rn
Evan: larkin
Brittany: wht about after? wanna come over?
Evan: cant

Mindy paused. Brittany seemed needy, and Evan never had liked that kind of girl. Mindy used to worry if he'd find a long-term girlfriend, but high school wasn't the time for that, anyway. In any event, Mindy didn't get the impression that Evan was buying Brittany any presents. To double-check, she scrolled backwards, trying to get closer in time to the cash withdrawal in March, but there were so many damn texts it was taking forever to load and she didn't want to get caught.

She thumbed to the other girls Evan texted, and touched the screen on the next girl's name, which was Maddie:

> **Maddie: i thought we were going to rita's**
> **Evan: cant make it**
> **Maddie: why where r u? mall? we can meet you**
> **Evan: w the guys**
> **Maddie: where?**
> **Evan: movies**
> **Maddie: want us to come?**
> **Evan: no gotta go**

Mindy shook her head, feeling sorry for the girl. She wished Evan didn't lead them on. She scrolled backwards to see if the earlier texts showed a relationship that would justify gift-giving, but she wasn't finding anything. It looked as if Maddie was always asking for Evan's time, but he wasn't coming around. Mindy knew the feeling.

She thumbed back to the list of girls Evan texted and touched the third name, which was Amanda, a name she didn't recognize. It must've been one of the girls who didn't go to CVHS or a girl in a different class. The text opened, and the screen filled with a nude photo of a girl— showing her full breasts, tiny little tummy, and a completely shaved pubic area. Her legs were partly opened, a crudely pornographic pose.

Mindy recoiled, shocked. This was a *sext,* for God's sake! What were these girls thinking? What the hell was going on? The photo didn't show the girl's face, but it was a selfie of her body, and she had a tattoo of a dream catcher on her side, too, like Miley Cyrus.

She scrolled backwards through Evan's texts with Amanda:

> **Amanda: ur at movies? don't u kno what ur missing?**
> **Evan: oh man**
> **Amanda: did u forget?**
> **Evan: no way**
> **Amanda: get here. im so wet.**
> **Evan: cant**
> **Amanda: i need u. get over here. i need it hard**
> **Evan: gimme ten**
> **Amanda: dying 4 u luv u**
> **Evan: luv u 2**

Mindy felt aghast. She scrolled backwards, and the texts were a blur of dirty talk and nude selfies—Amanda's perfect butt, fleshy breasts, tan tummy, and a belly button as taut as a frown. It was positively pornographic, but Mindy couldn't help but look at the girl's waistline with envy. Her own waist had never looked like that, and her belly button was a thing of the past.

Mindy went into contacts, looking for more information about Amanda. She searched under A, but there was no other contact information but a phone number. Mindy took a picture of the contact information, then went back to the screen of people Evan texted, touching the next girl's name. She wanted to make sure there weren't any other girls he was buying presents for, or whatever was going on.

She went through one girl, then another, and then finally the third, but it was getting late. Plenty of those girls had sent him naked pictures, but something told Mindy that Amanda was the one Evan was buying gifts for, or maybe he was even giving money to. Mindy had to figure out what to do, but she couldn't do it now.

She turned off the phone, left the bathroom, and headed back toward Evan's bedroom. She crept inside, replaced the phone, plugged it in, and slipped out, closing the door behind her. She headed down the hallway, turned into her bedroom, and crawled under the covers beside her snoring husband.

She stared at the ceiling and realized she still didn't know for sure who was withdrawing the money, since both Paul and Evan could withdraw from the account. It seemed more likely that it was Evan, but she didn't know why, and that left the question why Paul had lied to her about Carole's birthday.

You have to let it go. We've been through the mill. We've worked through it, and we did everything we were supposed to do. We're past it now.

Mindy didn't know if she'd ever get to sleep.

Chapter Thirty-three

Sunday morning dawned sunny and cool, and Chris joined the back of the crowd filing into the modern church. Dr. McElroy had sent the CVHS faculty an email saying that Abe's passing would be mentioned at the church service this morning, the first Sunday after his death on Friday night, since he and his partner Jamie Renette had been such active members of the congregation. Chris had decided to come and follow up on Abe's suicide because he couldn't put his doubts to rest until he had investigated from this angle.

Meanwhile, he'd worked all night reviewing his tapes and research files, but learned nothing more about Dylan or Trevor. The Rabbi was setting up the work-around on the Kiefermanns', but that wouldn't happen until tomorrow, if then. Chris was running out of time.

He spotted a man he assumed was Jamie at the front, talking with the female pastor and a group of teary men and women, presumably close friends of the couple. There were also faculty from CVHS, among them Dr. McElroy, Courtney and her husband, Rick Pannerman and

his wife, and Coach Natale and his wife. Behind them
was a weepy clutch of students but so far, Chris didn't see
anybody from the baseball team.

They filed into the church, a modern building made of
sandstone-faced bricks with stained-glass windows depict-
ing flowers, trees, sunny skies, and a cross. A tan spire
soared at its center, and the glass entrance was flanked by
banners that read *Everyone Is Welcome at Our House of
Worship.* Chris had been raised without a religion, and as
an adult, his career infiltrating neo-Nazis, drug cartels,
and human traffickers had provided him ample evidence
that God needed to do a better job.

Chris reached the church and entered a hall with an
American flag, a Pennsylvania flag, and a rainbow flag.
The congregation filed into sleek oak pews, greeting each
other with hugs, then settling into seats. He sat on the end
of a pew in the back, and the church was shallow and
wide, so he could keep an eye on Jamie, his friends, and
the CVHS faculty. The pastor appeared on the elegant al-
tar, flanked by banners with an embroidered cross and a
white dove. Live music began, a string quartet in the balcony.

The pastor crossed to the pulpit. "Ladies and gentlemen, friends of our church. We welcome those who are
here today to support Jamie in the heartbreaking loss of
his partner, our beloved Abe. We thank you all for being
here at this difficult time."

Chris heard sniffling, and Dr. McElroy patted Jamie
on the back.

"Before we begin the service, allow me to remind you
that God does work in mysterious ways, and at times like
these, we are at a loss to understand the mystery of those
ways." The pastor's voice softened. "I say this because
there is no one in this congregation who does not have an

Abe Yomes story. Mine is the time he told me I shouldn't wear green vestments because 'nobody looks good in green except leprechauns.'"

Chris heard teary chuckles and wished he had gotten to know Abe better.

"Abe was a fixture at all of our volunteer efforts—he happily doled out the carbohydrates at our Thanksgiving Day meal, he worked on our voter-registration drive, and he delivered Christmas gifts to the children of those less fortunate." The pastor smiled sadly. "He was the least credible Santa Claus, because he was way too thin and refused to wear the beard."

The congregation laughed, and there was more sniffling and hugs. Chris realized that Abe had earned this tribute by his relationships with everyone—a partner, a set of friends, students, and a larger community, grieving together. Only the Rabbi, Flavia, and the twins would show up for Chris's funeral.

"Abe's death is especially difficult to understand because it came by his own hand." The pastor paused. "I don't want to avoid that topic because this church is about honesty. No one of us knows the struggles that others undergo. Abe experienced hardships, but they made him a better servant of God and a better friend to us. They gave him the empathy and the sensitivity that carried him through every day, through his volunteer work, his teaching, and his home life."

A group of female students burst into tears, and Dr. McElroy, Courtney, Rick, and Coach Natale tried to comfort them. Chris realized that no one from the baseball team had come. He couldn't seem to puzzle out the connection between the team, the plot, and Abe's death, but that only told him that he needed to keep digging.

"Our church has always been about love, and today we

celebrate our service to God and rededicate ourselves to His community, as we know that Abe would want us to. And now, let us begin."

Chris watched as the pastor led the congregation in prayer, hymns, and a homily about universal understanding. The service ended in signs of peace, and he hugged the people near him, relieved that he wasn't wearing a shoulder holster. He filed out of the church, and the congregation went outside. Dr. McElroy, Courtney and her husband, Rick and his wife, Coach Natale and his wife, and a weepy group of friends and students clustered around Jamie, and Chris approached the group, who turned and smiled at him.

"Chris, how wonderful of you to come," Dr. McElroy said, reaching over for a hug. She didn't have her knee scooter anymore, but her big black orthopedic boot was on, matching a black dress.

"Deepest condolences, Dr. McElroy."

"Thank you." Dr. McElroy gestured to Coach Natale. "I assume you've met?"

"Yes. Hi, Victor." Chris shook his hand. "Sorry about this loss. This is very sad."

"It sure is." Victor gestured to his wife. "Please, meet Felicia. I think I mentioned her to you. She knew Abe, too."

"Yes, of course, the reading support specialist." Chris shook Felicia's hand, and she smiled back.

"Hi, Chris." Courtney gave him a hug, her eyes puffy, without her usual sparkle. She had on a black pantsuit and sagged against her husband, a blocky linebacker type with blond hair. Chris remembered that Abe had called him Doug The Lug.

"Courtney, I'm very sorry about your loss."

"I can't believe he's really gone. I *don't* believe it."

Courtney rallied to motion to her husband. "Please, meet Doug."

Doug extended his hand. "Chris, nice to meet you. So I heard you're from Wyoming."

"I went to school there. Are you from Wyoming?" *Please don't be from Wyoming.*

"No, I'm from here. Abe was a great guy, and it's nice that you came today. It's been hard on Courtney."

"I'm sure." Chris noticed a crestfallen Rick standing next to an attractive Japanese woman with long dark hair, presumably his wife, Sachi, dressed in an artsy black smock. Chris turned to greet them, extending a hand. "Rick, I'm so sorry about Abe."

"Thanks. You, too." Rick squeezed Chris's hand. "It's not possible. It doesn't seem real. We were just together. Remember, we were joking? 'Mr. Y?'"

"I know." Chris turned to Rick's wife. "And you must be Sachi."

"Yes, nice to meet you." Sachi smiled sadly. "Have you met Jamie, Abe's partner?"

"No, I haven't." Chris extended a hand, and Jamie shook it, managing a shaky smile. His brown eyes were bloodshot, and grief etched lines into his smooth face. He was trim and compact in a sharply tailored dark suit with a crisp white shirt and blue-patterned tie, a stylish stand-out in the crowd of outlet gear.

"Oh, you're Chris Brennan. It's so kind of you to come today. Abe told me about you."

"I'm so sorry about your loss," Chris said, meaning it. "Abe was a wonderful man, and you have my deepest condolences on his loss."

"Thank you." Jamie's eyes glistened. "He was *so* excited about you. No one from Wyoming ever comes out here. He hadn't lived there in so long, but he was nostalgic about the place. He had even pulled some pictures for you."

"How nice." Chris felt touched.

"You know, a few of the other teachers and our closest friends have set up a little brunch back at the house. I'm not ready to be alone, and my friends know that. Why don't you come back to the house? It would mean so much to me if I knew that you saw the pictures. He wanted you to see them."

"I'd love to, thank you."

"Terrific. You can follow us."

Chapter Thirty-four

Heather cracked an egg into the Pyrex bowl, humming happily to herself. Susan Sematov had known of three job openings, one as an assistant in ValleyCo's corporate office and two from the outlet stores for Wranglers and Maidenform. She had already applied online for all three jobs and was planning a shopping trip to get a nice interview outfit.

Heather scrambled the eggs, making a yellow funnel so perfect it could've been in a surf movie. She wasn't Ina Garten yet, but she was on her way. She was going to surprise Jordan with French toast because he needed cheering up. He had been sad about Mr. Y's suicide, returning home from practice subdued and staying in his room all day. She'd tried to buck him up at dinner, telling him the good news about her job prospects, but that hadn't worked.

Heather added a dash of vanilla, feeling good about herself for the first time in a long time. If she got an office job, with nine-to-five hours, she could be home and make dinner every night. From recipes. With fresh herbs. And pretentious butter from Whole Foods. She'd spent last night fantasizing about that ValleyCo job, which could become a stepping-stone to a real career. ValleyCo had a scholarship program for employees, and Heather vowed she'd never be in a dirndl again.

She lifted a piece of bread into the egg mixture, then sprinkled on cinnamon, and let it soak, her thoughts straying to a fantasy that had nothing to do with gainful employment. She'd found herself thinking about Chris, more and more. He was a total hunk, and sensitive, but in a manly way. He listened to her, learned about her, and he'd coached her, to boot. And he was so good to Jordan. She knew that it was an inappropriate fantasy, but no fantasy worth having was appropriate. The man was Marriage Material on Wheels.

"Hey, Mom." Jordan shuffled into the kitchen in his Musketeers T-shirt and jersey shorts that hung around his knees.

"I'm making French toast!" Heather looked over, expecting applause, but Jordan was reaching for the pot of brewed coffee in the machine.

"Good, thanks."

"I even have powdered sugar for the top." Heather's mood was too good to be brought down that easily, like a balloon that refused to pop.

"Great." Jordan set his phone on the counter, reached into the cabinet for a mug, and then filled it with coffee. Just then, a text alert sounded on his phone, and Heather glanced over, reflexively. The text was from Evan, and it read **sharing is caring**—underneath a photo of a woman who was completely nude from shoulder to thigh. Her face wasn't showing, but her breasts and private parts were crudely exposed.

"Jordan! What is *that*?" Heather almost dropped the fork. "Evan is sending you naked pictures?"

"Mom, wait." Jordan reached for the phone, but Heather grabbed it first and went to the table, where the light was better. The photo was like something out of *Playboy,* but a real girl. She had a small dream-catcher tattoo on her side.

"Jordan, what is going on here? Is this a girl Evan knows? Do you know this girl?"

"I don't know, I never got one of these from him."

"One of *these*? What does that mean?"

Jordan flushed. "I heard that sometimes he sends pictures to the guys on the team."

"Are you kidding me?" Heather felt shocked. She'd seen this on *Dr. Phil.* "Do you swear he never sent a naked picture before?"

"I swear. It's a group text to the team. I was never on it before. Mom, you don't need to freak."

"Yes, I do! This is terrible! This is *wrong!*" Heather felt disgusted. She had been happy that Jordan had become friends with Evan, but no longer.

"The girl sent it to him—"

"I don't care! Two wrongs don't make a right. She shouldn't be doing that, but she doesn't expect him to send it around!" Heather tried to calm down. "I mean, how does this even happen, like, how does it work? How did you get this picture?"

"Mom, guys do it. It happens—"

"How. Does. It. Happen?"

"Well, she probably sent it to him by Snapchat or she texted it to him."

"What is Snapchat again?" Heather couldn't keep up.

"Snapchat is when you send a picture to somebody, and it disappears."

"A picture, like a sext? This is a sext, isn't it? I heard about that."

Jordan half-smiled. "Okay, yes it is."

"And if you send it by Snapchat, it disappears?"

"Yes."

"Do you have Snapchat?"

"Yes, but I never use it." Jordan rolled his eyes.

"Good." Heather felt a little better. "Okay, so why does Evan still have it if it was on Snapchat? Why didn't it disappear?"

"Either he took a screenshot of it or she didn't send it on Snapchat. She could have texted it to him. Mom, chill." Jordan put up his hands like he was being robbed. "I didn't do anything wrong. I'll delete it, okay? Now can I please have my phone?"

"You wait one minute." Heather went back in the kitchen, grabbed her phone, and before Jordan could stop her, she took a picture of the sext.

"Why are you doing that?"

"I want proof. This is outrageous." Heather wasn't exactly sure of the answer. It seemed like something a good mother would do, and she wasn't falling short anymore.

"Mom, it's not, everybody does it."

"*You* don't, do you?" Heather was pretty sure he was still a virgin.

"No, of course not."

"Jordan, I *never* want you to do this. Even if a girl sends you a picture like this, I don't want you to send it to anybody else. It's wrong. It's embarrassing. It's probably even illegal."

"Okay, Mom, whatever, can I have my phone?" Jordan held out his hand.

"Do you think Evan's parents know that he's sending pictures like that? Because if you were doing that, I'd want the mother to tell me. I should call her, right now."

"Mom, please, no, don't." Jordan's eyes flared.

"I think I should, I think I have to." Heather dreaded calling Mindy and telling her that her son was a dirtbag, which wasn't going to ingratiate her with the Winners' Circle. She didn't know if Mindy would believe her or if she would be furious with her. The messenger always got shot, didn't they?

"Mom, don't call his mother. Please, that would be so embarrassing."

"For who? For you? *You* shouldn't be embarrassed. *He* should be embarrassed."

"But Mom, Evan will be so pissed at me."

"And Evan will be in trouble if I don't. Which is worse?"

"Oh man." Jordan sighed, walking around to his seat at the table.

"I can't do nothing, Jordan. I'm not going to pretend I didn't see it."

Jordan sighed again. "Can we eat?"

"Damn!" Heather turned to the stove, but the French toast was already burned.

Chapter Thirty-five

Chris pulled up in front of the modern A-frame that looked like a European ski lodge, set off by itself on one of the wooded hilltops outside of Central Valley. He parked, cut the ignition, and got out of his car at the same moment as Dr. McElroy emerged from her Subaru, struggling because of her orthopedic boot.

"Oh my, I'm not doing very well," she said, leaning on the car.

"Let me help you." Chris went to her side.

"Thanks. I forgot that they have this damn hill."

"Not to worry." Chris took Dr. McElroy's arm and guided her up a gravel walking path that wended up in a gentle curve. Massive evergreens flanked the path and surrounded the house. "This is a major house, isn't it?"

"Yes, Jamie owns a real estate company. He does very well for himself, and he and Abe designed the house together and had it built. It's quite something."

"It sure is." Chris wanted to pump her for information because the newspapers had no details about Abe's suicide. "I'm sure it's going to be hard for Jamie to live in a place they designed together."

"Yes, though it wasn't a *complete* surprise to him. Abe did have a history of depression."

"Really. But depression is one thing, and suicide is another."

"Well, confidentially, Abe tried to end his life once before." Dr. McElroy lowered her voice as she labored to walk uphill with the cumbersome boot. "We kept it hush-hush at school and we thought he had recovered. Abe wasn't even in therapy anymore. It's just awful that this time, he succeeded."

Chris mulled it over. The previous attempt did make it more likely that it was suicide, but still. "I heard that he hung himself. Where did he do that? And was it Jamie who found him? I'd like to get the story before we go in, so I don't say the wrong thing."

"Of course. Jamie called me after it happened so we could figure out how to deal with it at school. Jamie is very responsible that way, and very caring."

"Good for him," Chris said, keeping her talking.

"Anyway Jamie told me that he came home late Friday night. He was showing some homes then met with the PR man from the Chamber of Commerce, out past Sawyertown. He didn't get home until one o'clock in the morning and the house was empty, so he assumed that Abe was out late. They have a great circle of friends and they love to socialize." Dr. McElroy sighed. "Anyway, when it got to be about three in the morning, Jamie started to worry. He knew Abe wouldn't be out that late, and also Abe wasn't answering any of his texts or calls. By the way, Abe's car was in the driveway but Jamie didn't think that was unusual because when Abe thought he might be drinking, he never drove. Jamie assumed he had a designated driver."

"Of course." Chris nodded, guiding her along.

"So Jamie called their friends, and Abe wasn't out with any of them. Then Jamie checked the cottage and that's when he found Abe, hanging from the rafter." Dr. McElroy shook her head. "He had hung himself with the power cord from his computer. Isn't that so horrible?"

"Yes, awful." Chris paused. "But what cottage are you talking about? I thought you said Jamie found him at home."

"They have a cottage out back, behind the house." Dr. McElroy motioned to the A-frame, as they drew closer. "Abe called it his writing cottage. You know he loved literature and he wrote short stories and poems. I think he might have entertained the notion of writing a novel."

"Really," Chris said, as they were approaching the front door. "So where is the writing cottage?"

"It's in the backyard. I'm terrible at measuring distances. That was where Abe did his writing, he used it as his own private retreat. Other writers do that, he told me once even Philip Roth did that."

Chris tried to visualize it. "If the writing cottage is in the backyard, I'm surprised that Jamie didn't see the lights on and know that Abe was there."

"The lights weren't on. Jamie told me he thinks Abe left the lights off on purpose, so he wouldn't see him and stop him."

"Oh, I understand." Chris still had his suspicions. "So I assume there wasn't a suicide note?"

"No, there wasn't a note." Dr. McElroy shuddered. "It's so sad to think of the pain that Abe must've been in. I'm glad he didn't leave a note, and the police told me that it's not uncommon for there not to be a note."

"Oh, you spoke with the police?"

"Yes, they came to the school yesterday and talked to

me about Abe. I told him about the previous attempt, but Jamie had told them already, too." Dr. McElroy sighed heavily. "So tomorrow morning we'll have an assembly, and grief counselors will be there, and Jamie told me that there will be a proper memorial service later this month."

"When is the funeral?" Chris had read the online obituary, but it hadn't given any details about scheduling.

"There's no burial. Abe wanted to be cremated, so Jamie honored that request."

"Of course." Chris masked his dismay. If Abe's body had since been cremated, it couldn't yield any further evidence about whether he had been murdered. Under state law, there had to be an autopsy, but it must have been routine, since suicide was suspected. A toxicology screen wasn't done routinely, but it would've shown if there was alcohol, tranquilizers, or another drug in his system, which could have incapacitated Abe and facilitated someone's hanging him. Now that evidence would be gone. It wasn't a mistake that a big-city medical examiner would've made, but Central Valley was a small town.

"I'm sorry this happened, so early in your time with us. We're usually a quieter town than this."

"After you." Chris opened the front door for Dr. McElroy, who stepped inside, and he followed her into a house brimming with guests.

Dr. McElroy got swept up with some students, and Chris got the lay of the land. The living room was of dramatic design, with glass on the front and back walls, and a ceiling that extended to the floor in an immense triangle. To the right was a living area furnished with tan sectional furniture around a rustic coffee table, and on the left was a glistening stainless-steel kitchen. A few casseroles, a sandwich tray, and soft drinks sat on a table, and a handful of guests talked in small, subdued groups. Jamie was in the kitchen, surrounded by an inner circle of friends that included Courtney and her husband and Rick and his wife.

Chris headed for the back of the house, so he could get a better look at the writing cottage. The backyard was lush grass, with a pool covered by a green tarp, and behind that was a smaller version of the A-frame main house, the writing cottage. He sized up the distance, and if the lights had been off inside the cottage at night, there would have been no way to see Abe inside. Ambient light would have been nonexistent, and there had been a cloud cover Friday night.

He eyed the cottage with more questions than answers, the obvious one being, who was the last person or persons to talk to Abe before he died? What had been his state of mind? Why now? Had he given any indication that he was about to commit suicide? Where was his phone? His computer?

Chris turned from the window, scanning the crowd. He didn't know any of the couple's friends, but he knew Courtney and Rick, and they seemed the best place to start, so he went over. "Hey, everyone, how are you all?" he asked, when he reached them.

"Horrible, I still can't believe it. He seemed fine to me." Courtney shook her head sadly, and her husband Doug put his arm around her, drawing her close.

"I know." Chris sighed. "You know, it's shocking because we all got together for lunch on Friday. Abe seemed fine."

"That's what *I* keep saying." Courtney looked at Rick, stricken. "Right, Rick? We can't believe it. His parents are so upset, too. They'll be here tonight. They're the nicest people."

Rick sighed. "They are. We met them when we went out there. It's just awful. But I get it, I understand. We went through it with him, last time he tried. He took pills. We all thought he was over it, but I guess he wasn't."

Chris remained skeptical, but hid it. "Had you noticed him becoming depressed again?"

"Honestly, I didn't," Courtney interjected, her blood-shot eyes bewildered. "I think he was having a hard time with the rejection though, I know that. He told me that."

Next to her, Rick nodded. "I think that's what did it. It put him over the top."

"What rejection?" Chris asked, keeping his tone less urgent than he felt.

"His poems," Rick answered. "He was trying to get his poems published. You should read them. But he kept getting rejection after rejection."

Courtney scowled. "These agents, they're really the worst. He wrote to one in New York, and the agent emailed him, 'We don't have time to take any more clients, and if we did, we wouldn't take you.' Isn't that so *mean*?"

"That's terrible." Chris supposed it answered why Abe would commit suicide now, but still. "Rick, did you talk to Abe Friday night? Did he call you or anything?"

"Well, yes." Rick's expression darkened, and a deep frown creased his forehead. "He did call me, but I couldn't take the call. I keep thinking, what if I had? What if I just taken the five minutes to talk to him? Maybe he wouldn't have—"

"Rick, no, don't say that." His wife, Sachi, rubbed his back, her expression strained. "We were at my mother's that night, and she's been in chemo, so she wasn't feeling well. Rick was helping me with her—well, you don't need to know the details. I asked Rick not to take the call right then, I thought it was a social thing. I never realized that . . ."

Courtney nodded, her eyes glistening. "Rick, it wouldn't have made a difference if you'd taken the call. Nobody knows that better than me. He called me that night, too, and I talked to him. He was upset about the rejection, but I never would've thought he would *kill* himself."

Doug chimed in, "Honey, like the pastor said, everyone has their own struggles. You did your best. You were on the phone with him a long time."

"Was I? I didn't think I was." Courtney reached into her purse, thumbed to her phone screen, and showed it to her husband. "Look, he called me at 9:35 P.M., and I was only on for fifteen minutes. I wish it had been longer."

Rick glanced at Courtney's phone, nodding sadly. "It must've been right after he called me."

Courtney nodded. "Probably, and like I say, he was disappointed but not *suicidal*. He even asked if we could get together Saturday night, last night. He wanted us to go out to dinner, but we couldn't."

Doug frowned, glancing at Chris. "I had a work thing last night. My boss's birthday. I couldn't miss that. We had to say no."

Courtney's eyes glistened with new tears. "But I feel like Rick does, what if I had said yes? What if we made the plans? He needed friends this weekend, and I wasn't there for him."

Chris still had no answers. "Courtney, you can't blame yourself for this. You were a wonderful friend to him, and so were you, Rick."

"Thanks," Rick said, miserably.

Courtney wiped a tear from her eyes. "I just really loved him. We all did."

"He knew that." Chris noticed over Courtney's shoulder that there was a lull in the guests greeting Jamie. "Folks, excuse me, I'd like to pay my respects to Jamie, okay?"

Chapter Thirty-six

Susan picked up the dirty laundry in Raz's bedroom while he showered in his bathroom, getting ready for their therapy session. Ryan was already at his therapist's office, and her therapist had wanted to see her and Raz together. She had agreed, though she couldn't deny the unease in the pit of her stomach. She knew the family needed professional help, but all three of them in simultaneous therapy put their crisis in relief—Neil's survivors were barely surviving.

Susan picked up sweat socks, which reeked, then his favorite jeans. It had been a long and difficult day yesterday, with Raz coming home after practice, emotionally drained about Mr. Y's suicide. Raz had even stayed inside last night, alone in his room. It was the first Saturday night he hadn't gone out in a long time.

You're the parent, remember?

Susan picked up a stained T-shirt and tried not to think about what Neil would've said about the mess in this room. He was the one who used to nag the boys about their room, their shower schedule, and whether their homework was done. He always had a running timeline of their quiz, exam, and midterm schedules. He checked their grades on the CVHS portal and he shepherded them through the PSAT, SAT, AP testing, and college application process.

She kept picking up clothes, going through the things that Neil used to do, and she hadn't even realized how many tasks there were until he had passed. She picked up a wet towel, then straightened up, suddenly assessing the scene. Raz's bedroom had always been a pigsty, but she found herself seeing it with new eyes, and for the first time, she realized that it bordered on hoarding.

Raz's bed was flush under the window, but the sheets looked grimy. Piles of dirty laundry lay around the bed on the floor and some had been stuffed under the bed, mixed in with sports pages, *Sports Illustrated,* empty cans of Red Bull, and Snickers and gum wrappers. Dirty underwear and sweatshirts were mounded on top of the television, and video games were strewn about. The controllers were buried under old CDs, which Raz never even bought anymore.

Susan blinked, appalled. She didn't know when it had gotten this way. She had to be the worst mother ever born. Her own son had been burying himself in filth and she hadn't even realized it until this very moment. She felt shocked at the realization, horrified at her own neglect. How had she been so selfish? So blind?

She resumed picking up the clothes, distraught. She collected a dirty T-shirt, a soiled blue Musketeers Baseball shirt, and another one identical to the first. She had no idea how Raz had accumulated so many Musketeers Baseball T-shirts, maybe he was buying them instead of washing them, or he was getting them from the team. Either way, she stepped from one pile of dirty clothes to the next, cleaning up his room, and when her arms were totally full, she went over to the hamper, which he kept in the closet.

The hamper overflowed, and she set the clothes she'd been holding onto the rug, looked inside, and saw that it was taken up by sheets and a blanket. She pulled the sheets and blanket out, but at the bottom, she felt something hard. Instinctively she withdrew her hand. It could be something crusty with mold, pizza crust, or God-knows-whatever. She had seen enough stiff socks to last a lifetime, mostly because Neil would find them and show them to her to make her laugh. Today, she wasn't laughing.

She reached her hand into the hamper again, but whatever she felt was hard and solid. She grabbed the object and pulled it out, shocked to see what sat in her palm.

A gun.

Susan felt thunderstruck. Where had he gotten it? Why was it here? Why was he hiding it? How had she lost control of her own home? They didn't have guns in the house. They didn't know anything about guns. Neil hadn't known a damn thing about guns. She didn't know much about guns, either, but she knew enough to know that this one was a revolver, with a silvery muzzle and a brown handle.

She walked the gun over to the bed and set it down carefully, with the muzzle facing away from her. She didn't know if it was loaded and she didn't know if the gun had a safety, or if revolvers even *had* safeties. She didn't understand why Raz had it or where he had gotten it. But she was going to find out. She went to the bathroom and heard the shower water still running. She knocked on the door and tried to open it, but it was locked. She didn't know why Raz had locked the door. Did he always do that? Did he ever do that? And why didn't she know?

"Raz!" Susan shouted, banging on the door. "Raz, come out!"

"I'll be out in a minute!"

"Now!" Susan shouted, louder, then got her temper in check. Being angry wouldn't help, and she wasn't angry, she was terrified. "Raz, please, right now!"

"All right!" Raz called back, irritably, and the next minute, the shower water went off.

"Hurry, please, I want to talk to you." Susan tried the knob again. She wanted him out of that bathroom. She wanted to see his face. Panic rose in her chest, for some reason.

"Mom, what's your problem?"

"Come out!" Susan turned the doorknob and pushed at the same moment that Raz opened the door, and she almost fell inside the bathroom. "Why is there a gun in your hamper?"

"A gun?" Raz's dark eyes went wide. A towel was wrapped around his waist, and he had barely dried off his chest, slick with water. She hadn't seen him naked to the waist in a long time, and she realized he wasn't a kid anymore, but a full-grown adult man, who had secrets.

"Raz, are you telling me you didn't know there was a gun in your hamper? Where did you get it? What's it doing there?"

"Oh, jeez." Raz stepped out of the bathroom, tucking the towel tighter around his waist.

"Is it loaded?" Susan pointed at the bed, but Raz made no move toward the gun.

"Yes, I think."

"Raz, you had a *loaded gun* in your room? Where did you get it?"

"From Ryan."

"Ryan!" Susan couldn't begin to process the information. Just when she thought it was bad, it went worse. Now both boys were involved. "Where did he get it from? And why do you have it?"

"Are you mad at me? Don't be mad."

"I'm not mad, honey," Susan said, realizing that the words were absolutely true. "I'm just trying to understand what's going on. You and Ryan have a gun? Why? How?"

"He got it from a guy that he knows."

"*What* guy?"

"He didn't say, I don't remember."

"You don't remember or he didn't say?" Susan thought he was lying.

"I don't know, it was, like, awhile ago, and he gave it to me and he asked me to put it in my room, so I did."

"Did he tell you what he got it for?"

"No."

"Do you have any idea?"

"No."

"Oh God." Susan found herself rubbing her face. She had put on makeup for the therapy session, but her foundation was coming off on her finger pads.

"Don't be mad," Raz said again.

"How do you know it's loaded?"

"He told me."

"Did it come that way or did he buy bullets?"

Raz smiled his goofy smile. "Bullets are like batteries. They're not included."

Susan didn't laugh. "This isn't funny."

Raz looked at her directly, seeming to focus. Then after a moment, he said, "I'm sorry."

"I am too," Susan heard herself say, her voice softening.

"What are *you* sorry for? You're just the mom."

Susan felt the words cut through her chest, though Raz hadn't meant it in a bad way. "I haven't been acting like a mom, not for a long time, and I'm sorry about that."

Raz frowned. "It's all right, I get it. It's because Dad died."

"No, it's because he *lived*. I stopped being the mom

when he was still alive because he was such a good father. But you still needed me. You still needed a mom."

"It's not your fault." Raz swallowed hard.

"Yes, it is. I'm sorry I let you down. I'm sorry I didn't notice your room was getting this bad. I'm sorry I didn't know how sad you were."

Raz blinked, and for a moment he didn't say anything fresh or come back with a wisecrack. "I am sad."

"I know, honey. I know that now." Susan reached out, hugged him, and held him again, the same way she had the other day in the car, and she stopped herself from saying *I'm sad too*. Because it couldn't be about her anymore, not for another minute. She held him close, her youngest son, as wet and slick as the day he was born and she had held him in her arms for the first time, and she realized that she had hugged him more in the past two days than she had probably in the past two months, and when she let him go, they both wiped tears from their eyes.

"I just had the gun for safekeeping, Mom. I wasn't going to do anything with it."

"I'm afraid you were," Susan said, her heart speaking out of turn.

"No, I would never hurt anybody."

"I know that." Susan kept her tone quiet, even grave, which wasn't hard to do because it was exactly how she felt. Deep inside, she knew the answer to the question she was about to ask him, as if her very soul housed the two of them, mother and child, the way her body once had, long ago, back at their very beginning. "I know you'd never hurt anyone else. I'm worried you would've hurt yourself. Did you ever think about that, honey? Did you ever pick up that gun and think about that? About hurting yourself?"

Raz nodded, then his lips began to tremble, and tears came to his eyes. Susan reached for him again, hugging him closer while he began to cry, and they sank to the floor together, surrounded by the debris of their lives. She cradled him against her chest while she told him that she loved him more than she had ever loved anybody in her life, that he was her special and spirited son, and that she would always be there for him and that they were going to sort this out together, the three of them.

As a family.

Chapter Thirty-seven

Chris made his way to the kitchen and shook Jamie's hand. "Jamie, thanks for having me today. I really am so sorry about Abe. He really was such a nice guy."

"Thanks." Jamie met Chris's eye, his gaze sad, but strong. "I'm glad you could come. It was so kind of everyone to bring the food, and they won't leave me alone, which is fine with me. And Abe would have loved that you came and got the pictures. I know you two would've been great friends. The Wyoming thing and all."

"I think you're right." Chris felt guilty. He realized that, unlike his typical operation, he was undercover among a wonderful group of people, a true community. It affected him in a way he'd never experienced, conflicting him. But he reminded himself to stay on track.

"It's just so hard to imagine that we're here, but he's not. I mean, I know he was depressed and I guess you heard he tried once before, everybody knows, he was open about that. He even volunteered at a suicide hotline."

"He didn't give any sign or anything, this time?"

"No, I knew the rejections were starting to mount up. He counted them and there were twenty-one." Jamie shook his head. "I think the number just got too high. He felt hopeless, like it would never happen for him."

"Did you talk to him Friday night?"

"Yes. He called me around eight o'clock, asking me how long I'd be, and we spoke for about five minutes. I couldn't talk longer, I had people. He sounded bummed about the latest rejection, he told me about how there were twenty-one. He said he wanted to talk to me when I got home."

"Did he say what about?"

"I assumed it was about the rejections."

"That's what Courtney and Rick said, too. I wonder if he talked to anybody else."

"No, he didn't. I asked everybody. So when I came home, that's why I figured he wasn't here, that he went out to forget about it and have a drink. But otherwise he was looking forward to summer." Jamie paused. "And those pictures he pulled for you, he couldn't wait for you to see them. I'd love to show them to you but," Jamie hesitated. "They're in the cottage. I guess you heard that's where he . . ."

"Yes, I did. That must be so difficult for you."

"It was, it is, finding him was the most horrific thing that's ever happened to me in my life." Tears came to Jamie's eyes, but he tilted his chin up. "We designed this house together, and the cottage is where he loved to go. It was his man cave, only with books instead of a TV. I just ran out when I saw him and called 911. I left everything in there."

"What do you mean by everything? His phone?"

"No, his laptop. He probably had his phone on him when they took him away, and I assume the police or the funeral home have it. I know the Wyoming pictures are in the cottage because I saw them Thursday night, on his desk. He printed them out for you."

"If you want, I can go in there and get that stuff for you. I can see if his phone is there, too." Chris kept his tone low-key, but he was asking for legal reasons. A consent search was lawful, and if any evidence of foul play turned up, it would be admissible.

"Would you do that?" Jamie asked, hopeful. "I mean, I just don't want to do it myself. Our friends are already talking about me moving, but I would never do that. This was our house."

"Of course, you have memories here. I'll go look for his phone and get the pictures."

"Thank you, I'd love that. Don't forget about his laptop. He had a passcode that I don't even know, but I'd feel better if the laptop was in the house." Jamie gestured to a glass door at the end of the kitchen. "You can take the back door and go across the lawn to the cottage."

"Is there a key or is it open?"

"It's open. We never lock anything."

Chris didn't bother to correct him. Once again, the illusion of safety rendered people unsafe. "Be right back."

"Thanks again."

Chris headed for the back door, left the house, and walked across the lawn, then reached the cottage and opened the door, stepping inside and throwing the dead bolt behind him so he wouldn't be interrupted.

Chris looked around, sizing it up. It was an A-frame with one large great room, which was undisturbed, with no signs of a struggle or a forced entry. A cherrywood table dominated the room, cluttered with papers and a MacBook Pro. Books lined both sides of the room on matching bookshelves, and the tall triangle of the ceiling was constructed of the same rustic wood as the house, with three thick oak rafters.

Chris crossed the room and stood underneath the middle rafter. Sadly, it was easy to see that it was the one Abe had hung himself from—or had been hung from. A stain soiled the beige rug, and Chris surmised that it was from bodily fluids, postmortem.

Chris gazed at the stain, and it struck him as obscene that such a kind soul had died on this very spot, now flooded with sunlight. The back wall was also entirely of glass, offering a view of a flagstone backyard, two green Adirondack chairs, and the woods beyond. There was a back door, and Chris opened it and went outside, trying to understand how Abe could have been murdered.

He passed the patio and kept going to the edge of the woods and looked down. There were trees all the way down a steep hill, and at the bottom was a single-lane country road. He could see that the trees weren't that dense, so a killer could have parked along the road, climbed the hill to the back door of the cottage, and let himself inside. Escape would've been accomplished the same way, with the car left on the road below, which looked hardly traveled, like the roads he had taken on the way here.

Chris returned to the cottage, entered, and went directly to the spot, deep in thought. There was a random cherrywood chair sitting near the middle rafter. He looked over at the desk, seeing that the chair's mate was sitting in front of the desk and that it also matched the desk chair itself, which was on rollers.

Chris mentally reconstructed the murder. The killer wouldn't have chosen the desk chair because it had rollers, so the side chair was a rational choice. The killer could've entered the back door, surprised Abe at his desk, and either chloroformed or injected him to incapacitate him, then used the side chair to hang him. Abe would have kicked the chair over in his struggle or death throes. It was likely that the police, when they came to cut him down and take the body away, would have righted the chair.

Chris reasoned there had been more than one killer, because Abe would have been too heavy for one person to lift and hang from a rafter, deadweight even if he wasn't struggling. Chris walked over to the desk but didn't touch anything, looking around. His first impulse was to go to the computer, but Jamie had said it was under passcode that even he didn't know.

The bright sun illuminated the cluttered desk, covered with correspondence, pages of poetry in draft, and notes written on lined paper. He read the notes to try to see if they contained any clues, but no luck. He slid his phone from his pocket and took pictures of the papers, the desk, the rafter, the stain, and everything else, to be reviewed later, in case he had missed anything.

Chris stood next to the spot, looking around in a 360-degree turn. The circular motion stirred up dust motes, the tiny specs visible in the solid shaft of sunlight, sending them swirling. It brought him to a realization. If killers had come in and hung Abe, there would have been signs of a struggle, even if they only had to hoist the body up. But the room was undisturbed, which meant that everything had been put back in order—and if that had happened, the proof could be in the dust.

Chris bent over and looked at the desk more closely. There was a clean square, book-sized, on the left side of the desk, and it was the only place not dusty. His gaze went to a paperback dictionary, which sat on top of another note-filled legal pad. It was the same size as the dictionary. So somebody had moved the book, and that wasn't something the police would do. They might have righted the chair, but they wouldn't have straightened up a desk.

Chris felt his heart beat faster. He continued scrutinizing the desk, finding more blank spaces where an object had been but was placed somewhere else. He didn't get the impression that the desk was searched, but merely put back in order so it would look as if Abe had simply been reading his rejection letters, rose from them, moved the side chair, and hung himself with the power cord.

Chris felt a bitter taste in his mouth, knowing it would be difficult to prove murder now that Abe had been cremated. But even so, he had to know who killed Abe and why. His gut was telling him that it was linked to the baseball team, but he couldn't connect the dots.

Chris moved papers on the desk to find the phone, but didn't see one, also consistent with his theory. The killers could have taken the phone, worried that it contained information or phone calls that implicated them. The police wouldn't have taken a personal effect, and the funeral home would have let Jamie know by now. Chris's best guess was that Abe's phone was in the hands of whoever had killed him, so cruelly.

Chris became aware that he was taking too long, so he picked up the laptop and gathered the Wyoming photos, taking pictures of them for later. They showed a scenic array of mountains, a lovely home in the woods, then Abe's parents and siblings, Jamie, Courtney, Rick, and their respective spouses.

Chris knew they would be grieving for years to come. He made a silent vow to the murdered teacher.

I'll get your murderers, Abe.

And I'm sorry I didn't get them before they got you.

Chapter Thirty-eight

Mindy glanced at the kitchen clock, on edge. It was 11:15, and she couldn't wait for Evan and Paul to get home. When she'd awakened this morning, having overslept through yoga, there'd been a note from Paul saying he and Evan had gone to play golf. She'd texted back, **come home ASAP, family meeting,** and he had texted back, **will be home after nine holes.**

She paced, getting angrier. She thought that Evan had withdrawn the money and spent it on Amanda, but it was still possible that Paul had, on his new mistress. She was going to confront them both at the same time. She wanted the truth to come out, unvarnished and unprepared for, once and for all.

She checked her phone, which showed one of the naked pictures she'd found in Evan's phone. There was more than one girl because they had pierced nipples, weird body jewelry, and tattoos, which she thought was disgusting. Plus you had to be eighteen to get a tattoo, so Mindy had no idea what was going on in the world anymore.

She heard the sound of Paul's car in the driveway and

reminded herself to stay in control. She didn't want to fall into the Hysterical Mom category, in which Paul and Evan were so willing to place her. They acted like she was the numbskull in the house, and she was finally over it. She hadn't had anything to drink, no G&T yet or wine. Deep inside, she was angriest at herself, for medicating herself with alcohol. For telling herself she had a happy marriage and perfect son, when she had neither. For not knowing what was happening under her own roof. That had to end, right now.

Mindy stormed out of the kitchen just as Paul and Evan entered the house, flush, happy, and sweaty in their golf clothes. "Boys, in the family room!"

Evan's smile faded. "Mom?"

"Honey?" Paul did a double-take.

"We're having a meeting in the family room." Mindy stalked into the family room, seeing it with new eyes—a cheery red couch with matching side chairs, a beautiful glass coffee table, three walls of eggshell white, and a red accent wall. She had decorated it herself, but right now, she wanted to set it on fire. Mindy pointed to the couch. "Sit down, both of you."

"Honey?" Paul said, in wonderment as he took a seat.

"Mom, you okay?" Evan asked, mystified, sitting next to him.

"No, I'm not okay, and I'll tell you why." Mindy scrolled to the saved photos on her phone, held up her phone to face them, and started an XXX-rated slideshow for her son and her husband. "Evan. What in God's holy name are these photographs doing on your phone? Who is Amanda? Why are there so many different ones? And are you texting the photos to anybody else, because if you are, Heaven help you, I am going to rearrange your very handsome face."

"Oh no!" Evan's eyes flew open.

"Oh no," Paul said, aghast.

"Oh, yes," Mindy corrected. "And Evan, before you answer, I also want to know who you're buying presents for, and what you're doing with the money, because you've withdrawn ten thousand dollars from your account over the past three months. So either you're buying drugs, buying women, or buying tattoos—"

"I can explain, Mom—" Evan interrupted, panicky, but Mindy wasn't finished venting yet.

"Evan, why are these girls sending you these photos?" Mindy stood above Paul and Evan, folding her arms, and she had never felt more powerful in her life. "Do you ask or do they offer? If you sent them to anybody, you're transmitting child pornography, do you realize that? You can go to jail! Everybody you sent them to can go to jail, if they send it on. If you have an explanation, you better start explaining right now!"

"I can explain," Paul interjected, his tone quiet, and Mindy wheeled around to him.

"Paul! Don't tell me you *knew* what this is about! If you knew and didn't tell me then you're going to have more to answer for than Carole's real birthday, because the one you told me was a lie!"

Paul grimaced. "Honey, I didn't know about the pictures—"

Evan interjected, "Mom, Dad didn't know about the pictures, he didn't know about any of it—"

Paul shook his head. "I knew about the money, Evan. I can explain about the money—"

"Dad, you don't have to." Evan put a hand on Paul's arm, and Mindy could see they were trying to protect each other. Boys will be boys, covering each other's asses against Mean Mommy, the Disciplinarian, the Mother of Us All, the *Boss Bitch*.

"No more games, either of you!" Mindy barked. "I want the truth and I want it now."

Paul sighed, then said, "Honey, as I started to say, I can explain about the money, it went to pay for—"

"I got a girl pregnant," Evan said, finishing the sentence.

Mindy almost fell over. She wasn't sure she had even heard him right. "You *what*?"

Evan reddened, flustered. "Mom, I'm sorry, I'm really sorry. It was an accident. I always use protection, I do. I know you told me, I know all about it. But this one time I didn't, she was drinking, and I was drinking, and it was legit consent, but we didn't use protection, and then she told me she was pregnant and she wanted to, well, end the pregnancy—"

"An abortion?" Mindy groaned, stricken. She had a million thoughts at once. An abortion, a baby. Evan got a girl pregnant. A baby had been aborted. Her son's baby. Her *grandchild*. It was too much, and she sank into the couch opposite them, suddenly powerless, helpless, useless.

"Mom, don't be upset, really, it's all fine now, we took care of it, that's what the money was for." Evan leaned forward urgently. "When it happened, when she told me, I went to Dad and I told him that the girl didn't want the baby. Believe me, I didn't have a choice even if I wanted a baby, she wasn't about to have it and neither were her parents—"

Mindy listened, appalled. Paul knew. Her parents knew. Everyone knew but Mindy. She didn't know what to say. She didn't interrupt her son, who was talking a mile a minute anyway.

"—I went to Dad because I didn't want to upset you, and he said I had to pay for it out of my own money because

that's my fault and I have to learn to accept the consequences and all that. So we took it out of my own account
and we knew you never look at my statements, so we
thought it would be fine."

Mindy's mouth had gone completely dry, and she
turned to Paul. "You thought this would be *fine*? You paid
for a girl to abort your son's first child and you didn't even
tell me? And you thought *that was fine*?"

"Yes, I'm sorry, honey." Paul kept his surgeon's demeanor, experienced at delivering bad news. "I thought it
would be the best way to handle it, just Evan and me. I
didn't want you to get upset, and we knew that you would.
So we took care of the problem ourselves."

"The problem?" Mindy shouted. "It wasn't a problem,
it was a *baby,* our *grandchild,* and I had a right to know
that baby existed. You didn't tell me because you thought
I would say no, because I could stop you, so you just ignored the fact that I exist. How could you? How could you
keep it from me?"

"I thought it was best, considering, that last year was
so difficult—"

"Ha! Oh, I get it! So, because you kept your affair a
secret, which almost ended our marriage, you also decided to keep this a secret, too. Which therapy session
did we cover that in? Because I must've missed that
one!"

Paul frowned, glancing at Evan. "Honey—"

"What?" Mindy knew Paul didn't like that she'd just
let Evan know about his affair, but she was beyond caring. "Yes, Paul, you had an affair, and now Evan knows it,
too. Our son is not a child anymore, since he *made a child
of his own*. The jig is up, wouldn't you say, *Gramps*?"

Evan said nothing, without looking over at his father.

Paul sighed, contrite. "I'm so sorry, honey. I should've

told you. I just wanted to make it easier on you, and that may have been a mistake, but I own that."

"Oh, you *own* that?" Mindy hated that Paul used therapy-speak but had learned zero in therapy. "Don't you think that's wrong, that that's *terrible,* that your son got a girl pregnant? When did you buy him the BMW, before or after?"

Evan made a little hiccup, his eyes suddenly brimming with tears. "Mom, I'm really sorry, I really am. I would never do it again, and if I could take it back, I would—"

"Evan." Mindy felt unmoved, turning to him, shaken to her very foundations. She felt as if she were seeing him with new eyes, as if she had been sleepwalking through her own life. "Evan, I don't know what to say to you. I don't know what to do about this."

"Mom, you don't have to do anything, it's over now."

Paul nodded. "Honey, it is over. I swear to you. It's over. We dodged a bullet, and we came out fine."

"You don't even know how bad it got," Evan added.

"No, I don't, why don't you tell me?" Mindy realized that she had never disliked her son before, and now she hated him. Hated her own child. Hated the man he was growing into, or had already grown into. Hated her son and her husband. *Hey, Facebook, how do you like the Kostis Klan now?*

"Mom, she started to ask for more money because she wanted to get the abortion in New York so nobody would know, and we said yes, because we were worried that everybody at school would find out—"

Paul interrupted, "And at the club and the hospital, too. We didn't want it to get around."

"Oh God." Mindy moaned. Her phone rang in her hand, and she glanced down to see who was calling, but it was a number she didn't recognize, so she pressed the screen to send it to voicemail.

Evan was saying, "Dad took care of it. We gave her as much money as we could, and she took, like, two weeks off from school. She stayed at a hotel in New York, it cost a lot."

Paul nodded. "I cut her off at ten grand in cash, and she accepted it, and so did her parents, and it's over. They don't want it to get around, either. It's a terrible chapter in our lives, but it's over."

"It's not over for me. It's just begun for me."

"What do you mean, Mom?" Evan asked, his voice cracking. He wiped the tear from his cheek.

"What's this girl's name, Evan? Is it Amanda, the girl sending you the naked pictures? Excuse me, *one* of the girls sending you—"

"Mom, no, it's not Amanda."

"So it's a *different* girl? You got one girl pregnant, and another one's sending you naked pictures? You told Amanda you love her, and she said she loves you!" Mindy couldn't even follow. "What's the name of the girl you got pregnant?"

"Mom, what's the difference? She's not from here. She goes to a different school."

"How dare you! You answer this question! What is her name? Which one is she?" Mindy reached for her phone. "Is she one of the girls in this phone?"

"No, I said, I don't see her anymore."

"Evan, what's the matter with you?" Mindy exploded. "What are you, a sex addict?"

Paul interjected, "Mindy, you don't need to know her name."

"Why, Paul? Because you don't want me to look her up, to call her? You better tell me her name or I'm going to divorce you on the spot. You can go up and pack right now." Mindy pointed upstairs again. "Right now."

Evan answered, "Okay, her name is Cynthia Caselli. She goes to Rocky Springs. But, please don't call her. You're just gonna make everything worse."

Paul chimed in, "Honey, he's right. I dealt with these people. The Casellis are lowlifes. Let it go."

"The hell I will!"

"Mom!" Evan jumped up, as tears spilled from his eyes. "You shouldn't've been in my phone in the first place! You invaded my privacy! How do you even know the passcode? Why do you have to stick your nose into everything? Why can't you just let it go?"

"How dare you!" Mindy rose, squaring off against Evan. "I can't let it go because you're my son. Don't throw a tantrum about me not trusting you—if you're not worthy of trust!"

"Mom, you didn't know that when you went in the phone. You were just snooping around in things that aren't your business." Evan started to move toward the door, and Mindy went after him.

"You're my business, and everything you do is my business!"

"I've had it with you! I've had it with you *both*." Evan stormed out the door, letting it slam behind him.

"Don't walk out when I'm talking to you!" Mindy started to go after him, but Paul appeared at her side, holding her arm.

"Let him go, honey. He needs to cool down. Let him think it over."

"Oh, what do *you* know?" Mindy wrested her arm out of his hand as if he were a complete stranger, which was exactly how she felt. "He can't walk out on me when I'm talking to him. That's rude and disrespectful, and he needs limits. When are you going to figure that out? When he gets another girl pregnant? How many BMWs can you buy him, *Dr. Kostis*?"

"Min—"

"He's sick of the two of us? I'm sick of the two of *you*!" Mindy turned and ran upstairs to her bedroom to figure out whether the Kostis Klan could be saved.

Or should be.

Chapter Thirty-nine

Susan went downstairs as soon as she heard Ryan come home from therapy and head into the kitchen. She'd called and postponed her and Raz's session until later this afternoon because the situation needed to be dealt with immediately, not by a therapist, but by her. She had the gun wrapped in a pink towel from her bathroom, without really knowing why. She didn't feel angry anymore, only sad, and underneath that, she had a renewed sense of purpose. To put the Sematovs back together, however reconstituted, after Neil's death.

Susan entered the kitchen, and Ryan was standing in front of the refrigerator with the door open, staring at it like it was a television. He'd been doing that since he was little, and she used to yell at him for wasting electricity. Not today. He looked predictably drained, his skin pale and his blue eyes washed-out. He looked so much like her, with her dark brown hair, which he wore short, and he had a longish nose with thin lips, which right now were pursed.

"Ryan, hi."

"Hi," Ryan answered, without looking over. He was very tall, six-foot-four, but he hunched rather than stood, his head slightly forward. He'd lost weight since Neil's death, which emphasized his bad posture, or maybe he'd just been downcast since then.

Susan set the wrapped gun on the kitchen table. "You hungry?"

"Just thirsty. I did a drive-through on the way home."

"Oh, good," Susan said, not sure she believed him. She'd have to stop herself from second-guessing his every move. It wouldn't be productive right now. "Why don't you grab a soda and come sit with me? I want to talk about something."

"Really, Mom?" Ryan sighed. "I'm kind of talked out."

"I'm thinking there's no such thing. Grab something to drink and come on over."

"Fine." Ryan closed the refrigerator door without getting anything to drink, making a point, but Susan didn't remark on it. He was so much like her it wasn't even funny.

"What is it?" Ryan flopped into the chair and pressed it away from the table with an annoying scraping sound. Behind him, a small strip of sunlight came into the kitchen through the narrow window over the sink, and Susan felt bothered by that, for the first time. The kitchen was large, but it was dark, with walnut cabinets that made it seem darker. It needed more light. More windows. Maybe she could renovate and blow out a wall, later.

"How you feeling?" Susan asked, testing the waters.

"Okay."

"How was your session?" Susan liked the way he met her eye directly. She was pretty sure that he hadn't been drinking today. She realized how much she had missed the steadiness of his gaze, and the intelligence there. He was the rational one, and she'd always been able to talk to him. Even though he was closer to Neil, he was *of* her.

"It was okay. I liked it better than yesterday."

"Good." Susan peeled aside the corner of the pink towel revealing the silvery metallic barrel of the gun. "I just found this in your brother's room."

Ryan's face went white, and he sighed again, audibly.

"I'm not mad, I just want to understand. Did you give it to him?"

"Yes, I did."

"When?"

"After Dad died, like a month or two."

"Where did you get it?"

"I don't know, Mom." Ryan shook his head, newly impatient.

"Ryan, you have to know where you got it." Susan softened her tone, nonaccusatory.

"Honestly, I don't."

"Did you buy it in a gun shop?'

"No, from a guy."

"What guy?"

"I don't know." Ryan averted his eyes. "I don't remember."

"Ryan, you bought a gun and you don't remember who from?" Susan maintained her calm tone, for which she deserved an award. She didn't have to be a detective to know that he was lying. "Okay, when did you buy it?'

"Like, a month after Dad died."

"How is it that you remember that, but you don't remember who sold it to you?"

"Because." Ryan hesitated, returning his focus to her, with a frown. "I was at a party, Mom. I drank too much. I blacked out, and I bought the gun."

"How much was it?" Susan asked, incredulous.

"Like I say, I don't know."

"Who was at the party?"

"A lot of guys I don't know, mostly guys, some women, I just didn't know the crowd."

"Whose party was it? Where was it?"

"Just some people I met at this bikers' bar, in Rocky Springs. They said you want to come over and party, and I went to some house, I don't remember where it was. All I know is that I got drunk and I bought the gun."

Susan tried to understand. "But a gun has to cost a couple hundred dollars. You never have more than twenty dollars on you. You weren't working then, either. Who's going to sell you a gun for twenty bucks?"

Ryan blinked. "I don't know, I don't remember."

Susan bore down. "Honey, I love you. I just don't feel like you're telling me the truth. It doesn't make sense."

Ryan fell silent, and she could see him going inward, which was his way. Her way, too. She got that from her father. Her side of the family kept it all inside, until they exploded.

"Ryan, just tell me. I won't be mad. I've been thinking about a lot of things and we are going to make a lot of changes here for the better." Susan hesitated, then tried to explain, the way she had with Raz. "We're all hurting since your dad died, and we've lost our way, as a family. Me most of all. I think I delegated so much to him, he was the true head of our household, and without him, well, there's been kind of an emptiness, a power vacuum."

Ryan seemed to be listening, and Susan realized that he was probably unused to her taking the time to sit down with him this way, not to mention being so vulnerable, so she continued.

"You know, there's an expression, 'nature abhors a vacuum.' That means when there's a power vacuum, things go wrong. The world gets out of whack. Well, I think our world has been out of whack. I haven't stepped into that power vacuum yet, but I'm going to now. I have to be the head of this household. I made a lot of mistakes, but I'm going to try to get it right from now on. So please, tell me where you got the gun and why."

"I stole it," Ryan answered, after a moment.

"You *stole* it?" Susan asked, unable to keep the incredulity from her tone. Ryan was her mild child, the rules follower, the one who never did anything wrong—until his father had died. She arranged her face into a mask of calm, but inwardly, her emotions were all over the map. "How did you steal it? From where? From a store?"

"No, from a guy. I mean, everything I just told you about the party was true, and we all drank too much and I didn't know those people, but there was this guy and he fell asleep and I saw the gun sticking out of his jacket pocket, and I just took it and I left."

Susan knew it was the truth, as shocking as it was, because his gaze stayed level and his voice had a ring of authenticity. "Okay, why did you steal it, then?"

"For protection."

"Why did you think you needed protection?"

"Not for me, for you," Ryan answered softly.

"For me?" Susan said, touched.

"I mean, after Dad died, I felt that way . . ." Ryan's forehead buckled with pain, and his voice trailed off. "Okay, maybe it's like you said, I felt like I needed to be, like, the man of the house. I had to protect you and take care of you, and Raz, too. Then when I thought I was going back to school, I gave it to Raz, so he could protect you, and himself, and the house."

Susan felt speechless, then realized it wasn't the time for words anyway. She got out of her chair, went around the side of the table, and put her arms around her beloved firstborn, holding him close to her. He turned and wrapped his long arms around her waist, and neither of them said anything, clinging to each other. She didn't have to say anything to him, unlike Raz, because he knew her so well, and deep inside, she knew that he was coming back, returning to her again.

And more important, coming back to himself.

Chapter Forty

Chris drove away from Abe and Jamie's house, feeling a pang. He hadn't known Abe that long, but the teacher had made an impact on him, maybe in the way of all teachers. Chris had always loved school because it was his only constant; it was always him and a teacher, even as the schools changed, because he never had many friends. He'd earned good grades, eager to please those who had provided him even a temporary sanctuary, and he realized now that Abe had become for him every teacher who'd helped him, sheltered him from the hell of his home life, and encouraged him to go to college and find a career that actually helped people, in return.

Chris knew in his bones that Abe had been murdered, but he didn't know who had done it or why. He sensed it was connected to the baseball team, but he couldn't tie the two together. There was a piece of the puzzle missing, and he had faith that he would find it—just not in time. The Rabbi still hadn't gotten back to him about the workaround on the Kiefermanns' farm, and he still didn't know where Dylan had been last night, when he sneaked out of his house.

Gravel popped under his tires as he accelerated onto the country road. He had been in this situation before, but he'd been part of a larger operation and had access to the full array of ATF resources—other special agents would be deployed, police records and other official records subpoenaed, CIs, or confidential informants, questioned, and there would have been electronic surveillance for months, plus visual and cyber surveillance. The general public had no idea how much personnel, resources, techniques, and electronic fact-gathering was demanded by a major ATF operation. But that wasn't Operation Varsity Letter, manned by one undercover agent.

Yet as Chris drove, he felt more motivated and determined than ever. In other operations, he had been instrumental, but he'd also been a cog in the wheel, working with the Rabbi and other agents. This time, he was completely on his own, with only his wits and experience to guide him, and it struck him that he felt like a cowboy, from Wyoming of all places.

Chris whizzed by farmhouses, cornfields, and horses grazing in pastures, seeing all around him that which he wanted to protect—innocent people, this beautiful countryside, his homeland. The buildings of Central Valley rose in the distance and he couldn't wait to get home to study his audios, lay out the information he knew, review the photographs he had taken and all the mental notes he had made, to try to make sense of things, to find the missing piece, solve the puzzle, and connect the dots.

Suddenly the text alert sounded on his phone, and he looked over. The text was from the Rabbi, and it read:

**Something is going down. Meet us in 15 mins.
Same place.**

Chris felt a surge of new energy. Information must be coming in, and the "us" referred to Alek, so it must be big. If Alek and the Rabbi had the missing piece, they could bust the conspirators. Nobody else had to die, nobody else had to get hurt. Central Valley could go on living its quiet life. Jordan would be safe, and so would Heather.

Chris turned the car around and raced toward the abandoned development.

Step Three

Chapter Forty-one

"You can't shut me down!" Chris said, furious.

The Rabbi and Alek stood opposite him, with the Rabbi looking pained and Alek in his stupid ball cap and aviator sunglasses, like the Unabomber on a federal payroll.

The Rabbi said, "Curt, we have to, this is big—"

"No!" Chris interrupted. "You were supposed to get back to me with the work-around. I'm *this* close, I'm one inch from the finish line. I'm telling you, the teacher was murdered. It wasn't a suicide. And I caught one of my suspects sneaking out last night. All I have to do is put it together."

The Rabbi shook his head. "I hear you, but this is bigger, and we need you up north. I'm going up myself. You fly with me."

"Are you serious?" Chris guessed that Alek had made the Rabbi do the talking, because this wasn't a conversation, it was a sales pitch.

"There's no time to waste. We believe it's about the

Oklahoma anniversary. We have one day to figure it out, and it's all hands on deck."

"Where up north? Why?"

"I can fill you in on the way."

"Fill me in now. Because I don't want to get pulled off this."

Alek interjected, "Curt, we don't need to justify this to you."

"Yes, you do," Chris shot back. "I've taken it this far, I know I'm close. I'm not gonna drop everything just because you say so."

Alek pursed his lips. "I'm your boss. You work for me."

"I work for ATF, not for you. There was a you before you and there'll be a you after you. You're all the same guy. I'm doing the right thing."

"Keep it up and I'll fire you."

The Rabbi stepped between the two men as if he were separating two boxers. "Curt, hear *me*. Here's what we got. About two hours away from here, the northern part of the state, that's part of Marcellus Shale, you ever heard of that?"

"Not really," Chris said, though he had. He just didn't feel like cooperating, even with the Rabbi. If they wanted him to drop everything, they were going to have to lay it out. He'd been on too many wild goose chases sent by bureaucrats like Alek who had no idea what they were doing.

"The Marcellus Shale is one of the largest deposits of natural gas in the country, and it's one of the major fracking sites. In fact, the most fracking sites in the entire country are in Pennsylvania, on the Marcellus in Susquehanna County and a bunch of others. Towns like Dimock, Montrose, Springville, Headley. As you know, the gas companies use explosives to drill and they have the FELs."

"Okay, I got it, what's the point?" Chris knew that FELs stood for Federal Explosives License, which allowed companies to buy and sell explosives necessary in the course of their business.

"So you know that under the regs, the gas companies have to monitor their inventory of explosive devices and detonators, like blasting caps. If over a certain number get lost or stolen, they have to report that and they're subject to fines."

"Yes, so?" Chris knew all this and it bored him. It was part of ATF routine monitoring under the new Homeland Security regulations, but it was administrative and handled by a separate team in the office.

"So you know how this works, we send agents out there, they inspect the gas companies' operations. We fine any company that has an excessive theft report, which, business being what it is, sometimes they cheat. They underestimate the number of blasting caps that were lost or stolen to avoid the fines."

"Okay, so what? Somebody is lying about the blasting caps? Take away their FEL. Recommend they be prosecuted."

"If that's all it was, we wouldn't be shutting you down."

Alek interjected, "Yes, we would."

The Rabbi ignored him, continuing, "So we got a report from a resident of Headley, a town up there, that while he was hunting, he found a burn site. He figured it was a burn pile or maybe kids playing with fire, but when he started digging, he found blasting caps. He called the locals, who called us."

Chris felt his gut tense, knowing that it was a valid cause for concern. Domestic terrorists who made IEDs typically field-tested their explosives, leaving burn sites and testing grounds, sometimes killing even small animals or neighborhood pets. Still he wasn't going.

The Rabbi continued, "We sent some agents up there to talk to the gas companies and double-check their inventory of blasting caps. Long story short, we found out that somebody's been stealing blasting caps, just under the amount that would trigger the reporting requirement, from different drilling sites in the area around Headley. And one of the companies reported theft of Tovex."

"Again, so?" Chris knew Tovex was a water-gel explosive used instead of TNT. "Are they finding reports of stolen fertilizer? They still need an oxidizing agent."

"No, but there's not much farming up there anymore." The Rabbi pursed his lips. "Curt, I know you're committed to your operation. I know you believe in it, and you think you're onto something. But it's time for triage. We need you up north. You have to admit, this alters the cost–benefit analysis."

"But you have no plan to deploy me. I can't get undercover in a day. And with whom? Do you have any suspects?"

"Not yet, and granted, we don't have a specific role for you as yet. We have to get up there, see which end is up, and figure out the best way to deploy you. It may not be undercover at all. We need all hands on deck."

Chris had a random thought. "What if the blasting caps are related to my operation? To my fertilizer?"

Alek interjected, "It's up north. It's two different places, two different *types* of places. One had nothing to do with the other."

"It's only two hours away," Chris said, thinking out loud. "Look, I *know* that one of my kids stole fertilizer, it's on that video. What if someone down here in farm country is getting the fertilizer, and someone up there is getting the blasting caps? Together they go boom. Let me work it from my angle, and you guys work it from yours. I need to get into that locked shed. Did you set up the work-around?"

Alek interjected again, "There's no work-around, I wouldn't authorize it. There's no point and there's no time."

The Rabbi's face fell. "Curt, we need you to come with us."

"I can't go, I'm not going," Chris shot back.

Alek threw up his hands. "You've lost your mind! We have *confirmed* intel that there's a testing ground upstate, but you're going to play with high-school kids?"

Chris stood his ground. "Alek, you said I had three days. I have one day left. Do without me for one day."

The Rabbi frowned, interjecting, "Curt, one day is all we have."

"It's all I have, too, and I've come this far. I swear to you, I'm close."

"We're closer. You're our best agent. We need you."

Chris had never gone against the Rabbi's advice, though he'd gone against orders from even more annoying bureaucrats than Alek. But Chris's gut was telling him to stay, and so was his heart. Maybe it was time for him to grow up. "Rabbi, I'd do anything for you. I'm sorry, I can't turn my back on these kids. If they're involved, if they're being used, then I'm gonna protect them. Because they're my boys."

"Curt, I'm your boss, too. Don't make me order you."

"Don't make me call in my chit. You owe me one. I'm asking now."

"You're gonna do that to me?" The Rabbi looked like he'd been punched in the gut.

"Yes, really." Chris didn't have to remind the Rabbi of the story. The only man Chris had ever killed was in his very first operation, when he and the Rabbi were undercover in a ring of dangerously violent gunrunners. One of the thugs had pulled a gun on the Rabbi, and Chris had revealed his identity as an ATF agent per procedure. The thug had taken deadly aim anyway, but Chris had tackled him, grabbed his knife from his ankle holster, and stabbed him in the throat, killing him. Chris had pulled out the blade too soon, a rookie mistake, but he had saved the Rabbi's life.

The bust had followed, the gunrunners had been arrested, and an investigation by ATF's Incident Review Team followed. Chris had been exonerated when they'd found deadly force had been justified, since he'd had a reasonable belief that there was imminent danger of death or serious physical injury. And the Rabbi had never forgotten that Chris had saved his life. It gave Chris a chit that he'd never intended to call in, until this very moment.

Alek exploded. "Curt, you're an arrogant prick!"

"Keep me posted, Rabbi." Chris turned away and strode back to his Jeep while Alek ranted and raved, calling after him.

"Curt? Curt!"

Chris climbed into the Jeep, started the ignition, and hit the gas.

Chapter Forty-two

Heather sat at her kitchen table, trying to decide what to do. She had called Mindy, but Mindy hadn't answered, so she'd left a voicemail introducing herself and asking for a call back, but not giving any details. Heather had followed up with a text, but Mindy hadn't responded to that either. Then Heather had called Susan, but Susan hadn't picked up. Heather had left the same voicemail message and follow-up text.

Now she was fresh out of ideas. Jordan was sulking in his room, angry that she had confiscated his phone, which rested on the table in front of her. She'd taken his laptop too, so he couldn't text or G-chat. She didn't want any more online shenanigans until this mess was sorted out. She was beginning to hate the Internet altogether.

Heather sipped her coffee, which had turned cold, and her troubled gaze fell on the Friendly's sign outside the window. TRY OUR FRIBBLE MILKSHAKE FRESH AND FROTHY! She'd never eaten in Friendly's, though she could've recited every item on its menu, including made-up words like FRIBBLE and FISH-A-MAJIG, which appeared regularly on the sign. Maybe when this was over, she and Jordan could go over and have a Hunka Chunka PB Superfudge. Or maybe she could go over there with Coach Hunka Himself. Chris, her Inappropriate Crush.

Suddenly Heather got an idea. She could call Chris about the pictures. She wasn't even using it as an excuse. If Evan had really sent these photos to everybody on the baseball team, then somebody on the coaching staff should be made aware of it. Heather had never met Coach Hardwick and she felt intimidated by the horrible stories about him. But she knew Chris. It would make sense to contact him, though it wouldn't be the romantic beginning she'd been hoping for—*Hey Chris, did you see the dirty pictures the team is looking at?*

Suddenly Jordan's phone rang, and she reflexively looked over at the screen. It read **Evan Kostis calling,** and impulsively, she picked it up. "Evan, this is Jordan's mom."

"Oh, Ms. Larkin, is Jordan there? Can I speak to him?"

"Actually, no you can't, not yet." Heather thought Evan sounded upset. "Before I tell Jordan that you're calling, I need to deal with something. I've called your mother but I haven't heard back from her yet. May I speak with her?"

"Uh, I'm not home."

"Okay, well then." Heather hesitated. "I happened to see an inappropriate picture you sent to Jordan, and I'm very concerned. I think—"

"Mrs. Larkin, I'm really sorry, I already talked to my mom and dad about it, and they're angry, too. I know I never should've done that, and I'm very sorry. I apologize to you and Jordan."

Heather felt a pang of sympathy, but she wasn't about to let him off the hook. "Evan, I'm glad you feel remorseful, but this is a very bad thing. I don't even know the implications myself. There might even be legal issues—"

"I know, I know, my mom said the same thing, and I'm really sorry. Can I talk to Jordan?"

"No, you may not." Heather thought Evan was trying to rush her off the phone. "I would like to understand the situation better. Who else did you send the picture to?"

"Just the team."

Heather rued the day that Jordan finally made varsity. *Winner's Circle, my ass.* "Who's this girl in the photo? Is it your girlfriend? Does she know that you sent this picture around? Evan, this is a terrible thing to do—"

"Mrs. Larkin, my parents are all over it, so you really don't have to worry about it. Now can I please talk to Jordan?"

"No." Heather didn't like his attitude. "You can talk to Jordan when you've answered my question. You sent my son a photograph that can get him in trouble with the law. I want to know what you did—"

Suddenly the call went silent, and Jordan came rushing into the kitchen. "Mom, was that my phone? Was that for me?"

"Yes, it was Evan, and you'll be happy to know he sent that photo to the varsity players only, so only the best players will be going to prison."

Jordan's eyes flared. "Mom, did you just talk to him right now? Did you yell at him?"

"I didn't yell, but I told him 'no,' and if you ask me, it's about damn time."

"Mom, what are you doing? You're not his mom!" Jordan's mouth dropped open.

"His mom didn't call me back and neither did Raz's."

"You called *her*, too?" Jordan threw up his hands. "Mom, you can't do this! You're telling on everybody! Why did you do that? Evan's going to be so pissed at me!"

"First off, that shouldn't be your main concern, and second, Evan's parents already knew."

"How do you know?"

"He just told me."

"Mom, give me my phone, please." Jordan held out his hand for the phone, but Heather tucked it into her back pocket.

"You're not getting your phone or laptop 'til we figure this out."

"Mom, it's my phone."

"Not anymore."

"I paid for it. I bought it with my own money."

"It's under my roof, and so are you."

"Give it to me!" Jordan took a step forward, but Heather stood her ground, realizing for the first time that she wasn't big enough to stop him if he needed stopping. She realized that she and her son were crossing a parenting point-of-no-return. She looked him in the eye as fiercely as she could, for a woman who was accustomed to waiting for a living.

"And don't even think about trying to take it from me."

"You're ridiculous!" Jordan yelled, then walked out of the room.

Heather exhaled, wondering if other mothers had their sons walk out on them on a regular basis. She picked up her own phone and redialed Mindy. It was the right thing to do since she had just yelled at Evan. The call rang and rang, then went to voicemail, so she left a message: "Mindy, this is Heather, Jordan Larkin's mom, calling again. Could you please call me when you get a moment? It's very important."

Heather hung up, followed it up with a text, then phoned Susan.

Chapter Forty-three

Mindy sat on her bed with her laptop, scrolling through Facebook, but this time she wasn't posting or reading feeds. She typed Cynthia Caselli into the SEARCH window, and a long list of thumbnails of young girls, older women, and even a Maltese puppy came up. She scanned for local entries and found Cynthia Caselli, who went to Rocky Springs High.

Mindy clicked the thumbnail. Cynthia's face popped onto the screen, a gorgeous, blue-eyed blonde with a dazzling smile. Mindy thought of the baby and how pretty he or she would have been. Her grandchild. Mindy had looked forward to the day when she'd be a grandmother, since all of her older friends at the club talked about their grandchildren all the time. They said it was an experience like no other.

Mindy felt tears well up, but blinked them away. She looked at the Facebook page and, unfortunately, couldn't learn more about Cynthia Caselli, since the girl kept her page private except for the profile picture and the basic information.

Mindy opened a new window, went into White Pages, and typed in Cynthia Caselli, which called up a list of names and addresses. At the top was Paul and Gloria Caselli, 383 Hilltop Drive, Rocky Springs, PA, with a telephone number.

Mindy picked up her phone, then hesitated. She didn't know why she had the urge to call. On the one hand, it was a dumb idea, and she didn't know what she would say. On the other hand, she didn't like being left out of the equation, and at the very least, she owed them an apology. Paul could call the Casellis lowlifes, but Mindy and her spoiled son were no better than this girl or anybody else.

Mindy called the number, and the phone was answered after two rings by a woman. "Hello, is this Gloria Caselli?"

"Yes, who's calling?"

Mindy felt her heart start to pound. She couldn't believe that she was actually talking to the other grandparent of her grandchild, and it was strange to be connected through blood to a woman she had never met. But now that connection was gone, making it even stranger. "This is Mindy Kostis, Evan's mom."

"Oh, yes, how are you, Mrs. Kostis?"

"Please, call me Mindy. In the circumstances, I think it's appropriate." Mindy's mouth went dry. Now she had to think of what to say, and it was awkward. She wished she had a drink, but those days were over, so she had to tough it out.

"Okay, call me Gloria. Now, can I help you with something?"

"I don't know where to begin." Mindy felt so ashamed of Evan, Paul, and herself. "I guess I'm just calling to say that I didn't know what was going on with Evan and Cynthia, and I'm sorry about all of it. I am truly sorry."

"Well, there's nothing to be sorry for. They're young. It happens."

"It does?" Mindy asked, surprised. She would have expected Gloria to be furious with her and Evan.

"Yes, sure. They dated awhile, and Cyn was very hurt when Evan broke up with her. But she has a new boyfriend, so all's well that ends well. I don't like when teenagers get serious too soon, do you?"

"Well." Mindy felt flabbergasted. She'd been trying to be delicate, but it wasn't working. "I meant about the baby. I'm sorry that that happened. They didn't tell me about it. They kept it from—"

"What baby?"

"The baby, you know, their baby. Cynthia and Evan's."

Gloria gasped. "Wait. What baby? I don't know what you're talking about."

Mindy froze. Paul and Evan had told her that Cynthia's parents knew about the baby. But what if they had lied to her? What if the Casellis hadn't known? What if they were hearing it for the first time from Mindy? And now the baby was gone. Mindy didn't know what to say. Anything she said would break Gloria's heart.

"Mindy? What baby?"

"They got pregnant," Mindy blurted out, stricken. "Cynthia got pregnant and she had an abortion out-of-state, in New York. Evan and my husband gave her the money and put her up in a hotel. I thought you and your husband knew about it—"

"Are you *serious*?" Gloria sounded shocked. "That's not true at all! Cyn didn't become pregnant or have an abortion! Nothing like that happened."

"Yes, it did."

"No it didn't," Gloria shot back, firmly.

"I'm sorry if you're hearing this for the first time from me, but they told me you knew."

"There's nothing to know. It didn't happen. Trust me. You're wrong."

Mindy didn't understand. "I'm not, we just discussed it. They just told me. Maybe she just didn't tell you, or maybe she told your husband and not you. That's what Evan did, he told his father and not me."

"No, wrong. It's just false."

Mindy felt completely bewildered. Maybe Gloria was in denial. "Believe me, I don't mean to offend you, but sometimes we don't know what's going on in our own houses—"

"Mindy, if you really must know, my daughter had a torsed ovary at fourteen, and it was removed in emergency surgery. She's been on birth control ever since, to make sure she doesn't lose both of them. So the odds of Cyn's getting pregnant are slim to none. Now, I'm done with this conversation."

"Oh my, I'm sorry. Good-bye." Mindy hung up, shaken. She had no idea what was going on, but she didn't cry, and she didn't hesitate.

She got up, left the bedroom, and went downstairs to find Paul.

Chapter Forty-four

Mindy reached the bottom of the stairwell and didn't have to go any farther, because oddly, Paul was in the family room, where he never spent any time. He was sitting on the couch and staring at the ceiling, his head resting backwards in the cushion. A crystal tumbler with two fingers of Scotch rested near his hand.

Mindy entered the room, and Paul shifted his gaze to look at her. His gaze looked weary, exhausted, and bleary from the alcohol, but she still didn't feel sorry for him. In fact, she felt nothing for him.

"Paul, I just got off the phone with the Casellis." Mindy stood over him. "Would you like to explain to me what the hell is going on?"

Paul blinked, dully. "You called the Casellis," he said quietly. "Of course you did."

"What does that mean? What's going on?" Mindy didn't understand the way he was acting. He seemed to be decompensating, which was completely unlike him. "Did Cynthia Caselli have an abortion or not?"

"No, she didn't."

"*What?*"

"Evan didn't get her pregnant. It was a total lie."

Mindy had no idea how to react. She felt dumbstruck, astonished, and shocked. "Is this a joke? Are you kidding? Evan *didn't* get that girl pregnant?"

"No, he didn't."

"Did *you*? Did *you* get somebody pregnant?"

"Of course not, nobody got anybody pregnant." Paul sounded almost bored, reaching for his Scotch.

"Don't say 'of course not' to me," Mindy said calmly. She didn't feel the need to shout, with him acting so strange. "Are you telling me that you and Evan lied to me?"

"Yes. Well, to be precise, Evan made it up and I went along with it."

"What do you *mean*? Why? What's going on? Did you plan this?"

"No, we didn't plan anything. I didn't think you'd find the withdrawals and neither did he."

"Paul, why would you make up such a horrible story? I was so upset that he got a girl pregnant, that he aborted the child, our grandchild."

"I just told you, I didn't make up the story. He did, on the spot." Paul sighed. "He's a teenager. He was making it up as he went along. The good news is he's not that good a liar."

"Not as good as his father."

"No, not at all."

Mindy didn't like the way he was acting, almost comatose. She began to feel a tingle of fear. Something was terribly wrong with him. "Paul, tell me what's going on."

"You need to sit down."

"Don't tell me what to do, just tell me what you did."

"Mindy, this is bad. This is as bad as it gets. I suggest you sit down." Paul's unfocused gaze met hers, and something told Mindy to follow his advice. It wasn't a power struggle anymore, because Paul was acting absolutely powerless.

"What is it?" Mindy asked, sitting opposite him on the chair.

"I was trying not to tell you because I thought I had it handled. I thought it would blow over, but that's not happening. You're going to find out sooner or later because I'm going to be indicted next week. So there you have it."

"Indicted?" Mindy gasped.

"Yes, I've been the target of a federal investigation for the past six months, from the IRS and the FBI. Not one, but two federal agencies. Two." Paul held up two fingers like a victory sign.

"What are you talking about?" Mindy felt like she was in a bad dream. This didn't make any sense. It couldn't be possible. He could still be lying. She didn't know who he was anymore. Her husband, the stranger.

"I'm about to be indicted for Medicaid fraud, money laundering, and income-tax evasion."

Mindy felt the blood rush to her head, as if she would faint. She leaned on the soft arm of the chair.

"Would you like a drink? I know you drink." Paul held out his tumbler of Scotch, smiling crookedly.

"No." Mindy found her voice, choked. "Is this really true?"

"Yes. Next week, I'm going to be indicted." Paul didn't bat an eye. He stayed preternaturally calm, almost mechanical. "I took the money out of Evan's account. He didn't even know about it. I needed a criminal lawyer who specialized in white-collar crime. They wanted a retainer. I couldn't write them a check because I knew you would see it, and our assets are about to be frozen when the indictment is filed."

"Paul, no." Mindy reeled. It was too much to take in all

at once. Part of her still wasn't sure it was true. She felt gaslighted. "Are you lying again? Is this real?"

"Mindy, my dear, this is as real as it gets. They've been making my life a living hell every day since they sent me the target letter, you don't even know. That's where I've been, all these times I've told you I'm working late. I've been meeting with my lawyers and the IRS and FBI, trying to hammer out a deal."

"What did you do? Did you do these things?" Mindy struggled to process the information, all at once. If he was telling the truth now, he wasn't having an affair. He was doing something much worse, but all he felt was self-pity.

"Yes, I did these things."

"What, exactly? How?" Mindy couldn't wrap her mind around what she was hearing. Paul was a selfish jerk, but he never did anything illegal, that she knew of. And they had plenty of money to pay taxes with.

"I'll simplify it, because my lawyers aren't here to cite chapter and verse. I don't have to worry about your testifying against me at trial, even if you divorce me, because we're not going to trial. And you're in the clear, though you did sign our returns."

Mindy felt stunned. The words made no sense. *In the clear. Trial. Testify.* Her life was coming apart at the seams. She was too stricken to speak so she let him continue.

"Long story short, we've been charging for tests we don't perform and surgeries we don't perform, and we put the claims in and we keep the money. Of course we have to hide the money, which at this point is almost $7.2 million, and we've been dividing it equally among the three of us."

"*Seven million* dollars?" Mindy began to get her bearings, hearing the number. The money made it real. It was real. "Where's it all going?"

"Our share is over 2 million, and we've been spending it on this very couch, our club membership, Evan's BMW, and the Caymans vacation, which really was fun, I have to tell you."

Mindy had no idea why he would do such a thing. Money had never been a problem, so she didn't know why he would take such a risk.

"Mike, my beloved pal, told his lovely wife, Linda, and Linda made him tell the feds, who offered him a very sweet deal. In return for that, he became what's known as a CI, or a confidential informant. He's been wearing a wire under his lab coat for the past six months."

"Mike, your *partner*?" Mindy had always liked him and Linda. They'd been friends since Mike joined the group.

"Yes. They've also been tapping my cell phone and my office phone, and by the way, Carole was in on it too. We needed her cooperation to fake the billing. That's why we hired her and that's why I bought her the jewelry. To keep her happy and quiet. I know it's not her birthday." Paul sipped his Scotch, then made a clicking sound with his teeth, knocking it back. "Mike gave them the whole case. We would've gotten away with it—we *were* getting away with it—but he handed it to the feds on the proverbial silver platter. Which also happened to hold my head."

"Paul, did you really do these things?" Mindy asked in disbelief.

"Yes, I did."

"Why?"

"Money, primarily. The money is just too good. And frankly, I'm angry."

"You're angry about *what*?" Mindy shook her head, dumbfounded. "You have everything. We have everything."

"I'm angry at managed care, or rather, mismanaged

care. I'm sick of being told what tests I can run, what procedures I can bill for, what drugs I can order, and which drug companies I can use." Paul glowered. "So I found a way to get them back. I'm making up the money I would have been earning if they hadn't been interfering with my cases."

Mindy heard the self-pity eke into his voice and she began to grasp the implications of what he was telling her. "So what are you saying? You're going to prison?"

"Yes. I'm going to make a deal, Min. I'm going to plead guilty. I'll get twenty-two months."

"You're really *going to jail*?" Mindy felt incredulous.

"Yes, and the government is taking everything. Everything we own, everything in this room." Paul gestured around at the furniture. "It's going to be sold to pay the fines and make restitution. It's being seized, the whole house, the cars, everything we own."

Mindy felt her lips part in shock. Her hand went to her chest. Her heart thundered. She understood everything now, but she didn't care about the house, the car, or the couch. The only thing that concerned her was Evan. "What does Evan have to do with this? You didn't mix him up in this, did you?"

"No, he's in the clear."

"What do you mean 'in the clear'? Why did he make up the story? What happened?"

"After I got the target letter, he heard me talking on the phone, trying to hire a lawyer. He overheard the whole conversation and he asked me about it. I didn't mean for him to know. I thought it would never get this far, I didn't think they could prove their case. I didn't figure that Mike had turned into *their* partner, instead of mine." Paul shook his head, clucking his tongue again. "And I was so good to that jerk. I took him into the group when nobody else would have him. He's not that good a surgeon. He's practically a butcher, I'm telling you—"

"So then what happened with Evan?"

"Well, I suppose I confided in Evan from time to time, and he wanted to know. He saw what I was going through, and believe me, he's as angry about this as I am. He saw what they were doing to me." Paul sipped his Scotch, draining the tumbler. "It's been a nightmare, honey. You have no idea how much power the government has, and when it turns on you, you don't stand a chance. Not a chance."

"So you've been confiding in Evan all this time?"

"I needed the support, frankly."

"Your son isn't supposed to support you, you're supposed to support him." Mindy felt anger burn, like hot steel. "You shouldn't have told him, you should have told me."

"I didn't want to worry you—"

"Stop lying to yourself. You didn't want to *face* me." Mindy controlled her temper. Paul didn't matter anymore. Only Evan did. "So you let your son pay for your lawyer? You let your son take the rap for you? You let him lie to me? You let him hide what you did from me?"

Paul sighed heavily, shifting his gaze back to her, unfocused. There was no love in his eyes, nor was there any remorse. "I was about to tell you the truth, and if you think back, you'll remember that. I started to tell you, but he cut me off and he came up with this crazy story about an abortion, and I thought, why not go along with it? But I'm going to have to plead guilty. So you're going to find out sooner or later and you're finding out. Sooner."

"Where did Evan go?"

"I don't know. I have no idea."

"Is that really true?"

"Absolutely. Probably with his friends or one of his girlfriends. Our golden boy. He leads a charmed life."

"Does he?" Mindy said, rising. She began to panic. It was dark and they hadn't heard from Evan. She couldn't imagine him driving around for so long, and he had to be shaken to the core. He had lied to protect his father, who didn't deserve him. Or her.

"I'm sure he'll be fine."

Mindy's brain began to function. This was too heavy a burden for Evan, or any kid. His life was about to come tumbling down, and his father was going to jail. He would lose his home. Everybody at school would know, his teammates, his friends, his teachers. "Did you call him? Or text him?"

"No."

"Nice. Perfect. Great." Mindy reached for her phone and read the home screen. She'd gotten some texts from some moms but the text that jumped out at her was from Evan. She hadn't even heard it come in, maybe it came in when she was on the phone with Gloria Caselli. She swiped to read the text, which said:

mom, don't worry im fine. call u asap. love u

"Min, did he text you?"

"Yes, he texted me, but he doesn't say where he is or when he's coming home." Mindy took no comfort from the text. In fact, it worried her more. She called Evan again, but the call rang and rang then went to voicemail. She texted him.

call me asap please im worried about u

"If he texted, he's fine. He'll be home when he cools down."

"I wonder if he's with that girl, Amanda." Mindy went into her phone, scrolled to the photo she'd taken of Amanda's phone number, and called. The call rang and rang, then went to voicemail, a recorded message with a mechanical voice. She waited for it to end, then said: "Amanda, this is Evan's mother. Is Evan with you? Please have him call me right away. If he isn't with you, I want *you* to call me back right away. Right away!"

Paul called from the couch. "Min, who's Amanda?"

Mindy didn't bother answering, reflexively going to the window. Evan's BMW was gone, of course. He could be with Amanda or sitting alone in a car somewhere, distraught. She scanned the street, but there was no BMW. The moon shone on McMansions, manicured hedges, and mulched beds of daffodils. Everybody had a new car and a basketball hoop, and they all recycled. Mindy mentally kissed it good-bye. She only wanted her son back.

Her mind raced. She prayed that Evan wasn't running away. She looked down at the other texts and started opening them. Somebody had to know where he was.

Evan, where are you?

Chapter Forty-five

Chris worked in his home office, multitasking in high gear. He'd isolated the videotapes of the four suspects—Raz, Evan, Trevor, and Dylan—and was playing them. Their recorded voices echoed through the room while he reviewed the photos he'd taken of Dylan's house. It was the way he always worked a case, immersing himself in the investigation, reviewing all the facts and studying each detail. Every time, something popped out at him that he hadn't noticed before. He'd never been under such time pressure, but he performed better under the gun.

He shifted to the photos that he'd gotten from Abe's cottage and scanned each one. They showed scenes of white-capped mountains, a wildlife museum, Abe's older parents sitting in a porch swing, and Jamie, Abe, and the other teachers and their spouses at a pool in their bathing suits, smiling with their arms around each other. Abe stood happily at the center, and Chris felt a pang at Abe's loss, a sign of how deeply this operation had sunk into his bones. He couldn't let Abe's killers get away with murder and he had to stop them from killing anybody else. There *had* to be a connection.

Chris heard voices and a knocking at the door downstairs, but he ignored it. He wasn't expecting anyone. They must have the wrong building. It happened because the town houses in the development looked alike.

A woman called out, "Chris, are you home?"

Chris recognized the voice. It was Heather's. As much as he liked her, he didn't have time to deal. He waited, hoping she would go away.

"Chris, it's Heather and Jordan! Are you home? Your car is here!"

Chris would see what they wanted and get rid of them fast. He closed the file, hurried from his office, and hustled to the front door, buzzing them in. He stepped outside his apartment door to greet them on the landing, as they came upstairs. Heather looked stressed, her hair loose and her hands shoved into her jacket pockets, and Jordan lumbered behind her as if they weren't even together.

"Oh hello, guys," Chris said quickly. "Sorry, you caught me at a bad moment."

"Chris, hi." Heather flashed a tight smile, reaching the landing. "We're really sorry to bother you."

Jordan interjected, "Hey, Coach. My mom wanted to come, not me."

"Thanks, Jordan." Heather shot him a tense look, then turned back to Chris. "Chris, I wouldn't be here if it weren't important. Something came up that you need to know about, as coach. I didn't want to go to Coach Hardwick because, well, I don't know him, and I didn't want to call the principal if we could keep it to the team. Inhouse, as it were."

"Okay, how I can help you?" Chris resigned himself to dealing with it, then getting them out of here.

"Well, can we come in?" Heather blinked. "I don't want to talk about it out here."

"Oh, sure, right. Excuse my bad manners." Chris ushered them inside, but left the door open.

"Well, this is awkward to talk about, but here goes." Heather frowned, barely glancing around the apartment. "Jordan got an inappropriate picture in a text from Evan today. It's of a girl that Evan's dating, a sext. Jordan thinks they call her Miss Booty Call, but whatever. Evan sent it to the entire varsity team and apparently he has done this before. I don't know what to do, but we have to do *something*."

"I understand." Chris had no time for a high-school sexting drama. "I'll deal with this first thing tomorrow morning when—"

"I just want to say, it's the first time that Jordan ever got one of these pictures from Evan. Jordan wasn't on varsity before. I don't want my son to get in trouble for something that Evan is doing. Jordan needs a baseball scholarship and if this goes on his record—"

Jordan interjected, "But I don't want to get Evan in trouble. I called him but he didn't call me back."

"Jordan, really?" Heather shot Jordan another look, then returned her attention to Chris. "I called Mindy, Evan's mother, but this is the least of her worries right now. She's beside herself. She just found out that her husband's going to jail for tax evasion."

"Really," Chris said, surprised.

"Yes, and they had a big family fight. She doesn't even know where Evan is."

"Evan is missing?" Chris's ears pricked up.

"Well, not missing, just not home." Heather pursed her lips. "But Evan isn't my problem. That family can afford to write a check for college, but we can't, and I'm not going to let Evan hurt Jordan's chances to be recruited."

"I agree, Jordan shouldn't get in trouble. But it's Sunday night, so I can't contact Coach Hardwick, Dr. McElroy, or anybody in the office." Chris walked to the door. He sensed that something was going on with Evan and he had to get back to his desk. "Guys, I really appreciate your bringing this to my attention, but I'm in the middle of something. I will discuss this with them first thing in the morning—"

"Chris, I must not be making myself clear, this is so awkward." Heather took a phone from her pocket and scrolled through it as she talked. "Maybe you need to see what I'm talking about to understand. It's a *very* inappropriate picture. Look!"

"I assumed it was—" Chris started to say, but stopped when Heather held up her phone. Its screen showed the naked body of a woman whose face wasn't shown but whose legs were parted, leaving nothing to the imagination. She had a tattoo on her side, a dream catcher.

"Heather, let me see that." Chris felt something nagging at him.

"The sext?" Heather handed him the phone. "Kinda weird of you, but okay."

"Excuse me for one minute." Chris eyed the photo, handed her back the phone, and edged backwards toward his office. "Just wait here."

Chapter Forty-six

Chris hustled into his office, closed the door behind him, and hurried to his desk for the pictures from Wyoming. He found the one he was looking for, the photo of Jamie, Abe, and the other teachers and their spouses in bathing suits. His gaze went straight to Courtney, who was wearing a black two-piece suit. She had a tattoo on her side, and he looked at it closely but couldn't tell what it was. If it had been a digital photo, he would simply enlarge it, but he didn't have a scanner.

Chris tore open his desk drawer, found an old-school magnifying glass, and held it up to the photo. He moved it over Courtney's waist, and the ink came into focus. Courtney's tattoo was a dream catcher, and it was on her right side, in the same position on her body as in the nude selfie. He compared it with the phone, and it was a match.

Chris blinked. So Courtney was the woman in the sext, and she and Evan must've been having an affair. But something else was far more concerning. Heather had said that Evan's father was about to go to jail for tax evasion, a federal crime. Evan was so upset that he'd left the house. That could give Evan a motivation for a grudge against the government. But where was Evan? Could he be with Courtney?

Chris felt adrenaline surge into his system. He turned to his computer and plugged in Courtney's name and Central Valley PA, and the first address was hers:

Courtney Wheeler, 297 Mole Drive, Central Valley, PA

Then Chris's gaze fell on the third address, under **previous addresses of Courtney Wheeler,** and the entry read:

Courtney Shank Wheeler, 938 Evergreen Circle, Headley, PA

Chris's thoughts raced. Headley, PA. Where had he heard that name before? The Rabbi had said it. It was up north in Marcellus Shale. Courtney and her family were from the Marcellus Shale area. *She* could have been the connection to the baseball team—and if so, that meant Evan was the boy in the Musketeers Varsity T-shirt, stealing the bags of ammonium nitrate fertilizer from Herb Vrasaya's farm.

Chris felt the revelation electrify his system. If Evan was missing, it could be going down tonight. Or Evan could be in mortal jeopardy.

Chris reached for his phone and was pressing in the Rabbi's number when he heard the door opening.

"Chris?" Heather stood in the threshold with Jordan, her bewilderment plain.

Chapter Forty-seven

"Chris, what are you doing?" Heather asked, aghast.

"Excuse me." Chris hustled out of the office and closed the door behind him. "I'm sorry, but you both have to go, and so do I."

"What do you mean?" Heather recoiled, frowning. "What's going on?"

"I can't explain more. You both have to go. Please."

"But aren't you going to deal with this situation?" Heather folded her arms. "I'm not just going to let my son—"

"Heather, please. Evan could be in grave trouble." Chris grabbed his windbreaker from the hook and his keys from the side table.

"But what about Jordan? Jordan matters, too. I'm surprised you would treat him like he doesn't. I thought you cared about him. About us."

"Heather." Chris felt pained. He wanted to touch her but he didn't. Instead, he said, "Of course I care about you both. But please, for now, go."

"Why?" Heather asked, wounded.

"Coach, what's up? Why are you acting so random?" Jordan's lips parted, and Chris could see how hurt they were, which made him feel terrible. He had deceived her and Jordan, who had trusted him. They had been his unwitting, and he'd never felt bad about it before. He owed them an explanation.

"Heather, Jordan, there's something I have to tell you. I'm a Special Agent with the Bureau of Alcohol, Tobacco, Firearms, and Explosives, and I'm working undercover."

"Chris? You're a *what*?" Heather asked, astonished. "You mean, you're not really a coach?"

"Correct, I'm not a coach. That was a cover story. I have to go now. We all do." Chris had no more time to lose. He crossed the room and removed the false front from a shelf in the entertainment center, which concealed a small safe that he'd built into the wall himself.

"Whoa, Coach, I mean, for real?" Jordan gasped. "Are you kidding right now?"

"Jordan, I'm sorry I lied to you, but I had to." Chris dialed the safe's combination, opened the door, and took out his wallet and shoulder holster with his Glock. He closed the safe, walked back to Heather and Jordan, and showed them his ID and badge. "Here's my ID, so you know."

"It says Curt Abbott," Heather said, shocked. "Chris isn't your real name?"

"No, now that's all I can tell you and I shouldn't even be telling you that. I'm asking you to keep this completely confidential. Tell no one outside of this room. This is a federal matter, and we are handling it." Chris felt a wrench in his chest to see Heather edge backwards, her eyes showing the sting of betrayal.

"Chris, is this really true?" she asked, her tone newly hushed. "You lied to us to help Evan?"

"No, but I can't explain more," Chris rushed to say,

slipping on his shoulder holster and checking the snap on the thumb break, which held his Glock securely in place. "You'll be contacted by an ATF agent within the hour. They'll confirm what I'm saying. Now let's go, hurry."

Chris hustled them downstairs, then ran for his car, pulling out ahead of them.

It was go-time.

Chapter Forty-eight

Chris tore out of his development, heading toward Courtney's. Mole Drive was in the Murray Hills development, and he knew the way. He reached for his phone and called the Rabbi, who answered immediately.

"Curt, hi. I'm at the burn site, and we got nothing. Tell me something good. Improve my mood."

"Can do. I think the kid who stole the fertilizer is Evan Kostis, from my baseball team." Chris steered right, then left through the deserted streets. "He was having an affair with a female teacher at the high school, Courtney Wheeler, and she's originally from Headley. Her maiden name is Shank, and she used to live on Evergreen Circle. I'm going to her house in Central Valley right now."

"So they *were* connected. Nice work! You need backup? I'll get the locals over there."

"Yes, but I don't want them to tip her off if she's there."

"Think she will be?"

"No. She could be up there with Evan. You need to send people over to her family home in Headley." Chris told him the address.

"So you think the kid's in the conspiracy with the teacher?"

"Yes." Chris whizzed past the outlet malls, their stores darkened and closed. "His father is about to be indicted for tax evasion, a doctor at Blakemore Medical Center in Central Valley. Ask your AUSA and IRS pals what the deal is. That might be the source of Evan's gripe against the government."

"Okay. How are they traveling? You got a vehicle or a tag?"

"Not for Courtney, but Evan is driving a new black BMW. I'll text you photos of the tag, the car, and him." Chris had a photo of the BMW in his phone from that day in the parking lot, at school.

"What does this have to do with the dead teacher, Abe Yomes?"

"Not sure yet, but Abe was close friends with Courtney. You got anybody to call my unwitting, Jordan and Heather Larkin? I had to blow my cover, it couldn't be avoided. They need hand-holding."

"Text me the information, and I'll get somebody over there."

"Thanks. We have to assume any bomb plot is now in progress. If it was an anniversary bombing, they're not waiting anymore." Chris would fill him in about the sexting later, which would have accelerated the plot.

"Agree, they have to know we're onto them by now. Meantime we'll liaise with Homeland Security, the Joint Terrorism Task Force, and the FBI. They're all here. You need to get up here after you assess the situation at the Wheeler house."

"Okay. You going to send a helo for me?" Chris knew that getting a helo wasn't always easy for ATF, which no longer had an aviation fleet. It received air support from

DEA and U.S. Customs & Border Protection, through a Memorandum of Understanding, or MOU.

"Yes, we got all the toys up here."

"Good. Let me let you go. Call the locals and I'll meet them there."

"Stay safe."

"That's no fun," Chris said, hearing the bravado in his own voice. He used to say things like that all the time, but the words didn't fit so easily in his mouth anymore. He'd liked risk before, when he had nothing to lose. Now, it was different. Or it could have been.

Chris turned right, then left. At the first red light, he texted the Rabbi the photos from his phone. When the light turned green, he headed through the quiet suburbs late on a Sunday night, when everybody thought their biggest worry was work or school the next morning.

He had to make sure they were right.

Chapter Forty-nine

Chris turned into Murray Hills, and the development was quiet, the houses still and darkened. He turned onto Mole Drive, found the house, parked in front, and hustled out of the Jeep. He had beaten the local police.

The Wheelers' house was quiet, still, and dark, but a black BMW sat parked in the driveway behind a white Acura. It had to be Evan's. Chris hustled to the BMW, pulling out his phone and switching to the flashlight function. He reached the car, scanning inside, but saw nothing.

"Evan?" he called out, but there was no response, and Chris prayed the boy wasn't in the trunk, alive or dead. He would've popped it but he had to get inside the house. He jogged across the patch of front lawn, and when he reached the concrete steps in front of the door, he noticed that the front door stood partway open behind the screen door. The house was darkened inside.

Chris slipped his phone in his back pocket and pulled his gun from his shoulder holster, entering as quietly as possible. He found himself in a small living room and though the lights were off, he could see a dark figure lying motionless on the floor.

"Evan!" Chris rushed to the figure's side, kneeling and holstering his weapon. But the figure wasn't Evan. It was Courtney's husband, Doug, lying on his back. Blood soaked his T-shirt and the rug around his body, filling the air with its characteristic metallic odor.

"Doug!" Chris palpated under Doug's chin to feel for a pulse, but there wasn't any. The man's flesh felt cool, and his body remained still.

Chris began CPR, pressing down on Doug's chest, but there was no hope. The vast darkening stain on the rug showed that Doug had sustained a catastrophic loss of blood.

Chris kept compressing Doug's chest, but it practically caved in from the pressure. He could feel that Doug's sternum had been shattered and his ribs splintered, so there must have been two or three gunshots. Blood squeezed between Chris's fingers as he pressed down, and he glanced around to assess whether someone else was in the house, either dead or alive. He was taking a chance that he could be ambushed but he sensed he was alone and he had to give Doug every chance to survive.

"Come on, Doug," Chris said, trying to massage the man's heart back to life, but it wasn't happening. He finally stopped the compressions, feeling as if he were abusing a corpse.

Chris rose, wiped his hands quickly on his jacket, reached for his weapon, and began his walk-through. Courtney could be lying dead somewhere in the house, and so could Evan. He crossed the living room to the kitchen and scanned the room, but it was empty, its red pinpoint lights from the dishwasher, coffeemaker, and microwave clock glowing like a suburban constellation.

Chris hustled back into the living room and spotted a stairwell at the far left, so he went to it and climbed upstairs, looking around. There was a bathroom at the head of the stair, but it was empty, then he advanced down the hallway, ducking into the first room on his left, a master bedroom. Moonlight spilled through its two windows, and he could see there was no one else in the bedroom, which looked in order, not showing signs of struggle or ransacking, as if from a burglary.

Chris ducked out of the first bedroom and went to the second, evidently a spare bedroom with a single bed in the corner, and there was no activity or disturbance in there either.

So far, so good, Chris thought, relieved to see that Evan wasn't dead and neither was Courtney, at least not at this location. He left the bedroom, hurried back down the hall, and descended the stairwell. He spotted a side door, so he hurried inside, and down a set of stairs. He found himself in a finished basement with a bar, big-screen TV, and framed football jerseys on the wall. It was undisturbed, and there was no exit.

Chris ran upstairs and returned to the living room, where he saw Doug's body, and he looked down at the fallen man with a stab of anguish. Now two men had been murdered, and there would be more lives lost if he didn't succeed. He couldn't bring himself to even think the word *fail*. Suddenly he heard the sound of sirens a few blocks away. The local police were en route.

Chris walked to the front door and switched on the light switch with his elbow, illuminating the room to signal that he was inside. The locals must have reached the block because the sirens became earsplitting, and he spotted another light switch next to the door, for the exterior fixture. He flicked it on with his elbow too, casting a yellowish cone around the front door.

Flashing red-and-white lights chased each other around the walls of the living room, accompanied by the blare of sirens, and Chris realized his hands were covered with Doug's blood. He raised his hands palms up, standard procedure in case the locals hadn't gotten the message that he was on the scene, an occupational hazard for undercover agents. He knew of a case where two undercover agents almost killed each other, each believing the other was the criminal.

Chris positioned himself in full view as three police cruisers, with their distinctive brown-and-yellow Central Valley emblems, pulled up in front of the house and braked, their car doors opening immediately. Uniformed police officers jogged toward the house.

"I'm Special Agent Curt Abbott, ATF," Chris shouted, as loudly as possible to be heard over the sirens.

"Copy that! Everybody, stand down!" shouted the police officer who took the lead, and none of the locals drew their weapons, so Chris opened the front door and stepped outside, meeting the lead cop at the front step. He seemed stocky in his brown uniform, in his fifties.

"Hello. Special Agent Curt Abbott, ATF," Chris said, in case they hadn't heard him. "I'd shake your hand, but mine are bloody."

"Officer Mike Dunleavy," said the lead cop, his expression grim under the patent bill of his cap.

"We have a gunshot victim dead in the living room, name Doug Wheeler. I believe this is his residence. I performed CPR but it's too late and—"

"A *murder*?" Officer Dunleavy interrupted, shocked. "I don't think we have two murders in Central Valley in a year."

"I also did a cursory walk-through and found no other bodies, dead or alive. Your guys may want to double-check. I didn't have time to check the backyard."

"We'll follow up. But a *murder*. What's this about, do you know?"

"Sorry, Officer Dunleavy, I can't share that with you."

"You got any suspects?"

"I can't share that with you, either."

"Jeez, was it a bomb, guns, or something like that? I figure, since you're ATF—"

"Sorry, I can't explain further."

"I get it, if you tell me you have to kill me." Office Dunleavy chuckled, without mirth. Behind him, cops were shutting off the sirens, setting up a perimeter with yellow caution tape, and putting on gloves and booties. Lights went on in the other houses on the street, and heads appeared at windows.

"Officer Dunleavy, have your boss call my boss and they'll fill you in. They'll complete whatever reports you need." Chris motioned to Evan's car. "Before I go, I need to check inside the BMW's trunk."

"Let me go back to my cruiser, I got a crowbar." Officer Dunleavy jogged off, while neighbors began to file out of their houses to watch, their coats draped over their bathrobes and pajamas on the chilly night.

Chris kept his face down and walked over to Evan's car. He prayed Evan wasn't dead in the trunk and he bent over and checked underneath to see if anything was dripping, just in case the trunk's seal wasn't perfect. The driveway underneath the BMW remained dry.

Chris straightened up, coming eye level with the license plate, then he did a double-take. The license plate read RET-7819, but that wasn't Evan's license plate, unless Chris remembered it wrong. He slid out his phone, thumbed to the text function, and scanned through the photos. He found the one of Evan's BMW that he'd just sent to the Rabbi. The license plate was PZR-4720.

Chris pressed redial to call the Rabbi, who picked up after one ring. "Rabbi, I got good news and bad news."

"What's the bad news?"

"Don't you want the good news first? Everybody wants the good news first."

"Not Jews. We're tough. Give it to me straight."

"I found Courtney Wheeler's husband, Doug Wheeler, murdered in the house, three gunshot wounds to the chest. I tried to revive him but I couldn't."

The Rabbi groaned. "Okay, that's bad news. What's the good news?"

"I'm looking at Evan's black BMW, but it doesn't have the right tag. Evan's tag is PZR-4720, as in the picture, but now it's RET-7819."

"So they switched the plates."

"Exactly. You need to find the vehicle with Evan's old tag. My bet is it's on a van, and you know what I'm thinking." Chris didn't elaborate because a local cop was within earshot, unrolling crime-scene tape.

"The van is a bomb on wheels," the Rabbi answered, finishing the thought.

"Bingo. If you run the plate I'm looking at, it'll tell you the make and model of the van."

"And it'll turn out to be a stolen vehicle."

"Agree. I think I'm done here. Where's my ride?"

"In the air, ten minutes away. Where do you want him?"

"The baseball field at the high school, southeast of the main building. That will jerk Alek's chain."

"You're enjoying this, aren't you?"

"Only a little bit. And tell the pilot not to mess up the clay on the baselines. My boys just raked it."

The Rabbi chuckled. "Don't push it."

"Did you learn anything new? Or do I have to do all the work around here?"

"We're on our way to the farmstead now. Evidently the Shank family is well-known to the locals. Everybody knows everybody up here."

"Tell me what you got."

"The mother died a long time ago, and father about six months ago, heart attack. Two older sons, David and Jim, both barroom brawlers. The Shank brothers, everybody calls them. No neo-Nazi, biker, Christian Identity, or alt-right affiliations. No college degree, no criminal record. Anti-frackers. Write letters to the editor of the local paper. Go to the rallies. Courtney is the only one who graduated college, the youngest of three. She's the one who got away."

"Good to know." Chris noticed Officer Dunleavy returning with a crowbar. "I'm about to break into the BMW to make sure there's nothing in the trunk."

"Attaboy. Stay in touch."

"Will do. Good-bye." Chris hung up, and Officer Dunleavy reached him, extending the crowbar.

"Special Agent, you want to do the honors?"

"No, have at it. The anti-theft system is going to give you a headache."

"All in a day's work." Officer Dunleavy wedged the crowbar under the lid of the trunk, pressed down, and popped the lid. The car alarm went off instantly, beeping in a night already abuzz with activity. Neighbors lined the sidewalk, watching, talking, and smoking cigarettes.

Officer Dunleavy pulled a flashlight from his utility belt and shined it inside the trunk, and Chris looked. There was nothing inside but a baseball glove and a blue Musketeers ball cap.

Chris swallowed hard at the sight. "Thanks, I gotta go," he said, jogging toward his Jeep.

Chapter Fifty

Chris flew northward in the helo, an older Black Hawk UH-60 on loan from DEA, which was being piloted by a Tony Arroyo, an African-American subcontractor who'd served two tours in Iraq. A dizzying array of dials, levers, and controls filled the dashboard in the all-glass cockpit, glowing an array of colors in the darkness, and though the big rotors whirred noisily over head, the helo barely shuddered in Tony's experienced hands.

Chris kept his head to the window, his thoughts racing. The bomb plot was being rushed and that was when criminals started taking bigger risks—which made them even more dangerous. If the Shanks had killed Doug, they hadn't bothered to disguise the murder as a suicide or a home invasion. They could be setting Evan up as the fall guy. They had left Evan's car in the driveway, and the switching of the license plates would point to Evan's guilt. Maybe the scenario they were trying to sell was that Evan had killed Courtney's husband in a jealous rage.

Chris tried the theory on for size, and it worked. Reasoning backwards, that meant that the stolen vehicle, presumably a van, had probably come from the Central Valley area, because it would be a location to which Evan had access, not the Shanks.

Chris mulled it over as he looked at the land below. They were flying roughly along Route 81 to 476. The sky was dark, and they passed Allentown and were coming up on Hazleton, due north. The terrain below turned wooded, then rural, signified by vast dark spaces with only intermittent houses, towns, or signs of civilization. The moon shone brightly on the left side of the sky, and Chris found himself checking it as they flew farther north, knowing that its incremental sinking meant it was getting later. Soon the sun would rise, and it would be Monday morning.

Chris shuddered to imagine people going to work with their cups of coffee, phones, and newspapers, boarding trains and buses to get themselves to a city, to a building, and finally to a desk to start the workday. They wouldn't know that their lives and the lives of everyone around them were about to end in a violent death.

Chris thought back to the Oklahoma City bombing, the WTC bombing on 9/11, and a string of other deadly bombings that made him want justice for the victims and their families. It was his job to never let it happen again.

He clenched his jaw as the helo zoomed north, heading toward the Shank farmstead in Susquehanna County, and ten minutes later, he could see the change in the terrain. Bright white lights twinkled below in a regular grid pattern, like a box of connect-the-dots in the dark night.

"What's that, over there?" Chris asked Tony, speaking into the microphone in his headset.

"Drilling wells for natural gas. We're coming up on the Marcellus Shale."

"Tell me about it, would you?" Chris should know, but didn't.

"The Marcellus Shale runs under the Appalachian ba-
sin and includes seven states, like Pennsylvania, New
York, New Jersey." Tony pointed left. "Over there, that's
the fairway, where the shale's deep enough to extract."

"What's shale exactly?"

"Sedimentary rock that traps oil and gas in the layers.
In the old days, they tried to locate where the gas was and
drill for it, but now they frack for it." Tony pointed again.
"I fly over this all the time, doing VIP pickups. It changes
every year. More well pads and more drills."

Chris absorbed the information without judgment. He
knew fracking was a political hot button, but he'd always
been apolitical. His job was to save lives, and he couldn't
be distracted or people died.

"Ten minutes to landing," Tony said, and Chris
checked his watch. It was 4:32 A.M.

Dawn would be here before he knew it, and the first
order of business was to find the target. ATF and the
other federal agencies couldn't shut down every highway,
bridge, and tunnel in the Northeast. They couldn't issue a
warning to all federal buildings and state buildings. They
had to learn where the disaster was going to strike, so
they could avert it.

The helo began to descend in the night sky, tipping
forward.

Chris felt like a guard dog straining against a leash. He
couldn't wait until they touched down, setting him loose.

Chapter Fifty-one

Chris hustled from the helo toward the staging area, a white tent that had been erected on the front lawn of the Shanks' farmstead. Bright klieg lights flooded the area, illuminating folding tables, chairs, and laptops that had been set up. Federal agents hustled back and forth in blue windbreakers labeled JTTF, FBI, and ATF. The local uniformed police stood at the perimeter around their squad cars.

Chris looked beyond the staging area to the farm, a compound that struck him as a poor man's version of Skinny Lane Farm. Its layout was almost identical, with a stone farmhouse behind a pasture, an old barn, and several outbuildings, albeit in disrepair. Faded blue shutters hung askew on the windows, and its clapboard was peeling in patches. The roofs sagged, and the barn had faded to a dried-blood color. The pastures had been overrun by tangled overgrowth of scrubby weeds, and the fences missed boards everywhere. Farm equipment, a truck, and an old car sat rusting on cinder blocks.

Chris spotted the Rabbi running from the farmhouse to meet him. "Hey, you got anything new?"

The Rabbi reached him out of breath. "The joint is jumping, and the gang's all here. Let me brief you before we get inside. We're on top of each other in there."

"Okay." Chris hated that, too. Neither of them played well with others.

"Let me show you my phone. I got two videos. Check this out." The Rabbi held up his phone and pressed PLAY. "We ran the tag you gave us, and it belongs to a pickup, 2014 black Dodge dually, reported stolen from a used car lot outside of Central Valley. The locals sent us a traffic cam video."

"Good." Chris watched the video, in which a dark Ford Ranger pickup pulled up in front of a used-car lot and someone got out of the passenger seat wearing a black ski mask, black sweatshirt, and black pants. Unfortunately, the license plate wasn't in the frame.

"Now here's the video from the used-car lot." The Rabbi began thumbing through his videos, stopping at another one. He pressed PLAY, and the video showed the ski-masked figure breaking into the dually, with its characteristic double tires in the rear for bigger payloads. An old black cap covered its bed. The figure climbed inside and presumably hot-wired the dually, because he drove it out of the used-car lot.

"So far, so good."

"Stay tuned," the Rabbi said, and on the video, the dually drove away, but one moment later, was followed by the Ford Ranger pickup. The last frame showed the license plate of the Ranger before it slipped out of the frame.

"So you ran a plate on the Ranger."

"Yes, and it's Jimmy Shank's. So we got Jimmy on auto theft, and it got us into the farmhouse."

"You got anything on the target? And where's Evan and Courtney?"

"Nothing on Courtney or Evan, but come in and I'll brief you. We've narrowed possibilities for the target, and we put out a BOLO for auto theft. JTTF doesn't want to notify the public that we're talking about a domestic terrorist." The Rabbi headed for the farmhouse, and Chris fell into step beside him, checking his watch.

"But it's almost five o'clock in the morning. People are going to work soon."

"Tell me about it."

"Can't we issue some kind of general warning?"

"We're not calling the shots. JTTF is."

"But it's our operation."

"We know that but nobody else does." The Rabbi lowered his voice. "Humor them, Curt. It's the best way to get along. We divided the labor, and so far, we're living in harmony."

"So what's the division of labor?" Chris hid his frustration. He hated bureaucratic crap.

"Their guys searched the farm, and everybody's gone—the Shank brothers, Courtney, and Evan. We all went through the house, and the FBI found some of the files, and we found some others."

"What files?"

"I'll show you inside."

"Where's the burn site, the testing ground?"

"At a farm five miles away. Owner is Jason Zucker, and he's been in the hospital for a long time. Lives alone. Zucker is friends with the Shanks, so it makes sense that the Shanks would have used his backyard for testing while he was away."

"And nobody goes there?"

"It's in the middle of the woods. The FBI's command post is there. They think that's where the Shanks built the

IED but they haven't found any bomb-making equipment yet." The Rabbi picked up the pace as they approached the farmhouse. "The Shanks took their laptops. We know they had them because there are boosters in two of the rooms. They left nothing behind. They're not coming back."

"But they're not suicide bombers."

"No, I don't think so. They must have a getaway plan."

"They're going to make Evan do it, aren't they?" Chris felt his chest tighten. "They're going to make Evan drive that dually. They're going to kill that kid."

"You're assuming he's not in on it."

"He's not in on it."

"Even with the IRS indictment?"

"Even so, I just don't see it going that far. I just don't see him or Courtney going that far."

"Evidently they are."

"You don't know if Courtney or Evan's with them."

"I got a good guess." The Rabbi hurried along. "Another possibility is that Courtney and Evan went off together. Killed her husband and took off. Let the brothers bomb their hearts out, but the kid runs off with the teacher."

"The brothers wouldn't let them get away. They couldn't take that risk."

"You think they'd turn on their sister?"

"You tell me. I never had a sister."

"Instead of life in prison? Yes. And the youngest always gets picked on, especially a girl. I drove my sister nuts."

They reached the front door, and Chris followed the Rabbi into the crumbling farmhouse, which had thick stone walls, low ceilings, and small rooms that were typical of homes built during the colonial era, but the décor was hardly historic. The walls had been paneled and decorated with deer heads in baseball caps, and worn mismatched furniture and a fake leather recliner sat around an old television on a metal cart. Beanbag ashtrays overflowed with cigarettes, and the air smelled like stale smoke.

"Love what you've done with the place," Chris said, then his gaze fell on a grouping of family photos that hung at crooked angles. He spotted Courtney's pretty face, a bright-eyed young girl with missing teeth in her school picture, then a First Communion picture, and group pictures with her two older brothers, who had none of her good looks, though they shared her dark hair and dark brown eyes. Both brothers had broad smiles, which became flatter over the years.

The Rabbi pointed. "That's David, age thirty-eight, on the left and Jimmy, forty-five, on the right. We circulated a better one, but that gives you an idea."

"Got it." Chris took out his phone and snapped a photo, just in case.

"Come this way." The Rabbi led him from the living room and down the hall, past two crummy bedrooms to a back room, which appeared to be a spare bedroom. On the bed were piles of paper, correspondence in accordion files, and scattered court pleadings with blue backers.

"What's this?"

"More bad news." The Rabbi gestured to the papers. "The Shank family has had a dispute for the past five years with the Commonwealth of Pennsylvania, the Pennsylvania Department of Environmental Protection, the EPA, and Frazer Gas, which has leases to frack the neighboring farms. The problem is that three of the neighboring farms leased their land to Frazer Gas for fracking. Under Pennsylvania law, if three contiguous farms lease to frackers, the gas company can drill underneath your parcel, whether you leased or not. They drill horizontally."

"Really." Chris walked over to the papers, picked up the first packet, and started thumbing through the letter on top, to Frazer Gas, which read:

. . . You have ruined our home and our business. We used to sell top-quality horse and alfalfa hay, but then it was only good for mushroom hay and now even the mushroom farmers won't buy it. We can't sell it to anyone. You ruined our family business. We built a reputation as the best hay dealer on the quality of our hay and now that has gone down the tubes. We could not even give it away, not once they found out where it came from and we are not willing to lie to people to take their money like you will . . .

"Pennsylvania's law allows it, and the fact is, you can own the surface rights of your property, but not the mineral rights. Lobbyists and politicians strike again."

Chris picked up the second packet, looking at the date, 2010. It was scientific testing of some type, attached to a letter.

Dear Sir,
We demand that Frazer Gas, the PADEP, and the EPA cease and desist their drilling! They have destroyed our property and made us sick, especially my elderly father! We demand justice and we have proof! You can see by this report that the air is contaminated and killing us and our horses and dogs!!!!

Chris flipped to the report, skimming down the list of chemicals:

> **BTEX (benzene, toluene, ethylbenzene',
> m-xylene, p-xylene, o-xylene); carbon
> tetrachloride, chloromethane, methylene
> chloride, tetrachloroethylene; trichlorofluoro-
> methane . . .**

The Rabbi continued, "The Shanks claim that as soon as the fracking started, their farm went to hell. The air turned bad, the water turned bad, and Frazer Gas and the state government ignored them. The state eventually conceded on the water quality when it caught fire."

"The water *burns*? Is it methane?" Chris turned to the next letter, also to Frazer Gas:

> **. . . You give us water buffaloes but that's barely
> enough for us to drink but we don't have drink-
> able water for the horses and they all got so sick
> after you started drilling they were bleeding out
> their noses, losing weight, and refusing their
> grain until they died of starvation!!! My hunting
> dog died the same way . . .**

"Evidently. The same thing happened in Dimock, if you heard about that. So the Shanks and their neighbors complained and complained, and the state finally sent in some water buffaloes."

"Water buffaloes?"

"It's not an animal, it's a big tank of potable water. The water buffalo was for the family, not for the animals, and the Shanks had horses. They had no choice but to give the horses the water from the well, and over time, the horses got sick and died, except for one."

Chris felt for the Shank family and understood their grievance. Whatever the cause, it would've been disastrous to lose their farm and animals. He kept reading the letter.

> **. . . You sold my neighbors a bill of goods. You made our lives a living hell and now our houses are worth nothing. Nobody will buy them and we can't even move away. Your landsmen told them they would be getting royalties from the drill leases and that was a TOTAL LIE. They have yet to see a dime. You would say anything to get what you want, and that is a TOTAL CRIMINAL FRAUD that you perpetrated on . . .**

"They have forty-five acres, you'll see it out back. It's all open until you get to the well pads drilling the neighboring farms. It's not a pretty sight."

Chris looked out the window of the bedroom, but all he could see was darkness, and above it, the moon beginning to thin to transparency. Monday morning was on its way. He returned his attention to the letter:

> **. . . You were aided and abetted by the government! You know who to pay off and you have your lobbyists lining the pockets and kissing the asses of the politicians in Harrisburg and Washington. That is not LEGAL AND IT IS NOT JUSTICE. You don't care if you ruin family farms like ours. The Shanks have been in Pennsylvania since day one! Do you even know that William Penn named our beautiful Commonwealth Pennsylvania because that means Penn's Wood? He wanted it to be full of trees, not drilling pads . . .**

"Then about two years ago, the father, Morris Shank, develops nosebleeds, nausea, headaches, heart trouble. The Shanks start a letter-writing campaign, file suits, make all the noise they can. They get stonewalled by the state and federal government, Frazer Gas countersues them, and six months ago, Morris Shank dies of a heart attack."

"Oh boy." Chris eyed the papers, dismayed. "And they blame the gas company, the state, and the feds."

"Exactly." The Rabbi gestured at the papers again. "So what you're looking at is antigovernment animus. Motivation. The Shank boys get angry. David starts drinking too much, and believe it or not, they blame that on fracking too. And they don't have a bad argument. The locals tell me that alcoholism and crime increases in fracking areas. Also traffic accidents, because of the heavy machinery using roads not meant to carry the loads and noise."

"Really."

"I'm not making a judgment, I'm telling you what they're telling me. The locals say people who leased their land aren't happy and haven't seen a dime in royalties, but it's too late. And it's not our focus. The target is."

"Right, the question is, what's the target? The Shanks want justice, and I don't think they got it. The federal courthouse in Philly is the logical target."

"That's the consensus. JTTF sent everybody that way after you called me. It's only 160 miles away. Three hours by car. Remember, it's the Byrne Courthouse on the south side, twenty-six floors, and on the north, the Green Federal Building, ten floors—1.7 million square feet, all told."

"How many people work there?" Chris shuddered to think of the loss of life.

"In the courthouse about a thousand, including appellate and district judges, magistrates, clerks, and staff, but it's higher with jurors and visitors." The Rabbi looked grim, his lined forehead buckling and his mouth a flat line. Grayish stubble marked his chin. "The Green Federal Building holds regional offices of the FBI, IRS, DEA, Secret Service, U.S. Marshal Service, Federal Probation Services, and other federal offices. It has about the same number of employees but more members of the public. We think we're talking, all told with foot traffic, thirty-five hundred people. And that doesn't count the businesses nearby."

"Oh man. The FBI and the IRS are relevant to Evan." Chris regretted his words as soon as they left his lips. "But I think they're setting him up, framing him."

"Maybe," the Rabbi said, averting his eyes, and Chris knew he wasn't on board.

"Does the target change, given the fact that we're onto them?"

"Unsure. In terms of targets, if they change their plans, we're close to the New York state border, and Harrisburg, the state capital, is three hours away. There's an endless number of soft targets—train stations, bus stations, bridges, and tunnels. It could be anything, if they change tacks."

"You get no bang for your buck in Harrisburg." Chris set the file back down. "If you want to get attention for a cause and kill a lot of people, you go to Philly or New York."

"Luckily, there's no major bridge between here and Philly. There's a few tunnels through the mountains, but they aren't much. I'm guessing they're going into Philly, and most of the federal buildings are around our office in Old City and—" The Rabbi fell abruptly silent as a cadre of FBI agents lumbered down the hallway and into one of the other bedrooms. "Let's go back outside and talk."

"When can I go?" Chris wanted to get back in the air, heading to the courthouse.

"We have to wait for authorization from JTTF. They'll call Alek and he'll call me."

"Are you serious?" Chris couldn't control his impatience. "I have to ask permission to work my own case?"

"Go along to get along, Curt."

"Man!" Chris sighed inwardly. He followed the Rabbi down the hall, nodding to the FBI agents, a group of JTTF types, and two men in suits. The Rabbi opened the front door, but they both saw at the same moment that their staging area was full of uniformed locals helping themselves to coffee and doughnuts.

"Follow me." The Rabbi gestured to the right, and Chris fell into step with him. They walked toward the rusted cars in front of the abandoned pasture, with the red barn behind. Chris took a deep lungful of air, but it didn't smell like country air, but vaguely acrid and foggy. The Rabbi leaned against an ancient blue Taurus, fishing in his breast pocket and pulling out his cigar and lighter. "You're not asking where Alek is."

"Don't tell me, let me guess. He's with the cool kids."

"Yes. Taking credit for your investigation. All the *machers* are up here, and he's angling for a promotion to JTTF. He only used us as a stepping-stone."

"I feel so cheap."

The Rabbi chuckled. "The party line is that he was behind you every step of the way."

"Fine with me. Let's get him promoted out. The next Alek can't be worse than this Alek."

"Ever hear of the Billy Goat's Gruff?"

Chris shrugged it off. "Were you able to get an agent to the Larkins?"

"Yes, is that your crush? Heather Larkin?"

"Yes." Chris had forgotten that he'd told the Rabbi about her.

"I sent Marie over. She's a great agent, nicer than you."

"Thanks," Chris said, grateful. He flashed on Heather's pained expression when she'd learned his true identity. "I'm not sure Heather's going to be speaking to me after this."

"Och." The Rabbi waved him off. "You save the day, you get the girl. That's how it works."

Chris smiled, for the first time in a long time. "I didn't save the day yet."

"Added incentive." The Rabbi blew out a cone of smoke. "Was there ever any other? Every rock star in history says he did it to get girls."

"But they don't get shot at."

"There's that."

Chris looked around the pasture, noticing the bright lights in the distance and hearing the mechanical thrumming of drilling machinery, an unnatural sound. "Do they drill at night, too?

"I assume so."

"The Shanks were hay farmers." Chris eyed the abandoned equipment behind one of the old cars on cinder blocks. "That's nice equipment over there. A haybine, hay tedder, and that rusty thing with the round tines is a hayrake. That fluffs the hay into windrows."

The Rabbi turned, looking. "I always forget you're a country boy."

"I'm a country boy, I'm a city boy, I'm a whatever-you-want boy. I wonder why they didn't sell the equipment." Chris heard the distinctive sound of a horse nickering. "Somebody's unhappy."

"The horse? The FBI guys said he's crazy. They said he was going in circles. I told them, maybe he's hungry."

"When horses are hungry, they kick the stall door." Chris heard the horse nicker again. "That's strange. He's bothered. Something is bothering him."

"Probably the activity."

"No, he'd have gotten used to it by now." Chris found himself edging backwards to listen harder. "Let's go look into that."

"The FBI already did."

"Like I said," Chris said, heading for the barn.

Chapter Fifty-two

Chris heard the nickering of the horse as they approached the barn door, which stood open. "What's in the other outbuildings?"

"Equipment and junk. The FBI searched it pretty thoroughly."

They walked down the aisle between the empty stalls. The barn had eight stalls, four on either side, and cobwebs festooned the rafters like a Halloween ghost barn. The stalls were empty except for the one at the end, on the right. The manure odor was strong, so the stall hadn't been picked recently.

"That's funny," Chris said, thinking aloud.

"What?" the Rabbi asked, puffing on his cigar.

"If you have one horse, the normal thing to do would be to put him in the first stall. That way you don't have to walk to the end to turn him out." Chris gestured to the feed room, directly across in the first stall, the conventional layout. "And that's where you get the grain from. Why would you put the horse so far from the grain?"

"I don't know. Darryl and Darryl aren't Einstein?"

Chris approached the stall, and the horse stood tall, his ears facing stiffly forward at the intruders. "Ho, boy," he said, sing-song.

"You speak the language."

"You could too. Horses are easy to understand. They're flight animals, not fight animals. They're worried by new things, especially if they don't have a herd or buddy. You can get them a goat or a pony to keep them company."

"Horses have pets?"

"They don't like to be alone." Chris heard himself talking, realizing that maybe he was a fight animal. Maybe he didn't need a herd or a buddy. Maybe he truly was untouchable.

"There he goes." The Rabbi gestured with his cigar, as the horse circled the stall.

Chris looked at the straw, which had been so churned up that it had scattered to the edges of the stall, breaking up the manure. The hayrack was empty, and so was the feed bucket affixed to the side of the stall. The water bucket was empty, as well. "He needs hay and water. But something's up. He's bothered. Frightened."

"Is it the cigar?"

"I don't think so. The Shanks smoke, I smelled it inside." Chris turned on the barn lights, flickering fluorescents that needed to be replaced. The horse was an old brown draft, sweaty with nervousness. "He seems afraid in his own stall, which makes no sense. Their stall is the one place that horses are never afraid."

"Who knew?"

"Stand aside a sec, okay?" Chris lifted the nylon halter from its hook and opened the stall door, stepped inside, slipped the halter over the horse's head, and fastened the buckle. He led the horse out, and he quieted almost as soon as he stood in the aisle.

"That worked."

"Hold this." Chris handed the Rabbi the lead rope.

"Really?"

"There's no crossties." Chris returned his attention to the stall, walked back inside, and toed the hay that had been disturbed, revealing a layer of screenings, standard subfloor. He had bedded more stalls than he could count, and he recognized new shavings by their light gray color. They hadn't been here more than a day.

"Chris, what do I do with this thing?"

"Ride him or put him in another stall."

"He's looking at me."

"Maybe he thinks you're cute."

"He's scary."

"Put him away."

The Rabbi hustled the horse into the neighboring stall, and Chris dug the toe of his loafer into the shavings until he got to the floor, which was plywood. No stall that he knew of had plywood in the bottom. It should have been a rubber mat or dirt.

"You need to see this," Chris said, starting to dig. He cleared the hay, screenings, and manure to expose a plywood door locked with a padlock.

"Oh, whoa," the Rabbi said, over his shoulder.

"Can I get a pair of bolt cutters?"

"It could be booby-trapped."

"I doubt it. They were not expecting anybody to be here." Chris yanked at the padlock, then stood up and kicked it, but it wouldn't come off. It was new and shiny, unlike everything else on this farm. He ran his finger along the edges of the door. "They didn't just make this. It's been here awhile. Only the padlock is new."

"Be right back." The Rabbi took off, returning quickly with bolt cutters and some ATF, FBI, JTTF, and uniformed locals, who gathered in the aisle outside the stall.

Chris felt his heart pound as he cut the padlock, removed

it, and pulled the latch to open the door. It looked like the entrance to an underground bunker of some sort, but it was too dark to see anything.

"Here's a flashlight," the Rabbi said, handing him a small one from a uniformed cop.

He shined it inside the hole.

Chapter Fifty-three

"Courtney!" Chris shouted, when the jittery cone of light found her bound and gagged on the floor, her body facing him. Blood clotted her hairline, and dirt streaked her lovely face. Her eyes closed above a red bandanna covering her mouth. They opened, squinting in the sudden light, and she began to make whimpering noises.

"It's the sister?" the Rabbi asked, urgent. "Is she alive?"

"Yes, Courtney Wheeler, alive." Chris stuck his head in the hole and shined the flashlight around. Evan wasn't there. The bunker contained a plastic table cluttered with bomb-making equipment—a leftover pile of white ammonium nitrate fertilizer in crystalline form, a soldering iron, wiring, wire cutters, pliers, and other tools—plus ashtrays, an old CD player, and empty soda cans. There were two folding chairs, one knocked over. The bottom floor was earth, about six feet or so away.

"Courtney, it's Chris, I'll be right there!"

Courtney responded with frantic sounds, writhing, and Chris jumped down through the hole, landed hard, and rushed to her side. Tears came to Courtney's eyes, and she tried to get up, making whimpering noises as he elevated her upper body, undid the bandanna over her mouth, and dug out a sock that had been cruelly stuffed inside it. Instantly she began to cough, a hoarse hacking that wracked her chest.

"Chris . . . Chris . . ." Courtney tried to talk between coughs. "Thank God . . . somebody came . . . they put me here . . . to die . . . my *own* brothers . . ."

"Where's Evan?" Chris helped her sit up, then scrambled to untie her hands from behind her back, putting the flashlight between his teeth.

"They took him . . . they made him go . . . oh, Chris . . . Chris . . . it's all my fault . . . I'm so sorry . . ."

"Your brothers took Evan? Where? When?" Chris untied the rope around her shins, bound on top of her jeans. She only had one shoe.

"To . . . Philly . . . the courthouse . . . don't know when . . . they're going . . . to blow it up . . ."

"Rabbi, did you hear that?" Chris shouted out the open lid, taking the flashlight out of his mouth.

"Got it!" the Rabbi called back. "Get her underneath the door. We'll hoist her up."

"Courtney, can you stand? Hold on to me." Chris took her arm, looped it around his neck, and supported her as she struggled to her feet.

"Chris, you don't know what . . . they've done . . . they killed Doug." Courtney started to cry, but Chris couldn't let her lose it now.

"Courtney, keep it together. We have to get you out of here. Let me lift you, then reach up, okay?" Chris positioned them under the door, hoisted her up, and lifted her upward.

"I can't, I can't . . ."

"Climb on my shoulders, you can do it."

"Help me!" Courtney struggled to get her legs onto Chris's shoulders, and in the next moment, she was pulled up through the trapdoor into the stall. He grabbed a chair, stood on it, and boosted himself out of the hole. The Rabbi helped a weepy Courtney to a sitting position against the wall, as he identified himself and Mirandized her. Behind him, ATF, FBI, and JTTF agents started videotaping her with their phones. Somebody handed Courtney a bottle of water, which she drank thirstily while Chris went to her side, kneeling.

"Courtney." Chris knelt at her side. "You're okay, you're gonna be fine. We need you to help us now."

"Chris, I don't . . . understand." Courtney's eyes brimmed with tears as she took in the crowd. "Who are . . . all these people? What are you doing here?"

"I'm an ATF Special Agent and I was working undercover at the school. My real name is Curt Abbott. I have to stop your brothers and find Evan. You're sure they're going to blow up the federal courthouse in Philly?"

"Yes, but . . . Chris? Curt?" Courtney's bloodshot eyes flared with disbelief. "Really, is this you? You're not . . . a teacher?"

"It's true but we don't have time to talk about it. When did they leave? How long have you been down there?"

"I don't know . . . what time is it now? What day is it?"

"It's almost six in the morning, Monday morning. You've been there since when?"

"Since midnight last night." Courtney began to cry, her chest heaving with hoarse sobs. "I didn't know they were going to do it, I swear . . . I thought they were going to blow up the well pads, but not when anybody was around . . . that was what we all said . . . that Frazer was going to pay for what they did to my father"—Courtney's words ran together in one anguished stream—"we were never going to kill anybody . . . that's what I told Evan . . .

he went along with it because of me, because of his dad . . . I asked him to do it, he did it . . . he helped steal the fertilizer to blow up the pads, but not a courthouse . . . not with *people* in it . . ."

"I understand," Chris said, glancing at the Rabbi, who looked grim.

"They *killed* Doug . . . right in front of me, they *shot him* . . . they had a gun and I didn't even know they had . . . a silencer on it." Courtney sobbed, her skin mottled. Tears streamed down her face.

"Where is the bomb? Is it in the dually, the black dually?"

"Yes . . . Evan came to my house and Doug wasn't supposed to be there . . . he was supposed to be away for the weekend . . . but he came home early."

"Then what happened?"

"Jimmy *shot him* . . . and I got hysterical . . . but they said they would kill me and Evan if I screamed . . . I never saw them like that . . . they've gone crazy, they've lost their minds."

"So then they put you in the dually?"

"Yes, we were in the dually . . . and they had a gun to Evan's head, and in the back of the dually was the fertilizer . . . the bomb we were going to use to blow up the well pads, but I was crying . . . and they said 'change of plans, that's not what's going on.'" Courtney dissolved into tears, breaking down completely, her head drooping. "Nobody was supposed to die . . . nobody was supposed to get killed, ever . . . I think they killed Abe, too . . . They said they didn't, but I think they did."

"Why did they kill Abe, Courtney?"

"It's my fault, it's all my fault . . . he found out about me and Evan, he saw me texting Evan and he was so . . . upset with me, so disappointed . . . and I was so stupid, I told my brothers that Abe knew . . . but I think they *killed him*."

"How are they going to bomb the courthouse? They can't all be in the same van."

"Jimmy has a pickup . . . it's black . . . and he's going to follow the dually to Philly. Evan's going to drive the dually to the courthouse . . . and they're going to blow it up . . ."

"Does Evan know that?"

"No, they told him that they would kill his parents . . ." Courtney hiccuped sob after sob.". . . if he didn't go with them . . . they told him that they'd get him out . . . before they blew the dually up . . . but that's not what's going to happen . . . they have a remote control . . . they're going to blow him up in the dually."

"Courtney, hang in." Chris touched her shoulder, and she looked up at him.

"Chris, don't let them hurt Evan . . . He did it for me . . . I got him into this . . . I know it was wrong to have the affair but . . . he gave me so much attention . . . and I felt young and pretty again . . . Doug was never home . . . and now, he's dead . . . all because of me . . ."

"Okay, hang in." Chris rose, having all the information he needed and not a moment to spare. "Rabbi, I gotta go, authorization or no."

"Agree. Your helo's waiting." The Rabbi left the stall with Chris, and they hurried down the aisle, clogged with law-enforcement personnel, including ATF. The Rabbi directed them on the fly. "Mark, get Ms. Wheeler some medical attention and take her into custody. Don't move her from the farmhouse until you hear from me. Don't let anybody talk to her unless they're authorized by me or Alek. Jenny, call Alek and brief him. We're supposed to run everything through JTTF."

Chris fell into step beside him. "And somebody, please feed and water the horse."

"I did already." The Rabbi winked. "He's my buddy now."

"Nice." Chris glanced at the sky as they left the barn, which was warming to a soft rosy blue, an unwelcome sight. Time was running out.

Meanwhile, the Shank compound had become a scene of controlled pandemonium, since word had spread the target had been confirmed. JTTF and FBI personnel met in groups, raced back and forth, clustered around laptops, and talked on phones or walkie-talkies. Police cruisers and black SUVs appeared out of nowhere, parking on the overgrown pasture, and three other helos sat waiting on the field with his.

Chris asked, on the run, "So what happens now? Do they cut off I-95? I-76? Inform the public, now that we have confirmation?"

"I don't know. Not our call." The Rabbi shook his head. "JTTF makes all the decisions. They liaise with Homeland Security, the FBI, the Philly police, the Pentagon, and the White House." They hustled toward his helo, and Chris felt the gravity of the situation. "I'm thinking of those tourist attractions across from the courthouse, like the Liberty Bell Pavilion. School field trips go there from all over. Plus the Federal Reserve Bank, the Bourse, the African-American History Museum, WHYY—"

"They *have* to tell the public." Chris spotted his pilot, Tony, running toward the helo.

"They don't want to induce panic. It's a major American city, 1.5 million people. If you go public, the residents, businesses, employees, and tourists freak out. It would be mayhem, dangerous for them and us." The Rabbi shook his head. "And the Shanks might switch targets. The courthouse is on the other side of the Ben

Franklin Bridge to Jersey. They could decide to blow up the bridge or hop on it to New York. They could stop at any exit, hide out, wait, steal cars—"

"They'd terrorize the entire Eastern Seaboard. Paralyze business." Chris watched Tony climb into the helo, and in the next moment, the rotors whirred into life. "Looks like I'm good to go."

"Okay." The Rabbi hugged Chris impulsively. "Good luck, son."

"Thanks," Chris said, touched. He raced for the helo.

Chapter Fifty-four

The helo flew toward Philadelphia, and Chris kept an eye on the horizon like a stopwatch. The sky was cruelly clear, and the rising sun streaked it in rosy swaths. It promised a beautiful day that could end in a horrific loss of life. Chris would never forget 9/11, which was one of the loveliest mornings of September until it became the most tragic.

Chris scanned the terrain below as the helo flew south down Route 81. The Shanks had an overwhelming head start, and he assumed they were already in the city. Nevertheless, he kept his head down and his eye on the traffic, looking for the black pickup or the dually. As they flew southward, Route 81 widened and grew more congested with cars, trucks, tractor trailers, school buses, and vans. Chris ran possibilities in his mind for the next step, trying to formulate a Plan A and Plan B.

"Curt?" Tony's voice was transmitted through the headset into his ear. "I have a phone call for you from Supervisor Alek Ivanov. I'm going to patch him in. You'll hear his voice next in your headset."

Terrific. "Thanks." Chris heard a crackling sound, then a click.

"Curt? Are you in the air?"

"Yes, headed toward Philly. What's going on? Are they going to close the courthouse? Are they going to inform the public?"

"No decision yet. There are a lot of moving parts. JTTF will liaise with the other agencies and the city, and those decisions will be in their very capable hands."

"Okay." Chris thought Alek sounded unusually official and assumed that his boss was speaking for the benefit of others overhearing the conversation.

"Curt, you may not have been told that ATF is no longer primary in Operation Varsity Letter. JTTF is. JTTF didn't authorize your deployment to the target zone. You've done a great job, Curt. I couldn't have asked for more. But JTTF has its own people in the air, handpicked. Turn around and return to the Shank farmstead."

"No." Chris hadn't come this far to quit. "JTTF doesn't know how this may go down. Anything can happen. I may be needed. I'm the only one who knows Evan. I have his trust and his confidence—"

"Curt, Evan Kostis is a domestic terrorist, armed and dangerous, engaged in a conspiracy to blow up a courthouse and murder thousands of innocent people—"

"No, you're wrong, he's not a willing participant. They're using him as a human shield. Courtney confirmed it to us, just now. Call the Rabbi, he'll tell you. Evan is a *hostage*." Chris felt fear tighten his chest. He could read between the lines. They were going to shoot to kill Evan. The boy was about to become collateral damage. If Evan didn't get killed by the Shanks, he'd get killed by the feds.

"Curt, we're talking about one person as against thousands."

"No, it's not that way. I would never sacrifice thousands of people for Evan, but I don't think we have to sacrifice anyone. I want to stop the Shanks and get Evan out of there." Chris had to sound reasonable or he would never convince Alek. "You already put the word out about the dually and the pickup. We're going to start getting sightings. We'll be able to locate them. They've got to be in the city or close by. When you start to get those sightings, we can coordinate our extraction of Evan—"

"There's no *extraction* of Evan. That's not JTTF's plan. Their order is for you to come back."

"But JTTF needs me. What if they have to defuse the bomb? I can do that. I'm a certified explosives specialist. You know that—"

"Again, not JTTF's plan. Bomb squads are already headed to the target. Turn around and come back to the farmstead." Alek's tone turned angry, but controlled for the sake of the others listening.

"No, I can't. I'm asking for one shot. I'm not gonna let you kill this kid. There's no reason to. He's a victim, not a perp."

"Pilot, return to the farmstead."

"No, don't," Chris told Tony, then said to the headset, "Alek, please, I promised Evan's mother I'd bring him home and I want to try—"

"Pilot, turn around and return to farmstead." Alek's tone hardened like steel. "That's an order."

"Roger that," Tony answered.

"Over and out," Alek said, then there was a click on the headset.

Chris turned to Tony in appeal. "Please, don't go back. They're going to kill a kid for no reason, a seventeen-year-old boy. I can get him out of there. I've got to try. Let me try."

Tony looked over, grim-faced. "I'm not going back. I heard you. We're going to give it a shot."

"Wait, what?" Chris didn't get it.

"I don't take orders from your boss, I'm a subcontractor. I'm a father, too. I'll follow your lead."

"Thanks." Chris's hopes soared. Evan had been given a stay of execution.

"I can switch channels and listen to the chatter from the other pilots. We'll hear about the sightings as soon as they do. Nobody will know we're in the sky until they see us." Tony shot him a warning glance. "But if it goes south, I'm turning back. I'm not going to let you get us killed."

"Fair enough," Chris said, turning to the city.

Chapter Fifty-five

Chris spotted the cluster of Center City buildings he knew so well—City Hall topped by William Penn, the spiky ziggurat of Liberty Place, Commerce Center, and the Cira Center to the west, and to the east, Carpenter Hall, the U.S. Mint, and the Federal Detention Center. Straight ahead was the redbrick and smoked-glass tower that was the target, the James A. Byrne U.S. Courthouse and the William J. Green Federal Building.

Chris shuddered to think about the horrific loss of life if the Shanks succeeded, and the deaths would extend to people in the nearby office buildings, retail shops, restaurants, and tourist attractions clustered in the historic district of Philadelphia. It made him sick to his stomach. He wished the helo could move faster, but they were flying as fast as safely possible.

Chris listened to the constant crackling chatter through the headset. There had been no sightings of the dually or the pickup, according to the bulletins from the Philadelphia police and the other federal agencies, all with their own lingo and codes, telling the story of a major American city under terrorist threat, unfolding in real time. The public had been just been notified of a credible bomb threat on the federal courthouse, and Homeland Security had issued a severe threat level for the City of Philadelphia, shutting down the airport, and train, subway, and bus lines.

The Ben Franklin, Walt Whitman, Betsy Ross, and Tacony-Palmyra Bridges had been closed, and cars stuck on the bridge at the time of the closure were being escorted off by Philly and Port Authority police. The federal courthouse and all municipal offices and courts had been closed, and all employees, judges, staff, personnel, and jurors evacuated. People flooded the streets and sidewalks in panic, waiting their turn to be bused to shelters uptown. But none of this could be accomplished quickly, and tens of thousands of people were terrified, frantic, and in mortal jeopardy.

Tony looked over, eyes narrowed. "You seeing anything below?"

"No." Chris watched the traffic as they flew over I-95 south, six lanes of wall-to-wall traffic, the drivers honking in fear and driving erratically as they fled the city. A fleet of Black Hawks and bigger helos from JTTF, FBI, and the Philly police filled the sky, searching the highway traffic, main streets, side streets, and parking lots for the dually and the pickup.

"This is JTTF. Pilot, identify yourself," crackled an authoritative voice in the headset.

Tony looked over. "Tony Arroyo. I'm a subcontractor for DEA."

"Who are you with, Arroyo?"

"Special Agent Curt Abbott, ATF."

"Special Agent Abbott, do you copy? We were told you returned to base."

"Negative," Chris said, and just then, the voice was overridden by an urgent voice through the headset:

"Subject vehicles sighted at Ninth and Race Streets, heading east." Suddenly the headset exploded with orders, reactions, and sightings, a frenzied cacophony of official business as every helo in the air and vehicle on the ground started barking orders, notifications, and alerts.

"They found them!" Chris said, his heart pumping.

"Copy that. We're on." Tony steered the helo eastward. The other helos turned and headed east as if on cue.

Chris and Tony's helo was among the closest and they beelined for Race Street, flying over the concrete complex of buildings that was Hahnemann Hospital, then the Roundhouse, Philadelphia police headquarters. They zoomed east on Race Street and fell into formation with the other helos in hot pursuit.

Chris scanned the city streets. He didn't see the dually or pickup. Traffic was being stopped in a ten-block radius around Race Street. Race Street was in the process of being cleared by police cruisers blaring their sirens, herding motorists off the street or to the curb.

Chris scanned the city streets as they descended, flying over Chinatown, which was bisected by Race Street. They flew directly over the ornate red-and-green gate that was the entrance to Chinatown, then zipped over Ninth, Eighth, Seventh, and Sixth Streets, where Chris spotted the police chase and felt his heart leap into his throat.

"There!" Chris pointed to the black dually and pickup, careening down Race Street at high speed. Blue-and-white Philadelphia police cruisers, boxy black SUVs from JTTF, FBI, and ATF, and emergency vehicles raced after them at top speed. Adrenaline surged through Chris's system.

"Uh-oh." Tony shook his head. "They're not turning for the courthouse. They're heading for the Ben Franklin Bridge."

"The bridge is full of traffic." Chris felt his heart sink,

looking at the Ben Franklin, the massive blue suspension bridge arching over the Delaware River. Cars, trucks, and Bolt buses sat stopped across its span like a parking lot.

Meantime, the Shanks kept trading positions on the street, sometimes driving side by side, sometimes one leading the other.

"This does not look good." Tony clenched his jaw.

"Stay with the dually." Chris saw with horror that one of the unmarked helos was aiming a long gun out of the window, a sniper getting ready to take a shot.

"No!" Chris cried out, too late. The rapid popping of gunfire filled the air. He looked below on the street, stricken. Bullets ripped through the pickup. It zigzagged down Race Street and crashed into a line of parked cars.

Tony said grimly, "They're shooting to kill."

Chris said into the headset. "This is ATF, Special Agent Abbott. Do not fire on the dually. Repeat, do not fire on the dually. The dually contains a fertilizer bomb. Firing on the dually will result in its detonation and drastic loss of life and property."

"Special Agent Abbott?" several voices replied, crackling with static. "To whom do you report?"

"Supervisor Alek Ivanov at the Philly Field Division, ATF. In the dually is domestic terrorist David or Jimmy Shank and also a hostage, minor Evan Kostis. I need to get the hostage out of there. If the bomb goes off on the bridge, you're going to kill thousands of people and destroy the Ben Franklin Bridge. Do you copy?"

"Stand by," "Negative," "Affirmative," came a torrent of replies, crackling with static.

Chris turned to Tony. "You got binoculars? I need to see inside the dually."

"In the compartment at your feet."

"Can you get me to the passenger side of the dually? I want to see if the boy is driving or in the passenger seat."

Chris opened the compartment, found the binoculars, and trained them on the dually as they bounced along.

"Going south, hang on." Tony swung the helo around, provoking excited chatter in the headset, which Chris ignored.

"This is Special Agent Abbott, going in for a visual to determine location of the hostage and detonator." Chris ignored the responding chatter and looked through the binoculars, trying to focus in the bumpy ride.

Suddenly he spotted Evan in the passenger seat, hair blowing back from his terrified expression. A large pink bruise distorted the right side of the boy's face, swelling his right eye. Evan's hands were handcuffed in front of him. He wasn't holding the detonator. Chris tried to see if Shank had the detonator, but had no luck. There was no time to lose. A protective fury gripped Chris's chest, the closest he'd experienced to a paternal feeling.

"This is Special Agent Abbott. Preparing to extract the hostage. The hostage does not have a detonator. Do not fire on the hostage or the dually. Repeat, do not fire on the hostage or the dually." More excited chatter crackled through the headset, and Chris heard a few "copy thats" from the other helos. He turned to Tony. "You got a ladder?"

"Sure, behind your seat."

"If I hang a ladder outside, can you get me down to that dually?" Chris climbed out of the seat and into the belly of the helo, opening the trunk and rummaging to find a rope ladder of yellow nylon.

"You'll see the clips on the wall there."

Chris located the clips, secured the ladder to the helo wall, and opened the door. Wind buffeted him crazily, but he grabbed the handle and righted himself, saying into the headset, "This is Special Agent Abbott. Deplaning to extract the hostage."

Frenzied chatter came nonstop.

Chris looked over at Tony. "I'm going. Thanks."

Tony nodded, tense. "I'll keep talking to them. Go with God."

"Thanks." Chris slid off the headset, grabbed the ladder, and climbed out of the helo.

Chapter Fifty-six

Chris got hit full force by a powerful wind current. It almost blew him off the rung but he kept his grip. The ladder swayed sideways as their helo swept toward the Benjamin Franklin Bridge, a major span of seven lanes with a center divider heading to and from Camden, New Jersey. Two massive anchorages stood at either end of the bridge, and along the span were arches with lighted signs to shift lanes in off-peak hours.

Chris climbed down the ladder, flying over the sign that read **WELCOME TO THE BENJAMIN FRANKLIN BRIDGE, DELAWARE RIVER PORT AUTHORITY.** Below him, the black dually barreled around the curve at Fifth Street onto the bridge. Tony steered their helo farther south, overshooting the dually, then circling back toward the city for the one pass that Chris would get to grab Evan.

Chris kept climbing down the ladder, buffeted by the wind and the wash from the other helos, circling like hornets. Again he spotted a long gun poking through the passenger-side seat of one of the helos.

He couldn't stop them now. He could only hope that

the gun was aimed at Shank and not Evan or the bomb. His feet reached the final rung, and he flew through the air at the end of the ladder.

Tony turned the helo west, then south to complete the circle, at the same time lining up with the dually.

Pandemonium broke out on the bridge. Drivers sprang from the parked cars and abandoned them, running for their lives toward the nearer side of the bridge.

Suddenly Chris realized that their helo was zooming toward one of the arches over the bridge, which would crush him. Tony jerked the helo upward just in time, sailing Chris over the top of the arch, but they'd missed their first pass.

The other helos circled or hovered, creating major turbulence, setting Chris swinging crazily on the ladder. He could barely manage to hang on.

Below, the dually barreled up the incline of the bridge. Shank started firing at the helos. The helos returned fire or jerked out of the way, evading the bullets. Chris was still armed, his Glock in his shoulder holster, held securely by the thumb break.

He kept his eyes on the dually as Tony began another pass, circling again to the north, then toward the west, and then south again, ultimately beginning his descent to the dually. It would be Chris's last chance to save Evan.

He spotted another long gun poking through the back door of one of the larger Black Hawks. He intuited that they were waiting for him to get in position to take their shot. Meanwhile, Shank kept firing on them.

The dually sped to the summit of the bridge, and Chris kept an eye on Evan as Tony flew their helo closer, within fifty feet, then forty, then thirty.

Evan looked out the passenger-side window, spotting Chris, his eyes wild with fright. He shouted, "Help, Coach!"

The helo was twenty feet from the passenger side, then ten feet, and Chris could see Shank pull Evan away from the window.

The second arch of the bridge zoomed toward Chris at warp speed, and he made his move. It was do or die.

Chris linked his legs through the bottom rung of the ladder, flipped down and backwards, and reached both hands down. The ladder swung toward the dually with him facing away and upside down. Momentum carried him to the passenger side window. He arched his back and stretched out his hands toward Evan.

"Evan, catch!" Chris shouted, on the downswing.

Evan thrust his handcuffed arms out the passenger side of the dually and grabbed Chris's arms.

Chris grabbed him back, gripping Evan's arms as tightly as he could, and in the next moment Tony flew their helo up and away, lifting Evan from the speeding dually and clearing the second arch.

The air filled with a lethal barrage of automatic weapons fire. The snipers must have hit Shank. The dually veered to the left.

Chris secured his hold on Evan, straining with all his might to hold on to the boy as they flew through the air. Evan looked up with terror in his eyes, his hair blowing wildly, locking his fingers around Chris's forearms.

"I got you!" Chris shouted to Evan.

Below, the dually barreled toward the cars that had been abandoned, parked every which way, along the north side of the bridge. Motorists scrambled safely out of its path.

Chris watched the scene unfold with his heart in his throat.

The dually headed straight for a Corvette and drove squarely onto its low front end, kept going onto its hood like a ramp, and took off over the side of the bridge. The dually soared away from the bridge into thin air, its wheels still spinning, then plummeted into the Delaware River.

Chris held his breath. There was a muffled *boom*. The fertilizer bomb exploded underwater, producing a massive bubble of white water and ripples in all directions. The bridge shuddered at the percussive wave, but the explosion was far enough from its anchorage not to damage them.

People fled toward both ends of the bridge, but none of them was harmed or injured.

"Yes!" Chris cheered inwardly, keeping a tight grip on Evan as Tony completed his final circle.

Flying them toward safety.

Chapter Fifty-seven

Their helo flew back toward the Philadelphia side of the bridge and descended slowly. The ladder dug into the back of Chris's knees, cutting off his circulation and weakening his leg hold. The ache in his shoulders and arms intensified, supporting Evan's weight.

Chris felt Evan grow heavier, as if the boy could no longer hold himself up, the handcuffs hobbling his grip. Chris formed his fingers in a vise, praying that they landed soon. He feared that Evan had been beaten, suffering internal injuries.

The street below was being hastily cleared and a makeshift helipad was being formed at the base of the bridge, in front of a small grassy park that contained a monument to Benjamin Franklin, a silvery lightning bolt piercing the sky. Their helo descended slowly, and Chris worried whether they'd clear the lightning bolt, but he had confidence in Tony, who'd more than proved his mettle.

Both Chris and Evan hung their heads, looking down at the chaos below. JTTF, FBI, and ATF vehicles, Philly and Port Authority police, firefighters in heavy coats, and EMTs and other emergency personnel clustered around a slew of fire trucks, ambulances, and a bloodmobile. There were SWAT team members in boxy paramilitary vehicles, white Bomb Squad trucks, and bystanders, gawkers, and other civilians, who must have left or been evacuated from their offices, businesses, and homes.

The helo dropped lower and lower, and each person watched the sky or held up a smartphone, iPad, or tablet to videotape the dramatic descent. A throng of reporters and media stood filming from white vans bearing network and cable-TV logos.

Chris realized that it was the biggest news story that had ever happened in the Philadelphia area and it was being recorded, filmed, and photographed by professional outlets as well as guys with flip phones. He looked back at the smartphones, lenses, and cameras with the sickening knowledge that he was blown. His undercover career was over. His face, his image, and his true identity would be posted online, shared, and broadcast everywhere around the country, maybe even the world, starting right now.

Chris Brennan/Curt Abbott was about to go viral, and there would be no more hiding in plain sight. No disguise would be good enough, not after today. Chris had saved Evan but he'd lost his job, and the only life he knew.

And it struck him that if he didn't know who he really was, he was going to find out.

Chapter Fifty-eight

Chris didn't release Evan from his grip until the boy's feet touched the street, then all hell broke loose. Philadelphia police, JTTF, FBI and ATF agents, federal marshals, and EMTs rushed Evan from all directions, crouching to avoid the rotors and wash of the helo as it hovered above the street.

"Coach, Coach!" Evan shouted, as they hustled him away, his voice lost in the din of the rotors and blaring sirens.

"Get him to a hospital!" Chris shouted, as Evan was whisked into the nearest ambulance, its back doors hanging open at the ready.

Chris kept his grip on one side of the ladder, unhooked his legs from the rung, and swung his feet down to the street, righting himself as a noisy slew of official personnel engulfed him. He scanned the crowd for an ATF windbreaker, but there was too much of a commotion. The rotor wash subsided as Tony pulled the helo up and began his ascent, still trailing the yellow ladder.

Chris looked up, and Tony flashed him an okay sign, then climbed higher and steered northward.

"Special Agent Abbott, come with us, this way!" shouted one of the Philly police, barely audible over the din. "Special Agent Abbott, this way! There's a command post at the United States Attorney's office. We've been instructed to take you there unless you require medical attention."

"I'm fine, let's go!" Chris shouted back, jostled in the crowd, and the cadre of police whisked him to a waiting cruiser surrounded by more cruisers, emergency vehicles, and paramilitary vehicles. The media and the civilians beyond the perimeter surged forward, trying to get a look at him and cheering, applauding, or shouting to him.

Chris hustled to the backseat of the cruiser, closing the door behind him. The sirens kept blaring, preventing conversation with the uniformed officers in the front seat. He didn't feel like talking anyway. He worried about Evan and how the boy would be dealt with by the law. It wasn't a fate that Chris could save him from, but maybe the time for saving Evan was over.

The cruiser began to make its way through the crowd as official personnel cleared a path for it to pass. Chris couldn't hear anything because of the sirens and the people cheering, clapping, or calling to him, though he couldn't make out any of the words. They waved at him or flashed him thumbs-up. One woman blew him a kiss, and another one held up a hand-scrawled sign that read MARRY ME!

Chris looked away, thinking of Heather. He didn't know what she'd think of him now or if she still felt betrayed. Same with Jordan, which hurt, too. Chris didn't want to be untouchable anymore, but he might have blown his chance.

The cruiser inched along, and he looked out the window at the cheering mob. His thoughts were in a quieter place, Central Valley. It struck him then that everything he'd said to Dr. McElroy in his job interview was absolutely true. He'd thought he'd been lying to her, but he'd been lying to himself. Central Valley *did* feel like home to him, and it was the kind of place where he'd want to settle down and raise a family.

He just didn't know how, or even if, he could ever get back there.

Chapter Fifty-nine

The next few hours were a blur, during which Chris was escorted to the United States Attorney's office, a concrete monolith on Chestnut Street in Philadelphia. The Rabbi gave him a relieved hug and Alek shook his hand, acting as if Chris had followed his orders to the letter, a charade in which Chris played his part. After that, Chris, the Rabbi, and Alek met with the heads of JTTF, Homeland Security, FBI, and ATF, in addition to the United States Attorney for the Eastern District of Pennsylvania, the Middle District of Pennsylvania, the mayor of Philadelphia, and the police commissioner. Chris met so many members of the top brass that he lost track of the names, the uniforms, the suits, and the badges.

Everybody needed to be briefed, and he answered all the questions they had, though they answered none of his. The most he could get out of them was that they were getting ready to give an official press conference at six o'clock today, at which he was expected to speak. Chris couldn't ask the Rabbi and Alek about it because they weren't alone until the end of the day, when he hustled them down the hall to the first private room he could find, which was a large supply closet.

"Why do I have to speak?" Chris asked Alek and the Rabbi, closing the door behind them. "That's not how we roll. We don't parade the details of our undercover operations in front of the public."

Alek looked at him like he was nuts. "Operation Varsity Letter is a major victory for federal law enforcement. You're the hero. You're a celebrity. You're truly the new Eliot Ness. You *are* The Untouchable!"

"Curt, listen to me." The Rabbi placed a hand on Chris's shoulder, his lined face weary. "I know you hate the limelight. But you got it done, and this was a major operation. We thwarted a domestic terror attack. We need to explain that to the media and the public."

"We never did anything like this before, had an undercover agent speak."

"Correct, and you know why?" the Rabbi asked, patiently. "Because this scenario is unprecedented. We didn't stop the Oklahoma City bombing. But we stopped the Philadelphia bombing, and you're blown anyway."

"Rabbi, I know that, but what about the next undercover agent? How many questions are we going to answer? How much of the story are we going to tell? Rather, am *I* going to tell?"

Alek dismissed him with a wave. "Just the basics, Curt. Nothing granular. This is ATF's time to shine. If you don't do it for yourself, do it for them."

"You mean *us*. You're still ATF for another hour or two, aren't you?"

Alek's smile faded. "I'm still your boss, Curt. You're still reporting to me. You'll go to that press conference and you'll say what ATF needs you to say."

"On one condition." Chris had gotten an idea during those endless debriefings with the nameless suits. In fact, it was his own personal Plan B. "If I can't work under-cover anymore, I still won't work a desk. After the dust settles, I want a different job."

"What do you want?" Alek asked, his smile back, though he was still ugly.

"I want to start a field-training program for undercover agents, over and above what we had at Glencoe, based on my experience. It could start as a pilot program in Phila-delphia and extend to the other divisions around the country."

Alek hesitated. "A field-experience program? That job doesn't exist."

"I know, I want to create it. I want to teach everything I know to undercover agents coming up."

Alek frowned. "Curt. This is the government. We don't create jobs willy-nilly, and you won't get any more money."

"I don't want more money. I'll stay at my pay grade." Chris was a GS-13, making a little over a hundred grand a year.

The Rabbi interjected, "I think that's a great idea, Curt. You know so many tricks of the trade, and I think it would be great if you could impart that knowledge to our newer agents."

"Thanks." Chris returned his attention to Alek. "If I can look forward to a new job, I'll be happy to speak at the press conference."

"Oh, I get it. We're negotiating." Alek folded his arms. "You never give up, do you?"

"Lucky for you, no."

Alek thought a minute, then his grin returned. "Curt, a field-experience program is an *excellent* idea. I was just thinking the same thing myself!"

Chapter Sixty

Police guarded the doors, and Mindy sat in the waiting room of the emergency department waiting for Evan to come back. He had taken ten stitches through his eyebrow and had bruises on his right cheek, though his orbital bone hadn't been fractured or his eyesight impaired. He was being X-rayed because they suspected two cracked ribs, but otherwise, he would be physically okay.

Mindy had cried all the tears she could cry. She could never live with herself if more people had been killed. She felt exhausted, sitting next to her new lawyer, Maxwell Todd, Esq., of Logan & Dichter. Todd specialized in the legal problems of the children of their corporate client CEOs. Mindy would never have guessed there were enough spoiled brats to support a law practice, but maybe affluenza was contagious.

Evan was in police custody, and he was going from here to the Federal Detention Center until his arraignment. The charges against him had yet to be decided upon, but Mindy would be there for him, not to excuse him, but to help him deal with whatever sentence they gave him. A mother was a lighthouse in a storm, and she would stand with him always. And even though, if she'd said yes to him before, when she should've said no, they both still had time to turn it around. She could change, and so could he.

She glanced at Paul, sitting several rows away from her with his criminal lawyer. They were the only people in the waiting room, which had been cleared by the police. Her phone rested in her lap, but she didn't look at it. She'd stopped checking Facebook when the posts about Evan started appearing in her feed, mostly horrible and vile. She was ditching Facebook and going back to real books.

Mindy's gaze found the TV mounted in the corner, playing on mute. There was a car commercial, and the screen returned to the the courthouse and the rescue, above the banner BOMB PLOT FOILED. Then came a shot of Evan's latest school photo, then photos from his Facebook and Instagram accounts, a continuous slideshow of media coverage.

Mindy watched the coverage, having an out-of-body experience. She couldn't believe that Evan was on TV, that hers was the family they were talking about, that she was *inside* the news, even though they were real people. They weren't a story. It was her, Evan, and Paul.

The screen switched to a photo of Coach Brennan above the title UNDERCOVER HERO CURT ABBOTT. Mindy watched as the video in which Coach Brennan—she still called him that in her mind—flew upside down like a trapeze artist, holding on to Evan as they soared over the Benjamin Franklin Bridge.

Mindy felt tears come to her eyes. Coach Brennan had saved Evan's life, as well as the lives of thousands of innocent people, and risked his own. Her first impulse had been to call him and she'd gotten his cell phone from the Booster directory, but her lawyer had advised her not to call him.

Mindy picked up her phone, scrolled to the text function, and typed a message, straight from the heart.

Coach Brennan, this is Mindy Kostis. I'm not supposed to be communicating with you, but what's right is right. Thank you very much for saving Evan's life. God bless you.

Mindy swallowed hard. Her attention returned to the television, and she found herself watching her own Facebook album, the Kostis Klan in the Caymans.

"Mrs. Kostis?" said a female voice, and Mindy looked up to see the doctor entering the waiting room, with a professional smile.

"You can see Evan now. He's asking for you."

Chapter Sixty-one

Heather tossed the salad, alone with her thoughts while Jordan sat in the living room with the television blaring CNN.

". . . this is Wolf Blitzer, welcoming our viewers in the United States and around the world. We're only five minutes away from our coverage of the press conference, which we will be bringing you live from Philadelphia, regarding the terrorist bomb plot that was thwarted today by federal law enforcement, working in connection with state and municipal law enforcement . . ."

Heather screened out the TV, trying to process her emotions. She couldn't wrap her mind around the fact that Chris wasn't who he said he was. She had a crush on a guy that didn't exist. Worse, Chris, or Curt, had used Jordan to get information. She still didn't know the details and she didn't care if she ever found out. The bottom line was that she had been lied to, and so had Jordan.

She kept tossing the salad, bringing up the tart scent of the apple-cider vinegar, which she'd never used before. She'd finally had the time to make an Ina Garten recipe, a corn salad made from real corn, not canned, with red pepper, red onion, and fresh basil. She'd never used kosher salt either, so she'd gone to Whole Foods to buy some, celebrating the fact that she had a job interview on Wednesday, as an administrative assistant in the corporate headquarters at ValleyCo.

Heather smiled to herself. She felt confident about her prospects, considering that her boss would be Susan, who had all but told her that she'd get the job. Almost overnight her life had changed, and she had the possibility of a new job with a desk, a nameplate, and a tuition-matching program. Not only that, she could wear whatever she wanted as long as it came from a ValleyCo outlet, which was where she shopped anyway. She was even baking a poached salmon filet, filling the small apartment with an expensive, culinary aroma known only to home cooks, like her.

". . . stand by for a briefing from the Director of Homeland Security, who will be outlining the details of today's breaking news, the thwarting of the bombing of the James A. Byrne U.S. Courthouse and the William J. Green Federal Building in Philadelphia, which would've caused thousands upon thousands of deaths in and around the building. The loss of life and property would've been catastrophic, but for Operation Varsity Letter. You will hear from Special Agent Curt Abbott of the Bureau of . . ."

Heather screened out the name, which was much less appealing than Chris Brennan. She wondered how he had chosen his alias, and if he had actually looked up online for friendly-sounding names that would fool single mothers who were desperate enough to believe anything.

She tossed the corn salad and tried not to think about it. Jordan had come home from school early and had spoken with her only briefly before he went to his room and closed the door. He'd been shaken by the fact that Evan had almost been killed, as well as being involved in a lethal terrorist plot. In fact, he had come out of his room only ten minutes ago, to watch the press conference on TV.

"Mom, it's about to start," Jordan called from the living room.

"I'm making dinner. I can hear it from here."

"Mom, are you serious?"

Heather didn't answer, and in the next moment, Jordan appeared at the entrance to the kitchen in his baseball sweats.

"Mom, you're not going to watch?"

"I've heard it all day, the coverage has been nonstop. You've been at school, you don't know."

"We had it on there, too. That's all anybody's talking about. It's major, Mom. You have to watch."

"They're not going to say anything new. It's all the same thing. We know it all. We lived it all. It's about *us*."

"Don't you care about Evan? They *arrested* him. He wasn't in school today. I think he might be going to jail."

"Of course I care about Evan." Heather felt terrible for Mindy, for what she must have been going through. Heather never would've thought it could happen to a family like the Kostises.

"Everybody says he was in with those guys, but I don't think he was."

"I'm sure he wasn't," Heather said, though she wasn't sure. She didn't know Evan, but her father always said, *If you go through life with your path greased, you could end up on your ass.*

"I mean, it's so random that it was Madame Wheeler in the picture, but Evan is not a *terrorist*. He wouldn't *kill* anybody, he wouldn't blow up a courthouse." Jordan glanced at the TV, where CNN was teasing the press conference. "Mom, come on. I want to see what happens."

"Jordan, I'm cooking—"

"Why are you being so weird?"

"I'm not being weird." Heather kept tossing the salad like a madwoman. Maybe she *was* being weird. A weird version of Ina Garten.

"You're acting like you're mad."

"Well, I *am* mad." Heather turned to him. "Aren't you? How do you feel? You went in your room and vanished after school. Do you want to talk about it?"

"Okay," Jordan answered, less certainly. "It's a big deal, and I think you should watch the press conference. Don't you want to hear what the coach has to say?"

"He's not *the coach*."

"Okay, I know that. Whatever."

"Curt. It sounds like Chris, but it's not Chris."

Jordan cocked his head. "Are you mad at him?"

"Aren't you?" Heather told herself to calm down. She let go of the serving fork and spoon. "How do you feel about it, Jordan? You believed he was a coach, didn't you?"

"Yes."

"And you believed he liked you, that he was showing interest in you as a friend. As a coach. Isn't that right?"

"Okay, yes." Jordan shrugged uncomfortably. "Why are you acting like a lawyer? You sound like a lawyer."

"I'm trying to understand how you feel. Don't you feel angry that you were lied to? That he lied to us both? Did he ever ask you questions about Evan or the other boys on the team?"

"Yeah, I guess. Once."

"So he was using you for information. He was pumping you for information. He was only pretending to be your friend, and mine. Doesn't that make you angry?"

"Um, it's not great, I admit."

"It's more than *not great,* Jordan. It's a lie. I teach you not to lie. I don't like people who lie. But he lied to us, and I'm mad at him, so you'll understand if I don't want to watch the stupid press—"

"That's not what I think," Jordan interrupted her, which he rarely did, especially to offer his thoughts.

"What do you think?"

"I know he lied and all, and that's not right, but I still think he liked us." Jordan blinked sadly, and Heather felt a wave of guilt for her son, let down not only by his father, but by his father figure.

"Maybe he did, I'm sure he did. But I don't like being lied to."

"Mom, he *had* to lie, don't you see?" Jordan gestured at the TV, where Wolf Blitzer was counting down. "He saved Evan's life and he saved the lives of all those people. Like they just said, thousands of people would have been killed."

"But he deceived us. He pretended to be somebody he wasn't."

"He had to, for the greater good. He did what he had to do to save people's lives. It's like he really was a coach, and we're all the team. Mom, he did the right thing for *the team*."

"But he's not a coach," Heather said, softening, thinking back to that night in this very kitchen, when Chris had coached her to think about her skill set.

"It doesn't matter if he really was. He did what a coach would do, a really great coach. He went to the standard, Mom. The standard did not go to him. It's seventeen inches, Mom."

"What?" Heather had no idea what he meant.

Jordan shook it off. "It doesn't matter. All I'm saying is, he flew upside down through the air holding on to Evan. He *rescued* him. He achieved *excellence*."

Heather felt a glimmer of new pride in Jordan. "You

know, you should express yourself more often. You make sense."

"So you agree?"

"No."

"Mom, come on." Jordan took her hand and tugged her into the living room, where they sat down in front of the TV, side by side, something they hadn't done for some time.

Wolf Blitzer continued, "We take you directly to Philadelphia, where the press conference is beginning." The screen morphed to a man in a suit standing behind a lectern with a cluster of men in suits. To the man's right was a tall ugly guy, a shorter older man, and on the end, Chris.

"There's Coach!" Jordan leaned forward, resting on his knees.

"Not a coach," Heather said reflexively, though her gaze went immediately to Chris and stayed there. It was so strange to see him in such a different role, on TV to boot. She couldn't deal with the fact that it was the same man. She couldn't help but think, *If nothing he said was true, is it the same man?* Then she answered her own question, *Of course not, you idiot. But he's still hot.*

"My name is Ralph Brubaker, Chief of the Joint Terrorism Task Force. I'm here to brief you on the thwarting today of an act of domestic terrorism whose goal was to destroy the James A. Byrne U.S. Courthouse and the William J. Green Federal Building in Philadelphia, murdering the persons inside and causing considerable property damage. The plot was foiled by JTTF and many other law-enforcement agencies, but first mention goes to the Philadelphia Field Division of ATF, headed by Group Supervisor Alek Ivanov, Special Agent David Levitz, and the hero of Operation Varsity Letter, Special Agent Curt Abbott."

Jordan hooted. "Woohoo!"

Heather grumbled. "Hmph."

". . . Law enforcement scored a major victory today in our ongoing battle against domestic terrorism. We have no reason to believe that there are other conspirators or participants in this plot, so the City of Philadelphia and the region remain safe. Structural engineers are inspecting the Ben Franklin Bridge, and it will remain closed until further notice. We will retain the severe threat level, out of an abundance of caution. Most important, no confirmed lives were lost today in connection with this plot, except the perpetrators, brothers James and David Shank of Headley, Pennsylvania."

Jordan looked over. "Mom, can you believe Madame Wheeler sent Evan that selfie? I *knew* I should've taken French."

Heather rolled her eyes. "Spanish is more useful."

"Ha!"

"I'm just wondering why Evan was dumb enough to send you all her picture. Why didn't he just keep it to himself?"

Jordan snorted. "Mom, are you kidding? Did you *see* her? If I got a girl who looked like that, I'd send it around, no doubt."

"Don't tell me. I don't want to know."

Chief Brubaker continued, "We have taken into custody Ms. Courtney Shank Wheeler, the younger sister of the Shank brothers and a teacher at Central Valley High School in Central Valley, Pennsylvania. We also have in custody a seventeen-year-old junior at Central Valley High School. Neither Wheeler nor the minor have been charged, as yet. We are investigating their participation in the plot and it is unclear at this time."

Jordan looked over with a worried frown. "What does that mean? Why don't they say his name?"

"Privacy, I guess? Because he's a minor? Anyway, it means they haven't figured out what Evan did yet."

Jordan grimaced. "Do they really think he's one of the bad guys? He doesn't know Madame Wheeler's brothers. They beat him up. You could see his face in the videos."

"Shh, let's listen."

Chief Brubaker continued, "There are many details of this Operation Varsity Letter that we do not have or cannot make public for security reasons. We are holding this conference before we have the totality of the facts because we want to inform the press and public, giving correct information rather than the rumors circulating online or in social media."

Jordan turned to Heather. "He has to say that. Twitter is blowing up."

Heather kept looking at Chris/Curt. She wondered if he was even single. Maybe that had been a lie, too. Her gaze went to his left hand, but she couldn't see if he had a wedding ring. Maybe he kept it at home, with his wife. And seven children. Also a dog and a cat.

Jordan listened as the spokesman continued, but Heather kept her eye on Chris/Curt, trying to read his mind. He was probably thinking that he was a hero, that he did his job even if it meant telling a whopper. He may have served the greater good, but still, she didn't like being lied to. The *lesser* good still mattered, and she and Jordan were the lesser good. She wondered if she'd ever hear from Chris/Curt again, then if she *wanted* to hear from him again.

Suddenly she realized that the odor of salmon was permeating the apartment, and the fish was burning.

"Dammit!" Heather said, jumping up and running into the kitchen.

Chapter Sixty-two

It wasn't until midnight that Curt got home to his spare, one-bedroom apartment on the second floor of a row home in the Italian Market, a city neighborhood of open-air stalls selling fruit, produce, and fish, packed cheek-by-jowl with old-school Italian restaurants. The air always smelled like fresh basil and rotting food, but the neighborhood suited him. He could pick up prepared foods anywhere, and it was easy for him to blend in, since the Market bustled with employees, shoppers, and tourists.

He'd come home tonight completely unnoticed, the shops closed, tarps drawn over the stalls, and the few tourists inside the restaurants. He'd kept his ball cap on just in case, after having spent the day feeling like a celebrity poseur, being clapped on the back, congratulated, and even hugged by a pretty lawyer in the U.S. Attorney's office, who reminded him of Heather.

Curt flopped on his bed, which was made by the cleaning lady who came in every other week, whether he was home or not. There was nothing on the white walls of his bedroom because he'd never had time to decorate, nor had he truly cared to, but tonight it looked lame, beyond bachelorhood into psycho hermit. Oddly, he missed his apartment in Central Valley, and by now, other ATF agents would be routinely fingerprinting, taking photographs, collecting his laptop and going through his videotapes and audiotapes for the government's case against Evan. None of the possessions in that apartment belonged to him, except the clothes, but he would leave them behind, shedding the Chris Brennan identity like a snake does its skin. It had never been a problem before, but now, he felt vaguely like a real snake.

He picked up the remote, turned on a news channel, and watched the coverage of the operation on mute. There was one talking head after another, then the screen played the video of him flying upside down, with Evan hanging on.

Curt felt odd. He had never seen himself on television before. The camera focused on the sheer terror in Evan's battered face, and Curt's heart went out to the boy. He thought of the text that Evan's mother Mindy had sent him earlier today, thanking him. It made him feel good inside, but still he worried about Evan, and of course, Jordan and Heather.

The TV screen changed to a replay of the press conference, and Curt watched himself on the dais, knowing that he had been thinking about Heather the whole time. He wondered if she had been watching and what she must be thinking of him. He thought about calling her, then glanced at his watch. It was 2:15 A.M. He'd lost track of time with so much going on.

A wave of exhaustion swept over him, and Curt let his eyes close, thinking about her. He wanted to apologize to her, and to Jordan, and to all of them—for the first time ever, he felt guilty after an operation was over, even though by any objective measure, it had been successful. But he didn't feel successful, he felt like a jerk. He had gotten justice for the murders of Abe and Courtney's husband, Doug, but justice never was an eye for an eye, not for him. All that was left was death and destruction, leaving him feeling more alone than ever.

Curt drifted to sleep, knowing that it would never be any other way—unless he changed something. And so three nights later, after the hoopla was subsiding and he was returning to a normal schedule, with his new position as yet unspecified, Curt found himself lying on his bed again, looking up Heather's phone number online in the Boosters' directory, pressing in the numbers, and waiting while the call rang.

"Hello?" Heather answered, her tone vague, probably because she didn't recognize the number of his new phone, since he'd turned in his old one as evidence. Still, hearing her voice brought him back to Central Valley, and knowing she was on the other end of the line made him feel different, too. Better, the way he had felt back then.

"Heather, it's Chris, I mean, Curt." Curt thought he had gotten used to using his true name again, but evidently not.

"Oh, hi." Heather's voice sounded cold, which he had expected.

"I waited a few days but I wanted to call you to say, well, I'm sorry. I'm sorry that I lied to you about who I was. I hope you understand—"

"I get it."

"It's my job. It *was* my job anyway."

"I said, I get it." Heather paused. "Jordan gets it, too. Team player, greater good, seventeen inches. Got it."

Curt didn't, but let it go. She sounded unhappy talking to him. "I wanted to apologize to Jordan too, but I didn't want to contact him without asking your permission first."

"Fine with me, if you call him."

"Good, thanks."

"You should. You lied to him, too."

Curt felt a pang, hearing the sting in her words. "I'm sorry. I know it must've been really strange for you, both of you, to find out I was undercover."

"It was."

"Is there anything you want to ask me? I mean, you're entitled to know the truth."

Heather didn't answer except to chuckle, not in a good way.

"I mean I never contacted anybody after an operation before, but this is different."

Heather didn't say anything.

Curt felt he should explain further, especially because she was saying so little. "I usually work undercover with drug dealers and thugs, but this time, I was infiltrating good people, like you and Jordan."

"So?"

"So—" Curt hesitated, unsure what to say next. "So it's unusual for me, and I know it must be for you too, finding out that I'm not a coach or a teacher."

"Yes, it was. It was for Jordan too, although mostly he's concerned about Evan."

"Sure, right." Curt had been relieved that both Evan and Courtney were negotiating plea deals to a whole list of charges, since circumstances had shown that they had voluntarily and completely renounced their participation in the conspiracy.

"School is just now getting back to normal."

"Did you ever get a new job?"

"Actually, yes. I start at ValleyCo as an administrative assistant next week."

"That's wonderful!" Curt thought he heard a softening

in her voice, or maybe he imagined it. "Well, I was wondering if you ever wanted to have dinner with me."

"Why would I do *that*?" Heather asked coldly, which gave him his answer. It had been a terrible idea, calling her. He had lost her, as he feared. But he couldn't ignore his feelings for her. He'd been thinking about her all the time and he wanted to give it his best shot.

"Heather, I really liked meeting you and getting to know you, and I have more of a normal life now."

"I have to think about it," Heather interrupted. "I'm not sure that's something I want to do."

"I understand," Curt said, disappointed, and the sad part was, he really did understand, completely.

"Now, excuse me, I have to go. I have something on the stove."

"Sure, but can I give you a call again in a few days?"

"Try a month," Heather said, hanging up.

Curt hung up, defeated.

Luckily, he had a Plan B.

Chapter Sixty-three

Curt waited a month to put Plan B into action, wanting to show Heather that he respected her wishes. He put the time to good use, hammering out his job description with a ridiculous number of bureaucrats and filling out a ton of paperwork, and serving as the de facto assistant to the new head of Philadelphia Field Division, the Rabbi himself, David Levitz. Curt couldn't have been happier that the Rabbi had finally received the promotion he deserved, and they were both delighted that Alek had gotten kicked upstairs to JTTF, never to be heard from again. At least until the next terrorist attack, which gave them an ulterior motive to keep the country safe.

Curt couldn't look out the window since the shades were down. Central Valley was finally returning to normal, and the story had just begun to fade from the headlines. He turned down the requests for interviews, as well as offers of movie and book deals. Evan and Courtney had begun serving their sentences—Courtney for twelve years, and Evan for five.

Curt had spoken with Raz, who was doing better than

ever, taking over Evan's position as catcher for Jordan, who was pitching a winning season for the Musketeers. Curt had even gone to a game, and Coach Hardwick had greeted him with a completely unexpected bear hug, thanking Curt for his service and inviting him to come to practice anytime he wanted—even if he had to come late. Curt and Jordan texted each other all the time, and Jordan had helped arrange this date tonight. Or at least, what Curt had hoped would be a date.

"Mr. Abbott, can I get you anything besides the water?" the waitress asked, hovering over him with a smile.

"No, thank you." Curt smiled back, having gotten used to being sociable, as a matter of necessity. He'd met more people in the past month than he'd met in his entire life. He couldn't remember the last drink he'd bought himself and he wasn't complaining. Everywhere he went, people shook his hand, thanked him, and wanted a selfie with him. It was forcing him to come out of his shell, and Curt was learning that he actually liked the people he had sworn to protect.

In fact, his fame was one of the reasons that he'd been granted this favor tonight. He'd asked the restaurant to close to everyone except him and Heather, because he knew that if the regular crowd were here, they wouldn't get a private moment. He'd offered to pay for shutting down the place, but they'd done it as a personal favor, living up to their name.

Friendly's.

Curt checked his watch. It was 6:30, and according to Jordan, this was the exact time that Heather would be coming home from her new job and heading into the kitchen to start dinner. He couldn't look out the window so he didn't know if she was coming. They'd closed the shades so no one would see that he was inside, and he kept them closed. He had asked Friendly's to take down the usual promotion on their sign in favor of something special, and he wondered if Heather had read it yet:

**H, PLEASE MEET ME HERE FOR
DINNER TONIGHT? CURT**

Curt checked the table to make sure everything was in place. He'd brought a bag of Chips Ahoy, two bottles of water, and two nice glasses. He'd also bought a bouquet of a dozen long-stemmed red roses in a clear glass vase, but when he'd gotten here, he realized that the color of the flowers inadvertently matched Friendly's logo. He'd messed that up, but okay. He was new at romance, and it wasn't easy. On the contrary, it was easier to hang upside down from a helo.

Curt sipped his water, trying not to be nervous, a new sensation for him. He'd met a lot of nice, smart, and attractive women in the past month, and he'd gotten plenty of fan mail, emails, and photos from them. He was red-blooded enough to look at the photos, but none of the women appealed to him like Heather. She was nice, smart, and attractive in a way that felt *real* to him, and he couldn't explain it any better than that. If she felt the same way, she would be walking through the door in the next few minutes.

So far, no luck.

Curt felt his heart beat faster, giving him a tingle that he'd never experienced before. He never thought he could get a tingle from anything but his job, but that was about adrenaline. This time, it was about emotion. About feelings that went to the core of who he was, flowing to and from his heart, like the very blood that gave him life. He was only just now finding out who he really was, meeting new people and trying a new job, but he wanted to go deeper than that. He wanted to be the man he was meant to be, for himself, and for Heather and Jordan. Maybe he could be a husband and father. Maybe he could have a family, with an overweight dog of his own.

Curt looked up, and his mouth went dry when he saw the door opening and Heather walking in with a surprised smile. She looked adorable with her hair down, wearing a blue dress, and when she met his gaze, her eyes smiled at him, too. With real happiness.

He found himself on his feet and heading to the door to thank her for coming.

And to introduce himself to her, for the very first time.

Acknowledgments

Here's where I get to say my favorite words in the English language, namely, thank you. So many people helped me with this novel because it required information that was outside my fields of expertise, which are basically law, dogs, and carbohydrates. But because this book has so many twists, I don't want to give spoilers to those of you who read these before you finish the novel. (You know who you are, and frankly, I'm one of you, so no judgment.) So I'll thank some people here without explaining exactly what they did to inform this novel. I owe them a huge debt of thanks, and all mistakes herein are my own.

First thank-you goes to Shane and Liam Leonard, the teenaged sons of my best friend and assistant, Laura Leonard. I have had the great privilege to watch these two young boys grow from babies to high school scholar-athletes who know everything about baseball. Shane and Liam answered all of my questions and even coached me. Coincidentally, this happened to be the year that I was asked to throw out the first pitch for my hometown Philadelphia Phillies, and Shane and Liam actually helped me acquit myself on major-league game day. Thank you so much, guys.

Thank you so much to Coach Matthew Schultz of Great Valley High School Baseball program, who also spent hours with me answering all of my dumb questions about baseball, as well as letting me attend team practices and games. Thanks to the members of the Great Valley varsity baseball team, a group of terrific and talented young men.

Thank you to Dr. Heidi Capetola, principal of Great Valley High School, for leading a truly wonderful high school and for taking the time to teach me how it works. Thanks to the amazing teachers Gerry McGrath and William McNamara, who allowed me to sit in on their Government classes. And it goes without saying that the fictional teachers, coaches, and players in this novel are completely products of my own imagination.

Thank you to Anthony Tropea and Steve Bartholomew for their expertise and time. Thanks to Mark, who taught me the chemistry behind explosives, and rest assured that I revealed nothing herein that couldn't be found on the Internet, a fact which is both interesting as well as scary. Thank you to Lisa Goldstein, M.D., a psychiatrist who treats adolescents and helped me develop the psychology of the characters.

I'm a lawyer, but criminal law wasn't my field, so I always touch base with my dear friend, the brilliant public servant Nicholas Casenta, Esq., chief of the Chester County District Attorney's Office.

Also, thanks to Dan Bankoske.

Thank you to my wonderful friend and editor Jennifer Enderlin, who is also the Senior Vice President and Publisher of St. Martin's Press, yet she still finds the time to improve my manuscripts. Thank you so much, Coach Jen! And big love and thanks to everyone at St. Martin's Press d Macmillan, starting with the terrific John Sargent and lly Richardson, plus Jeff Dodes, Lisa Senz, Brian Heller, ff Capshew, Brant Janeway, Dori Weintraub, Tracey uest, John Karle, Sara Goodman, Stephanie Davis, ncy Trypuc, Anne-Marie Tallberg, Kerry Nordling, izabeth Wildman, Caitlin Dareff, Talia Sherer, Kim dlum, and all the wonderful sales reps. Big thanks to ichael Storrings, for outstanding cover design. Also hugs d kisses to Mary Beth Roche, Laura Wilson, Samantha elson, and the great people in audiobooks. I love and preciate all of you!

Thanks and love to my agent, Robert Gottlieb of Tri- nt Media Group, whose dedication guided this novel into blication, and to Nicole Robson and Trident's digital me- a team, who help me get the word out on social media.

Many thanks and much love to the amazing Laura onard. She's invaluable in every way, every day, and has en for more than twenty years. Thanks, too, to Nan aley for all of her research assistance on this novel, and anks to George Davidson for doing everything else on e farm, so that I can be free to write.

Finally, thank you to my amazing daughter (and even author), Francesca, for all of her support, laughter, and ve.